THE BOY WHO KNEW TOO MUCH

by
Jeffrey Westhoff

ISBN-13: 978-1-940758-05-3

Cover Design by Instinctivedesign

Published by:
Intrigue Publishing, LLC
11505 Cherry Tree Crossing Rd. #148
Cheltenham, MD 20623-9998

Printed in the United States of America

Dedication

This book is dedicated to the three authors who most directly inspired it: Robert Louis Stevenson, Elleston Trevor (who wrote the masterful Quiller novels under the pseudonym Adam Hall), and especially Ian Fleming. I stole from all three; I pray I did it artfully.

THE BOY WHO KNEW TOO MUCH

CHAPTER 1--WINNER

Brian Parker was about to open his laminated map of Lucerne, just to verify the square they were nearing was the Mühlenplatz, when his friend Tim Gifford elbowed him in the ribs and announced, "That guy right there. He's a spy!"

Entering the square, Brian scanned the café to locate the spy Tim had spotted. He locked on to the target immediately and knew why Tim suspected the man: jet-black hair, commanding eyes, strong jaw. He was the type of continental smoothie Brian pictured lounging in a *piazza* in Rome, not a *platz* here in Lucerne. The man wore a dark blue suit but no tie. He leaned across his table with practiced casualness to light the cigarette of his companion, a breathtaking blonde. Brian was too far away to see what kind of lighter Tim's supposed spy used, but he saw a flash of gold in the man's hand. Maybe a Colibri, just like Foster Blake used.

Brian turned back to Tim, who was grinning in triumph.

"Not a chance," Brian said.

"Oh, come on!" Tim said as they walked past the man and his gorgeous companion. "Look at that guy! Killer looks. Sharp clothes. Hot blonde in a teeny dress. I bet he's carrying the blueprints for a next-generation laser cannon in his briefcase."

Brian laughed. Tim always made him laugh. The two best friends from Wisconsin had been playing "Spot the Spy" since their European trip began four days earlier in Austria. They had dreamed up the game during study halls back in Wauwatosa East High School while they were selling candy bars to pay for the trip. So far Tim was ahead in the spy game. Way ahead. According to him, every third person who walked through their hotel lobby in Innsbruck had been a spy, plus the entire population of Liechtenstein.

Brian, however, had yet to spot a single spy.

"I keep telling you real spies don't look like tuxedo models," Brian said as they walked toward Hug bakery, another café across the Mühlenplatz from their disputed spy. "They don't want to draw attention to themselves. They want to look ordinary."

"Lighten up, buddy. This isn't real; it's a game."

"So you want me to cheat?"

Tim shook his head. "Foster Blake would be very disappointed in you."

"How could I disappoint a fictional character?"

"Look, you've read all his books eight times—"

"I haven't read any of them eight times. Six at the most."

"Whatever. You own at least three copies of every book. You've plastered your bedroom walls with Foster Blake movie posters. You've memorized the DVD commentary tracks. Yet here you are, Wisconsin's biggest Foster Blake fan, losing big time at "Spot the Spy" because you want to be *realistic*." Tim paused to deliver his coup de grâce. "Face it, pal, Foster Blake ain't real."

Brian rolled his eyes. He knew the world of Foster Blake wasn't realistic, although not right off the bat. Four years ago, when he was eleven, Brian caught *Clandestinely Yours* on HBO and was forevermore hooked on Foster Blake. He saw more of the movies and then started checking Foster Blake novels out of the library. Soon he was collecting the varied paperback editions of the novels and buying the movies on DVD. Foster Blake turned Brian into a spy buff. He DVR'ed espionage documentaries on the Military Channel, spent hours scanning real-world intelligence websites and grew to appreciate the serious spy novels of John le Carré and Len Deighton.

But even as Brian realized how far-fetched Foster Blake's adventures were, his imagination always came back to Agent 17K. "K for killer" was the spy's catchphrase. Who wouldn't want to be Foster Blake? Equally suave and tough, unflappable in the midst of danger. And scoring with exotic women by the truckload—the "Blake Beauties," as film publicists called them in the days before political correctness. Brian never knew such a time, but his mother assured him it wasn't so long ago.

"Even if I know Foster Blake isn't real," Brian said to Tim, "I still want to enjoy the fantasy."

"That's what I'm saying," Tim replied. "You're the one who wanted to come on this trip to live out his spy novel fantasies." He grabbed Brian by the shoulders and shook him. "So fantasize, buddy, fantasize!"

Brian brushed back a lock of blond hair that had fallen into his eyes. "You do want me to cheat, then," he said. "Gotcha."

As Brian and Tim approached Hug, a smiling waitress in her early twenties seated them at a glass top table alongside the Reuss River. They ordered coffees, and the waitress returned with two mugs. Tim took his first sip and nodded toward his spy across the square. Brian shifted his gaze in time to see the man and the blonde share a laugh.

Tim said, "You have to grant me that in the fantasy world of Foster Blake, that suave stud over there could be a spy."

"A superspy."

"OK, then, another point for me. But I still expect you to spot a spy before the day is over." He poked his mug at Brian for emphasis. "You're due, man."

Brian chuckled again and sipped his coffee. Even if Tim had just equated spotting a spy with scoring a base hit, he understood Brian's Foster Blake obsession. Few of Brian's other friends did, not really. Nor were they willing to leave the cocoon of the suburbs, preferring to hang out in 'Tosa on the weekends.

Luckily, Tim shared Brian's wanderlust. Tim was always up for a Saturday afternoon trip into Milwaukee to hunt for classic spy novels in the used bookstores downtown. Tim's enthusiasm allowed Brian to be adventurous. They always had a blast exploring the city, sometimes journeying to the East Side for an anime festival at the Oriental Theatre.

And here they were in a city 4,400 miles away from home, on their own again. The rest of their high school group had gone to lunch at a fondue restaurant. That was another of the side trips the tour company sprang on them in every city. Most were too expensive for Brian, who decided to save his money to collect complete sets of Foster Blake paperbacks in German and French. Tim skipped out on the fondue restaurant, too. "We're from Wisconsin, for God's sake," he had declared. "Why would we pay that much to eat cheese?"

As the others left that morning, Miss Weninger, Brian's French teacher and the head chaperone, told Brian and Tim, "Don't go too far from the hotel." Luckily, nothing in central Lucerne was too far from their hotel. Brian and Tim spent about an hour hitting the nearby shops before arriving at the Mühlenplatz for late-morning coffee. It had been a productive excursion for Brian. His backpack now contained three more Foster Blake paperbacks in German.

As the waitress walked past, Tim leaned back to allow her a good look at his University of Wisconsin T-shirt. If Bucky Badger impressed her, she didn't let on. Brian grinned. Unlike Tim, he didn't want to dress like a tourist. He wore his standard outfit, a polo shirt (dark green today), a pair of Levi's 501 jeans, and black Adidas Sambas. The shirt, like all his others, bore no small animals or insignias because it was nobody else's business where he bought his clothes.

The waitress returned and Tim ordered a cherry strudel to go. "I'll bring it to Stephanie. Maybe if I give her a pastry from Hug, she'll give me a hug." Tim had longed after Stephanie Tompkins since the eighth grade. The main reason he had signed up for this trip was to spend two weeks on a bus with her.

"You should pick up something for Darleen," Tim added.

Brian flushed. "I don't know …" Brian almost asked Darleen Miller to join him on this morning's book shopping excursion instead of Tim, but lost his nerve when Darleen said she was excited about the fondue restaurant.

"Yeah, yeah, you're waiting to make your move when we get to Paris, the city of love." Tim faked playing a violin as he said this. "But that's our last stop. You don't want to put it off until it's too late, pal."

"I'll think about it," Brian said, turning in his chair to hide his embarrassment. He looked across the Mühlenplatz for Brian's superspy and his femme fatale, but they were gone. Perhaps they were off to a secluded chalet to re-enact one of the scenes that always got cut when the Foster Blake movies played on basic cable.

Brian's eyes wandered to the entrance of the square and zeroed in on a newcomer, a man in a gray raincoat. The man walked deliberately but not hastily toward the river. Brian sensed the man was headed somewhere important but didn't want anyone to know the urgency of his appointment. He was a short man, about five-foot-two, with tortoiseshell glasses and a gray mustache. Wisps of gray hair poked from beneath his hat.

Gray coat, gray mustache, gray hair—he's the little gray man, Brian thought.

The little gray man noticed Brian studying him. Their eyes locked, and Brian felt a frisson race down his spine. The man's eyes first registered surprise, and perhaps a trace of fear, that Brian was watching him, then they narrowed to assess the boy. The man turned his head, breaking off eye contact. The look had lasted no longer than a second, but in that time Brian knew—he absolutely knew—his gaze had disturbed a man with a secret.

"That man right there," Brian whispered. "He's a spy."

Tim looked up. "Him? He's gotta be the most boring guy in the city."

"Exactly," Brian said. He watched the man enter the Spreuerbrücke, one of the city's two covered bridges built during the Renaissance. Brian's eyes followed the little gray man until his form became indistinguishable among the shadows on the bridge.

"I don't know if I can give you that one," Tim said. "I think you picked him out of desperation because I was making you look bad."

"You're not even going to give me a pity spy?"

"I'll have to think about it," Tim said. He drank the rest of his coffee and plunked down the mug. "Time to head back. You coming?"

Brian shook his head. "Don't want to cramp your style when you give Stephanie her strudel." In reality, Brian didn't want to see Stephanie snub his friend again. "Besides, there's one more bookstore across the river I want to check. I still need to find a German copy of *Snowfire*."

"Isn't that the one where the villain tries to melt the polar ice caps?"

"That was the movie. In the book he used icebergs as platforms to launch nuclear missiles."

Tim laughed. "You're a maniac." He picked up the bag

containing the cherry strudel. "I'll text you if they get back early. I know you don't want to miss the Mount Pilatus trip."

As his friend walked alongside the Reuss back to their hotel, Brian looked around. This slice of Lucerne fit the popular image of Switzerland so perfectly that Heidi could have skipped past at any moment. Skinny buildings with gabled roofs and rows of windows were squeezed together like books on a shelf. Many of the façades were painted with intricate frescoes. Biblical scenes and wine drinking were the favored motifs. Behind Brian, the Reuss burbled by. Beyond the rooftops were the snow-capped Alps, and beyond the Alps was the warm July sun in a cloudless sky. Brian smiled. He was in Europe! He felt like—no, he *was*— a man of the world. He hummed "The Foster Blake Theme" and tapped the staccato beat on the glass tabletop with his fingertips.

The 'Tosa East group had arrived in Lucerne late in the afternoon two days earlier. Yesterday a tour guide whisked them to the standard tourist sights. This afternoon the group would ride the inclined train up Mount Pilatus (Tim was right, this was a side trip Brian wasn't about to miss) and tomorrow morning they would depart for Munich.

Brian finished his coffee, left what he hoped was a generous tip, and hitched his backpack over his shoulders as he stood. Before the group left for Mount Pilatus, Brian had a mission. He was one title shy of a complete set of Foster Blake paperbacks in German. Even though he would be in Germany tomorrow, Brian figured he might as well try to complete the set here while he had some free time. One more book, one more bookstore. Seemed like fate.

Brian walked to the Spreuerbrücke. He recalled yesterday's tour guide saying the Spreuerbrücke was the older of the two wooden pedestrian bridges that spanned the Reuss. The other, the Kappelbrücke, was the more famous. With its picturesque water tower, the Kappelbrücke appeared on almost every postcard mailed from the city.

As he neared the Spreuerbrücke, Brian realized why it attracted fewer tourists. Historic though it may be, the Spreuerbrücke was a shabby-looking structure of dark, mismatched brown planks. Just as Brian was thinking that the bridge belonged in a haunted forest, he noticed the series of triangular paintings beneath the peaked roof. Each depicted the Grim Reaper interrupting a feast or ceremony. They reminded him of the German woodcarvings from his history book, the ones made during the Black Death. A plaque at the bridge's entry bore a poem:

> *"All living things that fly or leap*
> *Or crawl or swim or run or creep*
> *Fear Death, yet can they find no spot*
> *In all the world where Death is not."*

Cripes, Brian thought. *Can't a person cross a bridge without being reminded he's going to die?* The skeleton paintings were spaced every ten feet, and as Brian walked beneath them a sense of doom pressed down upon him. The only thing missing was the Headless Horseman hurling a flaming jack-o'-lantern.

Brian stepped off the bridge feeling silly that a tourist attraction could spook him. He pulled out his map. The bookstore was off to his left, near the train station. The map showed a series of narrow alleyways that curved behind the nearby Jesuit church. They formed a short cut that Brian followed toward the church.

The alleys were oddly barren. Brian saw only a few people dart across his path. A man wearing black jeans and a leather bomber jacket that matched his dirty brown hair stepped from a side alley and turned toward Brian. He carried an umbrella, even though no rain had been forecast that day. As they passed each other, the man glanced at Brian dismissively. Brian was struck by a pair of alarmingly pale blue eyes behind wire-rimmed glasses. Something else about those eyes unnerved Brian, but he didn't get a long enough look to figure out what it was. He turned to see where the man was going, but the man had already gone.

Moments later, Brian spotted someone slumped in a side alley. He had seen homeless people sleeping in alleys in downtown Milwaukee but didn't expect such a sight in tidy Lucerne.

Two realizations hit Brian at once: One, this was the same alley that the man with the pale blue eyes had just exited. Two, the person lying in the alley wore a familiar gray raincoat.

Brian rushed to the little gray man and was relieved to find him alive. He stooped beside the man and propped up his head. The man's eyes, also gray, focused on Brian. He said something in German, but the only word Brian recognized was *Mühlenplatz*.

Brian shook his head. "I don't understand."

"You are the boy from the Mühlenplatz," the man said. "American?"

"Yes," Brian replied.

"Please contact your embassy. Ask for Jack Silver." The man shook with every syllable. He was expending all his effort to keep talking. "You must. Urgent."

Brian looked him over quickly but could see no wound, no blood. "Relax," Brian said. "I'll get help."

"No time," the man said. "Tell Silver someone in Prometheus turned." He was grunting between words. "Tell him DeJonge doesn't suspect."

Brian was gobsmacked with panic and this man was talking in riddles. "Doesn't suspect what?" he asked.

The man's answer was a deep, guttural groan. He squeezed his eyes shut as his body shuddered. Brian looked down the central alley and saw a police officer. He waved frantically, and the officer came running.

The man's eyes reopened. "Tell Silver." His voice was a hoarse, obscene whisper. The strain of talking turned his face purple. "Skyrm." A final spasm convulsed through the man, and he went limp in Brian's arms.

Brian heard the police officer's steps echoing behind him. He lowered the dead man's head to the ground. As Brian's body went numb from the inside out, a grim thought hit him. He had won the game. He had spotted the spy.

CHAPTER 2--SILVER

"A man from your embassy should be here shortly," Lieutenant Markus Eisert of the Lucerne police said as he took his seat across the small table from Brian and Miss Weninger. "It seems one of their attachés is here in Luzern"—Brian noted the German pronunciation—"on personal business."

Brian's teacher had arrived about an hour ago, within minutes of Brian's phone call. He was fortunate to reach her before the group left for Mount Pilatus, but unfortunate to have his eardrum pierced by her high-pitched "What!?" when he told her he was at the police station near Obergrundstrasse and could she come right away?

"Well, that's lucky," Miss Weninger said, responding to Lieutenant Eisert's news about the embassy man.

"If you say," the lieutenant said curtly.

Brian was grateful that Miss Weninger insisted the police contact the U.S. Embassy in Bern. The officer Brian had signaled in the alley began to question him at the scene, but became nervous the moment he realized Brian was a young American tourist. The officer radioed his superiors, and Brian watched a police team photograph the dead man until Lieutenant Eisert arrived. After quickly conferring with the lead officer on the scene, Lieutenant Eisert drove Brian a few blocks to the police station.

As soon as Lieutenant Eisert brought him to this little white room, Brian asked to speak to his parents, Miss Weninger, and the U.S. Embassy. "Your parents and your teacher, of course," the lieutenant replied, "but there is no reason to involve your embassy. I must ask questions about how you came across this unfortunate man, certainly, but we accuse you of no crime and, in fact, it seems no crime had been committed." That last statement surprised Brian, as he had told the police at the scene about the man with the pale blue eyes.

But Brian had not shared the dying man's last words. Instead he told the police the man said a few things in German before he died. Withholding evidence left Brian feeling guilty and anxious—how many Swiss laws was he breaking? But the gray man had asked him to pass information to Jack Silver, and Brian didn't have to have read a library of spy novels to know those final words might be vital to the American government. Before he could tell the police what the man said, he wanted to clear it with Jack Silver, which meant contacting the embassy. When Brian persisted about calling the embassy, Lieutenant Eisert discouraged the idea. "It would take at least three hours for your embassy to send someone from Bern."

When Miss Weninger arrived, though, she also insisted the police contact the embassy, and Lieutenant Eisert relented once an adult made the request. With someone from the embassy en route, Miss Weninger moved to another subject.

"Have you identified the man...?" She hesitated. "The man Brian found?"

"Yes," Lieutenant Eisert replied. "He was Heinrich Tetzel." The lieutenant consulted the contents of the buff folder on the table before him. "A professor at the University of Neuchatel, in their physics department. We do not know why he was in Luzern." Lieutenant Eisert closed the file and looked up at them. "And that is all we know so far."

"What did he teach?" Brian asked.

Lieutenant Eisert furrowed his brow to show the question was a nuisance. But he reopened the file. "He did research in high-frequency radio waves. Microwaves."

Someone knocked on the door. A uniformed officer entered and whispered into the lieutenant's ear. "The man from your embassy has arrived," Lieutenant Eisert said. He went quiet for a moment, then added, "This room, I am afraid, will be too cramped for another person. Officer Riemer will escort you to my office while I greet our new visitor. Shall we go?" Lieutenant Eisert's excuse for moving the discussion to his office amused Brian. He knew the lieutenant did not want the man from the embassy to find two American citizens in an interrogation room.

Five minutes later Brian and Miss Weninger were sitting alone in Lieutenant Eisert's office when the door opened and, to the lieutenant's clear disapproval, the embassy man bustled past him without a formal announcement. He was tall—about six foot one—and burly. He looked as if he had been an athlete, probably a football player, who gave up on exercise years ago. His close-cropped hair was still more brown than gray, but not for much longer. Gray hairs only flecked his full mustache. The man's walk was peculiar. He favored his right leg, but he moved with more of a bob than a limp. Brian had a vision of a pirate trying to compensate for a rolling deck. The man smiled warmly as he extended his hand to Miss Weninger.

"Jack Silver," he said, and Brian sat bolt upright in his seat.

Jack Silver shook Miss Weninger's hand and finished introducing himself. "Attaché to the trade office at our embassy in Bern. Miss Weninger, I presume."

Brian couldn't believe it, but his teacher blushed. "Call me Betty," she said.

Silver turned to him. "And you must be Brian. How are you doing, son? Still shaken up?"

"I'm doing better," Brian said. "Still a little stunned, I guess. It's all been so weird."

"I'll bet," Silver said. His tone was sympathetic, but Brian felt the man's eyes measuring him. "You're lucky you reached me when you did. I was in Lucerne for a lunch appointment and was just about to hop the train back to Bern. Have you talked to your parents?"

"Not yet," Brian said. "I didn't want to call them until I had a clearer idea of what was going on."

"Gotcha. You didn't want to say, 'Hi Mom, I'm in the police station in Lucerne. I'll call you back when I know more.'"

"That's about it."

"Well, don't worry. I'm here to find out what's going on. The lieutenant briefed me on the situation, and his department wants to resolve this as painlessly as we do. Right, lieutenant?"

"Of course."

Silver positioned himself behind Brian and Miss Weninger. He placed his hands on Brian's shoulders, as if laying claim to him. "So I would like to know," he said to Lieutenant Eisert, "your intentions for this young citizen of the United States of America."

Lieutenant Eisert swallowed. "While we are almost certain that Professor Tetzel died of a heart attack and that no crime has occurred, we would prefer that Mr. Parker remain in Switzerland and be available to answer more questions until an autopsy proves the professor indeed died of natural causes."

Miss Weninger cut in. "How soon will that be? Our group is leaving Lucerne tomorrow morning for Germany."

It was not what Lieutenant Eisert wanted to hear. "We will expedite this, of course, but the soonest an autopsy can be performed is three days from now."

Everyone fell silent. *So much for Munich*, Brian thought bitterly. *Maybe even Paris.* Silver crossed his arms and leaned against the wall. Miss Weninger said, "Well, Brian, I guess I will have to make arrangements for the two of us to stay in Lucerne a few days longer while the rest of the group goes ahead."

Silver pushed himself from the wall and straightened his blazer. He said, "Betty, I have an idea that I think will cause the least disruption, at least for your tour group. Brian can come with me and be the guest of the embassy for a few days until Lieutenant Eisert gives the word, and then I personally will deliver him to you whether your group is in Munich, Dresden, Berlin, or Pago Pago." He turned to the lieutenant. "If the *Luzerner Polizei* finds that satisfactory."

Lieutenant Eisert pursed his lips and nodded.

Miss Weninger asked, "What do you think, Brian?"

Brian barely knew what to think. Fifteen minutes ago he had no idea how to reach Jack Silver of the U.S. Embassy, and now the very man was appointing himself Brian's guardian. Brian looked at Silver. Did he suspect Tetzel left a message for him? Brian watched for a hint of eagerness in Silver's behavior, but his face betrayed only empathy. "It's up to you, son," he said.

Brian simply said, "OK."

Miss Weninger nodded, but said nothing. She aimed her blue eyes at Silver, closed her mouth to a slit and almost imperceptibly puffed her upper lip. Brian perceived it. He knew the look from French class. This was how Miss Weninger collected her thoughts before scolding a student (usually Skip

Lewis). In low, direct tones, she said. "All right, Mr. Silver. I want to see every scrap of documentation you have. I want to talk to your superior at the embassy, and then I want to talk to your superior's superior. And Brian isn't leaving my sight until every person in this room has talked to his parents and received their permission."

"Very reasonable and very sensible," Silver replied, bowing his head a half-inch. "It's about time Brian talked to his parents anyway." He looked at his watch. "One-thirty here; it should be six-thirty in the morning in Milwaukee." He looked at Brian. "Would your parents be awake by now?"

"I think so," Brian said. "Dad doesn't leave for work until eight. They're probably just getting up."

Silver said, "Let's give them a few more minutes to at least down a cup of coffee before Brian lays this news on them."

"I'll need my suitcase," Brian said. "It's back at the hotel."

"Tim can bring it over," Miss Weninger said.

"He didn't go to Mount Pilatus?" Brian asked.

"When he heard what happened, he decided to stay behind in case you needed anything."

"We can send a car for the boy," Lieutenant Eisert said. "You may use my phone, Miss Weninger."

While Miss Weninger called the hotel, Silver pulled a cell phone from his inside blazer pocket. "Time to tell your parents the score," Silver said. He began punching numbers. "Milwaukee's area code is four-one-four, isn't it?" Brian nodded and Silver tapped the phone three more times before handing it to Brian. "You should finish it."

Brian looked at the string of numbers Silver had entered into the Nokia and realized it was the international dialing code. He entered his home phone number and hit the green send button.

As Brian waited for the ring tone, Silver said, "Just remember that no matter how unusual this situation is, Brian, you're safe and you've done nothing wrong."

Except withhold information from the police, Brian thought.

His mother answered after the third ring. To Brian's surprise, her voice was as clear as when he called for a ride home from the Mayfair Mall theater.

"Mom, it's Brian. Tell Dad to pick up on the other phone."

As hard as he tried to sound calm, Brian heard his voice tremble.

"Brian, what is it? Are you in trouble? Where are you?"

"I'm in Lucerne. In Switzerland. I'm not in trouble, not really. It's more like...once Dad gets on, I can explain."

There was a click and then his father's voice. "Brian, what's the matter?"

Brian told them, pausing for his mother's frequent interjections of "Oh my God!" When Brian finished, his mother wanted to talk to Miss Weninger and his father wanted to talk to Silver. Miss Weninger was using Lieutenant Eisert's phone again—talking to the embassy, Brian gathered—so he gave the cell phone to Silver.

And then Brian zoned out. The reaction was a defense mechanism. He was surrounded by adults trying to figure out what to do with him, and they didn't have much more of a clue than he did. Except for Silver, and Brian wouldn't be able to read Silver until they were alone, if ever. He stared at a coffee mug on Lieutenant Eisert's desk, wondering if the words on it were German for "World's Greatest Dad," and caught snatches of phone conversations. Miss Weninger, scrutinizing Silver as she spoke with the embassy, saying, "Please describe him for me." And Silver telling his father, "There's no need for you to fly over here, Mr. Parker." Brian cupped his hands around his elbows and started to rub his forearms as if to warm himself. For the first time since cradling Tetzel's dead body, he felt his bones turn cold. His mother's voice on the phone had been filled with worry, and Brian began to wonder if he should be scared.

Silver snapped him out of it. "Brian," he said, holding out his cell phone. "Your mother wants to talk to you."

Her voice had calmed. "So how are you feeling, Brian? Really?"

"I dunno. Weird."

"I wish I could be there with you, but your father and I are convinced you will be safe at the embassy with Mr. Silver. Just look at this as an opportunity to get to know Switzerland a little better, and do whatever Mr. Silver tells you, all right?"

"All right."

"We love you, Brian."

Brian turned his back to the others and lowered his voice. "I love you, too, Mom."

He handed the phone to Silver, who said, "Looks like we're all set." As Silver put the phone away, Brian noticed something unusual. It probably was a sleight of hand Silver had done hundreds of times before, something so quick Brian doubted Lieutenant Eisert or Miss Weninger caught it, but as Silver had returned the cell phone to his pocket he also removed the battery.

Three minutes later Brian stood in the hall holding his suitcase and enjoying a quick reunion with Tim Gifford.

"Dude, you should have gone to Mount Pilatus," Brian said. "I feel awful you stayed behind just to deliver my suitcase."

"Are you kidding? As soon as we heard you were at the police station, you became a sensation. When they get back, the girls will be swarming over me for information!"

Tim grinned, and Brian snapped at him: "If I had known it would improve your chances with Stephanie Tompkins, I would have stumbled across a dead body sooner."

Tim's smile disappeared. "God, I'm sorry, Brian. Was it really creepy? Are you OK?"

"People keep asking that question, and I don't know the answer yet. It's been a strange couple of hours." Brian decided not to tell his friend that Tetzel was the man he had identified as a spy in the Mühlenplatz. He didn't want Tim blabbing that coincidence to the group.

"It sucks I won't be with you guys for a few days," Brian said, "but I hope I'll be back by the time you reach Frankfurt."

They looked through the window into Lieutenant Eisert's office and saw Silver stand to shake the lieutenant's hand. Brian would be leaving soon.

"What about this guy from the embassy?" Tim asked. "This guy, Silver. You think he's a spy?"

"No," Brian lied.

CHAPTER 3--TAIL

"The train station is only a few blocks from here," Silver said. "Do you want to walk or hop on a tram?"

After two hours inside the police station, Brian didn't want to sit inside a crowded tram for even a few minutes. "I'd rather walk if doesn't bother you."

"If you're worried about my leg, don't," Silver said. "It's not as bad as it looks." They had traveled a block since leaving the police station, giving Brian a better sense of Silver's gait. He would take a regular step with his right leg, then swing his left leg around in a stiff but quick half-circle. He walked at a normal pace, but it did not appear Silver could bend his left knee.

"All right," Brian said, "but I have to tell you something right now because you'll probably want to take me straight back to Lieutenant Eisert as soon as you hear it."

Silver's eyes sharpened. "Eisert believed you were holding something back. What is it?"

"Tetzel did say something to me, in English, before he died. He wanted me to pass a message to you. He told me your name."

Silver nodded, showing no surprise. "Tell me on the train. We'll have privacy there."

"But won't the police want to know—"

Silver cut him off. "Kid, the police will want to say Tetzel died of natural causes and get you out of the country as soon as their laws and Lieutenant Eisert's sense of duty allow it. They don't want this turning into an international incident."

"I doubt I could cause an international incident," Brian said.

"Don't underestimate yourself."

Silver turned east at the corner. Brian noted the name of the street was Pilatusstrasse, a reminder of the mountaintop he was missing. They were in Lucerne's commercial district. The quaint medieval décor the tour guide had showed off yesterday was absent. The buildings were modern, or would have been in the 1970s. Pilatusstrasse was a thoroughfare of five-star hotels, art galleries, and furriers encased in concrete and glass.

Brian paused at a jewelry store and, pretending to look at the Rolex and Tissot displays, used the shop's window as a mirror to see whether anyone behind them stopped when he did. Brian figured Lieutenant Eisert would have someone watching them, but he didn't see anyone suspicious. Brian had to admit to himself he wasn't sure what behavior would look suspicious. When Brian moved from the shop, he found Silver appraising him with amusement.

"Were you checking for tails?"

Brian stammered, "I was wondering … well, if I was Lieutenant Eisert, I would have sent someone to follow us."

"He did," Silver said. "Next time you window shop, look across the street about a half a block back for a guy wearing a gold windbreaker."

Brian could resist no longer. "So are you Tetzel's case officer?"

"Case officer?" Silver was incredulous. "A lot of people over the years have asked if I were a CIA agent, but you're the first to ask if I were a CIA case officer."

"But you couldn't be an agent," Brian said. "Not if you're connected to the embassy. Agents are the foreign nationals that case officers recruit to reveal secrets about their country." Brian felt like a geek for saying "foreign nationals." He added hastily, "The Military Channel had a show on just last week called *Modern Spies*. The show said how CIA operatives were instructed to remove the batteries from their cell phones so their movements couldn't be traced by the phone company's satellite."

"What sharp little eyes you have," Silver said. "I hope the show also explained that all U.S. Embassy personnel receive extensive security training these days, so just because I can spot a tail and I take the battery out of my cell phone doesn't mean I'm CIA."

Silver's denial was convincing and smooth. Brian didn't trust it.

A Don't Walk signal stopped them at the next intersection. Brian looked down the cross street and saw the bookstore that had been his destination that morning, a million years ago. He sighed.

"What's up?" Silver asked.

Brian pointed at the bookstore. "That's where I was going ... before I found Tetzel."

"A bookstore? Not your usual tourist attraction."

"Well, I'm a huge Foster Blake fan, you see ..."

"That explains a lot."

"And I want to buy complete sets of Foster Blake paperbacks in German and French while I'm in Europe. I have all the German books now except a copy of *Snowfire*."

"Ah yes, *Schnefeuer*."

"You have a copy?"

"No," Silver said. "The movie was on TV here a couple of weeks ago. Rolls off the tongue, doesn't it? *Schnefeuer*. That doesn't happen often with German translations. *Snowfire* was a double feature that night with *An Emerald Eternity*, which the Germans mangle into *Eine Smaragdewigkeit*."

The signal changed and they stepped into the street. "It's funny," Brian said. "I just wanted to buy a spy novel. I didn't want to be in one."

Silver said, "Just do as I say, kid, and I'll make sure you're only in it for a few paragraphs."

Jeffrey Westhoff

CHAPTER 4--SKYRM

Standing outside the entrance to Lucerne's immense train station, Brian watched the buses roll into their depot across the Bahnhofplatz. A spider web of power lines looped above the bus station, moving the buses with the type of roof-mounted contacts Brian associated with trolleys and electric trains. He turned his attention across the street, where the man in the gold windbreaker sat at a café near the Hotel Monopol. The hotel was a grand old European building, a heavy Teutonic construction with a dome on top that looked like a helmet. Brian was dismayed that the restaurants off the hotel lobby were The New York Pizza Company and McDonald's.

"Britannia used to rule the waves," Silver said from behind him. "Now America rules the stomachs." He showed Brian their train tickets. "I got us a private compartment. Train leaves in ten minutes, so we better get on board."

Twenty minutes later, the red train had cleared Lucerne's suburbs and was snaking through Alpine passes. Brian, who sat facing the rear of the train, watched the mountain slopes grow steeper as they rushed past. The conductor punched their tickets, and Silver locked the compartment door when he departed. Down to business, Brian realized.

"So what did Tetzel say?"

"He didn't say much." Brian sipped from the bottle of water that Silver bought at a snack bar before they boarded the train. "He asked if I was American, and when I said yes, he told me to find you at the embassy. His exact words were, 'Please contact your embassy. Ask for Jack Silver.' He said it was urgent, then he said, 'Tell Silver someone in Prometheus turned. Tell him DeJonge doesn't suspect.' And then he died."

Silver looked at him blankly. "Is that it?"

Brian nodded.

Silver sat back, put a hand beneath his chin and ran his thumb back and forth beneath his lower lip. He said, "Well, I understand how that cryptic message would lead you to believe you walked into some heavy secret agent stuff, but I haven't the faintest idea what it means." Brian looked into Silver's eyes and this time believed he was telling the truth. "Are you sure that's all Tetzel said?"

Brian thought back. He placed his water bottle on the sideboard table near the window. "He did say one other word, but it must have been German because I didn't understand it."

"What was it?"

"It sounded like *squirm*."

Silver stopped stroking his lower lip. "Was it *Skyrm*?"

"Yeah. That's the word. What does it mean?"

"It's a name. S-K-Y-R-M. Describe the man you saw in the alley before you found Tetzel, the man with the pale blue eyes."

Brian did—the eyes, the dirty brown hair, the bomber jacket, and the umbrella. Silver said quietly, "That was Matthias Skyrm. A very scary man."

Then it hit Brian. The umbrella! Why hadn't he seen it before? "Do you think he stabbed Tetzel with the umbrella?" Brian said. "Injected him with poison like Georgi Markov?"

Silver shook his head. "Why am I not surprised you know about Georgi Markov? You know the difference between agents and case officers and you check for tails. When did they start teaching tradecraft in high school?"

"I learned a lot of this stuff from Foster Blake," Brian replied.

The train lurched as it switched tracks. Brian's water bottle wobbled. Brian and Silver reached for it simultaneously, but Silver's hand was quicker. He steadied the bottle before it could fall.

"Look, Brian, the less you think about all this right now, the better off you'll be."

Brian's skin prickled with fear as he realized what Silver was saying. "You think Skyrm killed Tetzel."

"Seems that way."

"Is he an assassin, this Skyrm guy?"

"That's more of a hobby for him," Silver said. "He's something of a freelance facilitator. He packages major operations, like bullion theft and, yeah, political assassinations. Everyone uses him: terrorists, organized crime, and certain governments that shall go nameless. Matthias Skyrm is one of Europe's most wanted criminals, but he operates completely off the grid. A phantom."

Silver tapped Brian's knee and said, "You probably got closer to him this morning than Interpol ever has."

Brian looked out the window and watched the world race away from him. He drank from the water bottle and turned back to Silver. "Am I in danger?"

"You're safe with me," Silver said. It was a flat, declarative statement with no air of bravado, only professionalism.

"So you are with the CIA."

"I neither confirm nor deny."

"The school trip is over in ten days." Brian took another sip. "Will you be able to return me by then?"

"I should," Silver said. "I hope so."

"I just better not still be here on July 21."

"That your birthday?"

"No, it's the next time I test for the black belt."

"Please don't tell me you're studying judo to be like Foster Blake."

"Not judo, tae kwon do. And it doesn't have much to do with Foster Blake, not really. My little sister started taking TKD a while ago, and when she started getting good, well…"

"You didn't like the idea that your kid sister could beat you up."

Brian felt his lips twitch as he smiled. "That's about it. She's still better than me, though. She made black belt last year. I'm stuck at red belt. I've tested for black belt twice and failed. I can do all the stances and forms and the sparring and board breaks, but the brick…I can't…no, I haven't been able to break a brick. I'm not visualizing myself striking *through* the brick, you know? You get two attempts, and if you don't get it right you're just slamming your hand into concrete. God, it hurts! I swear last time I was popping ibuprofens for two weeks. My instructor, Grand Master Kim, says he's seen it before, that I lack confidence under pressure. He says I'm thinking about it too much and those thoughts lead to doubt. 'Don't think, *do!*' he says. Sometimes Grand Master Kim sounds like Yoda..."

Brian realized Silver had gone silent and was letting him babble. The man was watching him the way a scientist watches a lab rat enter a maze. Suddenly self-conscious, Brian turned to look out the window. It took his brain a split second to catch up with his head. The sensation bewildered him. He turned back to Silver, and the slight movement made the world swirl. Silver twisted into a blur. Brian lost his grip on the bottle. His arm thudded to the seat and the bottle tumbled to the floor, splashing water across the compartment.

The water, Brian thought. *Something about the water.*

He said, or tried to say, "Did you drug me?" And then his chin crashed into his chest and his body lurched forward and carried him into oblivion.

CHAPTER 5--REAL TIME

As his mind emerged from a black hole, Brian Parker became aware of several sensations. First was the dryness of his mouth. It felt as if someone had scrubbed the inside of his cheeks with a cotton ball the size of a fist—and left the cotton ball.

Next, Brian sensed he was lying on his back. He couldn't yet tell what he was lying on. A floor? A bed? A cloud? One sensation was missing. After another moment Brian realized he was not feeling forward motion or rhythmic rumbling. He was no longer aboard the train.

He heard Silver's voice: "Who's Spider-Girl?"

Brian opened his eyes and rolled onto his side. He was lying on a battered army cot, a black polyester blanket pulled to his chest. The room was small, about five feet by six feet, with pale brown walls. A naked light bulb shined from the ceiling. There were two doors; Brian guessed one led to a bathroom. The only window was painted over with a shade of brown too dark to match the walls. He could hear birds chirping outside the window.

The contents of his suitcase and backpack were spread across the floor. The clothes were neatly folded, his Brewers cap on top. His comic books and German Foster Blake novels stood in separate stacks.

Silver sat in the far corner tapping his knee with a rolled-up comic. He repeated his question.

"Who's Spider-Girl? I never heard of her."

"She's Spider-Man's daughter." Brian was surprised to hear strength in his voice.

"Since when does Spider-Man have a daughter?"

"It's set in an alternate future, sort of." Brian said. He didn't have the energy to explain the whole thing.

"Christ," Silver said, "Marvel and all its alternate universes."

A DC guy, Brian thought. *No wonder I didn't trust him*. Brian closed his eyes tightly, hoping to squeeze consciousness back into his brain. He opened his eyes and sat.

The movement made Brian aware something else was missing, that extra snugness around his waist. His money belt was gone. He spotted it on the floor with his other possessions. His cash was next to it, an untidy pile of euros.

Silver saw where Brian was looking. "It's all there. I'm not about to rob a kid. But I will be holding on to these." He pulled Brian's passport and cell phone from inside his jacket, wagged them at Brian, and then slipped them back.

"Where are we?" Brian asked.

"Not telling," Silver said.

Brian noticed he was still wearing his watch. As an interrogator, Silver should have removed the watch to deprive Brian of his sense of time and disorient him. Brian shrugged and checked his watch. It was just after four thirty. But which four thirty? He could hear birds, so it must be the afternoon. Brian was too groggy to have been asleep for only a few hours; he must have been out for an entire day. He tried to calculate how far they could have traveled in that time.

"Are we still in Switzerland?"

"Could be," Silver said.

Brian knew what Silver was playing at. By withholding information, by taking Brian's passport—hell, by kidnapping him—Silver was demonstrating his power over Brian. The mind games were designed to keep Brian off balance and liable to let secrets slip. Except that Brian had no secrets. He had told Silver everything he knew about Tetzel's death, and he doubted the CIA man (Brian was now certain of that) wanted to learn more about Spider-Girl.

Silver handed Brian a white, plastic-foam cup filled with coffee. "You'll need this. You've been out for a while."

"Like I'd take something from you after you drugged me," Brian said.

"I needed you asleep then. I need you awake now. Always know what the other guy needs, so you can exploit it. It's one of the keys to surviving this game."

Brian took the cup. It was warm, not hot. "When did you drop knock-out pills into my water on the train? I didn't notice."

"I didn't put anything into the bottle." Silver wiggled a thumb. "I rubbed a sedative around the lip."

"Right after I mentioned Skyrm?"

"You got it," Silver said. "Now drink up."

Brian drank. Silver was right; he needed the coffee. It washed the dryness from his mouth and the lethargy from his mind.

"I'll bring you dinner in a few minutes, but I have to show you something first," Silver said, looking at his watch. "If you want water, you can get it from the bathroom," Silver said, nodding at the nearer door. "You won't find anything you can use as a weapon in there. Unless you're strong enough to rip the toilet from the floor."

Silver chuckled at his own joke, and it occurred to Brian the man was a little drunk. Silver's chuckled faded as he looked down at the stack of Foster Blake novels.

"You weren't kidding about being a Foster Blake fan," he said. "Agent 17K. 'K for killer.' I read those books when I was your age too. Read 'em all at least three times." He looked up. "Which one's your favorite?"

"*Lightningrod*," Brian answered.

"That's a good one. My favorite was the one in Mexico, *Dying on Borrowed Time*. Who was the woman in that one?"

"Fabiola Montez."

"Oh yeah, Fabiola Montez. Did I dream about her! And that was before the movie."

Wistfulness filtered into Silver's voice. It creeped Brian out but fascinated him, too.

"I really bought into the superspy thing," Silver continued. "That's why I applied to the CIA right out of college. I wanted to be Foster Blake. And don't think the Agency doesn't work that angle. They play up the cloak and dagger thing when they set the interview. 'Go to Room 204 of such and such motel at so and so time. Don't tell anyone you're coming, not even your family.' Once you get the job, they send you to the Farm—you know what the Farm is?"

Brian nodded. "The CIA's training center. In Virginia."

"You are a well-informed young man." Silver laughed as if

that were a joke and then went on. "They take you to the Farm for almost a year and teach you how to parachute onto a three-foot round target in pitch dark. And how to smash your car through a roadblock at sixty miles per hour. They get you thinking you'll get to do the cool spy stuff from books and movies, all that Foster Blake shit."

Silver looked at the floor. "Then they post you overseas, give you a drab office in godforsaken Bangladesh so a JMB thug on a motorbike can run you down and you're sent to some Third World doctor who doesn't know how to reset your shattered leg. As a reward, you get reposted to boring, neutral Switzerland and told to scout out schlubs you can bribe or blackmail into giving up their country's secrets."

Now Brian did feel disoriented. He was the captive, yet Silver was confessing. Brian doubted it was another mind game. Silver was complaining about his job like any disgruntled employee. Well, as long as Silver wanted to be informative, Brian decided to keep him talking.

"Was Tetzel a schlub?" Brian prodded. "Was he one of your joes?"

Silver snorted. "No one calls them joes except in le Carré novels. We call them *assets*. Tetzel was one of my assets." Silver paused, then added softly, "My million-dollar asset."

"He was on his way to meet you, wasn't he? That's why you got to the police station so fast. You weren't in Lucerne for a lunch date. You had a rendezvous with Tetzel."

Silver refocused his gaze on Brian, a different kind of sadness in his eyes. "You see, that's why you're in this mess, Brian," he said. "Because you use words like *rendezvous* and *case officer*. If you were another kid who spent all his time playing with his Xbox, I could have handed you off to the State Department and let them baby-sit you while I searched for Tetzel's killer. But you had to have read these spy thrillers written years before you were born. You had to have watched Military Channel documentaries about who killed Georgi Markov. You had to know too much about the spy game. I couldn't risk leaving you at the embassy."

Then it hit Brian: Silver didn't want to make him talk. Silver wanted to keep him quiet.

The theme from *The Munsters* screeched from inside Silver's jacket, and Brian jumped. Silver answered his cell phone, a Motorola and not the Nokia he had used yesterday.

"You've got him? Great job. Give me five minutes and then you're on."

Silver turned to Brian with a graveness that made the skin between Brian's shoulder blades tingle. "Like it or not, Brian, we have become partners. You need my protection, and I need your cooperation. I know you can't trust me. So I have to make you obey me."

Silver turned on a laptop computer on the small table beside his chair and then stood. "Take a seat. I've prepared a little slide show for you."

Brian sat in Silver's chair. Silver reached over his shoulder to start the PowerPoint presentation. Brian caught a whiff of alcohol as Silver leaned over him. Then the program began and Brian gasped as his transcript from 'Tosa East filled the screen.

"While you were sleeping, I had time to get to know you. Brian Eric Parker. Age fifteen. Sophomore at Wauwatosa East High School in Wauwatosa, Wisconsin. Son of Raymond and Victoria Parker. Older brother of Cecelia."

The image changed to a picture of his mother leading a field trip to the Milwaukee County Zoo. The photo had appeared in the Milwaukee Journal-Sentinel last December.

"Your mother teaches seventh grade at Whitman Middle School, also in Wauwatosa. Your father is an accountant at the law firm of Milner, Fields, Bolander & Henderson in Milwaukee. Apart from having a black belt in tae kwon do, your sister, age twelve, was last fall's highest scorer in her division of the Milwaukee Kickers."

The picture changed to one of Cecelia driving down a soccer field. The photo had run in the sports pages of the Wauwatosa News-Times last October.

The image changed again and Brian groaned. He was looking at his house on Lloyd Street, but it was bathed in the eerie green of night vision. A note at the bottom of the photo claimed it had been shot at 4 a.m. Central Time, which Brian guessed was a few hours ago.

The computer screen changed to show a city street, but the

cars were moving and Brian could hear the traffic of another Milwaukee rush hour. Silver spoke from behind him: "It's almost 5 p.m. where we are. That means it's almost 9 a.m. in Wisconsin. You're watching this in real time."

The time code flashing at the bottom of the screen said it was 8:56 a.m. Central Time. The camera moved in a slow arc to show the surroundings, and Brian recognized the spot on Wisconsin Avenue just east of Water Street. The person operating the camera was standing outside the office building where his father worked. The camera panned. When it stopped Brian saw his father walking toward him.

"My friend is shooting this with the latest in buttonhole cameras," Silver said. "Incredible technology, isn't it?"

Brian had to agree. As his father approached, Brian could see he had nicked his chin shaving again. His father's face, seen from a low angle, filled the screen and Brian heard the voice of Silver's accomplice.

"Excuse me. What time is it?"

Brian's father glanced at his watch and smiled at the stranger. "It's about eight to nine," he said and walked past.

Silver hunched down so his mouth was next to Brian's ear. "Your dad's watch is four minutes slow," he said. "I hope you get the chance to tell him to reset it."

Brian understood the stakes now. If he didn't follow Silver's orders, the people he loved were at risk. Although they were thousands of miles away on the other side of an ocean, Silver had just taken Brian's family hostage.

CHAPTER 6--ESCAPE

Sitting on his haunches, Brian examined the locked door to his cell and contemplated escape.

It was shortly after midnight, ninety minutes since the hallway light went out and one hour and ten minutes since Silver last made a sound. Holding his penlight in his mouth, Brian had spent the previous ten minutes quietly assembling an escape kit in his backpack. He had bought the penlight on a whim after spotting it in the checkout line at Target when his mother took him shopping for vacation supplies.

Thank God for whims, he thought.

Kneeling next to the backpack, Brian had assembled the items he thought he would need: three changes of clothes, windbreaker, Milwaukee Brewers cap, sunglasses, collapsible umbrella, rain poncho (still in its package), shaving kit, and Fodors guides to Switzerland, France, and Germany (just in case he was in one of those countries). He restocked his money belt and fastened it around his waist. Then he began his examination of the door.

The hinges were on the inside. The easiest way to open the door would have been to pop out the pins holding the hinges together. But Brian's penlight revealed the hinges were flanged on the bottom as well as the top. Only a bolt cutter could take them apart.

Brian had already ruled out breaking the window because Silver said it was alarmed. He might have lied, but Brian didn't want to chance it. The only way out was the door, and the only way to open the door was to pick the lock. When Silver had left four hours earlier, Brian heard him lock the door but did not hear him slide a bolt or a chain. Brian moved the beam to illuminate the crack between the door and the frame and hoped he wouldn't see a deadbolt. If the lock was a deadbolt, Brian could do nothing but climb back into the cot and wait for morning.

Not that it was going to help him open the door, but Brian was grateful Silver had left him his watch. It allowed Brian to track the hours as he lay on the cot contemplating everything Silver had said that evening, trying to separate the credible threats from the bluffs.

Brian had challenged Silver immediately after seeing the video feed of his father. "It's illegal for the CIA to operate within the United States," Brian said, but Silver quickly responded, "It was illegal for me to kidnap you."

Following a bland dinner of microwaved burritos and Spanish rice, Silver told Brian to get a good night's sleep because they had a busy day tomorrow. Sleep—what a joke. Brian didn't need sleep after being sedated for so long, and he was too wired anyway. He turned out the light but lay awake mulling the situation that he and his family were in. He felt certain Silver had only the one person watching his family; Silver did not have the time to mount a full surveillance operation. Nevertheless, Brian thought it prudent to assume Silver's man would tap his family's home phone, cell phones, and e-mail accounts and might even intercept and read their mail.

After four hours of deep, deliberative thought, Brian was certain he would not put his family in danger if he escaped Silver, not unless he tried to contact them after he got away. Still, Brian wrestled with the notion of whether escaping Silver was wise. He would be alone in a foreign country (which one, he didn't know) without his passport. He wouldn't be able to return to his school group because Silver would be monitoring them. He wouldn't be able to go to the local police or the nearest U.S. consulate, because no one would believe his story and he eventually would be handed back to Silver. If he did get away, Brian would have only his wits, the supplies in his backpack, about eight hundred dollars worth of euros, and a single name to pursue: DeJonge. Escape was a foolish prospect.

But staying with his kidnapper might be a deadly prospect. Brian fixated on Silver's offhand comment about Tetzel being his "million-dollar asset." He had an idea what that meant, and he suspected Silver might sacrifice his captive to save his own skin. Brian couldn't risk being Silver's pawn. He needed to be a player. He needed to escape, so he smiled when his penlight revealed a spring latch and not a deadbolt.

Brian knew the difference between the two locking mechanisms from helping his father install a new back door on their house. More importantly, he knew how to pick this type of lock from reading Silver's favorite Foster Blake novel, *Dying on Borrowed Time*.

Inserting a curved bar or length of plastic behind the slanted side of the latch and quickly pulling it back should spring the lock. Brian had a curved piece of plastic. In fact, he had two. He reached into his backpack's side pocket and retrieved the sunglasses. He folded the glasses so that one curved temple stuck out, then wriggled the temple behind the latch. It fit perfectly, but the plastic was too flimsy. When Brian pulled, the temple bent and slid back over the top of the latch without springing it. He needed something to hold the temple steady from the bottom. If Brian had a longer, more flexible length of plastic, he would have been able to thread it around the latch and pull both ends of the plastic. Thread! That's it! Brian blessed his mother, because he was finally going to use the dental floss she insisted he pack.

If this worked, Brian would have to move fast. After cutting off a six-inch length of floss, he replaced his shaving kit and hoisted the backpack over his shoulders. The floss was waxed, which made it easier to manipulate. Brian folded the length of floss in half and stuck the looped end into the crack just beneath the latch. It took four attempts to maneuver the temple behind the latch so that the tip was caught inside the loop. He pulled the floss taut and felt it tug the temple. So far, so good. Brian placed the impromptu apparatus in his left hand and gripped the knob with his right. He twisted the knob. It held firm, but would give once the latch popped. Brian counted in his mind. One. Two. Three!

He yanked on the floss and sunglasses, and the latch retracted with a snap that sounded like a gunshot to Brian's ears. The doorknob gave and turned left. Brian had beaten the lock.

He held the door closed and kept the doorknob in the open position as he slipped his sunglasses and penlight into his jacket pocket with his left hand. He listened intently for two minutes but heard no sound. Calling upon his tae kwon do training, Brian closed his eyes and took deep breaths to center himself. Rising from his crouch, Brian pulled the door open and was met instantly by a merciless electronic screech.

Silver had been sleeping in a chair at the end of the hall, but the high-pitched alarm woke him and he kicked over a bottle of Captain Morgan rum as he came after Brian. Silver blocked the only passage. Brian put his head down and ran to bull past him, but the hallway was too narrow. Silver grabbed his arm. Brian tried to counter, but the weight of the backpack threw off his balance. Silver only had to pivot on his heel to send Brian crashing into the wall. Brian went down on one knee and tried to recover when he saw Silver reach for something inside his belt and, God, would that horrible monotone whine ever stop? Brian recognized the device in Silver's hand as a stun gun a split second before Silver pressed it into his chest. With a crackle, Brian's body arched into a rictus and he collapsed to the floor.

Next, Brian had the sensation of bouncing. Silver had thrown Brian over his shoulder. Brian wanted to push away, but his flaccid limbs would not respond. All he could do was loll his head to the side and watch as Silver switched off a simple door alarm that consisted of two magnetic sensors. The racket ceased, yet lingered inside Brian's head like the cry of some vicious bird.

Silver said, "I picked up that alarm at a Home Depot the last time I was home visiting my mother in Bayonne." He carried Brian back into the room.

"Only thirty bucks. Not a bad investment," he said as he dropped Brian onto the cot.

CHAPTER 7--CATCH

"You can take off your blindfold."

Brian guessed the trip had lasted ten minutes by the time Silver said those words, his first since they got into the car. Or perhaps fifteen minutes. Brian was a lousy judge of time, and Silver had taken his watch as punishment for the escape attempt. Silver also took his money belt before they left the safe house that morning, but Brian had anticipated that. Once the effects of the stun gun had worn off, Brian replaced the money in the belt with torn pages from the Spider-Girl comic. Brian's cash was now hidden in his socks and sneakers.

Most of the drive had been downhill, along twisting roads. During the last few minutes the roads had straightened, Silver had braked more frequently, and the traffic noise had grown louder and closer. They were nearing a city. Brian could hear another sound pushing from beneath the buzzes and whirrs of small European engines. Was that? Yes, the sound of waves rolling into a shoreline. He felt the sun's warmth, magnified by the windshield, on his face. He smelled fish and seaweed and ... something else. A tangy scent he never encountered while in-line skating along Milwaukee's lakefront.

And then, while the car was idling, Silver told him to take off his blindfold.

Brian did and was dazzled by blue.

Silver said, "Not quite like Lake Michigan, huh kid?"

Brian nodded dumbly. Even on the brightest and clearest day, the waters of Lake Michigan were tinted dark green. But the waters now filling his view were the purest blue Brian had seen—a blue purer than he had imagined possible. The waters seemed to radiate with a mysterious energy, as if this sea were the source of all the blue in the universe. Only a distant oil tanker told him where the sea ended and the sky began.

Brian knew this was the Mediterranean. He guessed that the unfamiliar, tangy scent was the salt in the sea air.

He thought he had been staring at the bright turquoise sea for twenty minutes, but when Silver put the car in gear and jerked him back to reality, Brian realized his reverie had lasted only seconds. He looked around to figure out where they were. A harbor filled with yachts and sailboats was to their left. A steep hill whizzed past on their right. As they rounded the hill a columned monument came into view. The road signs were in French, and on most cars a white *F* stood beneath the circle of stars next to the license plate numbers. These "eurobands" were one of the first things Brian and his schoolmates had noticed about Europe's vehicles. The letters signified what country each car was from, and *F* stood for *France*.

"Figured out where you are yet?" Silver asked.

This had to be the French Riviera, so Brian named the first city to enter his thoughts.

"Monte Carlo?"

"You're only eight miles off," Silver said, "but you got the country wrong. Monte Carlo is part of Monaco, one of those pocket principalities stuck between Europe's borders like a gob of spinach stuck between your teeth."

Brian decided it was a good thing Silver didn't work for the State Department.

"What's your next guess?" Silver said.

Brian knew of only three French cities on the Mediterranean. He knew Cannes because of its film festival, but this city seemed too large. And he knew Marseilles because many a thug in the Foster Blake novels—how did Clive Hastings usually phrase it?—"had brawled his way up through the Marseilles drug trade." But Marseilles wasn't on the Riviera.

Through process of elimination Brian said, "Nice."

"You got it," Silver said. "The jewel of the Cote d'Azure. I've never been here on a day when the weather wasn't gorgeous."

The car passed the steep hill and the road straightened and widened into a seaside thoroughfare.

"Great view, huh?" Silver said.

Again, Brian had to agree. Golden beaches stretched for miles alongside the blue sea. Brian saw hundreds of figures swimming, wading, or sunbathing. Tim would be giddy to know his friend was looking at probably dozens of topless women, even if Brian couldn't make anything out from this distance.

To their immediate right were buildings that had changed little since the nineteenth century. Houses and shops were packed together. They had skinny windows and shutters and the type of red-tiled roofs Brian associated with Mexico.

Silver made a hard right turn into this older neighborhood of thin, pastel-colored buildings. Traffic was slower on these narrow streets, but Silver didn't seem to mind. He made another right turn at the next intersection, followed quickly by a left. The car rolled past shops, taverns, and open-air markets. Another right and two more lefts and the car passed four churches within three blocks.

Silver made another left. They passed the first church again and Brian wondered why Silver was driving in circles. Then he understood. He said, "Are you making sure we haven't picked up a tail?"

The CIA man nodded. "If you want to play junior spy, you might as well make yourself useful. There's a yellow Citroën Deux Cheveaux back there that I've seen too many times for comfort. Keep an eye out for it." He added, "A Deux Cheveaux looks like an old Volkswagen Beetle, except flatter."

Brian was about to say he wouldn't be playing junior spy if Silver hadn't kidnapped him, but something below the dashboard caught his attention. It was the car's cigarette lighter. Silver wasn't using its receptacle to charge a cell phone or laptop or MP3 player. The knob of an actual lighter jutted from the console. It was on the passenger side, within an inch of Brian's knee. Just like in his mother's car, the old one she had inherited from her father.

In chapter eight of *A Whisper of Death*, Foster Blake uses a dashboard lighter to escape from Von Himmelsteen's henchman, Mr. Nix. The day after Brian finished reading the book for the second time, his mother drove him to the Mayfair Mall. Sitting in the passenger seat, Brian had wondered if he could mimic Foster Blake's sly maneuver of pushing in the cigarette lighter with his knee, then easing his knee back the millimeter required for the heated lighter to spring out without the usual popping sound.

The first time Brian tried the trick, not only did the lighter pop out noisily, it hit his knee in the same way as a doctor's mallet. Brian reflexively kicked the underside of the glove compartment and received a safety lecture from his mother. The second time he tried the trick, it worked. For weeks after that, whenever his mother gave him a ride Brian silently armed the lighter, secretly content that if his mother tore off a rubber mask to reveal herself as a S.C.Y.L.L.A. assassin, he'd have a weapon ready.

Then it had been a private joke, but could Brian do it now when his situation was urgent and the driver was not a suburban mom but a CIA officer? Fortunately, Silver was driving on crowded streets and making frequent turns to flush a possible tail. If Silver were roaring down whatever the French call a freeway, Brian couldn't attempt the stunt without getting them maimed or killed.

Brian assessed his situation. Silver had bound his ankles with plastic straps, but not his hands. Silver didn't want people to look inside the car and see Brian in handcuffs. Instead, he told Brian to sit with his backpack on his lap, figuring its bulk would hamper Brian's movements. The backpack would be in his way once the lighter was primed, but it still contained the escape gear from the night before and would be valuable once Brian got out of the car. He had to forget about his suitcase in the trunk.

The door locks were electronic, and the switch to unlock them was on the center arm console. That was another piece of luck. Reaching across Silver to unlock the doors would have been dangerous. Brian considered the timing. He couldn't control when the lighter popped; he guessed that once it did he would have thirty seconds before the inner coil lost the intense heat he needed. The safest time to act would be when they were stopped at an intersection, but Silver would be less likely to anticipate an escape attempt while the car was moving. Brian decided to do it while Silver was slowing to a stop. This opened the possibility that they would crash and the air bags would deploy. Brian didn't know how hard the air bag would hit him, but he would be prepared for the impact and Silver wouldn't.

Silver glanced from the driver's side mirror to the rearview mirror. He was preoccupied with spotting the phantom Deux Cheveaux, but that wasn't enough. Brian needed to distract him further. He started talking.

"What kind of gun do you carry?"

Silver shook his head. "That's one thing the books and movies get wrong. Few case officers carry guns. They invite trouble. You ever see me holding a gun, you'll know I'm desperate."

Brian tried another tack. "What do you think Tetzel wanted to tell you?"

Silver glanced at him. "Trying to help me crack the case?"

"Do I have anything better to do?"

"Point taken," Silver replied. "I don't know what Tetzel wanted to tell me, because I wasn't expecting his signal. Our next scheduled meeting wasn't for three weeks. The signal indicated he had important information, but that it wasn't safe to meet in Neuchatel. That was last Tuesday. On Friday night he contacted me and set up the rendezvous in Lucerne."

"And on Saturday he died."

"Right."

"What about Prometheus and DeJonge?"

"Prometheus could mean a few things, but my best guess is Tetzel was referring to a weapons program being developed by a European consortium. About eight months ago Langley told all case officers to press our agents for information on any foreign weapons program that took a quantum leap in development. Some military scientist had just died, and the Pentagon was worried his research had been stolen."

"How did the scientist die?"

"They didn't say anything, not even his name. The Pentagon doesn't want the CIA's rank and file knowing *their* secrets. Still, it didn't take much digging to learn that Prometheus is a weapon that uses something like microwaves."

"Microwaves were Tetzel's subject."

"How do you know that?"

"I asked Lieutenant Eisert."

Silver chuckled. "Maybe you can crack the case." He jerked

the car into a sharp right turn down a street Brian already had seen three times.

"And DeJonge?" Brian asked.

"Don't know. It's a common name in Central Europe, but with several spellings. Figuring out his—or her—identity is my next step."

Silver took another left turn, looking back through the driver's side window for the Deux Cheveaux. Brian slid his knee forward and depressed the cigarette lighter.

Now he had to drive Silver past distraction to aggravation. He said, "Then why smuggle me into France? Wouldn't it be easier to find all this information from your office in Bern? Or is this because you don't want your superiors to figure out your deal with Tetzel?"

Silver's voice hardened. "The hell are you talking about, kid?"

"Last night you called Tetzel your 'million-dollar asset.' Sounds like you had an *Our Man in Havana* scam worked out with him. Maybe you told your superiors he was a highly placed source, a gold mine with contacts in the Swiss aerospace industry."

Brian didn't know if Switzerland had an aerospace industry, but this was no time to slow down. "So you convinced them Tetzel was worth a premium in payoffs, and they started sending him large sums of cash every month. But Tetzel didn't have that much access, did he? You beefed up his reports and split the money with him and stuck your cut into a Swiss bank account."

Silver's neck turned red. Brian pressed on. "You weren't expecting Tetzel to ever learn anything big, but he did and he died for it. Your 'million-dollar asset' gets silenced and you have no idea why. All you know is that you had better figure out the answers before Langley starts asking the questions. You got scared, scared enough to snatch a fifteen-year-old tourist who wandered into your mess—"

"That's enough!" Silver's voice was a whip. "I don't want to hurt you, kid," he shouted, "but you're writing your death warrant here, and you'd better shut up before you sign it."

The cigarette lighter sprang free, silently nudging Brian's knee. Adrenaline coursed through him, but he acted calmly.

Disguising his movement as a reaction to Silver's rage, Brian sat up to move his knee clear of the lighter. He had to attack before the lighter cooled. The signal at the next corner turned from green to amber. Three vehicles were ahead of them, preventing Silver from gunning the car through the intersection.

In *A Whisper of Death* Foster Blake jabbed the cigarette lighter into Mr. Nix's neck, but Brian couldn't bring himself to do that. He had another method in mind. As the traffic light turned red, Brian looked over Silver's shoulder and said, "I think I see that yellow car you described."

"Where?" Silver asked. He looked out his window, away from Brian.

In one motion Brian swept his right hand forward to knock his backpack to his feet, scoop the lighter from its socket, and lob it into a high arc with a trajectory that would end in Silver's lap. The lighter's coil glowed bright orange as it spun in the air.

Brian said, "Catch!"

CHAPTER 8--IMPACT

Instinctively, Silver took his hands off the wheel to catch the lighter. He screamed as the hot metal seared into his palm. Brian hit the switch to unlock all the doors. Then he braced himself and shut his eyes as their car plowed into the rear bumper of the sedan in from of them. Their air bags fired instantaneously. It was like being walloped by a bounce house.

The air bags deflated as rapidly as they had deployed, and Silver automatically whipped the lighter from his hand. It ricocheted off the windshield. Brian ducked as the lighter flew toward his face. It bounced off his headrest and landed in the door well, which couldn't have been more perfect for Brian. He hit the button to unfasten his seatbelt and grabbed his backpack. Silver lunged as Brian opened the door, but his seatbelt held him back. Brian rolled out of the car and onto the curb. He snatched the lighter from the door well. It was still hot enough to melt the plastic strap binding his ankles.

Once his feet were free, Brian took off. Cars were backing up behind the accident, and people had gathered on the sidewalks, attracted by blaring horns and cries of *"Au secours!"* Brian looked back to see Silver exit the car with his wounded right hand jammed beneath his left armpit. He shouted, "Get back here, Brian! You have nowhere to go." Before Silver could follow, the driver of the rear-ended sedan grabbed his arm and let loose a tirade of what Brian guessed were the filthiest words in the French language.

Silver would be occupied for several minutes, hopefully longer, but Brian needed to be far from the scene before the police arrived. He ran down the sidewalk at full speed, dodging people as they jostled for a closer look at the accident. He slowed only for a second when he noticed that one of the cars caught in the jam behind the crash was yellow and looked like an old VW Beetle, except flatter.

Brian put the car out of his mind as he tore around the corner and flew past slender buildings of pink and ochre. He zigged down three blocks and zagged across two before darting into a music store. He walked swiftly to the back of the store and ducked behind a cardboard standup advertising two bands he had never heard of, The Acid Thwacks and Funky Lederhosen. Brian pulled all the euros from his left sock and jammed them into his pocket. He removed his jacket, sunglasses, and Brewers cap from his backpack and put them on. His appearance altered, Brian left the store. He walked at a normal pace to avoid attracting attention.

The exhilaration of the escape wore off swiftly. Brian was away from Silver, but he was alone in France and didn't know his next move. Maybe he could hide in a movie theater for a few hours then go to a library to try to find information on DeJonge.

Brian turned the corner and a solution presented itself. He was walking toward a bus station, and passengers were boarding a bus with the word *Cannes* above the windshield. Brian knew Cannes wasn't far, and Silver wouldn't expect him to leave Nice so quickly. The short bus trip should buy him enough time to determine a plan before Silver could find him.

Inside the station, Brian was pleased to discover his French was sufficient enough not only to buy a ticket, but also to learn the bus was leaving in five minutes and would arrive in Cannes thirty minutes after that.

The bus was half full. Brian took a seat toward the rear and overlooking the street. He watched for Silver, but the CIA man did not appear by the time the bus driver closed the door. Relieved, Brian settled back in his seat.

Someone pounded on the bus door. Brian sat up again expecting to see Silver as the door swung open. Instead, a tall man with black hair and a beige shirt stepped aboard. After an exchange of rude French with the driver, the man walked past Brian without glancing at him and settled into the rear seat.

As the air brakes sighed and the bus pulled away, Brian allowed himself a sense of triumph. He may be a fugitive in another country with little idea what to do or where to go next, but he was free. To celebrate, he pulled his iPod from his backpack, pushed the buds into his ears, and started his Gwen Stefani playlist (he had been a fan ever since her cover version of Roberta Flack's *Clandestinely Yours*, his favorite Foster Blake theme). Right now Brian was more excited than frightened, and he decided to enjoy that feeling for as long as it lasted.

CHAPTER 9--SEARCH

The feeling lasted two songs.

A few stanzas into the third song, Brian found the lyric "I'm walking into spider webs" ominous. He, too, was walking into spider webs, or at least riding a bus into them. What would happen if he got caught? Would his family ever learn what happened to him? Brian turned off the iPod and stowed it in his backpack. Morbid, fearful thoughts would paralyze him. He had to trust his intelligence and abilities and keep moving ahead.

His immediate goal was to learn the identity of DeJonge. Once in Cannes, Brian would find the public library, log on to a computer, and rely on his Internet search skills to locate DeJonge. He hoped it wouldn't take hours. A complication occurred to him. What if he needed a library card to use a computer? Brian doubted his freshman-level French would convince a librarian to let him use a computer. No, those were negative thoughts. Brian resolved to go to the library and simply try his luck.

He looked out the window to enjoy the remaining sights of Nice before the bus left the city limits. They were passing through the urban fringe. Buildings no longer crowded each other. Storefronts were glassy and modern and would fit in any American strip mall. Familiar fast food signs flickered by. Some shops remained distinctly European, like the Internet café up ahead. Brian smiled. Why hadn't he thought of it sooner? An Internet café would be better than the library. He would be any other tourist checking his e-mail or updating his Facebook status. No one would notice him. No one would remember him.

Brian consulted his French phrasebook. The translation for *Internet café* was *café Internet*. Simple enough. The book even said how to ask directions to the nearest one: "Est-ce qu'il y a un café Internet près d'ici?" He practiced the phrase under his breath.

Knowing what to do and say when he got to Cannes, Brian reclined in his seat to watch the scenery. Drab concrete condominiums obstructed the Mediterranean until the bus turned onto a wide thoroughfare with lines of palm trees running down the median. The sea, with its beaches and jetties, was on one side of the boulevard. On the other was a wall of expensive shops and belle époque hotels. Brian instantly recognized the Carlton because every May during the Cannes Film Festival a billboard advertising the next Foster Blake movie straddled the hotel's entrance. The palm trees flashed past like a tropical picket fence until the bus reached a massive, angular structure that resembled the Sydney Opera House after Godzilla had sat on it. Brian read the name of the building, the Palais des Festivals et des Congrès, as the bus passed and realized it was a glorified movie theater.

The boulevard curved to reveal a harbor where fishing boats bobbed alongside luxury yachts. The trip ended as the coach pulled into a station located between the harbor and the city hall, which looked exactly how Brian imagined a city hall on the French Riviera should. A modest, central clock tower topped by a shallow cupola divided the muddy yellow façade into symmetrical halves limned by a red-tile roof. The French Tricolour flew from the balcony two floors below the clock, with the main entrance directly beneath the flag.

Stepping off the bus, Brian hitched his backpack over his shoulders and looked for someone who could direct him to the nearest Internet café. His best bet, he figured, was to ask someone exiting the city hall, someone likely to be a resident. He approached a blonde woman in a light pink sundress who appeared to be in her late thirties (women nearing middle age always were nice to Brian, for some reason) and asked, "Pardonnez-moi, Madame. Est-ce qu'il y a un café Internet près d'ici?" She smiled, and in a mélange of English and French told him an Internet café was only a few blocks away in an old part of the city called Le Suquet. She pointed to an ancient church atop a nearby hill, which Brian gathered was Le Suquet's landmark. The woman added that if he said "pardon" instead of "pardonnez-moi," he would sound less like a tourist.

Brian thanked her and walked up the hill. He found himself inside an M.C. Escher print of narrow, tilting streets, some linked by tight stone stairwells that cut sharp angles between buildings. He had to ask directions twice more before finding the café.

Once inside, Brian paid for a half an hour on the computer and set to work. He called up the Google home page, typed in "De Jonge Heinrich Tetzel," and hit enter. More results than he expected came up, but they were in French. This wasn't going to work. Brian looked at the URL and saw the problem. It read "http://www.google.fr." He changed the "fr" to "com," and tried again. This time the results came back in English.

Well, almost in English. The first link led to a badly translated German academic site that listed physics professors in all European universities. Eight DeJonges were given, along with two Dejonghs, one Dejonghe, two De Jonges, five De Jonghs, and nine De Jonghes. Silver wasn't kidding about the multiple spellings.

Brian pulled his notebook from the backpack. It was one of those composition books with the dappled black and white covers that he mentally referred to as *Harriet the Spy* specials. He flipped past the now mundane journal entries describing rain clouds over Innsbruck and stamp dealers in Liechtenstein until he found a blank page. He transcribed the names from the computer screen and their corresponding universities. None of the professors worked at the University of Neuchatel, which didn't surprise Brian. Silver had smuggled Brian into France, which is where Silver must have expected to find DeJonge. Brian underlined the names of the eleven professors from French universities. Six taught in Paris, one in Toulouse, three in Lyons, and one in Aix-en-Provence.

Now to further cull the list. Brian typed in "DeJonge Prometheus" and clicked the search button. He was prepared to do this for every spelling of the name, but when the results appeared Brian saw that he got it right on the first try. Numerous entries highlighted the name Edouard DeJonge. One description read, "French researcher leads Europe's answer to America's Positive Enforcement program." Another said, "Breakthrough in Paul Sab laboratory pushes EU ahead of America in race to manufacture directed-energy weapon." The latter entry, dated six months earlier, was linked to the University of Toulouse's Internet domain. Brian hit the link and a French home page with the heading "Université Paul Sabatier/Toulouse III" came up. The article Brian sought was missing, and the link to the home page's English translation failed. He intuited that "Paul Sab" was a nickname for Université Paul Sabatier, which seemed to be connected to the University of Toulouse. That didn't bring him much closer to finding Edouard DeJonge, though.

Frustrated, Brian returned to the search results and looked for an entry with an American source. He clicked on a link to the archives of www.militech.org and was rewarded with the following, dated four months earlier:

U.S. LOSES P.E. LEAD

A breakthrough by a French physicist has allowed the European Union to leapfrog past the Pentagon in the development and likely implementation of a Positive Enforcement weapons system.

Prof. Edouard DeJonge, a researcher in microwaves and millimeter waves at Université Paul Sabatier in Toulouse, France, made this breakthrough roughly two months ago, although Eurocorps—a European Union military consortium based in Strasbourg, France—is mum about the nature of DeJonge's brainstorm. DeJonge has been put in charge of the program, called Project Prometheus, with Eurocorps footing the bill. DeJonge continues to be based in Toulouse, capital of Europe's aerospace industry thanks largely to the presence of Airbus.

America's Positive Enforcement program, in development for over a decade, encountered numerous setbacks following the sudden

death last year of the program's chief researcher, Dr. Roland Eck, in a plane crash. Plus, Congress began to listen to critics who claimed the weapon could be turned into a torture device.

Eurocorps hints that its Prometheus device may be ready for public demonstration as early as this summer. If the EU continues at this pace, it could implement Prometheus within a year, marking the first time since World War II that Western Europe has deployed a new military technology while the Pentagon remained in the testing stage.

Brian blinked at the computer screen and shivered. Apparently he was hip deep in a covert war over some sort of next-generation super weapon. What sort he could only guess. Militech.org obviously was a website for military gearheads with prior knowledge of Positive Enforcement. The name Positive Enforcement was vague enough to be meaningless. Didn't it have something to do with training dogs?

He could worry about that later. Before Brian's computer time ran out, his priority was to learn how to find Edouard DeJonge and warn him. But warn him of what? The most likely scenario was that Matthias Skyrm, the man who killed Tetzel, was part of a plot to sabotage Prometheus. Skyrm may be planning to blackmail, kidnap, or murder DeJonge. Brian wondered how big the conspiracy was. Had Skyrm killed the American scientist, Roland Eck? Eck must have been the Pentagon researcher Silver had mentioned. Brian thought about Silver. Had he pinpointed Edouard DeJonge and put all this together yet? Not likely. Brian had escaped Silver only ninety minutes ago. Silver might still be in a police station filling out an accident report.

The news about an experimental weapon unsettled Brian, but the revelation about DeJonge and Prometheus also offered him a way out. If Brian got to DeJonge in time to warn him, this professor could protect him.

Brian navigated to an online telephone directory for Toulouse and pumped a triumphant fist when he found Edouard DeJonge listed. This whole mess could be finished before the day was through, depending on how long it took to travel to Toulouse by train. Brian had to assume DeJonge's phone was tapped, so calling him would be too dangerous. Brian wrote DeJonge's address in his notebook, which he returned to his backpack. A quick map search told him the Cannes train station was eight blocks northeast of the café. The clock at the bottom of the computer screen told him he had five minutes of Internet time remaining, five minutes to learn about the mystery weapon.

Brian returned to Google and typed "Positive Enforcement" into the window. Before he hit the search button someone stepped behind him and said, "Your time is up."

"I still have five minutes," Brian replied as he clicked the mouse. Then he turned to look directly into the face of Matthias Skyrm.

CHAPTER 10--STAIRS

As he stared into Skyrm's eyes, Brian knew why that subliminal chill had shot through him when he passed the man in the Lucerne alley. Skyrm's irises, so pale they were closer to white than blue, were unnatural enough, but they were made unholy by their outlines, hair-thin circles the same dark red as dried blood.

Brian could not tear his gaze away from these eyes. The world seemed to retract, leaving nothing but a frigid tunnel between his eyes and Skyrm's. Was this what it felt like to have a cobra stare you down? Skyrm looked back impassively. His irises flitted back and forth as if a subroutine in his brain were scanning Brian's face. After several seconds Skyrm's eyebrows rose and his mouth opened in recognition.

"The boy from the alley," he said. "This makes some sense after all."

Brian was confused for a moment until he realized Skyrm wasn't addressing him but a man standing behind him. It was the tall man with the beige shirt who had pounded on the door to board the bus in Nice. Things made more sense for Brian, too. Silver had been correct about being tailed. Skyrm and the other man were in the yellow Deux Cheveaux, and when Brian escaped, the other man followed him to the bus station and then to Cannes. The man must have overheard Brian asking directions to the Internet café, then called in Skyrm.

The two men formed a wall that hid Brian from the other customers. The tall man pulled a flick knife from his jacket and held it with the flat of the blade across his belt so that only Brian could see it.

Skyrm said, "You will come with Mr. Kralik and me to answer a few questions."

"Such as?"

"We would like to know your name."

Brian didn't answer.

"Very well," Skyrm said calmly. "You will tell us soon enough. Please rise and follow me. Mr. Kralik will follow you. Do not make a scene, because we are prepared to injure you."

When Skyrm said that, Kralik grinned like a demented jack-o'-lantern.

Repulsed by the grin, Brian turned back to the computer. The results of his search for American military technology glowed incriminatingly on the screen. Brian quickly clicked off the browser, but he had time to read a single headline: "Congress stalls funds for Pentagon heat ray." Had Skyrm seen it too?

Brian reached for his backpack, but Skyrm knocked his hand away. "I will carry that," he said as he lifted it from the floor. "Now, come."

Gripping Brian's backpack by the handle as if it were a briefcase, Skyrm led them out of the Internet café. Kralik took up the rear of their little parade. He remained just beyond arm's reach behind Brian—too far for Brian to strike but too close for Brian to make a run for it.

Brian kept his eyes on Skyrm's back as he followed him across the street. Skyrm wore the same leather bomber jacket from Lucerne and a pair of dark gray slacks. Neither man spoke. Brian needed to break the silence. Even though he knew the answer, Brian asked, "Were you following Silver in Nice?"

Without turning his head, Skyrm replied, "We have been following Silver since he arrived in Lucerne." Brian could not place Skyrm's accent. Maybe it had once been Russian or Polish, but Brian guessed it was the Central European equivalent of the uninflected diction taught to news anchors across America.

As they went up a short stairway to the next street, Skyrm said, "Until I recognized you a few minutes ago, we didn't understand your involvement. We thought Silver might be protecting you, but you ran away. That was puzzling. Now I see that Silver needed you to protect himself. And that makes you useful to me."

"I doubt that," Brian said without believing it. He wondered what had happened to Silver.

Skyrm was leading him across the street to another narrow stone stairway between two shops. "No more talking," Skyrm said. "My car is on the street above."

Stepping into a car with these two men would be the equivalent of stepping into a grave. Brian couldn't let that happen, even if he had to yell for the police. But no police officer was in sight as they crossed to the opposite sidewalk and Skyrm started up the stairs. This stairway was steeper and taller than the last, rising the equivalent of two stories. A metal handrail in the center separated up traffic from down, or it would have if anyone else were on the stairs. The steps took a sharp bend near the middle, so that the street above wasn't visible from the one below.

The layout gave Brian an idea. If he timed it right, he could get away from these men unharmed. If not, he at least would provoke a struggle that might attract the police before he was seriously injured. Brian shuddered at the possibility he might get hurt, but he had to risk it. He did not escape from Silver to be captured by Skyrm.

Choosing the right spot was crucial. Brian had to make his move after rounding the bend but before Skyrm reached the top. He could not give Skyrm the advantage of level ground. How Skyrm would react, and how quickly, was the plan's critical unknown. But Brian would worry about Skyrm once he took care of Kralik.

They trudged up the stairs in silence, too much like a funeral procession for Brian's comfort. He didn't dare turn around to measure the distance between himself and Kralik because that might signal his move. He listened to Kralik's footfalls, satisfied the thug was maintaining the same strategic distance as on the street. Brian had to lure him closer.

As he rounded the bend, Brian saw Skyrm had about twelve stairs to climb before reaching the street. Brian's moment was now. He started to run, perilously closing the gap between himself and Skyrm. As soon as he heard Kralik quicken his pace, Brian put his hands forward and dropped to a crouch. He gripped the step that his hands landed upon and pulled his right knee forward. With Kralik almost on top of him, Brian kicked backward like a mule. His foot smashed into Kralik's chest and sent the man flying. Kralik's body bounced off the railing before crashing to the stone stairs. Brian heard a satisfying grunt as Kralik tumbled past the bend and out of view.

Brian looked back up to see Skyrm's foot swinging at his face. He rolled under the railing, just avoiding the kick. Brian bounced to his feet with the railing between himself and Skyrm.

Skyrm leaned across the railing and snatched at Brian's jacket. Brian countered the move with a simple *bakat-marki*, an inside-outside forearm block. Skyrm cocked his head, a sign that he did not expect such a move from a teenager. Then he smiled.

"So you know some martial arts. I'd wager I know more."

As Skyrm said this, the thin red rings around his irises seemed to burn. Brian's confidence faltered. He turned to run, but Skyrm grabbed his jacket with his left hand and yanked Brian backward. Brian lost his balance. Falling, he twisted himself around to grab the railing before he hit the ground. He stopped himself from pitching headlong down the stairs, but Skyrm had gained the advantage.

Skyrm spiraled over the railing in a fluid motion that culminated in a roundhouse kick. Brian shoved himself from the railing, narrowly dodging the foot that would have crushed his ribs. Brian's momentum carried him into the stone wall behind him. He blinked at the impact, and Skyrm was in his face. Pinning Brian to the wall, Skyrm threw a flurry of blows at him. Brian deflected them with competence, but Skyrm was moving too fast to allow counterstrikes. The constant buffeting was hurting Brian's forearms and he knew it was only a matter of seconds before he faltered. That moment of doubt allowed Skyrm to score a knife-hand strike to Brian's left shoulder. Brian yelped as his upper arm exploded in agony, but the intensity of the pain focused his mind in time to twist away from a rabbit punch that would have dropped him had it connected with his stomach.

Skyrm resumed his boxing attack. As Brian continued to counter and dodge the blows he felt his left shoulder grow numb. That arm would soon be useless. His only hope was that someone would see the fight and call the police. But no one appeared. Brian wished he had picked a fight on a busier stairway.

Footsteps sounded from below. Brian didn't dare take his concentration off Skyrm, but maybe a rescuer had arrived. When Skyrm didn't break off his attack, Brian's spirits sank lower. He knew who was running up the stairs even before Kralik growled, "Let me have him!"

"Don't interrupt!" Skyrm warned, but Kralik wanted vengeance. Brian caught the flash of Kralik's knife as the man tried to step between the combatants. Skyrm turned his head toward Kralik. Brian punched Skyrm's larynx. The blow only stunned Skyrm, but it was all Brian needed. He grabbed the lapels of Skyrm's bomber jacket and spun him into Kralik. The two men tumbled together and landed in a heap halfway down the stairs.

Brian ran, scooping up his backpack and breaking to the left once he reached the street. At the corner he turned right and then took the next right so that he was running in the opposite direction he had shown Skyrm and Kralik. He was heading toward the train station, and though he was exhausted and had a numb left arm and a bruised right arm, Brian did not slow. This was the second time this morning he had run full bore through a city on the sunny Riviera. Not the way he expected to see France.

The Cannes train station was soon before him, its rectangular façade encased in decorative crosshatches of curved iron. Brian hurried inside and bought a ticket for the next train to Toulouse, which was leaving in forty-two minutes. He went into the men's restroom and peeled off his shirt to look at his injured shoulder. The bruise was huge, a violent mixture of black and purple, but the shoulder wasn't abnormally swollen. He sat down in one of the stalls and massaged the shoulder. This was painful, but the sooner normal circulation returned, the sooner the pain and numbness would dissipate.

Brian went to the snack bar and ordered a Pepsi. He drank it quickly and held the cup of ice against his shoulder for several minutes. Then he went into the gift shop and selected a *Michelin Green Guide* to France's Languedoc, Roussillon, and Tarn Gorges regions. The slim but heavy book contained a nineteen-page description of Toulouse, plus two street maps. Brian also wanted a cheap wristwatch to replace the one Silver had taken, but the only inexpensive, plastic watches the shop offered were branded with the Superman and Batman logos. Brian looked at the balding man behind the counter and said, "But I'm a Marvel guy."

The man shook his head. "Je ne comprends pas."

"That's OK," Brian said to himself, "most people who speak English don't understand it either." He chose the Batman watch because black was much less conspicuous than red, blue, and yellow. Brian paid for the guidebook and watch then went down the escalator and boarded the train.

Exhausted from two getaways in one morning, Brian fell asleep as soon as the train left the station. He awoke six hours later in time to watch the sun sink into the Mediterranean, a circle of orange melting into wine-red ripples. He went into the bathroom and changed into a pair of olive drab cargo shorts and a black polo shirt. His left shoulder was still a deep purple, but with fewer black highlights. Brian returned to his seat and spent the remaining two hours of the trip reading about Toulouse and studying the maps.

By the time he arrived in Toulouse, Brian had learned that its train station was separated from the central city by the Canal du Midi, the manmade waterway that connected the Mediterranean to the Atlantic Ocean. Stepping outside the station, Brian saw the downtown lights half a mile away. He took the nearest bridge over the canal and then spent the next fifteen minutes crisscrossing streets and doubling back on himself to make sure he hadn't picked up another tail. Satisfied no one was following, Brian hailed a taxi in front of a hotel and showed DeJonge's address to the driver.

The cab headed south, which didn't surprise Brian. Université Paul Sabatier was south of the city. As the cab entered residential neighborhoods, Brian hoped his ordeal would be ending soon, that he would reach Eduoard DeJonge in time and that the professor would arrange for his protection. The driver told him they had reached DeJonge's street. Several vehicles were parked along the curb, including a dark red van. Brian imagined he saw the orange pinprick of a lit cigarette glow briefly behind the van's windshield. The cab pulled up outside a small two-story house on a street crowded with similar homes. Brian looked at his Batman watch as the cab pulled away. It was 9:27. "Gotham Standard Time," he murmured to himself.

Brian doubted the professor typically received foreign visitors this late, but what could he do about it now? He rang the bell, hoping the door led to his safety.

The door opened, and there, wearing blue jeans and a Ramones T-shirt, was the most beautiful girl Brian had ever seen.

CHAPTER 11--LARISSA

Her long, chestnut brown hair swept behind her neck and over her left shoulder, hanging low enough to partially hide the names Tommy and Johnny on her Ramones T-shirt, the ubiquitous one that spoofed the U.S. presidential seal. The girl's lips were dark pink and soft, her cheekbones high and radiant. Carefree bangs curled above her full eyebrows. Her eyes, a deep luxuriant brown that matched her hair, conveyed intelligence and wisdom.

Her hand still on the door, the girl asked, "Est-ce que je peux vous aider?"

She was his age. Brian tried to keep his eyes off the curve of her neck, which—despite all his recent trauma—now consumed his consciousness. Loud and fast punk rock, not the Ramones but similar, echoed from upstairs, probably from her bedroom. Brian's mind struggled to form a sentence in French. Haltingly, he said, "Est-ce que ce la maison d'Eduoard DeJonge?"

"He does not see students at our home," she said, switching to English, "and definitely not this late."

"I'm not one of his students. My name is Brian Parker, and I need to talk to your father about something important. Vitally important."

"He is not home. He is away on business—"

"When will he be back? This is urgent."

"He will not be back for several days." She began to close the door. "I am afraid, Brian Parker, I cannot help you anymore."

Brian's hand shot forward to stop the door. "Please," he said. "I think your father is in danger."

She stopped pushing the door shut, but didn't pull it back open. "What do you mean?"

"Your father is in charge of developing a weapon system

called Project Prometheus. I believe people are trying to sabotage it."

Her mouth opened slightly, forming a little bow. She looked at Brian as if he were mad. "And how does a teenage American boy learn such a thing?"

"For starters, he gets kidnapped by a crooked CIA officer."

"*Quoi?*"

"Did your father ever mention a man named Heinrich Tetzel?"

"I perhaps have heard the name."

"Heinrich Tetzel told me your father's name just before he died in my arms two days ago in Lucerne, Switzerland."

The girl stared at him. A new song started playing upstairs. Brian recognized it as "Alex Chilton" by The Replacements. This girl, scrutinizing him with her beautiful brown eyes to determine if he were crazy, was into old-school punk, and for the moment Brian cared little about rogue CIA officers, heat rays, or his throbbing shoulder. All he wanted that very second was for this girl to invite him in so they could discuss The Ramones and to see whether she would be impressed that he had several Donnas songs on his iPod. But if he asked that now, she *would* think he was crazy. Instead he returned her silence with silence and hoped his face expressed urgent sincerity.

Apparently it did, because she opened the door.

"I don't know how much I will be able to tell you," she said as Brian stepped inside. "I hear names sometimes when he speaks on the telephone. That is how I know of this man Tetzel, but my father speaks little of his work. I would not know about his Prometheus project at all if my friend Mathilde had not read about it in Le Figaro."

"Do you know where he is now?"

"In Spain."

"Will he be back soon?"

"No," she replied. "Not until next week."

Brian frowned. Next week might as well be next year.

The girl led him into the living room. The house's interior was smaller than the inside of an American home, even his family's modest brick bungalow. The room was furnished with a cluttered warmth that countered its Ikea-approved construction.

A rolled-up yoga mat leaned in a corner. Framed photographs dominated the bookshelves and end tables. Most were outdoor pictures of the girl in hiking gear with mountains in the background. In several pictures she was hugging a woman who looked like an older version of herself. The girl noticed Brian was looking at the photos.

"My mother," the girl said. She picked up one of the pictures and smiled at it sadly, which told Brian where her mother was.

"She died two years ago of cancer," the girl said. "This was from one of our hiking holidays in the Pyrenees."

Brian didn't know what to say. He blurted, "Did you go a lot?"

"Not with her. Only two times." The girl looked up at him. "I started trekking in the Pyrenees five years ago with friends, and I persuaded her to join us one summer. We went together once again, just the two of us, shortly after she was diagnosed with her cancer. Soon after that, she was too sick to return."

She looked back at the photo. "But we made wonderful memories on that last trip."

Brian stuffed his hands in his pockets and stood there, letting The Replacements fill the conversational void. How the subject changed from the girl's father to her mother, Brian wasn't sure, but changing it back seemed inconsiderate. He let a few more moments pass.

"I'm afraid I don't know your name," he said.

She looked up from the photo and came back to the present. "*Milles pardons*—I am sorry. My name is Larissa. And your name is Brian, correct? Where do you live in America?"

"Milwaukee. That's in Wisconsin. You know, where the beer comes from."

She shook her head. "I regret I do not know that."

He was flummoxed over how else to describe Milwaukee if she didn't know beer made it famous. "Well," he said, "it's the home of Harley-Davidson, too."

Larissa smiled. From that moment on, whenever Brian rode the Route 31 downtown bus past Harley-Davidson's headquarters on Highland Boulevard he would shout, "Thank you!" because Harley's name allowed him to see Larissa DeJonge smile for the first time. He knew it would be one of the greatest memories of his life.

"Harley-Davidson!" she said, her eyes lighting up to match her smile. "Such a coincidence! My mother and I used to talk about buying a Harley-Davidson, a Road King, and riding into the mountains and along the Canal du Midi because we knew it would make my father crazy."

Brian welcomed the chance to return the conversation to her father. "Do you enjoy making him crazy?"

Larissa smiled again. Brian hoped he would continue to say things that made her smile. "Only in a good way," she said. "He is much too serious. Especially lately."

"Like the last four months?"

"Yes." She paused. "How did you know that?"

"I know too much about too many things all of a sudden."

"Well, Mr. Brian Parker from the city of Harley-Davidson, please sit down and tell me why you think my father is in danger."

She was being sweet, but she was humoring him. Brian wondered how he might convince Larissa to take him seriously.

And then the front door crashed open.

CHAPTER 12--PEPPER

Larissa screamed. Brian froze. A terrifying thought shook him, that Skyrm had found him. Brian could not survive another fight with Skyrm.

But the man who burst through the door was a stranger. He looked like hired muscle, with thick chest and forearms and a flattened nose. His brown hair was unruly, and ragged sideburns outlined his cheekbones. A ruby stud glittered in his left earlobe, and Brian mentally nicknamed the man Ruby Stud.

Ruby Stud stalked into the living room, shouting at them in French. Larissa started shouting, too, at Brian: "Did you bring this man to my home?"

"No!" Brian cried. "There's no way anyone could have followed me!"

The man stomped toward them. He stood two inches taller than Brian and reeked of cigarette smoke. He wore a white T-shirt, khaki trousers, and scuffed construction boots. With the fingers of one hand splayed, Ruby Stud pushed Brian in the chest like a playground bully. He lowered his voice, but his French was too quick for Brian to follow.

"What's he saying?" Brian asked Larissa as she moved to his side.

"That he will not hurt us," she said, "but we must come with him."

"We can't."

"I know," Larissa replied as her right foot lashed up toward the man's groin.

Ruby Stud twisted away in time so that Larissa's kick caught him in the pelvis. He grunted, then spun back to swat Larissa. The blow connected with her chin, and she gasped as she fell sideways over the arm of a stuffed chair.

Brian went hot with rage. He straightened his right hand, imagining it as rigid as a blade, and chopped Ruby Stud's neck as the brute grabbed for Larissa. The man turned on Brian. His eyes narrowed into a simian glare. Like a gorilla, he raised his arms to crush Brian, but he was slow, much slower than Skyrm had been, and Brian fired two straight punches to the man's solar plexus. Ruby Stud faltered. His arms fell ineffectually. With all his strength, Brian clapped his hands together and boxed the man's ears. Stunned, Ruby Stud's eyes glazed.

Larissa was moving. From the corner of his eye, Brian saw her run to the foyer. He figured she would head out the door, which was still open, but she stopped at a small console table in the entryway and reached into its drawer.

Ruby Stud shook his head, trying to regain focus. Brian still held the advantage and couldn't afford to lose it. Ignoring Larissa, he hopped to the side, spun on his heel and drove a roundhouse kick into Ruby Stud's stomach. The big man stumbled backward and crashed into a bookcase, which rocked back into the wall. Two framed photos fell from the top shelf and hit the floor with a sharp report of cracked glass.

Brian moved in on Ruby Stud, readying another assault on the man's unprotected stomach. But the thug swung his foot around and swept Brian's right leg out from under him. Brian twirled as he went down and rolled away from Ruby Stud as he hit the floor. He bounced up and assumed a Defensive Back Stance: his right foot stretched forward, his upturned fists held ready at his hips, and his injured left shoulder turned away from his opponent. Ruby Stud grinned and crouched into the traditional prizefighter's pose.

"Enough of this," Larissa said as she strode into the living room, a small tube protruding from her right hand. She walked straight at Ruby Stud. His brow crinkled in amusement as he turned to her. Brian was about to tell Larissa to get back when her hand came up and she filled Ruby Stud's face with pepper spray.

The man howled and clawed at his eyes. Larissa pocketed the pepper spray then took the yoga mat from the wall. She began swinging it at Ruby Stud like a baseball bat, herding him toward the door. Brian moved in from the other side, alternating punches to the man's abdomen and kidneys. Ruby Stud yelled at them ferociously, tears streaming down his face. He wiped his eyes with his left hand while lashing blindly with his right.

As they neared the foyer, Larissa dropped the yoga mat and went to the door. Brian shoved Ruby Stud forward. The man stumbled and fell at the threshold. Larissa stepped back quickly as Ruby Stud landed in front of her, but he lay still, snuffling and groaning.

With the big man writhing at their feet and The Replacements upstairs singing "Color Me Impressed," Brian and Larissa traded looks. Ruby Stud sat up, tears covering his cheeks and a five-inch trail of snot hanging from his nose. Brian threw a full nelson around Ruby Stud and lifted him. Gagging from the cigarette stench that clung to the man, Brian heaved him outside.

On the stoop and hunched over, Ruby Stud turned back to them. He could keep his eyes open for only a second or two at a time. Larissa aimed the pepper spray at his face and sharply ordered, "*Allez!*" He backed away and hobbled quickly toward the street.

Larissa closed the door and fastened the safety chain, which still worked. A small red welt showed on her chin. Brian placed his hand on her opposite cheek and lifted her face for a closer look. "You should put some ice on that," he said. "How bad does it feel?"

"It stings," she said, and covered the welt with her hand, "but I think I stung him more."

Relieved that Larissa wasn't seriously injured, Brian said, "Yes, you did. Remind me to never make you mad."

She laughed nervously, and he moved past her toward the living room window. "You were very good, too," she said. "Was that karate?"

"No, that was tae kwon do. It's Korean." Brian pulled the curtain back about a half-inch to watch Ruby Stud stagger down the street. "Karate is Japanese."

Larissa stepped out of the living room. Brian's left shoulder was throbbing again, probably from lifting the big man off the floor. He heard a freezer door open and close, and Larissa reappeared holding a bag of peas to her chin. "I will call the police," she said.

"No, don't," Brian said softly, again looking through the gap in the curtains. Ruby Stud was leaning against the dark red van Brian had seen just before the cab dropped him off.

"But that man broke into my home and attacked us."

"If the police pick him up, his employers might panic and do something to your father."

Larissa crossed her arms. "If that is the type of man threatening my father, I doubt he is in danger."

Brian turned to her. "No, this man's low-level. He wasn't armed, either, which is strange."

"We should be happy he was not armed."

"I am," Brian said as looked out the window, "but it's strange." Outside, Ruby Stud pulled up the bottom of his T-shirt to wipe his eyes. Brian shifted his gaze to the van, the van that had been parked across the street before he arrived. Brian remembered the cigarette glowing behind the windshield, and he understood.

"I think he was watching your house," Brian said.

"What do you mean?"

"He was in a van across the street before I got here. Something like this happened in *Tears From Moscow*. Foster Blake couldn't figure out how Skorzeny had tailed him to a safe house, but he later found out the safe house had been under KGB surveillance for weeks."

"You know this from what happened in a spy movie?"

"Yeah, except it happened in the book, not the movie. Hollywood thinks safe houses and stuff like that are boring."

"Are you joking with me?" Larissa said.

"No. It makes sense." Brian met her skeptical eyes. "He had been watching your father's house. When he saw me pull up in a taxi, he called for instructions and they told him to grab me."

"So you *did* bring him to my home?"

"Sort of, but he was already here, really. In a red van. Do you remember seeing one?"

Larissa unpursed her lips and uncrossed her arms. She went to the bookcase and righted it. Then she started picking books off the floor and stacking them flat on the shelves. She didn't look at Brian. He decided to give her time to think. The music from upstairs stopped. "If you are correct," she said after a silent minute, "what do we do now?"

"We have to figure a safe way to contact your father."

"I can call him on his mobile right now."

"Not from here," Brian said. "They probably tapped your phone—and his." Brian was watching Ruby Stud once more. He worried that the man might grab a weapon from the van and return. But Ruby Stud remained outside the van, still wiping his eyes.

"Your father's in Spain, right?" Brian said.

"Yes, in Zaragoza. He's there for a type of military conference."

Brian nodded. A military conference fit with the Prometheus Project. "Do you know anything else about it?" he asked.

"No, he talks little about his work, as I told you before."

Brian looked at her. "Is there anything in the house that might tell us? His computer …"

Larissa shook her head. "Not here. When he started this new project he was not allowed to work on his home PC anymore. Some people from the university removed it, and now he uses only a *portable*—a laptop." She bit her lower lip in thought. "We perhaps could find something in his office at the university."

"Can we get into his office?"

"Yes, I know where he keeps his extra keys."

"Will you take me there?"

Larissa nodded. "We can go tomorrow in the morning." She picked up one of the shattered picture frames. It contained a photo of her mother. Her eyes on the picture, Larissa said, "You can stay here tonight."

Brian felt his cheeks flush. "Thanks," he said, "but..."

He didn't know what to say next. He didn't want to wait until tomorrow. He doubted it would be safe for them to remain in the house much longer. How could he persuade Larissa to leave with him, and soon?

The thunk of a car door sounded outside, and Brian looked back to the street. Ruby Stud was in the van's driver's seat. Brian expected the headlights to shine and the engine to growl, but nothing happened. Maybe Ruby Stud still couldn't see well enough to drive. A small light flickered inside the van. It shone bluish white and illuminated one side of Ruby Stud's face. His mouth was moving.

Two words hit Brian like a hammer: *cell phone*! He recoiled from the window. "We have to get out of here."

"What?"

"He's on his cell phone, probably calling in reinforcements. We have to get out of here fast. Both of us."

Larissa did not move. "What have you involved me in?"

"I'm sorry," he said. "I really am, but I think you were involved already."

She stared at him, her stance rigid. Brian feared she would refuse to leave. Then her shoulders dropped and she said, "All right. But where can we go?"

"If we went to your father's office this late, could we get in?"

"*Oui*, I think I can do that."

"Okay, that's enough of a plan to get us started."

Brian looked around the living room. "You may not be able to return here for a while," he said. "You should pack enough clothes for three or four days. And take any money you have."

"Anything else?"

"Yeah," Brian said. "Bring the pepper spray."

CHAPTER 13--LAPIN

Larissa packed quickly, stuffing clothes and toiletries into a black backpack. Its straps were covered with dime-sized pins advertising thirty-year-old punk and ska bands. So were the lapels of the denim jacket she threw on over her Ramones T-shirt. "We can take the Metro to the university," she said. "A station is nearby."

They left through the back door and cut behind several houses until they reached the sidewalk around the corner from Larissa's house. They walked quickly past the cypress trees of her neighborhood, Larissa leading the way. Neither spoke. Brian frequently glanced over his shoulder to see if they were being followed, but there was no sign of Ruby Stud or the red van.

After five blocks they reached the Metro stop, which was marked ST-AGNE in large black block letters. Larissa led him down a set of escalators and showed him how to buy a ticket from the automated dispenser. Brian checked his watch as they reached the subway platform; it was after ten. He counted seven other people waiting there, and Ruby Stud wasn't among them. Brian relaxed.

He was amazed moments later when the train emerged from the tunnel with only a quiet whoosh. Two years ago Brian and his father rode Amtrak to Chicago to see the Brewers play the Cubs. They caught the El to Wrigley Field at a subway station beneath State Street, and that train's arrival was deafening. Since then, Brian figured all subways carried the decibel level of a hurricane. He tried to relate this story to Larissa as their train doors opened with a chime, but her eyebrows dipped in confusion when he mentioned the Brewers and the Cubs.

"Baseball teams," he said. "The Brewers are from Milwaukee. They lost that day."

"I'm sorry," she said as they took facing seats in the nearly vacant car.

"Yeah well, they do that a lot," Brian replied.

His shoulder throbbed under the weight of the backpack. Brian slipped it off and dropped it on the seat next to him. He grimaced as he rubbed his shoulder.

"Are you hurt?" Larissa asked.

"Not badly. My shoulder was injured earlier."

"During the fight in my home?"

"No, I was in another fight, a worse one, this morning in Cannes."

"A fight this morning? In *Cannes*? But that is 450 kilometers away!"

"I've had a busy day."

Larissa leaned toward him. "Please tell me about it."

Brian did, starting with the game of "Spot the Spy" and Tetzel's death two days earlier. He recounted the subsequent events as quickly as he could, continuing his tale while the train rolled through two stops. Larissa did not interrupt, her deep brown eyes resting on his face the whole time, yielding more sympathy as he went on.

At the end of his story, Brian said, "The reason I came to Toulouse, apart from wanting to warn your father, is that I was hoping he could protect me."

"My father?"

"Well, I had hoped the organization he's working for, I think it's called Eurocorps, could offer me protection. From Silver, from Skyrm—cripes, from everyone. Like that guy who attacked us."

Larissa turned to look at the window even though nothing was visible in the tunnel beyond the Perspex. Brian studied the worried expression reflected in the blackened glass. Her eyes in the window shifted to him.

"Do you think this man Skyrm wants to hurt my papa?"

"Silver said Skyrm was some sort of freelance mechanic. That means somebody else hired him to run security for this operation," Brian said, "so Skyrm would only be following that person's orders."

She turned from the window to face him directly. "Whose?"

"I don't know," Brian said. "My guess is someone who wants to sabotage the weapon your father is working on. Or steal the plans. That's what spies do, steal weapon plans."

"Like they do in Foster Blake movies?"

"No, in Foster Blake movies enemy spies don't bother with the plans. They just steal the weapon."

The windows transposed from black to white as the train entered a station marked UNIVERSITÉ-PAUL-SABATIERE. Larissa stood, and Brian followed her off the train. As they walked across the platform and up to the street, Brian noted that the station seemed to have its own logo: a numerical pyramid with one 1 at the apex, two 2s underneath, followed by three 3s all the way down to a base of eight 8s. He wondered why the design didn't end at the logical conclusion of nine 9s, but mathematics wasn't one of Brian's strengths, as Mr. Burke, his algebra teacher, had reminded him all freshman year.

They came out of the station and strolled past a dormitory and student restaurant, still open at this hour, toward what Brian instantly recognized as an administration building. In front of the building was a long reflecting pool, although now it reflected only streetlights and the inky black sky. As they walked, Larissa explained that "Paul Sab," as the students and most professors (but not her father) called it, was part of the Université de Toulouse system. The main university, devoted to social sciences, was located in central Toulouse. Paul Sab was the scientific university, home to many of the most advanced research laboratories in France. Brian caught the hometown pride in Larissa's voice as she explained how the school benefited from Toulouse's reputation as the hub of Europe's aerospace industry.

She led him toward a row of long, narrow buildings. "We may encounter some guards," she said, "but many of them know me. When we come to the Physics Research building I will tell the guard that my father called to tell me he left urgent information in his office, and I must find it and read it to him immediately. Any guard will believe that Papa forgot something important. As I was on a date when he called, what else could I do but bring my date along?" She paused. "You are my date."

"I got that," Brian said.

"While I am talking to the guard, do not speak because your accent will give you away. And try not to move around. We do not want your American walk to give you away, either."

"My what?"

"Your American walk."

"There's no such thing!"

"There is and you have one. A very distinctive one."

Brian was about to object when Larissa spotted the guard through the building's glass entrance. "Ah bien," she said, waving flirtatiously at the young blond man. "We have luck. I know Marc well. Now be quiet."

As they entered the building, Brian noticed a sign that said "Recherché Physique." He adopted a sheepish look as he followed Larissa toward the guard. Her expression brightened. "Salut, Marc," she said, initiating a cyclone of French that whirled between her and the guard. Brian could pick out only a few familiar terms: *Papa, bureau, nuit, mon lapin*. The last phrase snared his attention.

Marc regarded Brian curiously at first, but subsequent glances were friendly. Brian nodded at Marc and stood with his hands in his pockets, as awkward and embarrassed as he figured Larissa's boyfriend would act in the situation. Did Larissa have a boyfriend? Brian hoped not.

Larissa ended the conversation with a laugh. She looped her arm through Brian's and guided him to a stairwell. The contact gave Brian a rush, and he wondered how long he could enjoy pretending to be Larissa's boyfriend.

Once out of the guard's earshot, Brian asked, "Did I hear you call me your rabbit?"

She chuckled. "Yes, *lapin* means *sweetie*."

"The things they don't teach you in high school French," Brian said.

Past the first flight of stairs, Larissa unhooked her arm from Brian's. *Oh well*, he thought, *it was fun while it lasted.*

"Papa's office is on the third floor," she said.

"How do you know the guards so well?" Brian asked. "I didn't get the impression you visited your father here often."

"No, not my father, but Mathilde and I visit her papa almost weekly. He is a professor of astronomy. That is why we had some luck that Marc was downstairs. He usually works in the astronomy complex, across the canal."

"Do French teenagers often visit their parents at work?"

"No, but Mathilde's papa is very amusing and we enjoy our lunches with him." She smiled slyly. "Also, it gives us the excuse to admire the sexy university boys."

Larissa opened the stairwell door at the third floor landing and led Brian down a corridor. They turned a corner to a hallway marked "Laboratoire Antennes, Dispositifs et Matériaux Micro-Ondes."

"Does *micro-ondes* mean *microwaves*?" Brian asked.

"*Oui*," she said. "You learn quickly."

They walked past five doors in the empty hallway before coming to one with a plaque that read "E. DeJonge." As Larissa unlocked and opened the door, Brian's subconscious registered that the room's light should not be on. But before that thought could take conscious form, they already had stepped into her father's office and discovered the stranger hunched in the corner.

CHAPTER 14--RING

A black woman was kneeling next to a file cabinet, her hands hovering above the papers and manila folders in an open drawer. Her mouth opened in surprise as Brian and Larissa entered the office, then snapped shut. Her expression made two more rapid transformations. First her eyes narrowed, fiercely intelligent and registering aggravation. Then her eyes widened and all guile vanished. One of these faces was a mask, and Brian had a fair guess which.

The woman's clothes were the reason Brian and Larissa didn't panic. She wore a cleaning woman's uniform, an indigo smock with orange piping over a canary yellow polo shirt and chinos. The shirt had a logo with a vacuum cleaner and feather duster that was partly hidden by the smock. It was not unusual to find a cleaning woman in an office building at eleven o'clock at night. It was unusual to find her rifling through a file cabinet.

The woman stood, but before she did, Brian saw her right hand pass over her left, as if she surreptitiously had dropped something into the open drawer. Stepping forward, she knocked the drawer shut with the heel of her foot. She approached them with her hands out pleadingly and began speaking a French that even Brian could tell was heavily accented.

"What's she saying?" he asked Larissa.

"She is saying that the drawer was open when she came in and that she was about to call the guard."

"That's crap," Brian said. "Ask her why the office door was locked if she was still inside."

Larissa asked, and the woman eyed Brian before responding. Larissa relayed the reply: "She said she did not know the door was locked. It must have locked behind her."

"More crap. Does she speak English?"

Larissa translated, and the woman shook her head slowly.

Brian looked back at the filing cabinet. The drawer hadn't closed all the way. "She's speaking with an accent, isn't she?"

"Yes," Larissa said. "Many African immigrants live in Toulouse."

Larissa asked the woman a question, and Brian didn't need a translation when she answered, "*Cameroun*."

To Larissa, Brian said, "Check the computer. Is it on?"

"No," she replied as Brian went to the filing cabinet. The woman's eyes followed him. On the floor near the cabinet were a rag and a plastic spray bottle filled to the top with blue fluid. No other cleaning supplies were in the room. He picked up the spray bottle. Its nozzle was dry.

"Ask her where her cart is."

"I don't understand."

"The hallway was empty. If she was cleaning the room, there should be a cart full of supplies outside the door."

While Larissa spoke to the woman, Brian pulled the cabinet drawer open and knelt beside it. The woman tried to keep her eyes on Larissa, but her glance often shifted to Brian.

"She said she had already moved up to the next floor when she realized she forgot to clean my father's office. She left her cart upstairs."

Brian wished Larissa hadn't identified this as her father's office, but the woman could have figured that out anyway. He began to pull files from the drawer and riffle through the papers.

"What are you looking for?" Larissa said.

"Ask her."

Before Larissa could ask anything, the woman started to speak rapidly and urgently. Brian pulled another file, flipped through the pages and put it aside. Larissa began translating before the woman finished. Their voices sounded as if they were in a race. "She is begging us not to turn her in," Larissa said. "She cannot afford to lose this job. She has three children she must feed and her husband cannot work …"

As Larissa spoke Brian pulled a file from the drawer that was heavier than the others. When he caught a gleam of metal amid the papers within, he knew he had found what the woman had dropped. He opened the file and was startled by what he saw.

"That's OK," Brian said as he stood. "I only have one more question for her." He held up the object and examined it for a moment. "How many Cameroon immigrants living in Toulouse wear a West Point class ring?"

The woman's pleadings halted. Her eyes, hard once more, were on the ring, but Brian couldn't read her expression. Larissa's was easy to read, though. She was incensed.

"Are you saying we caught a CIA agent spying in my father's office?"

Before Brian replied, it popped into his mind that Marceline Knight, the Blake woman in *Lightingrod*, had been a West Point graduate, and she worked for a different American agency.

"Not CIA," Brian said. "DIA."

The cleaning woman's eyes widened. She caught herself and instantly resumed a cool, inscrutable gaze, but it was too late. She had blown her cover.

Brian read the name inscribed inside the ring. "Ms. Lenore Harte here works for the Defense Intelligence Agency," Brian said. "That's the Pentagon's spy program, basically. Isn't that right, Ms. Harte?"

The woman didn't answer. She glared at Brian. He tossed the ring to her, unable to resist repeating a line from *Clandestinely Yours* that also referred to a telltale ring: "Vanity has its dangers." Harte caught the ring and slipped it into her pocket.

Larissa picked up the phone. "I shall call Marc," she said.

"No," Brian said. "Don't call security yet. Ms. Harte may be able to help us."

"And what makes you think I would want to help Encyclopedia Brown and Nancy Drew?" The lugubrious vowels of the West African accent were gone. Lenore Harte's voice was reedier than Brian expected, with an East Coast dialect. Almost Boston, but not quite. As she spoke she straightened her back and squared her shoulders. Those small adjustments altered her bearing entirely. One moment she was a poor African immigrant fearing for her job, the next she was a tough American intelligence operative dealing with two unexpected annoyances.

"Because if you don't," Brian said, "Larissa will call security and you will have to explain to your superiors in Washington how you were compromised by a couple of teenagers."

"*Compromised*? Who the hell are you and why do you talk like an espionage textbook?"

"My name is Brian Parker," he said, "I'm from Milwaukee, and I'm sort of a spy buff."

Larissa added, "Brian is a very knowledgeable Foster Blake fan."

"Foster Blake?" Harte rolled her eyes. "I knew I heard that line before. 'Vanity has its dangers.' Are you kidding me? Is that from *My Darling Assassin*?"

"*Clandestinely Yours*."

Silver would have been amused, but Harte exploded. "I take enough garbage from the sexist fools in this business who think it's hilarious to pull some smug Foster Blake shit. I am not about to take it from a Cheesehead tourist acting out some asinine college role-playing game."

Brian held up his hand. "We're not playing anything," he said. "We think Larissa's father may be in danger from a man named Mathias Skyrm."

Harte went rigid at the mention of the name. "How do you know about Skyrm?"

"He tried to kidnap me this morning in Cannes," Brian said, rubbing his sore shoulder.

"And that was after Brian escaped from a CIA agent in Nice," Larissa added.

"Case officer," Brian corrected.

Harte blinked then sat on the desk. "Are you saying you escaped two kidnap attempts today?"

"Three, counting the thug who jumped us at Larissa's house earlier tonight."

Larissa nodded. "Brian has had a busy day," she said.

"And one of your would-be kidnappers was CIA?"

"He did kidnap me, but I got away."

With a softer voice, Harte said, "I think you had better tell me about your day."

"Why should he?" Larissa interjected.

"Because, as Brian said, I can probably help you. But I'll need to hear your story first."

Brian started talking.

CHAPTER 15--ZOMBIE

Harte asked most of her questions toward the beginning of Brian's story. She had not heard of Tetzel and agreed with Brian's theory that Tetzel had been on the periphery of Project Prometheus and inveigled his way in to spy for Silver. She asked more about Silver. Working for a rival agency magnified Harte's contempt for the CIA officer who, to shield his own illegal deal, kidnapped a vacationing American minor (her word) and spirited him to another country. "That's taking even rendition too far," she muttered. She then assured Brian, "Don't worry, I'll see he burns for this."

Harte grew silent after Brian described his escape from Silver. She let him complete his story without interruption aside from a few verifications from Larissa near the end. When Brian finished, Harte simply asked, "How's your shoulder?"

"It's better," he said. "Still pretty sore, but better."

"I'll get you out of this, Brian," Harte told him.

Brian believed her. For the first time since Silver drugged him on the train, he felt safe.

Larissa, though, was not willing to bend. "This woman must explain why she broke into my father's office," she said.

"I don't have to," Harte replied. "But I will. If your father's in danger, we may be able to help him."

"How?" Larissa asked.

"We can work that out," Harte said, "but not here. We have to leave. You two have been up here too long already. The guard will get curious and may come to check on you."

Harte had a plan. She would leave the building after Brian and Larissa, and the trio would regroup ten minutes later at her car. "I'm in parking lot eleven, outside the gymnasium. Do you know where that is?" she asked Larissa.

Larissa nodded. Harte described her car, a twelve-year-old yellow Peugeot 205, and gave them the license plate number. Brian and Larissa then left and, as Harte had predicted, they met Marc coming up the stairwell on his way to find them. Marc escorted them back to the entrance as Larissa offered an explanation. The only words Brian picked out this time were *Papa* and *téléphone*. Larissa ended her account at the door by hugging Brian's arm and giving Marc a deep wink. The guard rewarded Brian with a jealous leer, and Brian felt his cheeks and forehead warm.

Still hugging Brian's arm as they walked away, Larissa said, "He thinks you are too shy."

"What did you tell him we were doing up there? Making out?"

"Why not? You are cute enough for the story to be convincing." She laughed. "I think I am getting good at this."

"Creating a cover story or making me blush?"

"Both," she said. She gave his arm one last squeeze and jogged ahead, leading Brian through a maze of stubby concrete buildings.

As he ran, Brian again found his thoughts closing on the beautiful girl sprinting before him. Despite her apparent delight in teasing him, Brian felt more at ease with Larissa than any girl back in Wisconsin.

Once in the parking lot, they located Lenore Harte's Peugeot easily among the seven cars present. Brian and Larissa waited about three minutes when Harte stepped out of the darkness.

"Hate to disappoint you," Harte said to Brian as she unlocked the door, "but there are no machine guns behind the headlights." She pulled off the blue smock, then put on a black nylon aviator jacket she retrieved from the driver's seat.

Larissa slid into the back seat and Brian was about to follow when Harte said, "One of you sit up front with me so I don't feel like a damn chauffeur." Brian obeyed.

Pulling out of the lot, Harte said, "I have one stop to make before we can go to my apartment. I have a secure line at the apartment, so it's the only place I can report to my control, but that's when we'll figure out how we'll keep you safe, Brian."

Brian nodded and said, "Thanks."

From the back seat Larissa said, "Fine. Now why were you spying in my father's office?"

Harte glanced over her shoulder to make momentary eye contact with Larissa before speaking. "This Prometheus system your father is working on is similar—in fact, almost identical—to a weapon the Pentagon has spent more than a decade developing."

"My father would not steal from America, if that's what you mean to say."

"I'm not," Harte said. "But there is a certain coincidence that can't be ignored. Nine months ago the chief research scientist for the Pentagon project—"

"Roland Eck," Brian interrupted. "He died in a plane crash."

"How do you know that?" Harte said.

"Google."

"Right," Harte continued. "Well, the Pentagon's program, which I'm sure Brian knows is called Positive Enforcement, stalled after Eck died."

Harte slowed as she drove through the university gates, then sped south from the campus. "Eck was flying his own plane when he crashed," she went on, "so we assumed his death was accidental. Then four months ago a European arms consortium made a research breakthrough on a similar weapon with specifics that mirrored Roland Eck's, a weapon they will be demonstrating three days from now in Spain."

"You had better not be implying my father killed your scientist for his research. My father has never been to your country."

Harte remained calm but raised her voice above Larissa's. "It is not my job to make judgments, Larissa. It is my job to uncover information and find connections. And there is one crucial thing that doesn't connect. Your father's specialty is microwaves, right?"

"*Oui.*"

"Well, both Positive Enforcement and Prometheus use millimeter waves. They are similar to microwaves, but different enough to arouse our suspicions when your father became enough of an expert in them four months ago to pick up where Roland Eck had left off, before his untimely departure."

Larissa interjected, "My father—" but Harte cut her off.

"My superiors do not believe your father had anything to do with Eck's death. But we think there is a strong possibility someone gave him Eck's research, or fed it to him in such a way he believed it was his own idea."

Brian, hoping to head off Larissa's anger, tried to redirect the conversation. "Silver told me he believed Tetzel was about to pass along information related to the death of a Pentagon scientist and his stolen research."

"Yes, I remember," Harte said.

"Well, if Skyrm killed Tetzel, he might have had something to do with Roland Eck's death. And if Skyrm is now after Larissa's father, how could Dr. DeJonge be part of Skyrm's cell? It doesn't follow."

Harte sighed. "Like I said, I am looking for connections. Larissa's father is connected, but we aren't sure how."

"Then why do you not just ask him?" Larissa said.

"We probably should," Harte said. "If he's in danger from Skyrm, we can protect him. Or offer to, anyway."

"He is in Spain," Larissa said.

"Specifically, he is in Zaragoza," Harte said. She steered into an industrial area. "In three days—" Harte looked at the dashboard clock. "Correction: In two days, your father will demonstrate the Prometheus machine during war games at San Gregorio field just outside Zaragoza."

Brian checked his Batman watch to confirm midnight had passed. "What does the machine do?" he asked.

Harte laughed. "Hell, Brian, I thought you knew everything about it."

"It's some kind of heat ray. That's all I could read before Skyrm interrupted me."

"Heat ray is about right. Some people call it a 'pain beam,' but if you ask me that's a sure way to end congressional funding. Positive Enforcement—and Prometheus, I suppose—are non-lethal weapons. They shoot a beam that tricks your nerves into thinking your body is on fire."

"What is the point of that?" Larissa said.

"Do you know what fight-or-flight is?" Harte asked.

Brian shook his head. Larissa was silent. Harte explained,

"It's the instantaneous decision your body makes when it realizes it is in danger. Do you stand your ground—fight—or do you run—flight? What these weapons do is take fight out of the equation. You feel such instant, overwhelming pain your only instinct is flight."

"That sounds horrible," Larissa said.

"No, because the moment you step out of the beam, the pain stops," Harte said. "And it beats getting hit with gunfire. Positive Enforcement was developed to disperse dangerous mobs. If you're familiar with *Black Hawk Down*, a Positive Enforcement beam could have saved those soldiers and greatly reduced the fatalities among the Somali rebels."

Harte parked outside a jumble of anonymous cinderblock buildings, each identical except for the numbers above their doors. "I just have to check in on my duck blind before we go to my apartment."

"Duck blind?" Brian asked.

"The team working on Prometheus used one of these buildings, which is suspicious because neither the university nor Eurocorps is leasing the premises, but a Barcelona holding company. I tried to bug the place, but there's some kind of Faraday cage inside."

"A what?" Larissa asked.

"Faraday cage," Brian said. "It jams electronic communication like radio waves and cell phones."

"Video cameras, too," Harte said. "So I placed a microcamera on the opposite building to keep track of who's been coming and going. I call it my duck blind."

Harte opened her door. "This won't take long," she said. She closed the door with her hip and vanished behind a corner.

Brian turned in his seat to look at Larissa. She glowered back. "I hope you do not believe what this spy has been saying about Papa."

"She's on a fishing expedition," Brian replied.

Larissa cocked her head. "I do not understand."

"She's looking for something, but she doesn't know what she's looking for."

"And she will not know until she finds it?"

"That's about the size of it." Brian saw Harte trotting back.

"Maybe she'll find something here."

Harte opened the door, but before getting back into the car she stooped to retrieve a notebook computer from beneath the driver's seat. As she slid behind the wheel, Harte pulled from her pocket a device Brian assumed was her microcamera. It looked exactly like a flash drive except for a black lens in the center.

Harte caught Brian's look and smiled. "Yes, sometimes even real-life spies get to have cool gadgets." She turned on the computer, which powered up instantly, popped the cap off the flash drive camera and pushed it into the computer's USB port.

"These will be time-lapsed pictures—every thirty seconds for the last twelve hours," she said. Brian marveled at the drive's storage capacity. "I don't expect to see anything significant because everyone working on Prometheus is in Spain right now," Harte continued, "so I'll speed through the images. We'll be on our way in a minute or so."

A door appeared on the computer screen, and as Harte flashed through the images only the shadows of the numbers above the door moved. Occasionally people appeared, but they were walking past the door. After several minutes Harte stopped on an image and gasped.

Brian gasped, too. On the screen, Jack Silver was emerging from the door with another man. They seemed to be arguing, and the time stamp at the bottom of the frame indicated the picture had been taken four hours earlier.

"There's a dead man who should not be walking," Harte murmured.

"Silver's dead?" Brian said sharply.

Harte looked up at him, the computer screen's luminescence highlighting the surprise in her face. She pointed at Silver. "Is this your CIA kidnapper, Silver?"

"Yeah," Brian said. "Who's the other guy?"

"This man," Harte said, tapping the figure on the screen, "is Roland Eck."

CHAPTER 16--DETOUR

Brian examined the blurred image of Roland Eck. The immediate impression was a body at odds with gravity. Thin and frail, Eck stood about three inches shorter than Silver. Eck's head—specifically, his face—appeared too heavy for his frame. Enormous brows, sallow eyes and a grimace pulled his features downward. If Silver slapped him between his shoulders, Eck would topple forward from the weight of his face.

Larissa craned her neck between the seats to look at the screen. Her cheek came within an inch of Brian's, and he felt his skin tingle.

"Are you sure this is Eck?" Brian asked.

"Positive," Harte replied. "I've had his face imprinted on my brain for the last two months."

"What about the plane crash then? How was his body identified?"

Harte sighed. "It wasn't, and I was never happy about that." She tapped her fingers on the steering wheel. "The thing is, the military liaison officers working on PosEn considered Eck a suicide risk. His wife had died fourteen months earlier, and shortly after that Eck began exhibiting mood swings. He flew his own plane, commuting between D.C. and Connecticut—his wife was buried in New Haven—on the weekends. So when his plane plunged into Long Island Sound, many assumed it was suicide."

"But the body?" Brian asked.

"Investigators determined that prior to the crash the plane caught fire. The fuel tank exploded before the plane hit the water. What was left of the body was disfigured beyond recognition. They identified Eck through his personal effects: the clothes he was wearing, his watch, his wallet, his credit cards, and the wedding band he wore as a pendant."

"If he faked his death, why do you suppose he is here?" Brian asked. "Trying to find the people who stole his research?"

"I think those are questions for your friend, Mr. Silver."

Brian agreed, but he doubted Silver was collaborating with Eck. It didn't jibe with Silver's claim that he kidnapped Brian to unofficially investigate Tetzel's death.

Harte advanced to the next picture. A third man had joined Eck and Silver. The frost that seized Brian's veins at the sight of the man carried into his voice.

"Skyrm," he said.

"That's Matthias Skyrm?" Harte asked.

"The man you fought on the stairs?" Larissa added.

"Yes."

"No intelligence service has ever had this clear a picture of him," Harte said.

Brian looked at the new image. Skyrm had appeared behind and between Eck and Silver. He gripped Silver's arm, and Silver was looking back at him with a scowl. Had Skyrm captured Silver in Nice? Silver appeared angry, but he didn't look like a prisoner.

Brian was still trying to read Silver's expression when Harte said, "Shit!" and snapped the laptop shut. She leaned forward to stash the computer beneath her seat with her left hand and to shove the key into the ignition with her right. Harte started the Peugeot, threw it into gear, and roared out of the industrial park. Larissa was tossed back into her seat as Harte shifted directly from first gear to third.

"What's going on?" Brian asked.

"What time do you estimate that thug attacked your house?"

"Shortly before ten," Larissa replied. Brian nodded in agreement.

"That picture was taken at ten oh seven," Harte said, "a few minutes after the attempt to abduct you failed." Brian remembered Ruby Stud using his cell phone. "I think Skyrm, Eck, and Silver just got the news when that picture was taken," Harte continued. "They know you're in Toulouse, Brian, so I have to make sure they don't find you."

"How?" Brian asked.

"I'm taking you to Paris."

"Now?"

"After we stop at my apartment. I still have to report in, but no matter what my control officer's instructions are, I will drive you straight to the Defense Attaché Office in Paris the minute I file my report. As I see it, your safety is now my first duty."

So Brian would beat his schoolmates to Paris by a few days. He wondered if he would be able to see them when they arrived. Maybe he would get a military bodyguard. That would blow Tim's mind.

Few other cars were on the road so early in the morning. Harte was driving fast but she wasn't flying. Didn't want to risk the police pulling her over, Brian figured. When they stopped at a red light, Harte turned to the back seat. "Miss DeJonge— Larissa—I realize I have no jurisdiction over you—"

"You don't have jurisdiction over me, either," Brian said.

"I realize I have even less jurisdiction over you," Harte went on, "but after the attack on your home, I believe it would be in your best interest if you accompanied Brian to the attaché office. It's in the American embassy compound."

"What about my father?"

"After I report in, my agency will contact your father immediately to offer him protection and to let him know you are willingly going to the DOD attaché office for safekeeping, provided you agree."

Brian turned to Larissa. "I could use the company," he said.

Larissa regarded him thoughtfully before saying, "All right."

Brian smiled at her then turned forward. Harte said, "Thank you, Larissa. I wouldn't feel right leaving you behind."

"I have something to ask," Brian said. He felt his face flush; he was embarrassed to say this in front of two women. "Can I take a shower at your apartment before we leave? It's been three days."

Larissa giggled. "If there is one thing we Europeans dislike about you Americans, it is your terrible bathing habits."

Brian didn't get the joke, but Harte let out a robust laugh that belied her nasal speaking voice. Brian joined in as the meaning dawned on him.

"That's OK, Brian," Harte said as her laugh subsided to a chuckle. "I have a lot to brief my control on. I'm sure you could get a shower in before I'm finished."

Harte merged onto a multilane highway. Brian watched the signs as they flashed by and learned they were heading north on the A 61. "Where are we anyway?" he asked.

"Near Castelnaudary," Larissa replied. She stifled a yawn before adding, "About sixty kilometers from Toulouse."

Harte sensed Brian's question before he asked it. "A little less than forty miles," she said.

Brian hadn't realized they had driven so far from the university. He was so surprised to see the dashboard clock's readout of 2:28 that he looked at his watch to verify the time.

"Time flies, huh?" Harte said.

"Sure does," Brian said.

"We should be at my apartment before sunup," she said. "Figure a half hour for me to report in and for you to shower, and then it will be another six hours to Paris and safety."

"Safety," Brian said. "I like the sound of that. Will I be able to talk to my parents?"

"Once we find the individual Silver sent to spy on your family, but after that, certainly."

"You sure it's only one guy?"

"More than one person would be too great a security risk," Harte said. "I'm amazed Silver even got one man to do it. It's career suicide for an FBI special agent to get caught doing off-the-books surveillance on American soil, but for a CIA officer? That's suicide, period."

From behind them, Larissa's breathing became a soft snore.

Harte glanced at Brian. Quietly, she said, "I have to admit, Brian, I'm impressed with your tradecraft instincts, particularly your escape and evasion skills. I know a few colleagues who would have failed to escape Silver or Skyrm the way you did."

"They underestimated me because of my age," Brian said. He was careful to keep the pride he felt from Harte's praise out of his voice. "They won't let it happen a second time."

"Well, you don't have to worry about a second time. You've got me on your side now."

Harte drummed her fingertips on the steering wheel again. "You're a fine young man, Brian. Too smart for your own good, but a decent young man. You want some advice?"

"Sure, why not?"

"When you're out of this, and that'll be soon, focus less of your attention on Foster Blake and more of it on girls like Larissa."

"That's probably good advice," Brian said.

"Damn straight it is. You should get some sleep, too. We'll be there in about twenty minutes."

Brian didn't sleep, but he let the remaining kilometers pass in silence. The lights of Toulouse appeared before them as the A 61 became the A 620, then the highway curved to make a wide loop to the west of the city. When the road angled back toward Toulouse, Brian could tell they were approaching the city's northern edge. The sky was still pitch black as Harte left the highway at a turnaround and bounced onto surface streets.

Larissa awoke with a grunt at the first jolt to the aged shock absorbers. She took in their surroundings and asked Harte, "Are we going to *le Quartier d'Afrique*?"

"All part of my cover," Harte said.

The streets grew narrower and the buildings skinnier. "My apartment is there," Harte said as they passed a grotty, three-story structure with a tiny restaurant named Café Couscous on the ground floor.

"Then why aren't we stopping?" Larissa asked.

"She's circling the block to make sure no one is watching the building," Brian said.

"Oh, more spy stuff," Larissa said.

"I thought you would appreciate the precautions," Harte said, looking down an alley as they drove by, "seeing as a known killer is looking for you two."

Harte drove around the neighborhood once more before parking a block from her building. "I'm going to make a final pass on foot," she said. "You two sit tight."

"Do you think all this is necessary?" Larissa asked Brian as Harte walked away.

"She knows what she's doing," Brian said. Harte disappeared down an alley and reappeared a minute later on the far side of Café Couscous. She walked past the entrance without glancing at it and headed back to the car. No one else was about this early. Brian reflected on Harte's professionalism. She was the opposite of Silver, who corrupted the rules to serve his own greed. Not Lenore Harte. She was ruled by duty.

As Harte walked toward them, Brian thought about how good that shower would feel. He was imagining the warm water washing away the grit of the last twenty-four hours when Harte passed beneath a streetlight and her eyes widened in alarm. Metal flashed and a thin brown taper appeared just above the top button of her shirt. Red seeped through the yellow fabric, and Brian recognized the taper as the hilt of a throwing knife jutting from her larynx.

Harte looked directly at Brian and mouthed, "Run." Then she fell to the sidewalk as the semicircle of blood on her shirt widened.

Larissa screamed and grabbed for the handle of her door. Brian reached between the front seats and stopped her. He pulled Larissa's arm, forcing her to drop along the length of the back seat as he ducked below the dashboard. She looked at him incredulously. "We have to help her," she said, struggling to rise as tears ran sideways down her face.

"We can't," Brian said, holding her down. He felt himself start to cry but knew they couldn't afford it. "That knife went straight into her throat. We can't save her. She told us to run. We can't let her die knowing that Skyrm got us. We can't let her die thinking she failed."

Larissa sobbed, but nodded. Brian released her.

"Keep your head down so they don't see us," Brian said.

"How do you know they haven't seen us already?"

"Because they haven't grabbed us." Brian wanted to peek over the window's edge, but decided it was too dangerous.

"Whoever threw that knife is on this side of the street," Brian said. "We have to get out through the driver's side, run across the street and keep running, OK?"

"OK."

Brian twisted himself beneath the steering wheel and got into a crouch next to the door. He heard Larissa slide to the rear door.

"OK," Brian said. "Now!"

They opened their doors simultaneously and barreled out of the car and into the street. Brian looked behind and saw Skyrm standing at the spot where Harte had fallen. Cars parked along the curb hid her body. Brian was grateful for that. Two men, Ruby Stud and someone Brian didn't recognize—a thick man with a cleanly shaved head and a Vandyke beard—ran toward Skyrm. The new man was unfolding a shroud of black nylon.

Body bag, Brian realized. *Bastards came prepared.*

Skyrm spotted Brian and Larissa instantly. "The boy and the professor's daughter!" he yelled to the others. "They were with Harte." Skyrm pointed at Ruby Stud. "Merz, after them!"

Merz, AKA Ruby Stud, slid across a car's hood to reach the street. Brian grabbed Larissa's hand and put on a burst of speed when a black car screeched around the corner and skidded to a stop in front of them.

Jack Silver stepped out of the car. "Brian!" he shouted. "Get in!"

"Like hell!" Brian yelled back as he and Larissa reversed direction.

Silver ran after them from the right, with Merz closing from the left. Brian and Larissa veered toward the nearest alley.

"Take the lead," he told Larissa as they ran down the alley.

"What! Why?"

"This is your city. You have to find us a place to hide." Brian looked over his shoulder and saw Silver and Merz enter the alley. "And fast!"

CHAPTER 17--SANCTUARY

The sensuous aroma of baking bread permeated the air. Toulouse's many *boulangeries*, seemingly one per block, were coming to life as the first hints of the sun tinged the sky. Brian closed his eyes and imagined hundreds of baguettes browning in dozens of nearby ovens. The fragrant air longed to embrace him, to pull him into sleep.

Why not? Brian thought. *Why Not?* He surrendered to the warm, buttery scent and felt his conscious thoughts melt.

Larissa shook him awake. "If you fall asleep, I fall asleep," she said. "And then we both will die."

They were in another alley, kneeling behind a stack of wooden produce crates. "Sorry," Brian said as he roused himself.

For thirty minutes they had sprinted through narrow streets and twisting alleys. Silver, with his bad leg, had been easy to lose, but Merz was tenacious. After doubling back into this alley, Brian and Larissa ceased to hear his footsteps pulsing behind them. Peering through the slats of the crates, they had seen Merz pass the mouth of the alley three times without entering it.

Brian looked at his watch. Merz had not appeared for half an hour. "Let's give it another fifteen minutes," he said, "then if the street is clear ..."

Then what? He had no idea. During their flight he got upset with Larissa because she didn't have an immediate list of hiding places. She snapped, "I live in the suburbs, not the city," as they ran, and he wasn't ready to press her again.

"If the street is clear," Brian repeated, "we just keep moving. When more businesses open, we can lose ourselves in the crowds of a department store or something. Then we can eat. You're probably as starved as I am."

Larissa nodded. "I know some suitable places," she said with a hollow voice.

"What's the matter?" Brian asked.

Larissa did not look at him, but continued to stare ahead. "Did she die because of us?"

"No. They were after her, not us."

Larissa turned to him. A tear drew a wet line down her cheek. "How can you be so sure?"

"Because Skyrm was surprised to see us." Brian placed a hand on Larissa's shoulder. "They were waiting for her." He realized neither of them were using Harte's name. Their guilt had turned her into a pronoun. "They even had a body bag ready," he continued. "They probably were going to search her apartment once they hid the body. I think that's why Skyrm brought a team."

"Why did that man Silver arrive late?"

"I don't know." Brian didn't want to share his anxiety about Silver's appearance, but their situation was far graver now, because they had witnessed one American intelligence officer at the scene of another's murder. Brian also worried about his own judgment. He had pegged Silver as a rogue, not a traitor.

"I think we were able to escape because getting rid of the body was Skyrm's top priority," Brian went on. "Otherwise he would have come after us himself."

"What do you think they did with it—I mean, the body?"

"I'd rather not imagine."

A nervous silence followed as they willed themselves not to imagine. Larissa's tears stopped, which left Brian conflicted. Clear-eyed determination was vital to their survival, but he hated wishing coldness into Larissa's heart. By any right, they should both be sobbing. He looked again at his watch.

"I think we can move now," he said.

The rising sun had thrown a shadow across one side of the alley. Brian and Larissa crept along the darkened wall. Brian peered around the corner. The city was waking, its early risers buying croissants, baguettes, and travel cups of coffee at the *boulangerie* across the street. Brian watched for several minutes, occasionally drawing back into the alley to scan the other direction. He saw no sign of Merz, Silver, or the others.

"All right," he said. "Now we find another hiding spot."

"How long will this hiding go on?" Larissa asked as they stepped out to the sidewalk.

"Until we come up with a plan."

"How long will that take?"

"I don't know. Do you have a plan?"

"Is it my job to think of a plan?" she asked with a rising voice.

"No," Brian replied as they passed a clothing shop, "but I don't have a plan, and if you do, I'm willing to listen."

Larissa shoved him so hard he bounced off the shop's door. The impact caused the *fermé* sign on the other side of the glass to swing in tiny drunken arcs.

"I'm kidding," Brian said. "See the smile? Kidding."

"Nothing about this is funny," she said.

He did not reply. Larissa's anger and fear were justified. Since Brian showed up on her doorstep last night, a goon had broken into her house and she had witnessed a murder. Saying another word now might cause her to crack, and Brian did not want a fight with his only ally on Earth. He remained quiet, hoping Larissa would cool off.

Brian's stomach growled, reminding him of his own fragile state. He was famished and exhausted. His emotions, too, were frayed. His horror at Harte's murder was conflated with deep shame; was he more distressed that she had lost her life or that he had lost his passage to safety? Brian wanted nothing more than to drop to the sidewalk in a fetal position. He kept walking because if he stopped, he would collapse.

They were following a street that twisted its way toward the Basilique St-Sernin. The tip of its steeple rose above the buildings just ahead. From the Michelin guide he had read on the train yesterday, Brian remembered that St-Sernin was Toulouse's landmark and that it was the largest remaining Romanesque church in the world. He didn't know the difference between Romanesque, Renaissance, or Rococo, but the fact that it was the world's largest stuck in his mind.

Knowing that fact didn't prepare Brian when their street angled in a new direction and St-Sernin stood before him, less than a block away. He did what was unimaginable only seconds earlier. He stopped. Brian said, "Holy …" As his voice trailed off, he realized the appropriateness of his unfinished thought.

Except for the bell tower, St-Sernin looked more like a medieval fortress than a church. Brian could picture archers, not priests, perched behind the small, narrow windows arrayed across the wide, pale stone. The roof was high—perhaps one hundred feet—but the structure was so broad it appeared squat rather than lofty. St-Sernin occupied an entire city block and was ringed by a street that might have been a moat ages ago.

Brian's eyes were drawn to the bell tower, which defied the rest of the building's reality. Even with his scant knowledge of architectural history, he could tell the bell tower had been added centuries later, some bishop's attempt to place a halo on a brute. The tower sprouted from the basilica's roof, exactly at the point toward the rear where the nave crossed the transept (terms Brian had learned just days ago touring Baroque cathedrals in Austria). The tower's features were more delicate than the building beneath it, more inspiring. It stretched skyward in arched tiers, like a tall, tapered wedding cake. The levels were capped by a needle-sharp green steeple, which in turn was topped by a cross that gleamed some two hundred feet in the sky. The bell tower appeared to be reaching toward heaven, miraculously lifting the hulking basilica with it.

Brian could do nothing but gawk. Larissa, who had kept walking, turned to look at him. "What now?" she asked.

"It's magnificent," Brian said.

Larissa looked over her shoulder at the church. "Yes, I suppose it is."

Her blasé attitude baffled Brian, but then he remembered reading that New Yorkers seldom look up at the Empire State Building and that Parisians go months without seeing the Eiffel Tower.

"My mother used to lead tours there," Larissa said as Brian caught up to her. "She taught me its secrets. I could show you around inside, but St-Sernin won't be open to the public for another hour and we might still be still running for our lives."

Brian hoped that was a joke, a sign that Larissa's mood was improving, but he couldn't tell. They had reached the street that circled St-Sernin, and they needed a plan or they would wander the city all morning.

Brian's stomach gurgled again. "We need to eat," he said.

Larissa nodded. "There are many shops and cafés on the far side of St-Sernin," she said. Her voice was stronger and the bitterness gone. "Food might improve our moods."

They waited for a break in traffic to cross the street when something about an approaching black sedan twigged Brian's memory. He looked at the driver. Recognition was instantaneous and mutual.

Brian cried, "It's Silver!"

Silver slowed sharply and steered for the curb, but a cacophony of car horns erupted behind him. The sedan accelerated and rejoined the flow of traffic because Silver did not want to attract the police. At least, that's what Brian assumed. Larissa grabbed his hand. "Come with me," she said, pulling him down the sidewalk. Brian looked back to see Silver turn at the nearest intersection and vanish.

"He's got to park," Brian said. "That buys us time, but I don't know how much. We have to hide quickly."

"I know," Larissa said as she yanked him off the curb into the path of an oncoming car. It squealed to a stop inches from them. Brian and Larissa ran, dodging sedans and convertibles as the air again erupted with caterwauling horns and irate Gallic shouts. They reached the opposite sidewalk and Larissa quickened her pace, leading Brian along a six-foot-tall iron fence toward the rear of St-Sernin.

"Where are we going?" he asked.

"Inside," Larissa said.

"I thought you said the church was closed."

"I know a door that should be open—if we have luck." As soon as she had said this, they came to a break in the fence and a walkway leading to the basilica. Larissa turned down the pathway so abruptly Brian nearly overshot it. The path curved slightly and ended at a doorway guarded by two large bushes.

"The first person who arrives in the morning usually leaves this door unlocked for the others," Larissa said. "My mother told me this." She pressed her thumb down on the latch and smiled when it clicked. "*Et viola*," she said. "We have luck." She opened the door just wide enough for them to slip through. Once they were inside, she quietly shut the door.

"OK," Brian whispered, "but if the door was open, then somebody is already in here. How do we avoid them?"

"Do not worry. No one will be where we are going."

"And where's that?"

"The crypt."

CHAPTER 18--RELICS

To Brian, *crypt* sounded like a dead end in every sense of the word. He glared at Larissa. "Are you kidding?"

"You said we had to hide, right?"

Brian wanted to suggest alternatives—maybe ducking beneath the pews—but he had no time to argue. Silver might have reached the street in time to see them sprinting toward St-Sernin. He might be heading down the path this very moment.

"Right," Brian said, "lead the way."

"We must move quickly but quietly," Larissa said in a low voice. "The smallest noise will echo like a bomb." She turned and headed toward the altar, sprinting on the balls of her feet. Brian followed.

He had only seconds to take in his surroundings, but the first impression was overpowering. If the exterior of St-Sernin was beastly, the interior was beatific. The church was brighter and airier than Brian had assumed. Looking down the aisles, he was stunned by the sight of white columns rising seventy feet to the arched ceiling, like proud trees in an alabaster forest. In the distance, perched above the main entrance, was the organ, dwarfed by clusters of shining silver pipes that framed the instrument. Statues of angels playing harps pranced atop the pipes.

Larissa veered behind the altar. Brian glimpsed a statue depicting a saint floating on a cloud before Larissa slipped into a doorway set in the curved wall beneath the raised altar. They descended a short flight of stone steps to a hexagonal chamber with a low, vaulted ceiling. Brian had just enough time to take in busts of saints recessed into the walls when Larissa grabbed his hand.

"We must go to the lower crypt," Larissa whispered. She

drew him down an adjacent set of stairs. Serving as a handrail was a thick rope, blackened by age and riveted into the stone wall.

"Oh, this just gets better and better," Brian muttered. A wood carving of six Apostles flashed in his peripheral vision near the bottom of the stairs. When they reached the crypt's floor, he saw that gray arches supported the low ceiling, like a cave designed by Michelangelo. Alcoves penetrated the walls, each holding what appeared to be a small coffin. Larissa headed toward one of the alcoves and lithely vaulted over the brass rail at its entrance. Brian copied her movements, glad that he nailed the landing despite his fatigue.

Larissa was stowing her backpack on a ledge behind the little coffin, which up close resembled two giant, bronze-plated Monopoly hotels joined by an annex.

"Toss me your knapsack," Larissa said. Brian did, and Larissa placed his atop hers and then plumped them as if fluffing a pillow. The gesture told Brian why Larissa led him to this spot.

"If anyone finds us here," he said, "we'll be trapped."

"No one will find us. I used to hide here from my mother, and she never found me. Once she was right there"—Larissa pointed just beyond the railing—"with a tour group, and not one of them realized I was behind the reliquary."

She looked at the narrow ledge and added, "I was smaller then, however."

Brian looked doubtfully at the ledge, which was about two feet wide. "Can we do this?"

Larissa nodded. "Fortunately, we are both thin. You first. Place your back to the wall."

They arranged themselves on their sides with Larissa lying in front of Brian, her back to his belly. The top of Larissa's head came up to his chin. "Pull your feet up," she said. "And hold me closer. Don't be modest."

Brian cinched his arms around Larissa's stomach. This was majorly unfair, he thought, to be pressed so tightly to such a beautiful girl on a cold stone slab. In a crypt.

To hide his embarrassment, Brian whispered, "So whose body are we hiding behind?"

"Not a body," Larissa said. "Relics."

"Oh, like teeth and knuckle bones? Well, whose relics are we hiding behind?"

"Philip and Jacques the Lesser, the Apostles."

"There was no Apostle named Jacques."

"You would call him James."

"Ah," Brian said. "Well then, saints preserve us."

"What?"

"It's a common phrase," Brian said. "In English." He resolved to leave the quips to Foster Blake. Luckily he didn't say it with a British accent, or he would have sounded like a total dink.

They remained silent for a while, until Larissa said, "I did not understand something she said, Lenore Harte."

"What's that?"

"She called us Nancy Drew and Encyclopedia Brown. I know of Nancy Drew, but who is Encyclopedia Brown?"

"Oh," Brian said. "He's a boy detective in a series of books. Each book has a bunch of short mystery stories. You're supposed to spot the clues and solve the mystery yourself, then check the answers in the back of the book. I remember one solution about polar bears being from the North Pole and penguins from the South Pole. I forget what the crime was, though."

"She should have called you Tintin," Larissa said. "You are more like him, running from criminals and spies."

"Oh yeah, that kid reporter who looks like a teenage Charlie Brown."

Her voice defensive, Larissa replied, "Tintin was being printed twenty years before Charlie Brown. You would be more accurate to say Charlie Brown looks like a young Tintin."

With no desire to pursue a cultural war over cartoon characters, Brian mulled his next words carefully. Before he could speak them, a noise from above echoed down into the crypt. Larissa tensed in his arms. They listened. *Thump kwish-ump. Thump kwish-ump.* Footsteps—the footsteps of a person with an irregular gait.

Silver.

The footsteps neared the altar. *Just keep walking*, Brian willed. *Don't come down here.* But then shoe leather clapped onto the first step leading to the crypt. Brian worried his feet were sticking out from behind the reliquary. Could he draw them up without knocking Larissa off balance? He felt Larissa's stomach clench as she held her breath. Brian did the same and pulled her tighter. He would risk leaving his feet where they were.

The footsteps continued downward then halted, probably in the upper crypt. Brian wondered why the intruder had stopped until he heard a second set of footsteps. These grew louder and more rapid as they approached the crypt's entrance. Then, from the top of the stairs, a man's voice:

"Monsieur! Monsieur! La basilique n'est pas encore ouverte de public."

Silver's voice replied, "I'm sorry, Father, I thought the church was open."

"No," the priest responded in English. "I am afraid St-Sernin will not open to visitors until eight-thirty." His shoes clicked down the stairs until he reached Silver. *Stay there!* Brian thought. *Both of you stay there!* Sweat beaded on his forehead.

"You are welcome to return in fifty minutes, of course," the priest continued, "but the crypt will not open until ten-thirty."

"Really?" Silver replied. "Because I thought I saw someone come down here, a boy and a girl." More descending footsteps sounded, Silver's followed by the priest's.

"No, that is impossible," the priest said. "I would have seen them. I assure you we are the only two people in the basilica."

Brian tried to get a fix on Silver and the priest's position, but the arched ceiling batted their voices about the alcoves. He guessed the men were a step or two above the wooden Apostles. Could they see into this alcove from there? Brian felt Larissa's heartbeat quicken.

"May I ask how you got in?" the priest asked tactfully.

"A side door was open. Over there."

The priest clucked his tongue. "I am always telling the cleaning staff not to leave that door unlocked." A moment's silence followed. Brian stared at the bronze box in front of him, still holding his breath. Then the priest said, "I am afraid I must accompany you out"—Brian pictured the priest placing his arm around Silver's shoulder—"and make sure the door is locked behind you. Please do not be offended."

"Not at all, Father," Silver said. The voices and footsteps headed upward. "I just thought the basilica was always open for people to pray."

"Yes, yes. That is how I wish it were. But unfortunately we must worry about vandals."

"We live in sad times," Silver replied before St.-Sernin's vastness swallowed their voices and footsteps. Brian and Larissa let out their breaths simultaneously, but they remained still. Brian feared the priest might return to investigate Silver's claim about a boy and a girl. Ten minutes quietly passed until Charlie Brown and his cousin, Encyclopedia, arrived to watch Nancy Drew and Tintin dance in a ballroom lined by towering white trees that held up the heavens.

Larissa sat up, startling Brian. The ballroom and trees vanished, replaced by the stone shelf and dull bronze reliquary.

"Whassamatter?" Brian said.

"Nothing," Larissa replied. She placed her hand on his shoulder. "You were falling asleep, but that is all right. You are exhausted."

She slid to the other end of the ledge. "No one will come down here for at least two hours. Sleep. I will wake you when it is safe to leave."

She rested her hand on his feet and smiled. He smiled back. "Thank you," he said.

Brian placed his head on the backpacks and fell into a cold sleep among the dead.

CHAPTER 19--TOURISTS

Brian woke to Larissa gently rocking his shoulders. The ambient noise in the crypt had increased while he slept. Murmured voices filtered from above.

"What time is it?" he asked.

"Nine forty-five," Larissa answered. "You have been asleep for nearly two hours."

"Wish I could say it was refreshing." Brian sat up, and a twinge of pain shot from his neck to his shoulder blades. He groaned.

"Is it your shoulder?"

"Mostly my neck is stiff, but it's aggravating my shoulder a little, yeah." Brian rolled his head slowly. "I guess that's what you get for sleeping on a slab."

Larissa placed her hands on the nape of his neck and rubbed. Brian winced when she pressed a palm into a sore nerve, but his muscles soon yielded as she rotated her thumbs between his shoulder blades. The pain subsided.

"How does that feel?" she asked

"Much better," he said. "Thanks."

"You're welcome." Larissa handed him his backpack and said, "We should sneak out of here before anyone comes down."

They shrugged on their backpacks and waited in the upper crypt until they were certain no one was near the altar. Then they slipped through the door and began to casually inspect the antiquities displayed in a semicircle behind the altar—more relics, Larissa told him.

A new fear hit Brian. What if Silver or the rest of Skyrm's men were inside St-Sernin waiting for them to emerge from the crypt? He moved behind a pillar near the altar and looked about. The only people he saw were tourists or old women in black shawls saying the Rosary.

Brian was relieved, but not completely. "If Silver suspected we were hiding in the crypt," he told Larissa, "they might be outside the church watching the exits."

"What do we do?"

"I'm not sure. We can't leave until we're certain we won't be noticed."

As he spoke, a group of about thirty tourists approached. A prim, middle-aged woman identified herself as the group's tour guide by wiggling the crook of an umbrella above her head. The crowd stopped before Brian and Larissa, and the guide turned to the altar to describe its elaborate furnishings. She spoke English with the exaggerated French accent of Warner Bros. cartoons and Disney Channel sitcoms, saying "Eet ees" instead of "It is," etc. *Maybe*, Brian thought, *she's giving her clients what they expect to hear.*

Several people at the group's edge ignored the guide and spoke softly to one other. Their voices were American, but Brian heard different dialects: a Texas drawl for sure, and another more difficult to place. Northern, but not quite Midwestern. He studied their clothes. Two women in their early twenties wore green T-shirts emblazoned with "Mercyhurst College—Erie." Across the crowd, where the Texas accent dominated, a young guy with blond stubble on his chin slouched in a hoodie bearing a cartoon miner and the initials UTEP. Brian figured it out. The guide was leading a combination of two tourist groups, one from Erie, Pennsylvania, and the other from El Paso, Texas.

"I think I know how we can leave," Brian said.

He told Larissa his idea. "Try not to speak," he concluded. "Your accent might give us away. I doubt anyone will notice your walk, though."

Larissa nodded, and they inserted themselves into the group as it moved to the next item of interest, a gold crucifix. Brian and Larissa would be unfamiliar to everyone in the crowd, but he hoped the people from Pennsylvania would assume they were with the Texas group and vice versa. A few women glanced at them curiously, but when no one spoke to them, Brian was confident his plan was working.

After roughly twenty minutes of lectures about statues,

frescoes, and more relics, the tour guide—by now Brian and Larissa knew her as Mlle Larreau—announced they would leave St-Sernin through the Porte Miegeville and head down the Rue du Taur to the Place du Capitole. Brian and Larissa maneuvered themselves into the center of the group as they exited the basilica.

On the steps of the imposing doorway, Mlle Larreau paused to speak about the Porte Miegeville's religious, historic, and artistic significance. Brian tuned her out and scanned the Place Saint-Sernin, the street that circled the basilica. He didn't look long.

"Oh crap," he moaned.

Across the street, on the corner where the Rue du Taur met the Place Saint-Sernin, stood Merz. With him was a man Brian didn't recognize, a pale, tall man whose shoulders hitched up like a vulture's wings. Their eyes were fixed on the Porte Miegeville. Merz lit a cigarette and began to smoke.

Brian nudged Larissa and nodded at the men.

"Who is the second man?" Larissa asked, keeping her voice low.

"I don't know. He's new." Brian fought the urge to duck back into the church. "They haven't spotted us," he said, "and I doubt they will as long as we stay in the middle of the pack."

After three agonizing minutes, Mlle Larreau concluded her lesson on the Porte Miegeville and waved her umbrella toward the street to indicate it was time to move on. Brian whispered, "Amen." He stole a look at Merz and the other man. They observed the tour group as it approached the street, but their faces were bored. Brian whispered, "Amen squared."

The two watchers were stationed on the southwest corner. By a stroke of luck, Mlle Larreau led her flock to the east side of the Rue du Taur. The people surrounding Brian obscured his view of Skyrm's observation team, but whenever he caught a glimpse of them, Merz and the tall man were ignoring the tour group and looking toward St-Sernin.

"I think we've made it," Brian said.

"The Place du Capitole is only two blocks away," Larissa said. "We will find something to eat nearby."

As the group walked south, Mlle Larreau explained the

street's history. "Rue du Taur means 'street of zee bull,'" she said. "Eet was along thees route that Saint Sernin met his martyrdom, tied to a bull and dragged to his death."

The tourists responded with variations on "Eww!" and "Gross!" until a masculine and unmistakably Texan voiced boomed, "Hell, that's just another Saturday night at the rodeo!"

Neither Mlle Larreau nor the people from Erie appreciated his humor.

CHAPTER 20--FIT

Brian and Larissa separated from the group when it reached the Place du Capitole. Their departure drew several curious looks but no comments. Brian briefly took in the scene, a wide stone plaza stretching to an official but attractive building with a long façade of pale red brick and white columns.

Larissa touched his elbow and said, "Time to eat." She took him to a nearby food court where Brian decided to stick to the familiar and wolfed down three cheeseburgers. Larissa ordered a salad topped with baked salmon. They agreed to stop at a convenience store and buy protein bars so they wouldn't be caught without food again.

Reinvigorated by the feeling of a full stomach, Brian said, "We should change our clothes in the restrooms—I mean WCs. You know, alter our appearance so hopefully they won't recognize us."

Five minutes later, Brian stepped out of the WC wearing a black polo shirt and olive drab cargo shorts. Man of action look, he mused. He had to wait another minute for Larissa. She emerged wearing her black Converse sneakers, blue jeans, and a pale blue T-shirt with the perennially placid cartoon dog Droopy saying, "Ce que tu sais? Je suis heureux."

"Here, try wearing this," Brian said. He handed her his Brewers cap. She put it on and pulled her ponytail through the opening in the back, a look Brian found adorable. He put on his sunglasses. They left the food court two different people.

"We have to talk out what to do next," Brian said. "We need to find a place where we blend in with a bunch of other people, but can move fast if we're spotted."

"I know of such a place," Larissa said.

A multitude of teenagers lounged in the narrow park that ran along the east bank of the River Garonne, which flowed through the center of the city. Laughing, chatting, holding hands, and getting some sun—the youth of Toulouse filled the riverfront. The park reminded Brian of a beach with grass instead of sand, and he knew Larissa was right to bring him here. They would be indistinguishable within this teenage mass, but they wouldn't be trapped if Skyrm or his men spotted them. Worst-case scenario, they could jump into the river and swim for it.

They sat beneath a tree, the river behind them. Brian pushed up his sunglasses and looked at the buildings of central Toulouse. They reflected one uniform color in the midmorning sun.

"It's very pink," he said.

"*Oui*," Larissa replied, rubbing a blade of grass between her thumb and forefinger. "It is because of those bricks that Toulouse is called *La Ville Rose*, 'the Pink City.'"

"I see," Brian said. His lowered his sunglasses and frowned. *Back to work*, he thought.

"Unfortunately," he said, "our first order of business is to get out of the Pink City."

"What is our second order of business?"

"We can discuss that once we have a plan to leave Toulouse, which won't be easy."

"You believe they are watching the train station?"

"And the bus station. Probably even the airport, though they must know I cannot get on a plane without a passport or credit card."

Brian took a twig from the grass and twisted it with both hands. "The thing is," he said, "we don't know how many people are working for Skyrm. Every time they turn up, there's a new face. The third man outside Harte's apartment. That guy watching St-Sernin with Merz. And Skyrm has had a few hours to call in more people to search for us."

"He cannot have that many."

"Logically, you're right, but we can't afford to be logical. We have to act like hundreds of people are after us, because the one place we assume they won't be looking for us is the place they will be looking for us. Paranoia has to be your new best friend."

Larissa leaned over and squeezed his elbow. "I thought you were my new best friend."

Brian's cheeks warmed. "Thanks," he said, "but I should be your new second-best friend. Paranoia will keep you safer. If it weren't for paranoia, we would contact your friends for help, but Skyrm is probably watching your friends and tapping their phones."

"But my father—"

"Is the last person we can contact now. Skyrm knows you will want to phone him, so his people *will* be watching him. They *will* be listening to his phone calls. If we tried to warn your father by calling him, we could put him in danger." Brian paused. "Well, more danger."

"I am not even sure what to warn Papa about. What do these people want with him?"

"My guess is Skyrm wants to sabotage your father's project, this heat-ray weapon, Prometheus." Brian waved the twig. "But so many things still don't make sense to me."

"The man Eck, the one who was supposed to be dead? Is he angry my father's design is too similar to his?"

"Maybe, but if he faked his own death, why risk being discovered by going after your father? I can't figure out Roland Eck's part in this at all, except that he is working with Skyrm."

"And Silver," Larissa said.

Brian hesitated. His instinct still told him Jack Silver couldn't be working with Skyrm, not willingly. Yet the evidence of the last twelve hours was damning.

"And Silver," Brian agreed.

"He did come closest to catching us," Larissa said.

"Which is why we have to get out of Toulouse quickly." Brian tapped his knees with the twig. "We know that trains and buses are out. Can you drive?"

"I can, but I do not have a license."

"We'd probably have to steal a car anyway. Even if I knew how to do that, it would put the police after us." He threw the twig aside. "So what can we do?"

"Ride bicycles," Larissa said decisively.

"And how do we get them?"

"We steal them."

Brian laughed. "So as soon as I rule out stealing a car, you want to steal a couple of bicycles?"

Larissa responded with a shrug. "Do you want to buy them? I do not think we have the money."

Brian weighed the consequences of being caught by Skyrm against the guilt of stealing a bike. It was no contest.

"All right," he said, "where do we steal these bikes?"

"The *université* is only two blocks from here. Even during summer sessions hundreds of students are around, and many ride bicycles. It should not take long to find two unsecured bicycles."

Brian looked for flaws in the plan. The only complication he foresaw was if an owner returned while they were stealing the bikes. He considered that chance slim.

"OK," he said, "where do we go once we take the bikes?"

"We ride north, along the Canal du Midi, to the next stop on the rail line, Launaguet, and board a train there."

"Is that a suburb, Launa-whatever?"

"Launaguet. *Oui*, it is a suburb of Toulouse."

"Let's be paranoid. What's the first stop that's more of a small town than a suburb?"

Larissa considered this. "Grisolles, about twenty-five kilometers away."

"That should be safe," Brian said. "How long would it take to ride there?"

Larissa pursed her lips as she calculated. "Two hours if we do not rest."

"We won't." Brian stood abruptly and held his hand to help Larissa up. "Now that we have the first part of our plan, let's steal some bikes. Lead the way."

They walked north along the riverfront. "What about the second part of our plan?" Larissa asked.

"We can discuss it along the way, but I'm afraid that sometime after we reach Grisolles we will have to split up."

Larissa stopped. "Why?"

Brian didn't answer immediately. He looked down at the Garonne, its wavelets flashing from dark green to black as the water rushed past. Its sound reminded him he was just as close to another river when this whole thing started, when he locked eyes with a doomed man in gray. How could Brian say what he had to say and convince Larissa he was right? How could he say it and convince himself?

He began, "You can't call your father to warn him his project might be in jeopardy, so you must do it in person. You have to go to Spain." Brian took off his sunglasses to look into Larissa's eyes. "But I can't go with you. Not without my passport. I think I should do what Lenore Harte wanted, go to the Defense Attaché in Paris and ask for protection."

"Will they believe what you tell them?"

"Eventually," Brian said. "I know too much to be making all this up, about Skyrm and Silver and Eck and Positive Enforcement. They'll definitely take me seriously once I tell them what happened to Lenore Harte."

"Then I should go with you."

"No, because by the time they verify my story, it may be too late for your father. Harte said he will demonstrate Prometheus in two days. You have to be in Zaragoza by tomorrow and find him. You know his hotel, right?"

She clutched his arm. "I don't want to go without you, Brian. I need your help."

"Believe me, Larissa, I'd rather go with you. I want to help you. But if you think I know what I'm doing, you're wrong. I'm just blundering along hoping a way out of this mess will turn up." He looked away. "And going to Paris seems like the only way out of this mess."

Larissa tightened her grip. "Who will tell me what Foster Blake would do? Who will tell me how paranoid I must be? You can't involve me in all this and then abandon me."

"I don't want to leave you! But how can I get into Spain? Silver has my passport."

Larissa released Brian's arm and went quiet. She rested her chin on her thumb and tapped her lips with her forefinger as she took a step back to appraise him. Brian felt self-conscious when her gaze rested on his bare legs.

"There is a way, Brian," she said. "And you seem fit enough."

"To do what?"

"To walk across the Pyrenees."

CHAPTER 21--TRANSIT

Thousands of hiking trails crisscross the Pyrenees, the mountain range that forms the natural barrier between France and Spain. Many of these trails, such as those that follow ancient Basque smuggling routes, snake their way back and forth across the two nations' equally serpentine border. For this reason the rugged frontier goes largely unguarded. Customs officials assume that nature walkers who begin their trek in France will end their trek in France and that Spanish hikers will do likewise.

Larissa explained all this to Brian on their way to the Université de Toulouse campus. "Why waste time checking the passport of a person crossing from France to Spain," she said, "if his route takes him back into France ten minutes later?"

"So you're positive I can cross into Spain without a passport so long as we're on a mountain trail?"

"Yes," Larissa said, "but for an extra precaution, and to honor paranoia, we will be somewhat off the trail when we cross the border."

"Sounds like you have a particular trail in mind."

"I do. We will follow the Comet Line. Not exactly but—" she searched for the word—"approximately." Larissa gave Brian a sidelong look and smiled. "I think you will appreciate our route, because it involves espionage."

That perked his ears. "Really? How?"

"During the Second World War, partisans in my country used the Comet Line to smuggle into Spain hundreds of American and British pilots who were shot down by Nazis."

Brian nodded. He knew from The Military Channel that downed Allied pilots would cross the Pyrenees to escape the Gestapo. Now he would be tackling these mountains himself.

Suddenly, Brian visualized Foster Blake climbing to Kang's

precipitous lair at the end of *A Tiger Hunts Alone*. So what if that happened in the Himalayas? A mountain's a mountain, right?

"Won't we need ropes and pitons and boots with spikes and all that?" he asked. "And maybe you think I'm in shape to climb a mountain, but I'm not so sure."

Larissa laughed. It was a wonderfully loud and musical laugh, but it ticked Brian off because the longer it lasted the sillier he felt. Finally, she draped her arm across his back. "You can relax," she said. "We will be walking. Uphill, but walking."

They arrived at the university's bicycle lot before Larissa could explain further. Conferring briefly, they agreed to locate a pair of unlocked bikes and take them simultaneously. As Larissa had correctly predicted, they found two suitable bikes in less than ten minutes. They mounted their bicycles, which were across the lot from each other, at the same time and rode off at a casual pace. Brian braced for shouts of "*Voleur! Voleur!*" and the need to apply a burst of speed, but no shouts came.

He followed Larissa up a tree-lined street hoping they would reach the canal soon so he could learn more about the Comet Line. They came to a bridge. Looking down, Brian saw a watery junction where the Canal du Midi approached the Garonne from the east then bent away to the north. Larissa led Brian over the bridge, across another tree-shaded boulevard, and down to the path that ran along the canal. They rode north, leaving Toulouse behind.

The trail before them was inspiring. A cortege of trees with long, curving branches created a green canopy over the water. Houseboats and small barges were docked on the other side of the canal, and people sitting on their decks waved as the teenagers cycled past. In the books Brian read and the movies he watched, spies were pursued through parking garages, dockyards, or narrow alleys at night. Here he was running for his life through paradise, and it wasn't yet noon.

Brian pedaled faster until he came alongside Larissa. "So how do you know so much about the Comet Line?" he asked.

"I heard about it from a guide in the Pyrenees. She said the leader of this dangerous escape route was a young woman, only twenty-four years old, named Dédée de Jongh—"

"Really!"

"I know what you think, but her last name is not the same." Larissa spelled it for him. "But you can see why I wanted to learn all about her. When I returned home I read everything I could about the Comet Line and Dédée de Jongh, who became my hero. She was from Belgium originally, like my father's family, and I hoped that despite the different spelling of our names, I would discover Dédée was a distant aunt, perhaps." She let go of her handlebars and shrugged with her palms up. "*Malheuresement*, that does not appear to be true."

"I know how you feel," Brian said. "I have the same last name as Spider-Man, but I'm pretty sure we're not related."

He wasn't certain Larissa would get the joke, but she laughed.

"My admiration for you just skyrocketed," Brian said.

"Because I know Peter Parker is secretly Spider-Man?"

Brian nodded.

"Even for an American you are a strange boy."

"That I do not deny."

The canal path ran smooth and straight. Encountering few other cyclists or joggers along the way, Brian and Larissa were able to ride abreast and discuss her plan.

In Grisolles they would board a train heading northwest to Bordeaux, and there they would catch another train south to Bayonne. This was a regrettably circuitous route, Larissa said, but the only one available by rail. From Bayonne they would take a bus to Hendaye, a Basque village on the Bay of Biscay and nearer the Comet Line. Once in Hendaye, they would buy the hiking and camping supplies they would need for the mountains. Brian raised his eyebrows when Larissa mentioned camping. She told him it would be best if they camped in the foothills that night then rose early the next morning to make for the border. Larissa hoped they would be hiking out of Hendaye that evening before sunset.

"Is that realistic?" Brian asked.

"If we have luck with the train schedules, yes."

Rolling into Grisolles an hour later, they discovered the train station was situated not in the small village center but on the other side of the Canal du Midi. They rode across a bridge and slowly approached the station from the north. The modest brick depot sat by itself with the canal on one side and a highway on the other. The building was so isolated that any of Skyrm's watchers would be obvious. Brian saw none, so they went inside.

They bought their tickets and learned the train to Bordeaux would arrive in forty-three minutes. Brian suggested they spend most of that time in the village, where they would be less conspicuous. They grabbed a quick meal of crêpes and lemonade at a café. As they pedaled back to the train station, Brian spotted a bicycle shop. He ducked inside to buy a chain with a padlock and key. At the station, he secured the bicycles to a rack near the parking lot.

"When we're on the train," Brian told Larissa, "you can write an anonymous note explaining that two bikes missing from the University of Toulouse can be found outside the train station in Grisolles. We'll send the note along with the key to the Toulouse police department when we reach Bordeaux."

"How will we know the address?"

"It's in my guidebook," Brian said. "We just mail a letter and—presto!—we erase the guilt of being *vélo voleurs*."

Larissa laughed. "*Très amusent*," she said and patted his cheek.

Brian smiled. First the Spider-Man joke and now a one-liner in French. Maybe he could quip after all.

CHAPTER 22--DANGER

Although the train schedules did not align as favorably as Larissa had hoped, forty-five minutes of sunlight remained when she and Brian stepped off the Rue Errondenia above Hendaye and entered the mountain trails of the Pyrenees.

The pair had slept most of the way to Bordeaux. In the Bordeaux station, they mailed the bicycle key and waited an hour to board the next train. Brian again nodded off during the shorter trip to Bayonne, but Larissa stayed awake to compose a shopping list. In Bayonne they had to dash to catch the bus to Hendaye. Aboard the bus, Larissa explained the rest of their travel plans: once in Spain they would find a highway and hitchhike to the nearest town, probably Irún, where they could catch a bus to Zaragoza.

"Hitchhike!" Brian cried. "Are you nuts?"

Surprised by his objection, Larissa asked, "Why should we not hitchhike?"

"In America," he said, "we assume anyone who picks up a hitchhiker is a serial killer. Boy, they sure didn't show you French kids the same safety videos in grade school."

"Hitchhiking is a common practice in the Pyrenees," Larissa said. "We will be safe if we are together."

"OK," Brian said, but he remained skeptical.

The bus arrived in Hendaye, and they marched to the nearest outdoors supply store. The pair spent half an hour selecting the items on Larissa's list. Brian understood why they were buying a tent, hiking shoes, and sleeping bags, but Larissa had to explain the need for other equipment. On the way to the cashier she made an impulse purchase, a maroon and navy FC Barcelona soccer jersey for Brian.

"You can wear this in Spain, and people will be less likely to think you are a foreigner," she said.

"Won't my American walk give me away?"

Larissa grinned. "The Spanish are not as sensitive to such things as we French."

In a nearby café, they had a light meal and transferred their supplies and their original backpacks into new, taller packs with aluminum frames. The shopping spree had sapped most of their cash, but except for bus fare and meals tomorrow, Brian doubted they would need much more money until they found Larissa's father. They put on their hiking shoes and pants in the café's WC (Brian was getting used to changing in public restrooms). After that, they walked out of the town and into the mountains.

Larissa indicated a wooden post marked with a white stripe above a red stripe. "We are on the GR 10"—she pronounced it *guh arr dee*—"a trail that extends the entire length of the Pyrenees, from the Bay of Biscay to the Mediterranean. It takes six weeks to hike the complete trail, which I hope to do next year. I have hiked only this section before, from Hendaye to Sare."

"With your mother?" Brian asked.

"*Oui*, with my mother."

They went in silence for a while. Brian used that time to adjust to walking with the higher, heavier backpack that raised his center of gravity. The hiking shoes, which looked like brown sneakers but had stiffer soles, required no adjustment period. Their comfort surprised him.

Larissa gestured toward peaks in the southwest. "We will be headed that way tomorrow, into Spain, but not up those mountains. Do not worry. No ropes or pitons required."

Brian shook his head. She wasn't going to let him live that down. They passed beneath a motorway and put the concrete world behind them. The evening sky was turning orange and salmon, dappling the landscape before them in darkening shades of green. Rounded summits hovered like gray ghosts in the distance.

"It's funny," Brian said. "I was just in the Alps a few days ago and figured all mountain ranges would be the same. But the Pyrenees seem less ... severe."

Larissa squeezed his arm. "We have a saying: *Les Alpes*

stupéfient, les Pyrénées séduisent. 'The Alps amaze, the Pyrenees seduce.'"

"I'm not sure I want to be seduced by a mountain range," Brian said. "It sounds painful."

Larissa laughed the throaty laugh he already adored. "Maybe you will change your mind tomorrow," she said, "when you see the Pyrenees in the daylight."

They walked out of a copse of trees into a meadow that stretched for miles. Shadow covered much of the valley, but the waning sun still illuminated a grassy stretch dotted with purple flowers.

"I wish we had arrived here an hour earlier," Larissa said. "This is my favorite place on Earth. It is so beautiful and so peaceful. Once I sat there"—she pointed toward a spot nearby— "singing along to 'Sheena Is a Punk Rocker' on my iPod. Only I changed her name to Larissa. There I was by myself in the middle of this quiet field singing punk rock until my lungs burst."

Her voice trailed off. Larissa had stopped walking and was smiling serenely, her hands clasping her shoulders as if to embrace the memory. Brian cupped her shoulder blade with his palm, his fingertips within an inch of hers. She relaxed into his arm and he smiled as well.

"I wish I could have seen you," he said. "I might have been terrified of this lunatic Ramones fan rolling in the grass, but I wish I could have seen you."

She laughed again and led him along the meadow's edge and back into the forest. "It will be dark soon," she said. "And we need to find the right place to set up the tent."

They were carrying flashlights by the time they came to a small clearing, about fifteen feet around. "We can camp here," Larissa said.

They set down the backpacks. Larissa pulled the furled tent from Brian's pack and unrolled it on the ground. She turned on a battery-powered lantern so they could see what they were doing.

"Do we even need the tent?" Brian asked. "This seems like a nice, warm night. Sleeping bags should do."

"The weather can change quickly in the mountains," Larissa said, handing him a compact rubber mallet. "You will be glad to be in a tent if it rains while we sleep."

Brian set to tapping stakes into the ground, pulling the tent's reinforced plastic floor taut as he proceeded. "Have we been following the Comet Line?" he asked.

"Not exactly," Larissa said as she screwed together sections of the tent's single, hard nylon pole. "If we followed the whole length of the Comet Line it would take two days. We are following only the section that crosses into Spain." She threaded the pole through a long, curving sleeve in the tent's fabric. "But we are not following it precisely. We do not need to. The forest is not filled with Gestapo agents pursuing us with their dogs."

"Good point," Brian said. Pounding in the last stake, he imagined the baying of hounds from a distant, desperate past.

"Which means we can take easier paths," Larissa said. "Help me with this, please."

They pushed the pole into a pin on one side of the tent and then pulled in the opposite direction to form a bow. "Also," Larissa continued, "if we stayed on Dédée de Jongh's actual trail we would arrive at a picnic area after crossing into Spain. I assumed you would want to avoid public places, at least until we reach the road."

"You assumed right," Brian said as they secured the other end of the pole. The arched pole now supported a mesh dome. They pulled a fabric skin over the skeletal tent and fastened it with Velcro straps, plastic clips, and a few more stakes.

Admiring the finished tent, Brian was about to say something lame like, "Home sweet home," when he looked up and was struck dumb. Beyond the treetops was a night sky his urban eyes had never beheld. More stars than he thought possible shined brightly and crisply, intense white specks blazing through infinite blackness. Brian realized he and Larissa were miles from any building. With no city lights to obscure it, the night sky glittered with endless beauty.

"You have not seen the stars like this before, have you?"

"Uh-unh. This is amazing." Brian wanted to add something profound, but his bedazzled optic nerves short-circuited his brain's speech function.

"It will grow more spectacular as the night continues," Larissa said as she turned off the lantern to complete the darkness. "This is merely prelude."

They stood for a long time in the black, still night gazing at the stars. Larissa pointed out constellations to Brian, who recognized only the Big Dipper on his own. When Larissa yawned, they knew it was time to retire.

She turned on the lantern, and they crawled into the tent, which was just big enough for the teenagers and their backpacks. They unrolled their sleeping bags and settled into them. The pair had a tacit agreement to sleep in the clothes they were wearing.

Not yet ready for slumber but always ready for a good spy story, Brian said, "So tell me more about Dédée de Jongh."

"They called her the Little Cyclone," Larissa said, "and it was she who ran the Comet Line. Dédée organized many people all the way from Belgium to San Sebastian in Spain. Most of those who worked for her were men, including macho Basque smugglers, yet they all obeyed the Little Cyclone. All but one."

"What happened?"

"One of the Basques betrayed her. The Gestapo captured Dédée and put her in prison, but they did not execute her because it was beyond their comprehension that a woman, particularly a young woman, could run so large and successful a resistance operation." Larissa paused, and her eyes flashed playfully. "The Gestapo were male chauvinists, just like Foster Blake."

"Hey!" Brian retorted, unprepared for the ambush. "That was uncalled for." Larissa's grin told him she was teasing, but it was still a cheap shot.

"Are you telling me you do not idolize Foster Blake for all the beautiful women he sleeps with?"

"That is a tired, unimaginative criticism." Brian tried not to sound defensive, but he had had this argument with girls before. "I could find lots more sex in other books and movies. And if sex was all Foster Blake had going for him, he wouldn't still be popular after all these years."

"So what besides sex makes him popular?"

Brian went quiet. He sat up to focus his thoughts. Finally he said, "I think it's the racing changes."

"Racing changes? What are racing changes?"

"I don't really know. But every time there was a car chase in one of the books, Clive Hastings would write something like,

'Blake threw his E-type into the hairpin curve and executed a perfect racing change before roaring into the straightaway.' I have only a vague idea what a racing change is—something you do with a stick shift—but it sounds cool as hell. *Racing change*. What matters is that Foster Blake knows how to do it, and he knows exactly the right moment to do it while cornering at high speed. Things like that. Like how he always knows the odds he'll be dealt a winning hand at baccarat. Foster Blake is in control of his world. That's what makes him so appealing. It's not just that women throw themselves at him or that he can kill with discretion, or that he gets amazing gadgets—those are extras. Foster Blake remains iconic because he has this, this masculine expertise that keeps him alive."

Larissa looked at him with wide eyes. A smile twitched at the corners of her lips. "I wonder if you have ever spoken at such length. You are very passionate about this, I see."

"I guess," Brian shrugged. "I've been a fan for a long time." Embarrassment rushed in, compelling him to parry. "Haven't you ever felt a connection with a fictional character?"

"Yes," Larissa said without hesitation. "Riff Randell."

"Who's he?"

"Riff Randell is a she, not a he. The heroine of *Rock 'n' Roll High School*. Don't you know your own culture? It is one of America's great contributions to cinema! Riff Randell worships the Ramones and persuades them to perform at her school. Then they blow it up."

Larissa's eyes glistened with fervor in the lantern's glow. Brian said, "Look who's getting passionate about a movie character now."

She nodded. "I have always envied Riff. I dream about getting the Ramones to play at my school, even though it is impossible now with Joey gone, and Dee Dee. But it is a wonderful thing to fantasize—the Ramones at your school."

"So do you understand then, at least a little, why I love Foster Blake?"

"At least a little, yes," Larissa replied. She moved closer. "But you are better than Foster Blake. You are not a chauvinist, and you are real, and you also know what to do to survive."

Brian snorted. "I know what to do because I've read so many

spy novels."

"No, you know what to do because you are smart. You have the wisdom to use your knowledge."

"Well, so do you. You knew how to get out of Toulouse. And you are the one who knows about Dédée de Jongh and the Comet Line."

"Then we make a good team," Larissa said, and she kissed him.

Larissa probably didn't intend the kiss as anything more than a sign of encouragement, Brian thought later, but as soon as their lips touched he felt a jolt he knew was mutual because the kiss intensified immediately. He pulled her tight; awkwardly aware of the bulky sleeping bags between them, yet deliciously aware Larissa was reciprocating his embrace.

He didn't know how long the kiss lasted before Larissa gently pulled away. "Brian," she said, her forehead to his cheek, "it's not that I wish to stop, but if we continue it may get ... dangerous." She looked up, smiling. "And you already have brought *beaucoup* danger to my life."

Brian chuckled. "But surely I can handle the peril."

"What?"

"It's from *Monty Python and the Holy Grail*. One of Britain's great contributions to cinema." He kissed her forehead. "But you're right, this isn't the time." Caressing her chin, he added, "I do want another kiss like that, though. Soon."

"I promise you that," she said as she retreated and switched off the lantern. "Goodnight, *cher* Brian."

"Goodnight, Larissa." Brian rolled onto his back and rested his head on his pillow, knowing it would be some time before he fell asleep.

CHAPTER 23--CURRENT

Shoots from the undergrowth traced early morning dew across Brian's bare calves as he and Larissa walked into the forest, their campsite behind them.

They had left the tent and sleeping bags in place, an idea that sparked a brief but fiery disagreement. Brian reasoned that taking down and repacking the tent would waste time. Furthermore (he actually used the word), they could move faster without the extra weight in their backpacks. Larissa protested they must not violate the camping law of "leave no trace."

"What's more important," he asked, "finding your father or leaving no trace?"

That had won the argument.

Still, Larissa was sullen in defeat. She remained silent for a full half hour as they hiked through corridors of poplar and fir, heading south by southwest to the Spanish border. Finally, she spoke, "Have you decided what we should do when we see my father?"

"Sort of," Brian said. "I have a Plan A. Hopefully I will come up with Plans B, C, and D by the time we reach Zaragoza, because Plan A hinges on a mighty big if. But I think it has the strongest chance of working."

"Which is?"

"We keep a watch on the front of your father's hotel—staying out of sight ourselves—until we see him come out. Then you go up to him on the sidewalk while I hail a taxi." Brian stepped over a large dead branch and then continued, "Hopefully the three of us will be able to get into a cab right away. This should catch anyone watching your father—Skyrm's men, the CIA, the DIA—by surprise, and we ought to be able to find a safe place to talk to him before they figure out where we went."

"But what if we do not see my father in front of the hotel?"

"That's the mighty big if and the reason I have to come up with Plans B, C, and D."

"It is a good plan, though," Larissa said. "Very clever."

"Thanks." Brian smiled, happy they were friends again. "But it's only clever if it works."

Larissa returned his smile and marched ahead to take the lead. They stayed within the forest, where high branches mottled the light of the rising sun. The woods smelled of damp mulch and, if Brian remembered his liquid soaps correctly, lavender.

Trudging upward through the woods, Brian realized the value of the hiking pole he did not want to buy. With the extra weight strapped to his back, the pole helped him keep his balance on the hilly trails. Mostly they headed upward, but their path sometimes jagged into a shallow gully. Whenever Brian skittered downhill, the contents of his backpack clinked and clanged. His concession during the argument was agreeing to carry the cooking equipment.

Their breakfast, consumed while dawn broke, had consisted of granola bars, coffee, and scrambled eggs. The eggs, like the coffee, were freeze-dried yet surprisingly tasty once mixed with boiling water.

After he had eaten, Brian slipped into the tent and changed into a pair of beige hiking shorts and a light gray UnderArmour shirt. He pulled on a pair of thick wool socks ("You do not want blisters," Larissa had said at the camping supply store when Brian objected that he already had socks), tied the strong, reinforced nylon laces of his hiking shoes, and tugged on his Brewers cap.

Larissa had bought her own cap, hunter green and free of team affiliation, in Hendaye. Her outfit matched Brian's except that her shorts were black and her UnderArmour shirt pale blue. Not that Brian could see her clothes now. As Larissa walked before him, her three-foot-tall backpack hid her torso. To Brian's eyes, she had become a green canvas sack with nicely toned legs. The canvas sack began to hum "Sheena Is a Punk Rocker." Brian whistled along.

An hour later they came to a level clearing. Larissa pulled off her backpack and handed Brian a protein bar. "We can rest here and admire the view." She pointed to a distant town below them. "That is Hendaye."

Brian looked down on their last port of call and the blue Atlantic beyond it. "I can't believe we're this high in the mountains."

"The slope was gradual, but between last night and this morning we walked uphill for two hours," she said. "And I hate to disappoint you, but we are not high in the Pyrenees at all."

Larissa took his shoulders and turned him away from the sea. Brian's head tilted as he looked up at the craggy wall. Green at their base and gray-blue with white striations near their peaks, mountains filled his field of vision. Brian knew then they were still near the great range's ground floor.

"How much higher do we have to climb?" he asked, fearing the answer.

"Actually, from here we go mostly downhill to the river."

Brian nodded and took a swig from his water bottle. Larissa explained that they would wade across the Bidossa River, which marked the border between France and Spain, just as more than eight hundred Allied airmen had done during the Second World War.

They rested another ten minutes before reentering the woods. As Larissa had predicted, their path soon sloped downward. The incline was gentle at first, but suddenly steepened. Brian had to use tree roots as steps like he did years ago playing in ravines near the Menominee River. Only then he didn't have a cumbersome backpack skewing his balance. Leaning against a tree to catch his breath, Brian looked down and watched with envy as Larissa nimbly descended the gully and disappeared behind a clutch of pine trees.

Brian sighed and followed. He quickened his pace, sometimes sliding on the damp soil but remaining upright. He heard a rush of water as he emerged onto a rocky floor. Larissa stood before him, her arms akimbo as she assessed the Bidossa River. Brian came alongside and was not happy to see Larissa scowling.

"There must be rain higher in the mountains," she said. "I did not expect the Bidossa to be so deep in July. I thought the water would come no higher than our knees."

"How deep is it?" Brian asked.

"To the waist, I think. Maybe a little more."

"That's not bad."

"Yes, but the current will be strong."

Brian looked across the swiftly flowing water to Spain, a mere thirty yards away. "Should we walk along the riverbank until we find a safer spot to cross?"

"No," Larissa said with a shake of her head. "We are now a few hundred meters from the traditional Comet Line crossing. If we go north, toward Dédée's true route, we might be seen from the highway bridge or one of the newer roads." She looked the other way. "If we cross any farther to the south, I am not certain I can find my way once we are in Spain."

"All right then," Brian said. "We cross here."

"We must be very careful."

"We will be."

Sitting on a boulder by the river's edge, they switched their socks and hiking shoes for rubber-soled wading shoes (another sporting goods purchase Brian had questioned). They tied their hiking shoes together by the laces and draped them around their necks. Larissa lashed her hiking pole to the side of her backpack, so Brian copied her. Without saying another word, they stepped into the Bidossa's chilly waters.

Larissa led, and Brian followed five feet behind. A quarter of the way across, the water was barely to their knees and Brian thought this would be easy after all. Larissa took two more steps and squealed as she fell into waist-high water. She pushed ahead. When Brian dropped to the same spot he felt the current, a roiling wraith bent on sweeping him away.

Larissa, now mid-river, turned her head. "How are you doing?"

"Just fine," Brian said, "but I should've worn my swim suit."

Larissa laughed and Brian stepped on a slime-covered stone that shifted beneath his foot. His knee buckled and he went down. He landed on his knees, his chin dipping into the water. Frigid wavelets lapped at his lower lip, and he shivered. His Brewers cap dropped into an eddy and sped downriver like a hydrofoil racer before he could grab it.

Larissa sloshed toward him.

"Stay right there," he said. "I don't want to pull you in. I'm OK. Just give me a second."

As soon as he stood, Brian sensed he had done it too quickly, failing to compensate for the surging water that buffeted him off balance. He twisted at the waist to regain his footing, and the current hit Brian square in the back and plunged him headlong into the cold river.

CHAPTER 24--SMOKE

Brian reflexively clamped his mouth shut as he submerged. He heard Larissa yell his name above the liquid maelstrom baffling his eardrums. Through the clear water Brian saw a thick branch jammed between two large stones just ahead. He twisted left to grab for it, but he missed and the undercurrent grabbed him lengthwise and rolled him like a log. The river's rocky gray bottom and the blue sky above its surface swirled in his vision. The backpack pulled him down, and Brian feared a strap would snarl on a branch and trap him on the river's floor. Or he would crack his head against a rock and lose consciousness.

Brian's eyes bulged as something grabbed his neck and throttled him.

His fingers automatically went to his throat to determine this new threat. It was, of all things, his shoelace. It had wrapped around his neck as he tumbled down the river. He looked back to see that one of the hiking shoes had snagged on a branch and was yanking the noose tight. The second shoe was pressing against his ear and cheek. The pressure in his lungs pounded at his ribs, and Brian's brain sounded a warning he would either drown or be strangled if he didn't act. He snatched at the shoe beside his head and tried to unwind it. The garrote tightened. Wrong way! He twirled the shoe in the opposite direction. The pressure on his neck loosened. His lungs wanted to explode with relief, but instinct stopped Brian from inhaling gallons of water.

Larissa's legs, phantom pale beneath the surface, moved toward him, and only then did Brian realize the nylon cord had turned him around when it seized his neck and, acting as a tether, now held him in place. He got his knees beneath his chest and pushed his head above water.

Brian gasped spasmodically, pumping blessed oxygen back

into his lungs. Larissa hollered his name, and Brian lifted a hand to show he was all right even if he could not yet talk. When normal breathing returned, he raised himself slowly until he stood, the waterline above his navel.

Larissa was on the verge of tears as she approached, and Brian wanted to assure her the danger was over. "I'm glad you insisted on the waterproof backpacks," he joked hoarsely. "At least my socks are dry."

Larissa held Brian until his legs steadied. She supported him as they moved toward shallow water and waded to the opposite bank. Brian collapsed onto flat, sun-warmed stones.

Larissa, still dry above the waist, crouched in front of him. "Are you all right?"

"I am now that I'm on land," he said. "And thanks."

She surprised him with a radiant smile. "*Bienvenue à l'Espagne.*" She kissed him on both cheeks. "Welcome to Spain!"

Brian looked up and down the empty riverbank, surveying the new country. It appeared no different from the country they had just left. He tipped a hiking shoe and poured a stream of water into the puddle spreading from beneath him. "*Olè,*" he said.

Larissa tossed him a camp towel, and he dried off the best he could. As Brian pulled the wool socks and hiking shoes back on, Larissa said, "We have to climb that." She pointed at a wooded gully that matched the one on the French side. "At the top, we can go behind trees and put on dry clothes. We won't be able to hitchhike like this." She pulled at her wet shorts.

"How kind of you not to mention this," Brian said. He waved his hand along his body, indicating his dripping outfit.

Larissa grinned, a sight that cheered his spirits. "I was being polite," she said.

The hill was steep, but tree roots again served as natural stairs. "The Irùn-Pamplona highway will be close by once we reach the top," Larissa said.

The sky darkened during their ascent. When they came to the crest, rain began to fall. "Where did this come from?" Brian asked, panting from the climb. "That sky was pure blue no more than fifteen minutes ago."

"I told you the weather changes quickly in the mountains,"

Larissa said. "But this is fortunate. It excuses our wet clothes and will make hitchhiking easier. Motorists will not question why we are giving up on hiking so early in the day."

How early, Brian wondered. He glanced at his watch. 8:48 blinked back at him.

They pulled forest green rain ponchos from their packs and slipped them over their already wet clothes before proceeding north. "We are heading back toward the site of the true Comet Line crossing," Larissa said. "We will reach the highway soon. No more than ten minutes. Follow where I walk because there are steep drops alongside the trail."

The rain was steady but not driving. It was a cleansing downpour that tamped down the smell of the soil and released the rich fragrance of the woods. Brian inhaled deeply, taking in the scent of sap, of pine needles, of lavender.

Of tobacco.

Brian clutched Larissa's wrist and pulled her to a stop. He put a finger to his lips to silence her question. Her confused look changed to surprise when she, too, caught the intrusive odor.

The wind carried the scent from the direction of the river. Brian slowly turned his head to the east, scanning the gaps between the trees for the telltale orange glow of a cigarette. Instead he saw a motion.

Ten yards away a man's arm rose and lowered. *Taking a puff*, Brian thought. The man knelt next to a tree with his back to them. He wore dark green clothes, but no rain gear. A plume of smoke drifted above his head. The man turned his face to wipe water from his eye. A pinprick of crimson flashed from his earlobe like a danger signal.

A ruby stud, Brian remembered. *Merz!*

CHAPTER 25--MISSTEP

Brian tipped his head and shifted his eyes to indicate Merz's position to Larissa. When she spotted the man, her eyebrows shot up and her mouth formed an O of surprise.

If they could see Merz, Brian reasoned, Merz could see them. Their rain ponchos provided camouflage, but Brian wanted to play it safe and put another line of trees between them and their stalker. Brian jerked his head toward a row of birches behind them, and, moving two crooked fingers across his other palm, gestured what he hoped was basic sign language for *walking*. He mouthed the word *slow*. Larissa nodded her comprehension.

As the pair inched backward, raindrops chattering on their poncho hoods, Brian continued to watch Merz. To Brian's relief, Skyrm's man kept his face toward the river. An eternal sixty-eight seconds later, Brian and Larissa ducked safely behind a pair of thick birch trees.

"That is the *méchant* who attacked us in my house," Larissa said at a volume just above a whisper. Brian was pleased to hear no panic in her voice.

"Yeah," Brian replied in equally low tones. "Merz."

"But how is he here? That is impossible."

"I don't understand either," Brian said, "but here he is. The good news is we're behind him and he doesn't know it. The bad news is he can't be alone."

Brian scanned the foliage. It took five minutes to spot the next man. "I see another one."

"Where?"

"About twenty feet north of Merz's position. He's hard to see because he's hidden by some thick branches."

"Do you recognize him?"

"No ... wait a minute."

The second man stood, stretched his arms, and limped to another tree.

"That's Kralik," Brian said as the man knelt behind the tree. "He's the one who tried to grab me in Cannes. I recognize his limp. I gave it to him."

Kralik, too, was looking east. Brian followed the man's line of sight and saw the edge of a picnic table through a gap in the trees. What had Larissa said last night about a picnic grove? A sickening realization hit Brian: if he and Larissa had followed the Comet Line faithfully, these men were in the perfect position to ambush them once they crossed into Spain.

Brian hastily decided to keep this intelligence to himself for now. No sense worrying Larissa over a possible coincidence.

"Do you see any others?" Larissa asked.

"No," Brian replied, "but we should assume at least six of them are nearby looking for us: these two, Skyrm, the bald man we saw outside Harte's apartment, the tall man with Merz outside St-Sernin, and Silver. There may be more. Let's hope we've outflanked them all."

"What do we do?" Larissa asked.

Brian kept focus on Merz and Kralik. Neither moved.

"You say we're close to the highway?" Brian asked.

"*Oui.*"

"We have to get to it, but stay inside the tree line and follow the highway south for at least a mile—two might be safer—and then hitch a ride." He touched Larissa's arm. "They were expecting to catch us here. They won't look for us a few miles away."

"But how could they be waiting for us here?"

"I don't know," Brian replied. "We just have to get away from them."

The teenagers backed slowly away from their hiding spot and headed south. After several steps Brian stopped and turned to see whether Merz or Kralik had noticed their movement. Kralik was out of view, but Merz remained a sentinel facing the wrong direction. Brian watched him take a puff of his cigarette, then followed Larissa through the woods. Soon they had doubled their distance from Merz. Brian could hear the thrum of car engines muffled by the trees and the rain.

Larissa turned to smile in celebration of the highway noise and tripped over a hidden root. She twirled toward Brian as she lost her balance and landed on her stomach with her legs draped down a ridge that bordered the path. From the underbrush, she gave Brian an embarrassed look that morphed into shock as she slid away. Brian dropped to his knees and extended a hand, grazing her fingertips as she plunged out of reach.

Larissa was slipping backward on her belly down a sudden incline. Her rain poncho flowered mockingly around her. Larissa grabbed at ferns and shrubs to slow her descent, but they pulled easily from the wet earth.

Brian dropped his backpack, stripped off his poncho, and snatched up his hiking pole. He stepped to the lip of the hill preparing to follow Larissa but was startled by the queasy sensation he was already moving. He looked to his feet and saw he was sliding down the slick mud as if on skates. Brian threw his legs forward and deliberately landed on his butt.

The slope was steeper here than the section they had climbed minutes earlier. Brian sped downhill after Larissa like he was riding an invisible toboggan. Twenty feet below him, Larissa grabbed at a bush. The branches held fast and halted her slide.

By leaning left, Brian steered toward a thin chestnut tree. He crashed into it with his hip and came to a stop a few feet above Larissa.

"Can you climb up?" he said.

"My feet cannot find a firm spot," she said. "I keep slipping."

"Are you hurt?"

"I do not think so."

"OK, good." Brian allowed himself to slide halfway past the tree to get nearer to Larissa. "I'm going to lower my hiking pole. Grab on to it and pull yourself up hand over hand."

He hooked his right arm around the tree trunk and leaned toward Larissa. Brian had no choice but to pull her up using his sore shoulder. He looped the hiking pole's nylon strap around his wrist and extended the pole.

"It's wet," Larissa said.

"Everything's wet," Brian said. "Just get a good grip on it."

Larissa reached for the walking stick with her left hand, nicking the end with her fingertips. On the second try she caught it, then shifted her body until she could reach her right hand above her left and grasp the pole.

Brian let out a whoosh of agony as he took the combined weight of Larissa and her backpack. His shoulder felt like someone struck it with an ax. He pitched toward Larissa, automatically tightening his hold on the tree trunk with his right arm. He groaned.

"Brian?" Larissa asked tentatively.

"Don't worry about me," Brian croaked. "Just climb!"

Brian stopped watching Larissa. He concentrated instead on the canopy of branches directly above that shielded him from the rain. *Most of the rain*, he thought as a drop splashed onto his cheek. Larissa continued to pull herself up the hiking pole hand over hand. Each time she grabbed hold, another spasm of pain flared through Brian's shoulder blade. He fixed his eyes on a gnarled branch and tried to transfer the pain outside his body, mentally burying it in the ground beneath his shoulder.

The weight on the walking stick eased. Larissa must have found footholds and now was using the stick only for guidance. Moments later, she flopped to the earth beside him.

"Oh Brian, your shoulder," she said and caressed his cheek.

"I'll be all right," Brian said. He pulled himself up until he could brace his foot on the tree, then rolled onto his stomach. "Just give me a moment," he said between deep breaths.

"Where is your backpack?"

"Top of the hill."

"I am so sorry I slipped."

"I fell in the river, you fell down a hill. We're even. Let's just get back up there and resolve to stay on our feet. We can make it. We have to move carefully, that's all."

They crawled up the ravine methodically, using exposed tree roots, low-hanging branches, and saplings like rungs on a ladder. Brian felt a jolt of pain when he reached with his left hand, but he knew that's all it was—pain. He was not injured. He simply had to push through the pain and reach the top. At least hitchhiking would be easier. Who wouldn't pull over to help two pathetic teenagers who looked like they fell down a mountain?

Brian gazed down past his shoulder. Larissa was just beyond his feet. Her cheeks were streaked with mud, but she smiled encouragingly. "Almost there," she said.

He looked up and saw she was right. The grassy ridge was only four feet above. Less than that. His right foot found a root and he pushed himself upward. Another step and he would be able to see above the rim. His left foot found solid earth, and Brian pushed up again to see past the crest and into the red-rimmed eyes of Matthias Skyrm, who towered over them with a sadistic smile plastered across his face.

As his every hope abandoned him, a curious fact registered with Brian Parker. Since this whole affair had begun, not until this moment had anyone pointed a gun at him.

CHAPTER 26--GUN

"Place your hands on the back of your neck and leave them there," Skyrm said.

Brian and Larissa obeyed. They stood in a clearing with Skyrm's crew facing them in a semicircle. Brian had guessed the number of men correctly, but not the roster. Merz and Kralik were present, along with the man from Harte's street and the man from St-Sernin. But the sixth man wasn't Silver. This was another new face—a hard face with a grim slit for a mouth and a notch missing from his right earlobe. The purple-shaded pouches beneath his stony eyes were sharply outlined as if scored by an X-Acto knife. While the other men were wearing various shades of dark green, the newcomer wore an army camouflage jacket. A genuine mercenary, Brian reflected. Each day Skyrm was pulling in deadlier accomplices.

Kralik held Brian's backpack by its handle. The tall man with the vulture shoulders had Larissa's pack. Skyrm had ordered the teenagers to leave their walking sticks at the ridge, denying them a possible pair of weapons. Brian was not allowed to put his rain poncho back on, so his clothes were soaked through again.

Skyrm stood four feet away and kept his pistol trained on Brian's chest. Brian looked at the muzzle. Reading hundreds of spy novels provides a rudimentary education on handguns, and Skyrm's pistol looked like a Browning nine-millimeter semiautomatic to Brian, though he couldn't be sure. The length of the barrel gave Brian the most important fact about the gun. Any shot at this range would be fatal.

Skyrm addressed Larissa. "Please lower your hood, Mlle DeJonge. I distrust hidden faces, and, besides, it is unfair that you remain dry while the rest of us suffer in the rain." He smirked. "Right, Mr. Parker?"

Brian replied, "It's not her fault you didn't bring your umbrellas."

Brian felt Larissa tense beside him. She must have thought he was mad to taunt the killer pointing a gun at him. But Brian wasn't playing Foster Blake for kicks. Skyrm, or his employer, needed them alive. Brian was certain of that. He had seen Skyrm operate, and if this man wanted Brian dead, he would have shot him five minutes ago on the hillside. Brian hoped a show of bravado might provoke Skyrm to reveal something useful—like why he was waiting for Brian and Larissa in this obscure spot in the Pyrenees.

The red rims of Skyrm's pale blue irises blazed for an instant at Brian's insolence, but cooled as quickly. "Please realize, Mr. Parker, this would be an ideal time to stop annoying me. In only a few days you have cost me much sleep and a considerable amount of money, and now I am standing in a rainstorm in the mountains at an hour when I should be enjoying breakfast."

Skyrm shook his head. "I do not admire your pluck," he went on. "I do not find you courageous. I find you bothersome. And if you do or say one more thing to bother me, my men will take turns snapping Mlle DeJonge's delicate fingers."

At the threat, Merz and Kralik looked at Skyrm in surprise, then nervously glanced at each other. With his back to them, Skyrm didn't see their reactions. But Brian did. *Well*, he thought, *that's interesting.*

"So," Skyrm said, "do we have an understanding?"

Brian nodded. He sensed terror radiating from Larissa and wished he could tell her Skyrm was bluffing, that her fingers were safe.

"Everyone has underestimated you," Skyrm continued. "Including that CIA buffoon. Certainly, you have been lucky, but this morning luck has left you."

"You're the one who's lucky," Brian replied, daring one more poke at the hornet's nest. "If we hadn't slipped down that hill, we would have gotten away from you."

Skyrm sneered. "'Gotten away from us?' What do you mean? You couldn't have known we were here."

"Oh, we knew," Brian said and nodded at Merz. "We smelled his cigarette."

Skyrm spun on his heel to glare at Merz. The man with the ruby stud raised his eyebrows pleadingly and opened his mouth to deliver an apology that never came, for Skyrm had lifted his pistol and fired. With the gun's single crack, a red hole appeared between Merz's eyes. Merz jerked backward, let out a strangled squawk, and crashed into the undergrowth, sparing Brian and Larissa the sight of the exit wound's carnage.

The small group remained motionless as the forest absorbed the gunshot's echo. Brian's stomach clenched. He glanced at Larissa and saw her quaking. Brian looked at the newcomer and saw he now held a pistol as well, but its barrel was pointed at the ground and the mercenary had angled himself toward Kralik and the others as if to head off any insurrection. None would come. The others stood languidly, displaying no remorse for their fallen comrade.

Skyrm pointed at Merz's body. "I warned him twice about his incompetence," he told his crew, his voice rigid. "I do not give third chances. Do you understand?"

The men nodded and grunted.

Skyrm looked at Brian. "Do you wish to register any further complaints against my associates, Mr. Parker?"

Brian slowly shook his head. His mouth was too dry to speak.

"Good," Skyrm said. He turned back to his men. "Voss, Carter, take Merz and throw him down that ravine. He should go undiscovered for days."

The bald man and the tall man went to Merz's body, giving Brian two more names, though he didn't know who was Carter and who was Voss. The pair roughly stripped off Merz's jacket and wrapped it around his head. This shroud would prevent a trail of blood leading from the clearing to the ravine, Brian realized. He watched them lift the limp body and felt a pang of responsibility. Trying to appear brave, Brian made a smart-ass comment that cost a man his life. A bad man, but a man nonetheless. Guilt infiltrated Brian's horror of the shooting.

Before Brian could examine his conscience further, a rustling came from the tree line. Everyone looked to the two men in orange rain ponchos and hiking gear who stepped into the clearing.

"'Ere, what's going on?" one of them asked, his accent

unmistakably Cockney.

They're British, was all Brian had time to think as he watched the hikers' eyes move from the two men hoisting a corpse to himself and Larissa standing as prisoners to Skyrm as he casually leveled his pistol at the new arrivals. The gun cracked twice more. The bullets' impact flung the hikers back into the woods. The momentary crimson bursts Brian saw as the men flew from sight would haunt him for years.

Larissa began screaming in French. Skyrm's head snapped around. "*Fermez!*" he said savagely. Larissa fell silent.

Skyrm fired off instructions to his men. "Dump these bodies as well. Kralik, you help. Make sure they are well hidden."

Kralik moved toward the dead hikers. Voss and Carter carried Merz from the clearing. "Meet us at the van," Skyrm called as they disappeared into the forest.

Skyrm turned to the remaining man, the hard-faced newcomer. "We must leave." He looked at Brian and Larissa with furious eyes, but spoke with a calm voice. "I will have no more trouble from either of you. Take your rucksacks and follow Masson."

The man in the camouflage jacket gestured with his pistol and took the lead. *So that's Masson*, Brian thought as he and Larissa marched forward. They moved like sleepwalkers. The towering trees, the rain, even the idea of Skyrm walking behind him with a gun pointed at his back barely registered with Brian. His mind was numb with the atrocities he just witnessed.

He wondered about the hikers, who died for stumbling upon a murder and a kidnapping. All Brian knew about them is that they were British. No, all he knew is that one was British. The other never got a chance to speak. They had appeared to be in their thirties. Were they married? Did they have children who would never see their fathers again?

A chill shook Brian's bones and his stomach convulsed. He fell to his knees and vomited. Reflexively, Larissa did the same.

"Have you finished?" Skyrm asked. Brian spat as much of the sour taste from his mouth as he could before nodding. He didn't want to speak to Skyrm.

"Then move," Skyrm said.

Brian and Larissa stood and resumed their march, now side-by-side. Talking might be dangerous, but Brian needed to communicate with Larissa. He took the risk.

"I'm sorry about that," he whispered. "The puking."

"Do not be," she replied, also whispering. "I am surprised neither of us did it sooner."

Brian responded with a shrug.

"What I still do not understand," Larissa said, "is how could they be waiting for us here?"

Skyrm hissed, "Silence!" before Brian could reply.

He was grateful for the interruption. Larissa's question made Brian uncomfortable because he suspected the answer, and this was not the time to share his suspicion.

CHAPTER 27--VAN

They came to a larger clearing where a maroon van was parked perpendicular to a black Volkswagen Passat. From the many tire tracks scoring the rain-soaked ground, Brian guessed this was a makeshift but well-established parking lot accessed from the highway.

Noting the Mercedes-Benz logo embedded in the front grill, Brian recognized the van's model as a Sprinter, its distinctly European design reminiscent of a bullet train. Sprinters were common back in Milwaukee, many still bearing the defunct Dodge ram and most driven by plumbers, electricians, or delivery people. Taller and slimmer than any American van, the Sprinter was a slender rectangle with a wedge-like snout. As Masson led them to the rear, Brian saw indentations along the cargo area where the windows would have been.

The Sprinter intrigued Brian because he had seen a similar vehicle recently. But where? Of course! Merz had been watching Larissa's house from a maroon van. Was this the same van? Brian dismissed the idea. This one's EU plates were branded with an *E*, for *España*. Using a Spanish van for surveillance in France would draw suspicion. Still, Brian considered it more than a coincidence that Skyrm's team would use two identical vans.

The small procession stopped at the rear doors, also windowless. A narrow ladder had been welded to the left-hand door, just inside the hinges.

"Do you have clean clothes in your rucksacks?" Skyrm asked.

"Yes," Larissa replied.

"You two should be presentable when you are delivered," Skyrm said, putting an ironical twist on the last word. He opened the rear doors. The empty cargo area yawned at them. Shelves built into one wall were bare. A black tarp covered the opposite wall. Dull light shone through a frosted window in the partition between the cargo space and the cab.

"Mlle DeJonge, you will change first," Skyrm said. "You have five minutes. Don't attempt anything subversive because I would welcome an excuse to damage Mr. Parker."

Larissa looked at Brian anxiously. "Go ahead," he said. "I'll be all right."

Larissa hoisted her large backpack into the cargo area and climbed inside. Skyrm closed the doors

"Where are you delivering us?" Brian asked.

Skyrm's answer was an impassive stare. Brian shrugged.

The other three men reappeared while Larissa was changing. They dropped the dead hikers' backpacks into a puddle. "By the time they're found, we shall be—" Kralik began, but Skyrm silenced him with a poisonous look. No one spoke again until Skyrm rapped on the door. "Your five minutes are up," he said and pulled open the door before Larissa could reply.

She was sitting on the floor, fully dressed and wiping mud from her face with one of the microfiber towels from the camping supply store. She wore black jeans and a brown Blondie T-shirt that featured a gauzy, Warhol-inspired portrait of Debbie Harry in full pout.

"You have quite a T-shirt collection," Brian said.

Larissa smiled at him. "The finest in Toulouse," she said. She stood to climb out of the van, but Skyrm raised a hand.

"Stay there," he said. "We don't want you getting wet again. And I cannot allow Mr. Parker any privacy, not with his habit of escaping. The doors will remain open."

"You pig!" Larissa shouted at him. "How dare you do this to Brian."

"Larissa," Brian interrupted. "Don't worry about it." He lifted his backpack and stepped into the cargo area. "It won't be much different from gym class."

Larissa nodded. "I shall close my eyes," she said. She handed the towel to Brian and turned her back to kneel facing the partition. Rain drummed on the van's roof.

Brian considered refusing to change, but he was drenched and desperately wanted out of his sodden clothes. Skyrm's game was to humiliate him, so the best response was to just get it over with and refuse to acknowledge a loss of dignity.

He pulled a second towel and his original backpack, which still contained his clothes, from the larger hiking pack. He made a mental note to leave the oversized backpacks in the van. They wouldn't be needed again. Brian changed quickly, pausing only to towel off. He avoided eye contact with the men watching him and ignored their chortling.

After he had pulled on another pair of cargo shorts and a navy blue polo shirt, Brian told Larissa, "I'm done." She turned around and rejoined him.

Masson spoke for the first time. "Both of you, hold out your hands with your wrists together." He leaned inside the van and bound their wrists with plastic straps.

Skyrm turned to his men. "I will join Masson in the van. You three follow in the sedan."

Skyrm hurled the doors shut. The impact knocked a corner of the tarp free. It drooped to reveal part of a concealed sign. Four large letters were visible: BARC.

Brian needed to see more. He rolled to the wall. Reclining on his back with his legs extended like scissors, Brian caught the tarp's trailing edge between his feet. He twisted on his hip and tore the tarp loose. It cascaded to the floor, exposing a vinyl banner held to the wall by magnetic backing. On a maroon background that matched the van's exterior, ten-inch yellow letters spelled out BARCELONA PAQUETE SERVICIO. Below the name was a phone number.

"Do you know what that second word means?" Brian asked.

"*Parcel*, I think," Larissa said.

"That sign is magnetic, and I bet there's a second one behind it," Brian said. "They can use those signs to disguise this as a delivery van. Skyrm made a joke about delivering us."

Both doors in the driver's compartment opened and closed. The van quivered as the engine came to life. The vehicle lurched forward and bumped along the muddy track. Brian and Larissa crawled to the partition and sat with their backs to it.

"Where do you think they will take us?" Larissa asked.

"My first guess is Zaragoza, because all this has something to do with your father's project. But I suppose Barcelona has become a possibility. Right now there's only one thing I know for certain."

"What's that?"

"That I'm glad to be wearing dry socks again. God, I hate wet socks. Walking around in squishy socks is the worst feeling in the world."

Larissa shook her head. "We have just been kidnapped, and you talk about socks?" she said evenly, almost dreamily.

"Doesn't matter what we talk about, we'd still be kidnapped," Brian said and let out an enormous yawn. Their exhaustion puzzled him for only a moment. From nearly drowning to plunging down the ravine to witnessing cold-blooded murder, their emotions had been amped up by adrenaline all morning. Now that there was a lull, their bodies were crashing. Like coming off a Red Bull rush.

Larissa curled into Brian and rested her head on his good shoulder. She whispered into his ear, "I am not wearing socks."

Brian glanced down at bare ankles peeking above her low-top Chuck Taylors.

"Tease," he said.

Then they were asleep.

CHAPTER 28--SCHEDULE

Brian awoke to Skyrm's voice.

"Today?" Skyrm said, repeating the word that had startled Brian from his sleep. Silence followed. Brian wondered why Masson wasn't responding then guessed Skyrm was speaking on a cell phone.

Brian looked about. The sunlight coming through the partition window was brighter, and rain no longer pounded the roof. He listened to the high drone of the tires and figured they were traveling rapidly along a highway. Larissa stirred next to him. Skyrm had woken her, too.

His voice muffled only slightly by the partition, Skyrm spoke again. "No, I agree. This added confusion does benefit our plan." Another silence came. Then, agitated, Skyrm said, "Both of them? I advise against that."

Skyrm didn't speak for a few moments. When he did, his voice had calmed. "All right. How much time do we have?" A pause. "We can just make it, but we will have to change vehicles. And we need new papers. Yes, we have them in the van. I will call again once they are in the car. Goodbye."

Skyrm exhaled loudly as the call ended.

"What was that about?" Masson asked.

"The demonstration has been moved up to today, three hours from now."

"What?"

"One of the high-ranking German officers must leave tomorrow morning. A family matter. He asked if they could rearrange the schedule and demonstrate the device today because, thanks to you, the equipment is already there."

"And this is not a problem?"

"I consider it fortunate. Failure can be blamed on advancing the schedule. People will be less likely to notice the switch. Best of all, this ordeal will be over a day sooner. Once I collect our payment, we will be free of any further dealings with our deceased friend."

Larissa nudged Brian and murmured, "Do they know we can hear?"

"Possibly," Brian said. "It's like he's speaking in code, not giving names. 'Our deceased friend' is probably Eck. It sounds like they are planning to sabotage the demonstration of your father's weapon."

Above and behind them, Masson spoke. "But something troubles you. If it is not the schedule change, then what?"

"We are to take them to the base."

"The boy as well as the girl?"

"Yes."

"That is unwise," Masson said.

"We have been doing many unwise things lately. Our employer is panicking. Partly because the operation is entering its terminal phase, but mostly because his conscience is conflicted." He paused. "Please, my friend, do not allow me to work for an idealist ever again."

Masson laughed. "This idealist will make us rich."

"If he stops acting sentimental. I must call the others and tell them we will transfer the boy and the girl to the car. This van cannot be seen on the base. And you will have to go without me. They shouldn't recognize me, but still I had better not show my face. Not there."

They laughed. Then Skyrm said, "I hope you have your credentials with you."

"Of course."

"Thank God one of my people prepares for emergencies." A pause. "But you'll need new papers, for them. That requires stopping at the warehouse." Another pause. "Take Kralik. Documentation is his expertise. I will call him now."

Skyrm called Kralik in the Passat and instructed him to rendezvous with the van at a rest stop outside of Zaragoza. Brian and Larissa exchanged glances when they heard the destination.

"What if they use us as hostages to blackmail my father?" Larissa whispered.

That possibility, among others, had occurred to Brian. He shrugged, taking note that the pain in his shoulder had subsided. "We'll just have to see what happens," Brian said. He looked around the vacant cargo area. "I wonder why Skyrm doesn't want anyone to see this van. It seems pretty nondescript, and there's nothing in here but those signs."

When Skyrm ended the call, Masson asked, "Do they understand?"

"As well as they can. As well as I can." Skyrm paused. "I feel uneasy about this job. So much has gone wrong in so short a time."

"You can relax," Masson said. "You are in Spain now, and the Spanish end of the operation has proceeded flawlessly."

"Perhaps," Skyrm replied softly, so softly that Brian had to concentrate to hear what followed. "But the boy hasn't been in Spain until now. Wherever he goes—Lucerne, Nice, Toulouse— my plans come undone. I don't like that he will be out of my sight once we reach Zaragoza."

Skyrm fell silent. Brian held his breath, anxious to hear the next words.

"You must watch him, Masson," Skyrm resumed. "Watch him as if he were your greatest enemy. Because if this job fails, it will be that damnable boy's fault."

CHAPTER 29--REUNION

Brian and Larissa climbed out of the Sprinter and saw they were parked behind a highway rest area far from other vehicles. Kralik, Voss, and Carter (whichever was which) were out of the Volkswagen and standing shoulder to shoulder on a diagonal between the car and the van. They formed a shield to block any rest stop patrons from seeing that the teenagers' hands were bound. The Passat's rear door was open on the passenger side, and Brian and Larissa were hustled into the car before anyone near the building could look their way.

Masson, who no longer wore the camouflage jacket, opened the driver's door. He heaved the teenagers' backpacks into the rear seat and settled behind the wheel. Kralik sat in the front passenger seat.

Skyrm approached Brian's door. The window, controlled by Masson, slid down with a whir. Skyrm stood with the sun over his shoulder, forcing Brian to squint up at him.

"Continue to behave for another twenty minutes, Mr. Parker, and Mlle DeJonge will be peacefully reunited with her father," Skyrm said. "Do not disappoint her." The window closed.

Masson started the Passat and pulled away from the van. Brian looked over at Larissa, who had begun biting her lip at the mention of her father. They did not speak. The stony presence of Skyrm's men told them conversation would not be tolerated. Instead, Brian smiled at Larissa lopsidedly to communicate hope, even though he, too, was confused by the promised reunion. Questions about Larissa's father had dogged his thoughts since morning.

Brian looked through the windshield and noticed three ungainly black insects buzzing in the sky. No, not insects. They were dual-rotor Chinook helicopters flying in formation over a far off hill. They appeared tiny from here, but Brian knew that up close the Chinooks were enormous transport aircraft. Perhaps a military air show was happening nearby.

The distant buildings of Zaragoza, dominated by a cathedral's spires, were directly ahead as the Passat hastened along the highway. Brian wondered which, if any, of the buildings was their destination when Masson startled him and took the first exit after the rest stop.

They came off a roundabout and headed into an industrial area with rows of warehouses. Masson pulled into a lot and parked where buildings shielded the car from the road.

Kralik exited the car and entered a door in the nearest warehouse. No sign or business name identified the door, only the number twenty-four above it. Brian filed this in his memory.

They sat in the Passat without speaking until Kralik emerged from the warehouse about ten minutes later. He handed a manila folder to Masson, then stepped to Larissa's window and produced a hunting knife. Larissa gasped.

"Relax," Masson said. "Kralik is just going to remove your bindings." He pressed a button on the center console and Larissa's window slid down.

"Raise your hands," Kralik said.

Larissa complied, and Kralik sliced through the plastic strap. He walked behind the car and repeated the process with Brian. Without another word, Kralik limped back to the warehouse. The two rear windows whirred shut.

Masson examined the papers, then twisted in his seat to look directly at Larissa. "You have a friend your age named Jerome Bertier." It was not a question.

"Yes," Larissa said. She narrowed her eyes quizzically. "How do you know?"

Masson ignored her question. He faced Brian. "When we get to the gate, the girl will go by her own name, but your name is Jerome Bertier. Repeat it."

Brian said the name.

"Good," Masson said. "I will talk for us all. Neither of you is to speak unless the guard speaks to you, and then the only word you will say is *sì*. Understand?"

"*Sì*." Brian and Larissa said it together without a hint of mockery.

"*Bueno*," Masson said, and then he started the car. As Masson steered through the warehouses, Brian mentally assembled pieces of the jigsaw that had been the last few days. Masson was driving them to a military base. That fit with the Chinooks flying nearby. But there was something else. Yes. Lenore Harte had said Larissa's father was supposed to demonstrate his device at a military base outside of Zaragoza. She even said the name. What was it?

Brian remembered. He asked, "Are you taking us to San Gregorio?"

As the name dropped, Masson's hands tensed on the steering wheel. The reaction pleased Brian. "I was told you were clever," Masson said through clenched teeth, "but you would have found out in a few minutes anyway."

"What is San Gregorio?" Larissa asked.

"The military base where your father is supposed to give his demonstration." Brian said. "Lenore Harte told us, remember?"

Larissa leaned forward anxiously. "Is my father all right? Have you people hurt him?"

Masson chuckled. "Your father is unharmed, although I imagine he is quite agitated at the moment."

Then Masson added, "He has been worried about you."

"How do you know that?" Larissa asked.

Masson didn't reply. The Passat crossed back beneath the highway and entered a street lined with trees.

"He's playing with us," Brian said. "Don't let him rile you."

Turning his head to confront his passengers, Masson said, "I promise I am not playing when I say you will not pull any tricks when the guard questions us. Otherwise the girl's father *will* be harmed."

Larissa fell back into her seat, her face pale. Brian squeezed her hand.

The trees along the roadside gave way to a seven-foot-tall cyclone fence topped with razor wire. Masson pulled up to a gatehouse. A young, dark-haired guard stepped from the hut, and Masson lowered his window to talk. The guard nodded, seeming to recognize Masson. A conversation in Spanish ensued. Brian understood none of it, except that the name DeJonge was repeated frequently. Masson handed over the papers from Kralik's folder. Brian's breath caught when he saw that his own passport photo identified him as Jerome Bertier. The papers could have been faked with any word-processing software, but only Silver could have supplied that picture.

The guard peered into the back seat.

"Larissa DeJonge?"

"*Sì*," Larissa replied.

"Jerome Bertier?"

"*Sì*."

The guard next searched the trunk. A second guard appeared to check the sedan's undercarriage with a mirror mounted on a pole. When their inspections were finished, the second guard walked away while the first guard returned their papers and handed Masson a parking pass and three visitor's badges on lanyards. He reentered the guardhouse and raised the barrier.

Masson drove past the gate and into a parking lot crowded with military and civilian vehicles bearing license plates from across Europe.

"How is your shoulder?" Larissa asked Brian as Masson parked the car. "Do you want me to carry your backpack?"

"No, I can manage. But thanks."

As they got out of the Passat, Masson handed them their badges and said, "I will tell you where to go, but you will walk before me."

He guided them through San Gregorio's parade ground, which was a brick-paved square symmetrically surrounded by four L-shaped Mediterranean buildings with arched doorways, tiled roofs, and twin clock towers at the entrance. The red and black bricks of the parade ground formed a geometrical pattern that appeared more Aztec than Spanish to Brian.

Past the ornate parade ground was a conventional military base with lines of barracks and soldiers driving past in Jeeps. The Chinook helicopters Brian had seen from the highway noisily hovered several hundred yards away. Masson directed them beyond the barracks, and presently a vast desert stretched before them. To Brian it looked like the Arizona development where his grandparents lived, minus the condos.

On their left was a soccer field without goals but with trailers along one side. Bleachers were set up at the far end and on the side opposite the trailers. The near end of the field remained open. Men and women wearing a variety of military uniforms mingled near the bleachers. Masson motioned Brian and Larissa toward the trailers. As they approached the first one, a middle-aged man stepped from its door and descended the metal stairs bolted to the frame.

Larissa ran toward him yelling, "Papa!"

CHAPTER 30--TEMPERS

Edouard DeJonge's thinning salt-and-pepper hair was brushed to a perfect left-side part. His thick mustache was expertly trimmed. The rest of his features belied his precisely groomed hair. His eyes, behind a pair of frameless glasses several years out of style, projected weariness. His cheeks were sallow, and his lips were chapped.

Brian could see only Professor DeJonge's face. The rest of him was hidden by Larissa as she hugged him fiercely. For a moment, as the professor closed his eyes and returned his daughter's embrace, his face was at peace. Then he opened his eyes and looked balefully over Larissa's shoulder at Brian and Masson.

Larissa stepped aside, revealing her father's blue business suit and the plastic identification badge hanging from his breast pocket. He spoke to his daughter in French, but Larissa answered in English.

"I had to leave the house, Papa. A man attacked our home."

She put her arm through Brian's and continued, "This is Brian Parker. From America. He helped me escape the attacker, and he has been helping me since."

"We've been helping each other," Brian said.

Larissa's father regarded him diffidently. "If you say so," he said as he offered Brian a quick, cold handshake.

Masson's voice interrupted them. "We should take this conversation inside," he said.

"Yes, of course," Professor DeJonge replied, and started up the stairs.

"But, Papa, he is working with the man who attacked our home!"

"Come inside," the professor said, "and I will try to explain in the little time I have."

They followed him through the door. The trailer was furnished like an office, with bookshelves containing technical manuals and a desk facing the wall opposite the door. Above the desk, a long window provided a view of the field. Brian saw that the military dignitaries were taking their seats in the bleachers. After Masson shut the door, Larissa said, "Explain what, Papa? Are these men blackmailing you?"

Masson barked a sharp laugh.

"We have an arrangement," Larissa's father said.

"An arrangement? What sort of arrangement? Papa, these men are wicked."

Professor DeJonge slammed his hand upon a stack of three-ring binders sitting on the desk, and his daughter fell silent.

"Lara, I have no time for this. I must be out there"—he waved toward the field beyond the window—"to demonstrate the Prometheus device I have been perfecting for many months. I am under stress already because they moved up the demonstration by a day. So I apologize for my brusqueness."

He took a breath, squeezing his eyes closed and pinching his nose beneath the bridge of his glasses.

"All this bad business could have been avoided if you had called me," he said.

"Brian believed that would have endangered you," Larissa said, calmly now. "He suspects these men want to sabotage your project."

The professor sighed. "I know the boy means well, Lara, but he has filled your head with wild conspiracies."

Masson, leaning against the door with his arms folded, said, "The boy has seen too many Foster Blake movies."

Brian wanted to groan. How many times had he heard those words, from jerks at school, from teachers he didn't like, and, when he aggravated her enough, from his mother? Brian's standard retort was, "There's no such thing as too many Foster Blake movies," but that wouldn't work now. He ignored Masson and looked at Professor DeJonge with all the conviction he could muster.

"I don't know what kind of arrangement you have with these men, sir, but the one they work for, Matthias Skyrm, is a killer.

He has killed five people in the last three days. One of his own men and two hikers this morning in the Pyrenees; an American agent, Lenore Harte, yesterday in Toulouse; and a man named Heinrich Tetzel three days ago in Lucerne."

Professor DeJonge's eyes snapped to Masson. "Tetzel?" he said.

"The boy lies," Masson said. "He craves the attention."

"Sure," Brian said. "I just love being kidnapped, being torn away from my school group, having my family threatened, getting beaten up, being chased across Europe, seeing people knifed and shot in front of me." Brian felt himself losing it, but he couldn't stop. His voice had been rising, and now he shouted, "Oh yeah, that's just the kind of attention I've been craving all my life!"

Larissa put her hand on his shoulder, and Brian shut up. He took deep breaths to calm himself. DeJonge and Masson watched him for several seconds, then faced each other.

"What is this about Tetzel?" DeJonge asked.

"He was about to go to the CIA," Masson said. "Skyrm had to deal with him."

"By killing him?"

Before Masson could reply, Larissa said, "It is true about the other deaths, Papa. I saw them."

Professor DeJonge's cheeks flushed with anger. "You murdered people in front of my daughter?" he bellowed at Masson. "Get out!"

"I have orders to watch the boy," Masson said.

"And I was promised the boy would be released to me. Now get out!" Professor DeJonge turned to the window. The bleachers were full. Several people were checking their watches. "I should be out there already," he continued, "and I don't want you in here with my daughter when I am gone. Or do you wish to explain to our superiors why you delayed the demonstration?"

A sneer flickered across Masson's face. "No, I don't want to interfere with a successful demonstration." Masson stepped outside, looking at Brian before closing the door. "Don't try to escape, boy, because I will be standing here." He pointed at a patch of ground at the foot of the steps. "In this spot."

CHAPTER 31--RIEN

When Masson was gone, Professor DeJonge said, "I am terribly sorry, Lara. I know you have many questions, but the timing of all this is diabolical." He gestured at the window. "All those officials are waiting for me, and I have been working toward this moment for so long."

"It is all right, Papa. Go."

"We will discuss everything when I return, you and I and Mr. Par ... Brian." As he moved to leave, Professor DeJonge took something from a shelf by the door, a curved white plastic gadget that looked like a flattened ice cream scoop. He tossed it to Larissa. "You will be able to hear the interpreter with this earphone."

Brian locked the door behind the professor. When he stepped back to the desk, Larissa turned on him. "You did not seem surprised to learn my father was working with them."

"I suspected it," Brian said.

"Why?"

"Who else would know you would follow Dédée De Jongh's trail through the Pyrenees? Skyrm's men were waiting for us at the exact spot the Comet Line crossed into Spain."

Larissa considered this and nodded.

"Why didn't you share your suspicions with me?"

"Would you have believed me?"

"No."

"Would you have been angry with me?"

She hesitated. "Yes."

"That's why." Brian shrugged. "Plus, I might have been wrong."

Applause from outside drew their attention to the scene framed by the window. Larissa's father walked into the center of the field carrying a wireless microphone. He spoke a greeting in Spanish. Larissa handed the earphone to Brian. "Here," she said. "I should understand most of what he says."

The earphone had a dial surrounded by tiny European flags. Brian turned the pointer to the Union Jack and held the device to his ear.

Professor DeJonge stood in the center of the field and began his address. A split second later, a British voice translated the professor's words through the earphone.

"As some of you may know," the interpreter said as Professor DeJonge inclined his head to the audience, "the project I have been spearheading on behalf of Eurocorps is a non-lethal weapon system that will drive back individuals, crowds, and perhaps one day even armies with a beam of millimeter waves that tricks the nervous system into feeling intense heat. Anyone hit by the beam will receive the sensation that his skin is on fire, and he will run. Once he is out of range of the beam, the pain stops instantaneously. The beam causes no permanent—or even temporary—physical damage. It harmlessly forces your enemy to flee."

Professor DeJonge paused to let this sink in. Brian took the opportunity to scan the crowd. About a third of the people in the bleachers also held earphones to their head. Brian wondered if a DIA operative was among them. If so, how could he establish contact?

The professor resumed: "The United States military have been working on a similar system, which they call Positive Enforcement, for years but have been unable to deploy it. We are on schedule to have the Prometheus device battle-ready by the end of the year, giving Europe an advantage in military technology over the United States."

This drew a paroxysm of applause and cheers. Professor DeJonge grinned and quieted the crowd by waving his palms downward. He continued his speech. "For their mobile version, the Americans have mounted their Positive Enforcement device on a Humvee, but we thought a more common vehicle would be stealthier and more tactically advantageous. So please welcome the Prometheus delivery system."

Professor DeJonge stretched his arm toward the barracks. The applause rose again as a maroon Mercedes-Benz Sprinter drove onto the field.

Brian dropped the earphone. Larissa clutched his arm. She said, "That is the van we were in!"

"No, it can't be the same one. They couldn't have got here in time," Brian said, "but—Oh my God."

"What?"

"They're going to steal it."

"What!"

"We thought Eck and Skyrm wanted to sabotage you father's project, but they were planning to steal it all along." Brian's words outpaced his thoughts. "Skyrm said moving the demonstration up a day would help the plan. He said people would be less likely to notice the switch. Sometime after the demonstration they're going to swap this van with a fake one. They can use those magnetic signs we saw this morning to disguise it as a delivery van. They could just drive away, and no one would notice."

While Brian spoke, a team of three technicians had opened the van's rear doors to reveal a small control center with video screens and panels filled with lights, gauges, and buttons. The technicians took their places in the control center and started to adjust dials.

Larissa stared at the scene in apprehensive silence.

Brian put an arm around her. "I don't think your father knows about the switch," he said. "This day is obviously too important to him. They're going to double-cross him."

"In his own way he can be quite naive," Larissa said.

Brian retrieved the earphone and listened. "The time has come to introduce you to Prometheus," the British voice said.

A section of the van's roof flipped over to reveal a device that looked more like an overgrown digital camera than a science-fiction ray gun. The front of Prometheus was a black box with two silver lenses, one twice the size of the other. Fanning out behind the box was a curved black reflector. A buzz of approval flowed across the bleachers as the weapon rose from the van on a telescoping pole with a thick electrical cord curled around it, much like a microwave antenna on a television news van.

"The van has also delivered our brave volunteers," the

translator said as the driver and a passenger stepped down from the cab wearing bathrobes. The audience laughed and hooted catcalls as the two men took off their robes to reveal they wore only swimming trunks and combat boots. Professor DeJonge guided them to an orange square spray-painted on the ground.

The professor lifted his microphone, and Brian listened to the English echo of his words. "Now, witness the extraordinary power of Prometheus."

The professor signaled the technicians. One of them pressed a button and a soft double beep sounded. The men in the orange square tensed their muscles in anticipation of the Prometheus beam's impact, but relaxed seconds later. They looked at Professor DeJonge and shrugged. "*Rien*," one said. *Nothing.* Some in the audience laughed nervously. Professor DeJonge impatiently signaled the technicians again. Once more the double beep, and once more the men in their bathing trunks stood unfazed.

Professor DeJonge trotted to the rear of the van as murmurs among the audience deepened. Larissa bit her lower lip as she watched her father adjust switches and speak urgently with the technicians. The double beep sounded, but again without any effect on the two targets.

For fifteen minutes Professor DeJonge and the technicians made adjustments. One technician climbed the ladder on the van's rear door and slid across the roof to check the firing lenses. The two test subjects fidgeted, clearly conscious of their ridiculous appearance. People began to drift out the bleachers. Twice Professor DeJonge promised the remaining observers that the technical difficulties would be resolved soon, adding plaintively that Prometheus worked perfectly the day before. Yet five more attempts proved fruitless.

Brian moved closer to Larissa, who bore her father's humiliation with quiet tears.

Finally, as figures with medals on their chests walked away with disgust on their faces, Professor DeJonge announced he would troubleshoot every last circuit and that he hoped to demonstrate the Prometheus device successfully the next day.

A tear fell from Larissa's cheek and splashed onto the desktop. Brian gently touched her elbow. "I'm sorry," he said.

"Do you still think they want to steal my father's project?" she asked.

"No," Brian said. "Maybe we were right about sabotage in the first place." He said that to comfort Larissa, but he questioned his own words. If Eck and Skyrm were working with Larissa's father, they had no reason to sabotage Prometheus.

Larissa watched her father, his shoulders sagging, walk off the field. Brian focused his eyes on the Sprinter, doppelganger to the one they rode in that morning. If Skyrm wanted to switch the Prometheus van with a phony, then the demonstration's failure had ruined his plot.

Brian touched Larissa's elbow again and wondered if she shared his fear for her father's life.

CHAPTER 32--TRUTH

When Professor DeJonge returned to the trailer, the part had disappeared from his hair and the edges of his moustache were ragged. He had unbuttoned his collar, and his loosened tie was snarled in his identity badge.

Larissa, still crying, threw herself into his arms. "Oh Papa, what happened?"

"I am unsure," he answered hoarsely. Brian noticed the professor was displaying a new habit, alternately licking and pursing his lips. That explained why they were chapped.

"I am sorry, Lara," her father continued. "You and Brian will have to wait here while I inspect the device. I do not know how long that will take. I will arrange to have your dinners sent to the trailer. It would be safest if you remain here, I think."

Brian thought so, too, but remained quiet. He looked out the window at the van, now guarded by two soldiers. They held submachine guns loosely at their hips, barrels drooping toward the ground, as if there were no urgency to protect a secret weapon that didn't work.

Professor DeJonge licked and pursed his lips. "I do not understand," he said. "I swear to you, Lara, that Prometheus functioned perfectly yesterday in the workshop."

"Where is this workshop?" Brian asked. "On the base or in a warehouse a few miles from here?"

The professor's head jerked around when Brian mentioned the warehouse. He narrowed his eyes at Brian and cocked his head as if a question were forthcoming. Then he waved a hand and said, "Please don't start this with me, young man. I am in no mood for wild conspiracies."

Larissa stepped back from her father so he could see her face as she spoke. "But Papa, there is something unusual about that van."

Professor DeJonge scrutinized the van. "What would that be?"

"We rode in one just like it this morning," Brian said, "after Skyrm's men found us in the Pyrenees, a maroon Mercedes-Benz Sprinter."

"The Sprinter is a common vehicle throughout Europe," the professor said. "That is why we chose that model, for its anonymity. I am not surprised you saw one this morning."

"But we didn't just see it, Professor," Brian said. "We rode it in. With Skyrm driving. And we had to switch vehicles. Skyrm told Masson he couldn't drive onto the base in that van."

Professor DeJonge was about to reply, but stopped. Brian sensed the professor might be on the edge of believing them.

Larissa must have sensed it, too. She added, "Brian also thinks he saw a maroon van outside our house the other night."

"I'm not so sure about that," Brian said. "But it could have been a Sprinter."

The professor licked his lips twice and pursed them. Slowly, he said, "So what are you suggesting?"

Brian hesitated. He didn't want his suggestion to sound like a wild conspiracy theory. "I'm not sure how to phrase it," he began.

Larissa leaped into the breach. "Brian believes those men planned to switch vans after the demonstration. To steal the weapon you developed."

Professor DeJonge let out a sarcastic laugh. "Steal that, that nonfunctioning disgrace?" he said. "Right now it isn't fit to haul cargo. Besides, why would Eck and Skyrm steal what is already theirs? It would not serve their purpose."

Brian and Larissa exchanged a look. It was the first time her father had acknowledged Roland Eck.

"What is their purpose?" Brian asked.

Before the professor could answer, the door swung open and Masson stepped inside the trailer. Brian wondered if he had been eavesdropping.

"I do not want you in here!" Professor DeJonge said.

"I won't be here long and neither will you," Masson said. "You must report to Skyrm immediately. All of us must go."

"Go? I cannot leave here. I must try to repair Prometheus."

"Skyrm wants to hear directly from your lips why the demonstration failed. I just spoke to him."

"How?" Professor DeJonge asked. "No one can use mobile phones on the base."

Masson grinned. "It seems I broke a law. Imagine that."

As the two men argued, Larissa stepped to Brian's side. "I don't trust him," she murmured.

"Your father shouldn't, either," Brian said.

"You two be quiet," Masson said. He jabbed a finger at Brian. "Especially you."

"You do not talk to my daughter that way," Professor DeJonge said. "Nor the boy. I refuse to deliver him back to Skyrm. That is not the arrangement."

"The boy will not be harmed," Masson said. "We will go to the workshop. You will report to Skyrm, then we will all return here."

"And what do I say to General Bayard?" Professor DeJonge asked. "I told him I would remain here all night if necessary to repair the prototype."

Masson was prepared for this. "Tell him you need diagnostic equipment from your workshop and you will return within the hour. It will take no longer than that; so do not anger Skyrm by delaying. He insists on debriefing you personally."

"*Debrief*," Professor DeJonge said. "Listen to you people. You say the boy has seen too many spy movies, but you are just as delusional. You should have heard the tale he was weaving before you interrupted."

Masson folded his arms and regarded Brian. "Please," he said with mock solicitude, "enlighten me, Professor."

Brian shook his head, and Larissa spoke his thoughts. "No, Papa."

But the professor pressed on. "Mr. Parker here says that you have another Mercedes Sprinter identical to the Prometheus delivery system, and he believes that sometime after the demonstration you were going to switch those vans."

Masson continued to stare at Brian, but Brian couldn't read his expression. It could have been curiosity or scorn. Brian looked back impassively.

Masson kept his eyes on Brian as he addressed Professor DeJonge. "Why would we take Prometheus from you when you assisted in its development?"

"I did more than assist, and Skyrm knows that."

"All Skyrm knows is the demonstration was a debacle," Masson said. He shifted his gaze to the professor. "All Skyrm knows is the assembled military experts of Europe consider Prometheus a joke and Eduoard DeJonge a bumbler. All Skyrm knows, and all that matters at the moment, Professor, is your machine doesn't work."

Masson turned to Brian with a smug smile. "So tell me, boy, why would we bother to steal something that doesn't work?"

And then Brian knew the truth. Masson's contempt gave it away.

"You wouldn't," Brian replied, "because you already stole it."

CHAPTER 33--BARGAINING

Brian's words had an electrifying effect. Larissa tensed. Her father gaped. Masson scowled. Brian kept talking. "That van out there is a dummy, isn't it? You switched it for the real Prometheus van yesterday, somewhere between the warehouse and the base? And you drove it yourself. That's why the guard at the gate recognized you."

Masson eyed the professor. "You don't believe this boy, do you?"

"You were the one entrusted with delivering Prometheus to the base yesterday," Professor DeJonge responded. He looked at Brian, "But ..."

"But why? He just told us," Brian said. "So that the assembled military experts of Europe would consider Prometheus a joke and you a bumbler."

Challenging Masson like this was dangerous, but Brian saw no alternative. He needed to win over Professor DeJonge quickly. He pressed on: "It's a brilliant trick, really. They got Eurocorps to fund the Prometheus weapon, and I bet convinced them to fast-track it to get a working prototype in the field before America could"—Brian was careful to omit the professor's culpability from the story—"and somehow they invited all those military leaders here to watch Prometheus shoot nothing more than sparks.

"After today's fiasco the military leaders will go home thinking Prometheus is a colossal waste of money, probably convinced it failed because they rushed it. And while blame is assigned, Skyrm's crew takes the original, working prototype and sells it to the highest bidder."

"It is true, Papa," Larissa said. "We heard them, he and Skyrm, say this plan would make them rich."

Professor DeJonge glared at Masson. Brian wondered how Masson would play it. He anticipated another accusation involving too many Foster Blake movies, but Masson's response was 180 degrees from Brian's expectations.

"The scheme will make us all rich, Professor," Masson said. "We couldn't tell you about the plot to switch vehicles beforehand, because we didn't trust your acting abilities. That is why Skyrm wants to meet with you now, to fill you in. And to tell you your share of the money."

Brian prayed the professor would recognize this was a lie. But the professor licked his lips and asked, "How much?"

"We estimate the Prometheus device will sell for at least five hundred million American dollars. Your share would come to ten million."

"Is that all?"

"We could see that you got none."

The professor stared at Masson. Brian could tell he was weighing the riches against the threat.

Larissa broke the standoff. "If you take any money from these men, Papa, I will never speak to you again."

Professor DeJonge looked to his daughter and smiled, wanly at first but with more confidence as he spoke. "It is all right, Lara. I have no intention of leaving with Monsieur Masson."

Masson moved toward Larissa. "If your daughter's advice means so much to you," he said, "perhaps I should change her mind."

Professor DeJonge threw himself between Masson and Larissa, but Masson grabbed the professor's shoulders and flung him into the desk. That gave Brian an opening. He rushed toward the distracted Masson and used the momentum to drive a corkscrew punch into his stomach. Masson doubled over. Brian delivered an elbow to Masson's exposed neck and dropped him to the floor.

Brian pulled the professor up and shouted to Larissa, "Out the door! Now!" He hoped his surprise attack would buy them enough time to flee the trailer and find safety outside. In no way did Brian plan to fight Masson.

Masson thought otherwise. He spun on the floor with his right leg outstretched and swept Brian's legs from under him. Brian fell backward into the wall but righted himself before hitting the floor. Larissa stepped toward him to help, but her father quickly pushed her through the door. It was the first sensible thing Brian had seen the man do.

Masson was standing again and reaching behind his back with his right hand. Brian feared he was going for his pistol and launched himself at Masson. His shoulder hit just beneath the man's ribcage. Brian saw the glint of the revolver as Masson's hand came around. He did the first thing that popped into his head. He grabbed Masson's right wrist with both hands, pulled it to his mouth, and bit.

Masson growled and clubbed Brian's neck with his left hand. Brian bit harder until the fingers of Masson's right hand sprang open and the revolver thudded to the floor. Brian lashed at it with his right foot, and the gun slid across the tiles and wedged beneath a bookcase against the far wall.

Brian loosened his jaw just as Masson spun about, throwing his hip into Brian's side. Brian grunted as he went clambering backwards. Struggling to maintain balance, Brian angled his trajectory toward the door. Masson wouldn't go for the gun as long as Brian was near the door and its promise of escape. Masson charged at Brian and trapped him in a bear hug. He aimed to drive Brian into the wall, but Brian twisted so the momentum carried them through the door. They crashed down the iron steps and Masson hit the ground first. They rolled over and Brian was underneath looking up at Masson, who had murder in his eyes as he cocked a fist above his head and pressed Brian into the dirt with his other arm.

Brian braced himself for extreme pain, but Masson relaxed his hold and looked left. Brian followed Masson's gaze and saw two soldiers round the trailer's corner with their submachine guns raised. Masson lifted his hands in surrender as Professor DeJonge and Larissa appeared behind the soldiers, whom Brian recognized as the men guarding the Sprinter. One of the soldiers pulled Masson up. Larissa ran to Brian and helped him to his feet.

She fussed over him, and Brian assured her he was all right, though he probably had collected a few more bruises. She smiled with a wisp of pride and said, "Papa summoned the guards."

Looking over his shoulder at Larissa, Masson snarled, "Papa just made a grave mistake." He turned away and said nothing more.

CHAPTER 34--PANIC

Before they had marched Masson away, one soldier kept the conspirator at gunpoint while his partner retrieved the revolver from the trailer (they had discovered Masson's empty holster). The same soldier then quietly conferred with Professor DeJonge off to the side.

After the guards and their prisoner disappeared, Larissa asked, "What did you tell them, Papa?"

"That Masson was part of a conspiracy to sabotage the Prometheus demonstration. Which is the truth. Now please collect your rucksacks. We must go."

Professor DeJonge was already on the move by the time Brian and Larissa came out of the trailer with their backpacks. He led them at a brisk clip toward the symmetrical buildings surrounding the parade ground.

"Are you going to the brig to make a statement?" Brian asked.

"That is where they are expecting me," the professor replied, "which is why we must be off the base before they wonder where I am."

Larissa shook her head. "Where do you expect to go, Papa? I have seen these people. They are ruthless. They will find us find us no matter where we go."

"Then we will keep moving," Professor DeJonge said.

"Forever?"

"If we must."

Each step carried Brian further into dread. Professor DeJonge was panicking, and panic was leading him down a suicidal path. Brian had to appeal to the professor's reason while some of it remained. He stopped walking.

"Professor DeJonge," he said, "running would be a mistake.

Right now this base is the safest place in the world for you, for the three of us."

The professor halted and faced Brian, glowering. Brian continued, "This base is the one place on Earth Matthias Skyrm cannot reach you." Brian looked to Larissa for support.

"He is right, Papa. Listen to him."

"And what am I supposed to do?" Professor DeJonge said. "Go inside my trailer and cower?"

"No," Brian said. "You should contact the American military attaché in Madrid."

Professor DeJonge goggled at Brian as if he just told him to jump off the Eiffel Tower. "And do what?" the professor asked.

"Tell them everything you know about Prometheus, about Positive Enforcement—and about Roland Eck."

"They will throw me in prison, or one of your CIA's black sites in the Near East."

"Not if you can deliver Eck," Brian said. "Then they will protect you."

"I can't deliver him. I do not know where he is. And how can you be sure they will protect me? What do you know? Things you have read in *romans policiers*?"

"In what?" Brian asked.

"Mystery novels," Larissa supplied. "Spy novels."

Brian shrugged. "You're right, Professor. I have no idea what the American government would do with you. But unlike Skyrm, they won't kill you. And Larissa will be safe."

Professor DeJonge studied Brian without speaking. He pursed his lips, and Brian believed he had taken a crucial step toward convincing him.

"Besides, Papa," Larissa added, "the Americans are investigating you already."

The professor's eyes clicked to Larissa and widened. "What?" he asked.

Larissa realized her mistake and looked apologetically at Brian.

"That's all right," Brian said. "Your father would have found it out soon enough." He spoke calmly, hoping to soothe the professor's nerves. "We encountered an American agent in Toulouse, Lenore Harte. She was with the DIA, the Defense

Intelligence Agency."

"You spoke of her," Professor DeJonge said. "The agent Skyrm killed."

"Yes," Brian said.

"How did she find you?"

"We found her," Brian said. "She was in your office at the university."

Professor DeJonge's mouth fell open, and Brian knew he had blown it.

The professor turned and walked toward the parade ground at a faster pace. "We must leave now, Lara," he said. Larissa looked at Brian, raised her hands hopelessly, and followed her father.

Brian didn't move. He had to make one last attempt. "You cannot leave the base, Professor. Contact the American embassy. It's the only way that's safe."

The professor spun around and stomped back, bending at the waist to bring his nose within an inch of Brian's. Curious soldiers looked at them. *They probably expect him to hit me*, Brian thought. *So do I.*

Instead, the professor spoke in a fierce whisper. "Safe? An America spy was in my office. Then she was killed. And what is your brilliant advice? Turn myself over to the Americans and tell them I have been working with—*conspiring* with—the man who murdered their agent. Do you think I am mad?"

Professor DeJonge stepped back. "Now, stop telling me what to do, you stupid boy—"

"Papa!"

The professor's hand shot up and Larissa fell silent. "If everyone knows I am at San Gregorio, I am not safe here. Larissa and I are leaving. You can stay for all I care, but I wonder what the base commander will think of you."

"Larissa?" Brian said.

"He is my father," she said. "I cannot leave him."

Brian nodded. The quaver in her voice told him she shared his anguish. He knew that when—if—her father calmed down, she would try to convince him to contact the American embassy. But how much time would they have before Skyrm caught up with them?

Brian considered his chances of helping them if he remained at San Gregorio. How would the Spanish military react to an American teenager wandering alone around their base in the middle of a war games exercise? Security would be in an uproar once they found Brian. He was in their country illegally, without a passport. The man who drove him onto the base under a false name was in the brig, accused of sabotage. How long would security question him before allowing him to contact his embassy? How long after that until the embassy allowed him to speak to the Defense Attaché Office? Long after Skyrm had found the DeJonges, probably.

Brian looked into Larissa's large brown eyes, now holding back tears. His eyes traced the contour of her nose to the bow of her lips. He remembered their long kiss in the Pyrenees, and an affection beyond any he had known before coursed through him. Brian shivered. Even if he were helpless to protect her, Brian would rather die than allow Larissa to face danger alone.

"I can't leave you either," he said.

CHAPTER 35--SUNSET

At the gatehouse Professor DeJonge spoke to the guard in quick Spanish sentences. The guard, older than the one who let them onto the base with Masson, gestured toward Brian and Larissa in the back seat of the professor's Audi A5 Coupe. The professor shrugged and spoke once more. In the moment the guard spent considering the professor's words, Brian willed him to check with base security and learn the professor was needed to question a suspected saboteur.

Instead, the guard raised the crossbar and waved them off the base. *I guess you can't mentally communicate with someone when you speak different languages*, Brian thought. He fastened his seat belt.

The professor turned north at the road, heading away from Zaragoza and into the countryside. The sun, now low on the horizon, hovered to their left.

Brian positioned himself so that he could see Professor DeJonge's face in the rearview mirror. "Did you tell the guard you needed diagnostic equipment from your workshop?" Brian asked. He kept his voice neutral, not wanting to antagonize the professor.

"Yes, I said exactly what Masson suggested," Professor DeJonge said. Then he smiled. It was the first time Brian had seen Larissa's father smile, and Brian could see that she did not inherit this trait from him. Where Larissa's smile was dazzling and positive, his was sickly and nervous. His upper lip vanished beneath his mustache and his lower lip curled crookedly to one side.

"When the guard asked about the two of you," Professor DeJonge continued, "I told him you were tired and I was taking you back to the hotel."

"Good thinking," Brian said.

The professor's eyes flashed to Brian's, checking for sarcasm. Satisfied that Brian's words were sincere, Professor DeJonge returned his attention to the road.

Brian glanced at the dashboard clock. It read 7:38. How long before San Gregorio's security team discovered Professor DeJonge had left the base? Spain's national police, the Guardia Civil, might be looking for them already. Brian hoped the authorities found them before Skyrm did.

After several quiet minutes Larissa asked, "How ... why did you ever become involved with those men, Papa?"

Professor DeJonge's story was more or less what Brian expected to hear.

The professor was first approached nearly two years ago by Masson, who claimed to be a researcher in millimeter waves on sabbatical from Ghent University. The initial encounters were innocent. Wouldn't it be a wonderful boost to European pride, Masson had suggested, if EU physicists could deploy a next-generation weapon ahead of the Americans? DeJonge agreed, of course. Each time Masson mentioned this dream, he described the Pentagon's Positive Enforcement system in more detail. The professor had listened eagerly.

After more than a month of this, Masson whispered that he could provide DeJonge with "found" research that would allow Europe to leapfrog past *les États-Unis* in the development of a millimeter-wave weapon. Because the Americans' work was similar to DeJonge's research into microwave weapons, the professor could credibly claim the breakthrough as his own—provided he could persuade Eurocorps to fund the project. Once DeJonge had agreed, Roland Eck emerged from hiding to explain his plan and reveal the organization commanded by Mathias Skyrm. All DeJonge needed to do was be the face of the Prometheus Project.

"Why would Roland Eck give his research to you?" Larissa asked.

"His Positive Enforcement program was languishing," the professor said. "For years Congress debated its funding, and it was losing priority within the Pentagon. He did not think the weapon would be deployed unless the Pentagon were in an arms race with another government."

"But couldn't Eck give you the research without faking his death?" Brian asked.

Professor DeJonge shrugged. "I thought it would be ungrateful of me to ask. I suppose he wanted to remove any chance he could be caught and tried for treason."

"Who came up with the name Prometheus?" Brian asked.

"Eck," the professor replied. Brian nodded.

Larissa sank back into her seat. "But why did you agree to this madness, Papa?"

"If the demonstration today had been successful, do you know who I would be right now? I would be the scientist who gave Europe a technological advantage over the United States military. I could command any position at any university on the continent. I could demand any salary." He turned to look at Larissa. "And I could give you so many opportunities, Lara. As I promised your mother."

"She would never have wanted you to become a fraud, Papa," Larissa said. "Do not deceive her memory, or yourself. You have done this only to reward your pride. And where has your pride placed us?" She bowed her head. "In a car running for our lives."

Uncomfortable with this family tension, Brian diverted his thoughts to watching the road for any sign of pursuit. A tail would be impossible to miss. The landscape was practically a desert, and the field of view was wide open. Except for an occasional vehicle heading south, toward Zaragoza, traffic had been sparse. Professor DeJonge had changed roads twice, but they were still traveling north. The Spanish side of the Pyrenees spread before them in the twilight like a jagged purple shadow. The professor was driving conservatively. A dark blue Mazda CX-7 had passed them minutes earlier, but the professor made no attempt to overtake the other car, even though it now coasted a teasing thirty yards ahead. *Good*, Brian thought, *don't draw attention to us*.

Still watching the road, Brian replayed Professor DeJonge's story in his mind. One question lingered. "How did Tetzel figure into all of this?" he asked.

"One of Eurocorps' conditions for financing Prometheus was that I assemble researchers from across Europe. Tetzel came to the team from Switzerland, the University of Neuchatel, with a specialty in high-frequency waves."

The professor wet his lips and continued. "I did not know him well, but he called me one day last week and said he had just learned of Roland Eck's death and feared the Americans might think we had stolen his research. I told him this was ridiculous, that researchers in similar fields often come to the same findings."

"Did you tell Masson or Skyrm about his suspicions?" Brian asked.

"No," Professor DeJonge replied. To Larissa, he added, "I swear to you I did not."

"They probably had Tetzel's phone tapped," Brian said. "Or yours. Or both."

The professor opened his mouth to protest, then closed it. "Perhaps so," he said.

"Where are we going, Papa?" Larissa asked, breaking her silence. "We cannot drive into France without being caught."

"There is a tiny village in the foothills of the Pyrenees called Nueno with a small inn where we can stay, practically a hostel. No one would look for us in such an obscure place. We can disappear there for a few days while I consider what to do." With an air of condescension, he added, "Do you accept this plan, Brian?"

"It sounds like a good plan, sir," Brian said, and he meant it. This would give Larissa time to persuade her father to seek help from the American embassy. And if the professor used a credit card to check into the inn, the Guardia Civil would find them quickly.

Brian's stomach gurgled, and he wondered how soon until they reached Nueno. The lengthening shadows of the road signs told him sunset was imminent. He saw no traffic coming from the opposite direction. Brian noticed they were gaining on the Mazda. Then he looked at the dashboard and saw the professor had the cruise control engaged and had not changed speed for miles. They weren't accelerating; the Mazda was decelerating.

Brian saw the trap as soon as they passed the crossroad. A hulking black Land Rover waiting at the intersection roared onto the road and pulled alongside the Audi. The blue Mazda was directly in front of them, blocking their escape. The Land Rover bumped the Audi's side. Professor DeJonge yelped and the Audi slewed to the right, but the professor straightened the car. Brian looked out the window and in the orange glow of sunset he caught a glimpse of Skyrm at the Land Rover's wheel as the SUV drew away from the Audi. Then the Rover came at the Audi with the mass and speed of a barreling rhinoceros. Its bumper clipped the Audi just above the front tire, sending the coupe into a diagonal skid toward the pavement's edge. Larissa screamed and the distant Pyrenees went sideways as the Audi pitched over and sailed off the road.

CHAPTER 36--BEEPS

How long they had sat in the darkened room was a mystery. From the hallway light seeping beneath the door, Brian could make out the shapes of the desk in the corner and the shrouded device suspended from the ceiling. He turned his head to look at Larissa, her silhouetted profile sharply defined despite the dim light. He couldn't see her hands but he knew that they, like his, were tied to the chair.

At least his strength was returning. Brian was able to keep his eyes on Larissa for nearly a minute before his neck muscles gave and his chin fell back to his chest.

She was sobbing again. Brian had tried to speak earlier, but all that came out was a gurgle and a line of drool that dripped from the corner of his mouth.

They had been drugged at the crash site. Not enough to put them to sleep, but enough to keep them docile so that the two men from the blue Mazda, Kralik and Carter (Brian had decided this was the bald man's name), could handle them like gunnysacks.

He had no memory of the crash, only rushes of emotion and flashes of images from its aftermath. Distress as blood welled from a gash in Professor DeJonge's forehead. Fear as Skyrm threw the professor into the Land Rover's rear seat. Anger as Kralik jabbed Brian's shoulder with a syringe. Helplessness as Larissa, who was being restrained by Carter, yelled after her father until her injection took effect and her limbs sagged. A surge of hope as a tow truck arrived, then a plunge into despair as Voss (the tall man's name by default) stepped down from the cab.

Skyrm drove off in the Land Rover as Voss started to hook up the professor's Audi to the tow truck. Kralik and Carter dragged Brian and Larissa to the Mazda. Before shoving him into the back seat, Kralik punched Brian in the stomach—payback for the limp, probably. Brian fell to the floor and rolled onto his back as the car made a sharp U-turn. His view for the rest of the ride was Larissa's sneaker hanging over the seat's edge.

When the car eventually stopped, Brian had given up on calculating the trip's duration. He attempted earlier to count the seconds, but always lost concentration somewhere around fourteen. Kralik opened the door, revealing a warehouse interior. He and Carter dragged their captives past forklifts and rows of wooden crates stacked five high. They came into an area where the floors were tiled with pale green Linoleum and the walls painted salmon. It reminded Brian of a doctor's office.

The men dropped Brian and Larissa onto the floor of the room with the desk in the corner and the device, covered in a light gray tarp, suspended from the ceiling. The two men left the room and returned with the type of folding wooden chairs Brian associated with church picnics. They positioned Brian and Larissa in the chairs and lashed their hands behind them.

Then the men did something Brian couldn't comprehend even as he watched. Each man tied a rope to an arm of Brian's chair and attached the other end of his rope to the facing wall. If Brian's chair were raised off the ground it would be suspended between the walls like a swing. But the chair was firmly on the ground. It made no sense. Brian expected them to truss up Larissa's chair as well, but they switched off the light and left.

Since then, nothing.

Brian raised his head again and counted the seconds. Two minutes passed before his neck muscles protested, but they were only twinges and he kept his head up. After another minute the twinges faded. The haze inside his mind lifted. He turned his head and tried to see the ropes that secured his chair to the walls, but they were invisible in the dark. He looked at Larissa. Her head was raised, too. He was about to test his voice again when the phone rang.

On the fourth ring the door opened and the lights came on. Brian squeezed his eyes shut against the sudden glare and didn't know who had entered the room to answer the phone until he recognized Skyrm's voice.

"Yes, I'm with them now. No, they have not been harmed."

Brian blinked until his eyes adjusted to the light. Skyrm was sitting on a corner of the desk, watching him.

"The boy is conscious," Skyrm continued. "The girl still appears to be under."

Brian looked at Larissa. Her chin was on her chest and her eyes were closed. Did the darkness trick him into seeing her head raised moments ago? Did he imagine her sobs?

"They probably gave her too strong a dose," Skyrm said.

Skyrm was silent for a few moments as he listened. Then he said, "I repeat my objections. I know your squeamishness, but they still represent a threat, especially the boy."

Silence again. Brian looked to see how his chair was attached to the walls. What he saw baffled him. They weren't ropes but bungee cords, the type with metal hooks used to secure cargo in pickup trucks. The cords were wrapped around each chair arm three times with the hook latched to the cord like a knot. The room had a chair rail, a green half-round two inches wide, and the hooks at the far ends of the bungee cords were wedged into the crack between the rail and the wall. Brian didn't get it. The only purpose the bungee cords seemed to serve was to prevent him from rocking his chair from side to side. He wondered if this were a booby trap that would spring if he left the chair. Or if Skyrm intended to turn the chair into a catapult, however unlikely that seemed. Whatever the cords' purpose, Brian could sense the tension pulling at the chair and felt like he was trapped in the world's simplest spider web.

Brian looked at Larissa's hands to see how she was bound. The rope was looped five times around the back of the chair, and the two ends tied her hands together. Brian tested the rope around his own hands. There was some give, but not enough to pull a wrist through. Still, if he were tied to the chair the same way as Larissa, all he had to do was stand to be free. This assumed he possessed the strength to stand, which Brian doubted. It also assumed he would be out of the chair before Skyrm shoved him back down, which Brian doubted more.

Skyrm spoke into the phone again. "Very well. No, I will not take my eyes off them." Another pause. "You can do that when you get here." Skyrm hung up.

Brian wanted to speak first, to gain a sense of advantage. "Was that your employer?" he asked. "Roland Eck?" His voice was hoarse. Brian sucked at his cheeks to generate saliva.

Skyrm stared at him coldly. "I told you once I do not find you clever. Don't press me when there is no one here to protect you."

"Eck is on his way," Brian said.

"He will not be here for several hours. Until then, you are mine."

"Where is Larissa's father?"

"Elsewhere. We are renegotiating our arrangement with him."

Brian glanced at Larissa. She hadn't stirred at the mention of her father.

"What about the two men who brought us here?" Brian continued.

"They are handling the renegotiation."

Brian's stomach knotted. He pictured a renegotiation that involved brass knuckles and hobnail boots. Or waterboarding.

"Please don't hurt her father."

"That is up to the professor now," Skyrm said. "Don't worry about him. Focus on your own, considerable, worries."

Brian hated where this conversation was going. He changed the subject. "How did you find us on the road?"

Skyrm allowed himself a self-satisfied smirk. "We planted a GPS device in the professor's car as soon as he began working for us."

"Planning for all contingencies, huh?"

Skyrm didn't respond. His face went blank, which frightened Brian. Skyrm came forward to inspect one of the bungee cords. He flicked it with his thumb and nodded with approval at the taut *thrum* it produced. Still looking at the cord, Skyrm said, "The chairs in this building are not as sturdy as I would like, so we had to improvise."

Skyrm went to Larissa. He crouched so that his face was inches from hers. He cupped her chin in his hand and shook it. When he let go, Larissa's head lolled to the side and she murmured as if reacting to a bad dream.

"Stop it," Brian said.

Skyrm shot him an icy look and turned back to Larissa.

"Your boyfriend is giving me an order, Mlle DeJonge," he said, "which angers me. Open your eyes and I won't kill him."

Larissa murmured again, but her eyes remained shut.

Skyrm nodded once more and went behind Larissa's chair. He tilted it backward, lifting the front legs, then pushed her across the room and parked her behind the desk. Skyrm stepped to the front of the desk, leaned his hips against it, and crossed his arms with the demeanor of an algebra teacher about to scold his class.

"Mr. Parker, do you know what it means to have a reputation?"

Brian snorted. "Of course I do. I'm in high school."

Skyrm ignored the retort. "I have a reputation, a reputation that is a great source of pride and a reputation that took more than a decade to secure. My reputation is this: I plan crimes. I do it better than anyone in Europe. Thieves, gangsters, spies, terrorists—they recognize this. Anyone with a criminal enterprise in mind knows they will succeed if they hire me. I work out the logistics. I recruit the talent. I procure the weapons and the equipment. I have never failed. And to the police and security agencies across the continent, I am no more than a rumor. My reputation is formidable, and it has made me rich. If this reputation slips, I lose work, and my personal wealth declines. Therefore, my reputation is sacred to me."

He took a step toward Brian. "So do you think my reputation might slip if potential clients learned this particular enterprise has been obstructed by a fifteen-year-old boy?"

Foster Blake would have cracked a joke at this point, but Brian was petrified. The red rings in Skyrm's eyes caught the light and glinted. His voice took on the tenor of a knife being sharpened. "Do you think I can allow this insult to my reputation to go unanswered?"

Brian forced the words out of his mouth: "Your employer told you not to hurt me."

"He will never know. And you can thank him for that."

As Skyrm said this, he raised his eyes to the device suspended from the ceiling. Brian's eyes followed. Under its gray cover, the contraption appeared to be about four feet long with a narrow snout and wide back end, almost a perfect cone.

The device was attached to a track that crossed the ceiling's width. The track was attached to twin runners along the ceiling's length. It was a larger version of the mechanism that moved the claw in the arcade machine. The nape of Brian's neck tingled as he realized what the tarp concealed.

Confirming Brian's fears, Skyrm reached up and pulled off the cover, revealing a Prometheus weapon identical to the one mounted atop the van at San Gregorio. No, not identical. This one would work.

"Our prototype," Skyrm said as he tossed the cover aside.

Up close the machine didn't appear anything like the sleek super weapons of the movies. It looked like it was built from oversized components purchased at Radio Shack. A curved black slab that looked like a miniature radar emitter extended from the back of the gun. The silver disk at the front appeared to be the muzzle. With that thought, Brian knew he was looking at a ray gun. An honest-to-God ray gun.

An honest-to-God ray gun currently pointed at the wall behind him and well to his right, although that would soon change. Skyrm picked up a device from the desk that resembled a model airplane's remote control. His fingers manipulated a joystick the size of a miniature pencil, and the Prometheus gun glided backward, humming as it went.

"They consider themselves idealists," Skyrm said, "Roland Eck and Eduoard DeJonge. They think they are giving the world a weapon that doesn't kill." The ray gun stopped moving backward and began to whir to the left until it lined up with Brian. "They will not admit this weapon's greatest potential use. It leaves no mark. It causes no physical damage. Yet it dispenses unimaginable pain." Skyrm was smiling now. "It is a torturer's dream."

Brian had no idea how to prepare for what was about to happen. His legs began to tremble and a film of sweat instantly covered his brow. Skyrm pressed another button, and the Prometheus gun's muzzle slowly tilted toward Brian.

"The longest anyone has been able to endure the Prometheus ray before jumping out of its path, Mr. Parker, is five seconds."

The ray gun stopped moving. It pointed at Brian's chest.

Skyrm's smile widened. "You are about to experience the

worst six seconds of your life."

Then, echoing louder in the small room than on the field in San Gregorio, two beeps sounded.

CHAPTER 37--HEAT

On a winter afternoon seven years earlier, Brian Parker and Tim Gifford huddled in Tim's basement and committed one of the high crimes of childhood: they played with matches.

They knelt facing each other, an ashtray between them and a bottle of Febreeze at hand to mask the scent. Tim took the wooden kitchen matches he had pilfered from the back of the silverware drawer and struck one down the side of the box. At the millisecond of ignition, a speck of phosphorous splintered from the match head and sailed onto the back of Brian's hand. The white-hot speck didn't just burn; it burrowed into his flesh. Brian leaped to his feet, slapping away the now blackened crumb. The heat only intensified. He ran to the bathroom and shoved his hand under a stream of cold tap water. Only then did the burning subside, leaving behind a white pinprick of a scar.

Brian never imagined he would feel a sharper pain or a more intense heat. But if that bit of phosphorous from seven years ago was an ember, the invisible beam now boring into his chest was an inferno. Every sinew in his body clenched at the concentrated blast, and his eyes squeezed shut. Air exploded from his lungs as if he were punched in the stomach by an armored fist.

"One," Skyrm said, beginning the count.

Brian lurched left, then right, instinctively trying to throw himself out of the beam's path. But the bungee cords held the chair steady. The heat in Brian's chest radiated through his body like wildfire. He screamed.

"Two."

Brian kicked backward, but the chair wouldn't budge in that direction either. As pain seared through him like a maelstrom, his besieged mind attempted to identify the sensation. It was like the worst-ever sunburn instantly turning every inch of his skin pink. No, it was like being tossed into an oven. No, it was like being tossed into a volcano.

"Three."

Heat consumed him, addling his senses. If he was being cooked alive, why couldn't he smell the smoke from his burning clothes? Why couldn't he hear his flesh sizzle? The only noise he heard was the ungodly wail of some strange animal. In an instant of terror, Brian recognized the wail as his own.

"Four."

Is this how Joan of Arc felt as she died? Except she was standing, not sitting. The muscles in his neck seized, and he arched his back in agony. Something snapped. Oh God, his spine?

"Five."

Brian Parker's reality was the conflagration raging through every cell in his body. He could do nothing but open his mouth wider and scream louder.

"Six."

Reality shifted.

Brian experienced an instant of weightlessness as every seized muscle went slack at once. His cry silenced by surprise, Brian opened his eyes to a new world. One moment he knew only fire and pain, and the next moment they had ceased. Utterly. The only remaining sensation was a tingling in his chest. His throat, raw from screaming, felt worse. And there was something new, a sharp soreness in his lower back. Was his spine broken? Brian concentrated on wiggling his fingers and toes. To his relief, they responded. He sat up straight and felt the back of the chair move with him. The ropes binding his arms loosened. He had broken the chair, not his spine.

Skyrm dropped the remote control onto the desk and pounced at Brian. He clutched the arms of Brian's chair, pinning him in place. Brian imagined he saw movement in the background, but Skyrm leaned in so that his face, hideous with a maniac's smile, filled Brian's field of vision.

"How did it feel?" Skyrm asked. His eyes glittered.

"Hurt like hell," Brian said, his voice scratchy.

Skyrm chuckled. "Hell. So appropriate. Yes, I sent you to hell. And I can send you again. Many times."

Brian flexed his arms, trying to keep the rope taut and the back of the chair steady. He didn't want Skyrm to know how close he was to freeing himself. Was Brian's scream so loud that Skyrm didn't hear the chair crack? Apparently so, because he continued his taunts.

"Your first trip to hell was solely for my entertainment," Skyrm said. "But there is one question I need you to answer, and that will require further visits."

Brian gaped back at Skyrm. The man knew everything about him. What was left to say?

"Have you told anyone else?" Skyrm asked.

"Anyone else? Told them what?"

"About your recent adventures, about this operation." Skyrm was no longer smiling. "We know you haven't contacted your family, because Silver's man is still in place. And we have been watching your school group, so we know you haven't contacted them."

Brian held his breath, fearing that Skyrm was about to threaten Tim or Miss Weninger.

"What I need to know," Skyrm went on, "is whether you have contacted someone else, maybe left a message with one of the girl's schoolmates, or sent a letter to a friend in Wisconsin."

"Who could I tell? No one would believe me."

"A reasonable answer," Skyrm said, still leaning over Brian. "Let's see whether you stick to it after another trip to hell." His smile returned. "Seven seconds, this time. Then eight. Then nine, until I am certain you're telling—"

Two beeps sounded, and Skyrm's face wrenched in agony. He squawked and pitched forward as the Prometheus ray scorched into his back. He jackknifed to the right to escape the beam, but lost his balance and fell to the floor. Brian already was moving and he felt the heat ray's sting for less than a second before he kicked away from Skyrm and dropped into a roll. His arms came free as the ropes fell away and the back of the chair skittered across the tiles. Brian's somersault carried him to the wall, ending with his heels touching the vinyl baseboard.

Lifting his head, Brian caught a glimpse of Larissa, awake and out of her chair. She stood beside the desk watching him anxiously over her shoulder. Her hands, still tied behind her back, lingered above the Prometheus gun's remote control.

Brian rose to his feet next to the bungee cord stretched between the wall and his chair. Skyrm was up, too. He advanced at Brian, then recoiled with a scowl as he stepped into the invisible beam. Skyrm took a step back and reached inside his jacket.

Brian reacted before Skyrm's pistol could appear. With straightened fingers, he chopped upward at the bungee cord's hook.

The hook tore away a chunk of the chair rail as it flew forward and smashed into Skyrm's larynx. Skyrm dropped his gun and let out a ragged gasp when the chair, yanked toward the opposite wall by the second bungee cord, cracked into his shins. Entangled in the cords and fighting to breathe, Skyrm tumbled over the chair.

Brian angled toward the desk and dived underneath the Prometheus weapon. He rolled to his feet and grabbed Larissa's chair by its front legs as he came up. Brian lifted the chair above his head. He shook the chair once to flatten it, and spun about to face Skyrm.

Skyrm was up on one knee, still tangled in the cords, and reaching for his pistol. Brian swung the chair hard into Skyrm's chest and knocked him onto his back. Skyrm kicked at Brian, but Brian swiveled out of the way. He brought the chair down again, clouting Skyrm's left temple. Skyrm went limp.

Brian threw the chair aside and picked up Skyrm's pistol. He hopped back out of Skyrm's reach and waited for the man to move. Skyrm didn't, except for the rise of his chest that accompanied his raspy breathing.

Brian stood there, gun in hand. He kept the barrel pointed several inches wide of Skyrm. Brian had played with many squirt guns and toy pistols (a few more recently than he cared to admit) but this was the first time he had held the real thing. It was heavier than he expected. The words on the grip read Astra Condor, a make unknown to him. Brian stared at the pistol as if hypnotized. All those spy novels had said holding a gun brought a feeling of power, but Brian felt revulsion.

"Brian?"

Snapped from his trance, Brian turned to Larissa and smiled.

"Thanks for the rescue. How long were you awake?"

"Since just before he came in," she said.

Brian placed the gun on the desk, relieved to no longer be touching it. He noticed the Prometheus controls and flipped the off switch. Then he started to untie Larissa's hands. He asked, "How did you remain so calm when he shook you?"

"I was using yoga relaxation taught to me by my mother," she said. "But it still was not easy. And you? Are you all right after what he did to you?"

"I'm fine," he said as he pulled the rope from Larissa's wrists.

"But that scream!" Larissa shuddered. "You howled like a wolf in a trap."

Brian ran his fingers through his hair. "Remember when I said wearing wet socks was the worst feeling in the world?"

Larissa nodded.

"Well, it's now a distant second."

Larissa chuckled. Brian was pleased to make her laugh again.

"Your father and Roland Eck delivered on their promise. As soon as Skyrm shut off the machine, the pain vanished just like that." Brian snapped his fingers.

He thought she would smile at that, too, but her face clouded. "How will we find my father?" she asked.

Brian placed a hand on her shoulder. "I have an idea. But first," Brian nodded toward the unconscious Skyrm, "we have to take care of him."

CHAPTER 38--DISPOSAL

Brian and Larissa trussed Skyrm up securely using the ropes, the bungee cords, and his own belt. They then dragged him into a stall in the men's restroom they located down the hall.

Brian pulled off Skyrm's tie and used it as a blindfold. He wadded up bits of wet toilet paper to plug Skyrm's ears. Recalling a bizarre medical fact he read in *Clandestinely Yours*—that people knocked unconscious by a blow to the head often vomit when they come to—Brian decided not to put a gag in Skyrm's mouth. "I hate this guy," he said, "but I don't want to be responsible for killing him." Finally, they searched Skyrm's pockets, finding a switchblade, a set of keys, and a wallet that contained 730 euros. Brian felt no guilt in taking the money.

In the hallway, where they were happy to discover their backpacks, Brian gave Larissa the switchblade and asked her to drop it in the ladies' room trashcan. "They won't look for it there," he said. "Oh, and the gun, too. I'll go get it."

"Shouldn't we keep the gun to protect ourselves?" Larissa asked.

"Would you actually shoot someone, even to protect ourselves?"

Larissa opened her mouth, but didn't speak immediately.

"Exactly," Brian said, "you'd hesitate. So would I. But anyone pointing a gun at us wouldn't hesitate. I'd say a gun would just give them a more compelling reason to shoot us."

Larissa nodded. "*Mais oui*, 'Don't pull a gun unless you are willing to use it.' I think I heard this in *The Godfather*."

Brian shrugged. "Haven't seen it."

He sidestepped another lecture on his pitiful lack of culture by returning to the office to retrieve the semiautomatic. Copying actions he had seen in many films (just not *The Godfather*),

Brian pressed a button on the pistol's grip and slipped the magazine from the butt. Brian figured Skyrm would carry a round in the chamber. He worked the slide and, sure enough, a bullet popped out and bounced across the desktop. Brian pocketed the ammunition, planning to dispose of it later. Larissa appeared in the doorway, and he handed her the pistol grip-first.

When Larissa returned from hiding the weapons, Brian was at the desk standing over the telephone. "I have an idea how we can get your father back," he said, "but we need to gather a little more intelligence. Roland Eck called Skyrm on this phone. Skyrm said he was hours away, so we have to learn where that call came from."

Brian pointed at the LCD display above the phone's numbered buttons. "Do you know how to bring up the number of the last incoming call? Everything's in Spanish, and I'd hate to delete it accidentally."

Larissa pressed two buttons and the number appeared on the display. Brian took a pen and memo pad from the desk and copied the digits. "This number is familiar," he said. "Do you recognize it?"

Larissa shook her head. "Only vaguely."

"Well, can you tell where the call came from?"

"There is no country code, so it must be from another city inside Spain."

"I guess we should call and find out," Brian said. "Can you put it on speaker?"

Larissa did, then triggered the automatic redial. The ring tone chirred three times before the call picked up and a recorded female voice recited a message in Spanish. Brian recognized three words: Barcelona Paquete Servicio.

Larissa translated. "It is saying, 'Thank you for calling Barcelona Paquete Servicio. We are closed for the day. Please call again during our business hours. If your call is urgent—'"

Brian cut off the call. "Yeah, I figured that's what she was saying," he said. "But that's where we saw the phone number, in the van. Apparently Barcelona Paquete Servicio is a real company, not just a name on a phony sign."

"Yes, I remember," Larissa said. "Barcelona Paquete Servicio—you would call it Barcelona Parcel Service in

America, I believe."

"It must be the name of their front company," Brian said, thinking out loud. "But if it's a real company, then they can hide the Prometheus weapon within a fleet of identical delivery vans." He nodded his head in admiration. "Hell, that's genius."

Larissa looked around the room. "Where do you guess we are?" she asked.

"We must be in that industrial park where Masson stopped on the way to San Gregorio," Brian said. "I saw tools in the warehouse area, so I think this is the workshop Masson and your father talked about."

"My father," Larissa said. "You said you had a plan."

"I do," Brian said, "but we have to work fast. We have to be done and out of here before Eck arrives." He looked into her eyes. "How long would it take for someone to drive from Barcelona to Zaragoza?"

"About three hours, but—"

"We'd better figure on two. Now, if we do this right, we'll be able to bargain with Eck to get your father back."

"Bargain?" Larissa's eyes widened. "Are we are going to trade my father for the man in the WC?"

"No, Eck wouldn't trade for him. But he will trade for that," Brian said, pointing at the Prometheus gun suspended from the ceiling.

"What are we going to do with that?"

"It depends," Brian replied.

"On what?"

"On how fast I can learn to drive a forklift."

CHAPTER 39--CALLS

As Brian listened to the harsh ring tones of Barcelona's phone system, his eyes lifted to the most astonishing and oddest building he had ever seen: La Sagrada Família, the church of the Holy Family. Larissa stood beside him, at the first pay phone they had found outside the Sagrada Família Metro stop, and she was also spellbound by the four spires that looked like titanic, hollowed-out taper candles scraping at the clouds.

From the guidebook he bought at the Barcelona train station that morning, Brian knew this church, still under construction after more than a century, had become Barcelona's symbol. But no guidebook's words or pictures could have prepared him for the experience of standing in La Sagrada Familia's presence. In many ways, it was the opposite of St-Sernin in Toulouse. St-Sernin was a squat, severe fortress that hugged the earth. La Sagrada Família was a soaring, surreal sand castle that yearned for heaven. With a façade of twists and crags and nodules, the cathedral looked organic, not man-made. It was as if God had reached into a coral reef and the spires miraculously formed as he withdrew his hand.

A crackle on the phone line tore Brian's thoughts away from heaven. The same woman from the recorded message answered. "Buenas tardes," she said. "Barcelona Paquete Servicio. En qué puedo ayudarle?"

Brian replied, "I would like to speak to Roland Eck."

The woman hesitated, then responded in English, "I am sorry, but no one with that name works here."

"My name is Brian Parker, and Roland Eck will want to talk to me. Tell him I will call back in exactly half an hour." Brian looked at his Batman watch: It read 2:35 p.m.

"I will see what I can do, sir," the woman said. Brian hung up before she spoke again.

Larissa had watched him during the brief conversation. He touched her arm and said, "Time to roll."

Brian took a last look at La Sagrada Família before they hurried down the steps to the Metro. In the station they passed a man playing a harp, his face serene as his fingers danced upon the strings. Earlier in the day, as the pair scouted Barcelona for pay-phone locations that suited Brian's plan, they had seen scores of street performers. This was the second harpist. Brian wondered how the man got the five-foot-tall instrument down the stairs.

A westbound train arrived moments after they reached the platform. Brian could still hear the harp music as they stepped aboard and the doors closed. The song was so familiar, but he couldn't place it. The melody was off—too slow, too lilting.

"Do you know that song?" he asked Larissa as they sat. "I know I've heard it before, but I can't name it." Worried about her father, Larissa had said little since they left the warehouse outside Zaragoza. Brian latched onto any lame attempt to start a conversation.

She nodded. "*Oui*. It is by the Beatles. 'Help!'"

"Help," Brian said. "We could sure use it."

The corners of her lips quivered upward. It was almost a smile, and Brian was relieved to see it. The train whooshed out of the station and the windows went black. Brian held Larissa's hand and closed his eyes. In his thoughts he reviewed everything that had happened since they first called Barcelona Paquete Servicio fourteen hours earlier in the warehouse.

As it turned out, driving a forklift was easy, not unlike a go-kart. From the pictograms on the dashboard, Brian figured how to operate the lift. Within ten minutes they had moved a crate, empty except for foam packing material, beneath the Prometheus prototype. Along the wall of the warehouse Brian had found the tools he needed to unbolt the weapon from the ceiling and let it fall into the crate. The device hit the foam padding with a giant *wuff* and a tiny snap. Brian didn't worry about the snap. The prototype did not have to be intact. It just had to be gone before Eck arrived. He and Larissa hastily nailed the crate shut and pushed it into the hall where the forklift, too wide to fit through the doorway, waited.

Only forty minutes had passed by the time Brian maneuvered the crate back into the warehouse. He already had discovered the gift Skyrm left for them, one of the maroon delivery vans. Brian grinned as he wheeled the forklift about and pointed the crate toward its destination. Fifteen minutes later, they were in the van and on the road.

Larissa drove. It was after midnight and the highway was a straight shot to Zaragoza, so they figured the odds of the police stopping them were microscopic. "This is like driving a truck, I think," Larissa said.

"Have you driven a truck before?"

"No, but we are sitting so high above the road," she said. "I am a bit nervous."

"You're doing fine," Brian said.

They crossed the Ebro River and entered Zaragoza's central business district. The spotlighted spires of a cathedral glowed several blocks to their right. Larissa pulled into the first parking lot they saw. They locked up the van, pulled their backpacks over their shoulders, and briskly walked away. Brian didn't care whether they were illegally parked. In fact, he hoped they were and that the van was impounded. The harder it would be for Eck and his men to find the van, the better.

Although it was 1 a.m., the streets were busy with people hopping from one nightclub to the next. Larissa hailed a taxi outside the Hotel Via Romana. "Train station, *por favor*," Brian told the driver. At the station, they learned the next train to Barcelona would not depart for two hours. Eck would reach the warehouse before they boarded the train. Brian frowned.

"What is the matter?" Larissa asked.

"I don't like waiting here this long. Eck might send someone to check the train station."

"Why would we take a train when we have their van? That is what they will think."

"I hope you're right."

"I am right," she said. She hugged his arm. "But we will remain vigilant."

Brian reclined and stretched out his feet. "Do you realize this will be my fourth train ride in as many days?" he said. "I should have bought a Eurail pass."

Larissa smiled—the last one Brian would see until her almost-smile on the Barcelona Metro—and rested her head on his shoulder. "Will we get my father back?"

"I hope so," Brian said. He wished he could be more positive, but he knew Larissa would not want to hear phony bravado.

The train ride to Barcelona lasted five hours. During that time Brian and Larissa caught up on some (but not enough) sleep, washed as best they could in the lavatories, and changed clothes again. Larissa put on a pair of black jeans and another Ramones T-shirt. It featured the band's first album cover, the one with them leaning against a brick wall in their leather jackets and exuding an attitude that mixed boredom and contempt and said, "We're about to change the face of popular music forever, but it will take twenty-five years before anyone realizes it." Brian changed into a pair of khaki slacks and the FC Barcelona jersey from the shop in Hendaye.

In the Barcelona train station, they bought a guidebook and a laminated map of the city and began their search for the two Metro stations where Brian would make his calls, as well as a fallback rendezvous point in case they needed one later. Brian had a feeling they would.

Now, with the first call made, they were back aboard the Metro and hurtling beneath an unfamiliar city toward the second call. As the subway train pulled into the Sants-Estacio stop, Brian squeezed Larissa's hand. She opened her eyes. "I wasn't sleeping," she said.

"I wouldn't blame you if you were."

They changed trains, switching to a southbound route and getting off at a stop called Poble Sec. As they jogged up the steps toward the street, Brian checked his watch. He had eight minutes until his deadline, but he made straight for the pay phone as soon as he spotted it. The last thing he needed was someone else grabbing the phone just before he called Eck. He spent the extra time taking in the scenery. Behind them rose the green hill named Montjuïc, a tourist attraction according to the guidebook. Aerial cable cars, just like the ones in amusement parks, flitted between the uppermost tree branches as they lifted passengers to the hilltop. Brian shifted his gaze and saw another, grander, cable car gliding above the harbor. *Such a beautiful city*, he thought. *If only I could be a tourist here.*

Brian wiped sweat from his forehead and took another look at his watch. Two minutes to go. He reached into his pocket and made a show of counting out the correct number of coins. Larissa watched him, her eyes pensive and her lips tight. Brian wished he could jump a few hours into the future and tell her this had all ended well.

At 3:05 he inserted the coins into the slot. He looked at Larissa. "Wish me luck," he said.

"*Bon chance*," she whispered.

Brian dialed the number. The phone picked up midway into the second ring. A man, not the receptionist, answered. "Is this Brian?" The voice was American.

"Yes," Brian said.

"Hello, Brian. I am glad we finally get to chat. I have heard much about you, as you might imagine. This is Roland Eck, by the way."

"Yeah, I figured that," Brian said. He was angry with himself. Eck had caught him off guard by answering the phone and speaking glibly. Brian had lost the initiative before opening his mouth. He needed to take control of the conversation. He said, "If you want to see—"

"I know, I know," Eck interrupted. "You have something I want. I have something you want. So we need to negotiate. But not over the phone. Too impersonal. We need to talk things over face to face, like men. I'm eager to meet you anyway. And I'm glad to see you're here in Barcelona, Brian. It makes getting together easier."

That was supposed to shake Brian up, the veiled threat that Eck had traced the call. Brian had expected it, though, just as he had expected Eck to suggest a meeting. This looked like his chance to take the initiative.

"All right," Brian said, "let's meet at the Columbus statue, near the harbor, a half-hour from now."

"You like these half-hour deadlines, don't you? But I'm afraid the time doesn't work for me. Why don't we make it four o'clock instead? That's still within the hour. Does four work for you, Brian?"

"Yes," Brian said, forcing authority into his voice.

"OK, so I will meet you at 4 p.m. at the Columbus Monument—that's what they call it, by the way, *monument*, not *statue*. I look forward to meeting you. Oh, and Brian?"

"Yes."

"Bring Larissa." Eck hung up.

CHAPTER 40--FALLBACK

"Not a chance," Brian replied to the dead phone.

There was never a possibility Larissa would accompany Brian when he met with Roland Eck. Splitting up at this point should guarantee her safety, and possibly Brian's. If he were walking into a trap, Larissa would be free to tell their story. Even if she couldn't rally the cavalry to rescue him, Larissa would be free. That mattered most to Brian.

He dropped the receiver into its cradle and related Eck's words to Larissa as they jogged back to the Poble Sec Metro station.

"So you know what to do now," he said. "You wait for me at La Boqueria's entrance at 4:45. And if I'm not there?"

"I walk away, and check back every fifteen minutes for the next hour," Larissa said, repeating the routine they had worked out that morning.

Brian had followed rudimentary espionage tradecraft to set up a fallback rendezvous. The place had to be public. Brian knew from the Travel Channel that the most public place in Barcelona was Las Ramblas, the broad thoroughfare that sprawled luxuriously from the harbor front into the heart of the city. Las Ramblas curved past hundreds of shops and cultural centers and was the rare attraction that drew as many locals as tourists, according to the guidebook. The book also stated the most public spot along Las Ramblas was an open-air food market grandly named the Mercat de Sant Josep de la Boqueria, or La Boqueria for short. During their reconnaissance, Brian and Larissa found La Boqueria packed with people. Without hesitation, Brian declared it their fallback spot.

"And if I still haven't shown by 5:45?" Brian asked, continuing the drill.

"I hail the first taxi I spot," Larissa said as they descended the steps to the station, "and go to the French consulate."

Brian figured if he hadn't made it to La Boqueria by 5:45, he would have been captured and Larissa should seek refuge at the French consulate. The deadline for their final rendezvous ought to give her enough time to reach the consulate before it closed to the public at 6 p.m. There she would tell her story. After her father's disappearance, Brian was certain the French authorities would protect Larissa and investigate her claims.

They boarded the subway and took facing seats. As the train approached Brian's stop, Drassanes, Larissa looked into his eyes sternly and said, "While you are talking with this man, if it becomes clear to you that you cannot help my father, I want you to turn away and run." Her voice caught. "I want you to run like mad to our meeting place, and then we will go to the French consulate together. Will you promise me that?"

"Je te promets," Brian said.

"Your pronunciation is beautiful," she said as she leaned in and kissed him. With her hands on his shoulders, she murmured, "You have been very smart so far, *cher* Brian. You must continue to be smart, especially now."

The train sighed to a stop, and, reluctantly, Brian left the car. He waved to Larissa through the window, the sensation of her kiss still on his lips. She responded with a sad semi-smile and a raise of her hand. Then the train pitched forward, slid into the tunnel, and she was gone.

Brian turned about and headed to the escalator. Larissa would exit the train at the next stop, Liceu, to be in place for their reunion. Focus on the positive, Brian told himself.

He brushed his lips while riding the escalator and reflected on Larissa's faith in his intelligence. Was he being smart? Brian did believe the missing Prometheus gun gave him leverage over Eck, and Eck had ordered his men not to harm him. Brian's plan hinged on that order remaining in effect. Even so, Brian had promised Larissa he would remain in a public area while with Eck. He would avoid dark alleys and wouldn't get into any cars. Were these precautions smart enough? Brian hoped so. He was tired of running, and as long as he had an advantage over his opponents, however slim, he wanted to press it.

Once Brian reached the street level, he saw the statue of Columbus levitating above nearby rooftops and trees. The famed explorer held a chart in one hand and pointed confidently with the other toward the New World. The statue was the sickly green of aged bronze, although it appeared someone had painted Columbus' hair white. As Brian drew closer, he realized the white wasn't paint but pigeon droppings. He also saw the statue was held aloft by a column that looked like a ten-story king's scepter. From the decorated base to the tip of Columbus' finger, the whole structure must have been two hundred feet tall. Beyond the monument, the black lines of the cable cars Brian had seen earlier stretched across the harbor. He watched as the two gondolas, little red buckets from this distance, approached each other and converged at a point behind Columbus' head.

The monument stood in the center of a small traffic circle. The meeting with Eck was still six minutes away, so instead of crossing to the island, Brian leaned against a plane tree at the foot of Las Ramblas and watched the people walking around the monument or sitting on the stairs at its base. He didn't recognize Eck, although all he had to go on were a few grainy images on Lenore Harte's computer screen. Brian glanced at his watch: 3:59. He looked behind him. The tree-lined passage of Las Ramblas stretched away, leading in his mind toward Larissa and the end to this nightmare.

Brian straightened himself and crossed the traffic circle. He walked in a counterclockwise spiral as he approached the monument, noting that eight life-size, polished bronze lions guarded the four stairways leading toward the column. He saw no sign of Eck. He looked toward the harbor then toward Las Ramblas, but Eck wasn't coming from either direction. When Brian turned back to the monument, the bald man with the Vandyke he had first seen on Lenore Harte's street—the man he had decided was named Voss—stepped from behind one of the lions and walked toward him.

"Where's Eck?" Brian asked.

"Elsewhere," the man replied. His accent was guttural Irish. "Where's the girl?"

"Shopping. You know how women are."

The bald man regarded him with less emotion, Brian

imagined, than Columbus' statue. He pulled out a cell phone and quickly placed a call. "The girl isn't with him," he said into the phone. After a moment he said, "All right." He killed the call and pocketed the phone. "I'm to take you to him," he told Brian. "Come with me."

"One question first. Is your name Voss or Carter?"

The man's brow furrowed. "Carter, why?"

Brian clicked his tongue. "Got it wrong." He sighed elaborately. "You know there's no way I'm getting into a car with you."

Carter showed him an eerie smile. "No car. We're walking." He turned away from Brian. "Now follow me."

Brian didn't like the smile. It was the smile of a bully savoring an impending punch that would knock his victim to the ground. Carter set out for the harbor, but Brian hesitated. Eck had just broken their agreement, and it would be smart to walk away now. Brian shoved his apprehension deep down and remembered this was for Larissa's father.

"No," Brian told himself, "this is for Larissa."

He followed Carter.

CHAPTER 41--HARBOR

Carter led him across a wide, busy street lined with palm trees, and they were at the waterfront. Brian now had an unobstructed view of the cable cars. They traveled from a tower far to his left, passed through a spindly center tower on a broad jetty directly before him, and vanished into what looked like a bunker halfway up Montjuïc.

Brian lowered his eyes to the Mediterranean and wondered why his itinerary had drawn him back to this sea. Hundreds of boats crowded the harbor. Two cruise ships were in port, dwarfing a quartet of single-masted sailboats that scudded past them. The water was choppy, even within the sea wall, and white-capped waves buffeted a small passenger ferry that had blue awnings above each of its two decks. Brian saw several such boats motoring about the harbor. A gust of wind, warm with the smell of salt, hit Brian and plastered the FCB jersey to his chest.

He had slowed to take in the scene, allowing Carter to get several paces ahead. Carter turned and barked, "Keep up!" as two in-line skaters whizzed between them.

Brian followed Carter past an ornate, cream-colored building that looked like it had time traveled from nineteenth century France. The words *Port de Barcelona* arced above its entrance. Carter rounded the building and headed toward the water. The naked masts of dozens of small sailboats bobbed alongside the jetties in the small, enclosed marina on the left. Carter led Brian across a footbridge decorated with curving blue iron waves supported by 20-foot-tall white pillars.

Brian considered the man leading him. If Carter was here, where were the others? He wondered whether Eck had a team looking for Larissa. For a split second, Brian worried that La

Boqueria was too obvious a meeting place, but he dismissed the thought. Barcelona was a major city with many meeting places equally as obvious. It would be like assuming Times Square was the only place two people would arrange to meet in Manhattan.

The bridge led to a small, man-made peninsula that curled into the harbor like the tail of a comma. A sign by the bridge identified the spot as Port Vell. They walked toward a wide, flat building with a glass façade. A slate-gray wedge rising from the roof bore the building's name, Maremagnum. An outdoor tapas bar spilled from the building, and Brian at first assumed Maremagnum was a hotel. Then he saw people stepping through its doors carrying bags marked Lacoste and H&M and Claire's. This was a shopping mall. Was he to meet Roland Eck in the food court? How anticlimactic. But Carter walked past the mall.

Beyond Maremagnum was an aquarium, also glass-fronted, but highlighted by a gleaming stainless-steel roof. Beyond the aquarium was an IMAX theater. As they approached the aquarium, Brian wondered. Foster Blake met one of his contacts in the Miami aquarium in *To the Point of Insanity*, but that led to gunfire and exploding shark tanks. Carter continued past the aquarium entrance without breaking stride.

"No exploding shark tanks today," Brian murmured.

Carter slowed his pace as they neared the IMAX theater. Brian frowned. Why meet in a movie theater? The aquarium, even the shopping center, made more sense. A mammoth poster, rippling in the wind, advertised a 3-D travelogue of Egypt. Maybe Eck had a thing for pyramids. Carter stopped, then folded his arms and stood impassively.

"Is this where we're going?" Brian asked.

"It is where I am going," Carter replied. "But not you." He looked toward the theater entrance and said, "Ah."

Brian followed his gaze and saw the tall man with the vulture shoulders—the man Brian now knew was named Voss—emerge from a throng of people in front of the IMAX building.

"You will go with him now," Carter said. He turned and fell behind a group of teenagers heading toward the Maremagnum. Carter did not look back as his disappeared into the crowd.

"Come," Voss said. Feeling like a baton in a relay race, Brian followed.

They were in the crook of the small peninsula, and after rounding the curve they headed back toward the city. The path angled through small gardens. Just off the path, a skinny young man with orange hair stood with a battered Fender Stratocaster plugged into an equally battered Marshall amp. Despite the heat, he wore a black leather jacket covered with buttons, skin-tight black jeans, and black Doc Marten boots. As Voss and Brian neared, the guitarist broke into a torrid Spanish version of "I Wanna Be Sedated." Brian filed away this scene to share with Larissa. It would make her smile.

When they reached the street, Brian looked to his left and saw in the distance the opulent Port de Barcelona building he had passed minutes earlier. Instead of following a straight line, Carter and Voss had detoured him through the harbor. Brian sighed. Roland Eck was playing more mind games. By prolonging their meeting, he wanted to unsettle Brian, leaving him confused, tired, and angry. Eck was succeeding, but Brian refused to show it. More in-line skaters buzzed past, swerving through a flock of bicyclists. The festive setting kept Brian's fear in check. The promenade was filled with people, most of them young, smiling, and energetic. If Eck's men kept parading him through tourist attractions, Brian should be safe.

Voss turned right, taking Brian east along the waterfront. Brian saw a large sculpture of a fish in the distance, its golden scales shimmering in the late afternoon sun. He could make out a beach near the statue. He hoped that wasn't their destination, because it would be a long, exhausting walk. He looked at his watch. 4:46. Larissa should have just stepped away from their first planned rendezvous. Brian had an hour to make the final one.

A larger marina was immediately on their right, and a broad building of peach-colored bricks and wide archways loomed before them, the Museu d'Història de Catalunya. In front of the museum stood Kralik.

Kralik looked at his watch and came forward. "Has he behaved?" he asked Voss.

"Yes," Voss replied. It was the first time he spoke since they left Carter. Voss turned and walked away in the direction they had come from.

"You should continue to behave while you're with me," Kralik said. "I haven't forgotten our encounter in Cannes."

"I'll bet," Brian muttered, noting that Kralik still trod with a slight limp. Kralik was leading him south again, back along the harbor. They were on another peninsula, a wider and longer one that tapered as it bent westward to form a natural protection for Barcelona's harbor.

A man pushing a drink cart approached from the opposite direction. A gust of wind blew the man's cap off his head. Seized by an impulse to defy his escort, Brian chased after the cap. The vendor smiled and blurted, "Gracias," many times as Brian returned it. He handed Brian a bulbous bottle of orangeade. Brian sipped his reward as he casually walked back to Kralik, who scowled and checked his watch. Brian read that as a sign this mystery tour may soon be ending.

As Brian came alongside him, Kralik increased their pace by a beat or two. He glanced at the cable-car gondolas overhead. "Skyrm was right," Kralik said. "We should have killed you in the mountains."

"How is Skyrm?" Brian asked with feigned nonchalance.

Kralik grinned. "Pray you never meet him again."

Brian hesitated for a step, then continued to follow Kralik.

In the marina, sailboats and small yachts rocked in the rough water. Brian looked out to the Mediterranean and saw larger waves crashing against the distant breakwater. Ahead of them, maybe six hundred yards, was the tower that was the eastern terminal for the cable cars. It was more a skeleton than a tower, as if someone had built a 300-foot lighthouse from a construction-grade Erector set and stuck a two-car garage on top. Brian couldn't see any significant buildings beyond the tower, just warehouses, more docks, and larger boats. He figured he was being led either to the tower or a boat. Brian was not going to board a boat—no chance of that!—but the cable car? It was tourist attraction. Would Eck dare harm him on a tourist attraction?

Ethereal music distracted him. Five men with dark reddish skin—Brian would have pegged them as South Americans even without their serapes—stood with their backs to the marina and played a reedy nocturne on pan flutes. The tones made Brian shiver. Kralik marched him past the group, but the ghostly melody caught the wind and trailed them toward the tower.

Once in the tower's shadow, Brian looked up over the harbor to see a gondola descending toward the station. It would arrive within a few minutes. Kralik increased his pace to a canter. He pulled out a cell phone, dialed, and said, "We're at the base," then hung up. About a dozen people were waiting at an elevator. The doors slid open, and Kralik pushed to the front of the line. When people protested, he snarled, "We are late for our shift at the restaurant." Brian hesitated at the elevator's threshold, but stepped inside once he saw three other passengers already were aboard. Six more people got on after him. Kralik punched the top button, which was marked Torre d'Altamar.

The elevator stopped at the cable car platform and everyone stepped out except Brian and Kralik. Brian saw the red gondola swing into the station as the elevator doors closed. Now it seemed he would be meeting Eck in the restaurant instead of the cable car. Yet as soon as they stepped off the elevator, Kralik turned to open a stairwell door.

"Down you go," Kralik said.

"After you," Brian replied.

Kralik grinned. "Of course," he said, then led Brian down a flight of stairs. Kralik opened the door to the station platform and guided Brian past the people queued up to board the waiting red gondola. Inside it was a single man. The man's face was hidden, but Brian knew it was Roland Eck.

The people at the head of the line began to realize they would not be allowed aboard this gondola. A few yelled at the attendant, who raised his hands innocently yet kept the people back. Kralik pointed toward the gondola's open door. Brian didn't move. This was a trap, but it hadn't yet sprung. He was about to throw himself into the queue when a hand clamped onto his shoulder from behind.

He spun around. It was Silver, who stepped forward and used his body to press Brian toward the door.

"Step inside, kid," he said. "We're taking a ride."

CHAPTER 42--HANGING

Brian stood at the rear of the gondola as it lifted from the station and watched the people continue to shout at the attendant.

"I bribed him, of course," Eck said from behind.

The gondola cleared the walls of the station, and suddenly the wind blew through the cable car with the same dull roar Brian heard whenever his father drove down the freeway with the sunroof cracked open.

Eck said, "As you see, I've gone to some trouble to arrange for a private conversation."

Brian turned to face the man who, veiled behind the scenes, had turned his life into a nightmare. The image from Lenore Harte's computer screen had been misleading. Though barely an inch taller than Brian, this man was not frail. Eck's face may indeed have been too large for his head, but what appeared sallow on the screen was bright with energy in the flesh. Eck's eyebrows were enormous. It was as if a doll maker had dipped his thumbs in ashes and scrawled two thick smudges across Eck's forehead. The gray eyes beneath these brows pulsed with an intensity that fixed Brian in place.

"You may not believe it, Brian, but I am happy to meet you at last." Eck took a step forward and gave Brian's hand a confident, if perfunctory, shake. "You know who I am, but I will introduce myself anyway. My name is Roland Eck. Of course, you know Jack Silver."

"Of course," Brian said, shifting his gaze to his former captor. Silver nodded. "Kid," he said in acknowledgement.

Silver stood in front of the door, as if to guard it. *Do they think I'm going to jump?* Brian wondered. The gondola had an octagonal floor plan and windows that started at chest height and rose to the ceiling. It was designed to accommodate at least twenty people and probably was cramped when it carried its full load. Carrying only three people, the gondola felt fragile, particularly with the wind rattling the windows. Brian's knees went weak with every quiver of the cable holding them aloft, literally hanging three hundred feet above the harbor.

"I asked Mr. Silver to join us," Eck continued, "because I thought he might help mediate an arrangement."

"You think I'm going to trust someone who kidnapped me and threatened my family?" Brian asked.

"That was a stroke of luck for me, that second thing," Eck said, wagging his finger. "With his surveillance in place my people were able to make sure you didn't contact your family. We wouldn't have been able to do it otherwise."

Brian glared at Silver, who stood poker-faced.

Eck went on, speaking rapidly. "Our time is limited, so I must come to the point. I know you came here hoping to arrange some sort of amnesty for Professor DeJonge, but I'm afraid I must inform you he has died from the injuries he suffered in his recent automobile accident."

Brian felt the blood drain from his face. Anguish and fear hit him like twin blasts of ice water. Anguish because he had come to negotiate Professor DeJonge's release, but now realized that was never in his power. Fear because, like an idiot, he had stepped into the very trap he swore he would avoid. He had failed Larissa twice over.

Eck kept talking. "Because his car was so smashed up, we deposited it at the bottom of a ravine in the foothills of the Pyrenees. It should be found in a day or two. The police will assume the professor went off the road."

As Eck spoke, Brian numbly stepped to the window and looked over the city sliding beneath him. In the middle distance were the distinctive spires of La Sagrada Família and the construction cranes rising behind them. To the left, the broad, tree-lined Ramblas were easy to spot, a twisting river of green flowing into the heart of the great city. Larissa waited somewhere along that lush path. She would be standing there not knowing Brian would miss their rendezvous, not knowing her father had died.

Several moments of silence lapsed before Brian realized Eck

had stopped talking. He turned from the window, and Eck resumed. "I know you may not believe me based on your last few days," Eck said, "but my overall aims are humanitarian, and I have no interest in harming children. I think we can make an arrangement."

"What do you want from me?" Brian asked.

"Two things. First, I want to know where I can find the van and the package you removed from the warehouse last night."

"You mean where did I put your ray gun?"

Eck showed a pained smile. "If you want to be childish about it, yes."

"All right," Brian said. "Then leave me and Larissa alone. Let me rejoin my school group and let Larissa settle with relatives, now that you've made her an orphan. Once I'm back in Milwaukee, and I've heard Larissa is safe, I'll send you a letter telling you everything."

"Sounds reasonable," Silver said.

"No. No it doesn't," Eck said. "I'm on a tight schedule, I'm afraid, and I can't wait that long. But since you mentioned Larissa, that leads to my second request. All parties involved should come to a mutual agreement, so I wish to talk with her as well."

"Not in this lifetime," Brian said.

Eck looked at Silver. "Such loyalty at a young age."

"In my experience," Silver said, "that's the last age anyone has loyalty."

"But I'm sure your profession has colored your experience," Eck responded. He turned back to Brian. "It will be much easier for Larissa if she joins us willingly."

"She won't be joining us willingly or otherwise," Brian said.

"Perhaps, perhaps not. But we are of course watching the French consulate."

Brian flinched. Immediately he tried to mask his reaction as a loss of balance in the swaying gondola, but he knew Eck had caught it.

"We may not know where she is," Eck said, "but we know where she's likely to go."

CHAPTER 43--SHUTDOWN

Brian stared at Roland Eck and seethed, but his anger was directed inward. How could he be so stupid? He had allowed Eck to stay one move ahead, and he had left Larissa in harm's way. When this ride ended, Brian had to get away from these two men and find Larissa before 5:45. He could think of no other way to stop her from going to the French consulate.

"You need to make a decision quickly, Brian." Eck said. He looked out the front window. The gondola was halfway to the center tower. "You've got about six minutes."

"And then what happens?" Brian asked.

"We arrive at the Montjuïc station, where Mathias Skyrm awaits us. He doesn't share my qualms about harming children."

"Yeah, I found that out last night when he tortured me with your heat ray."

Silver stiffened his shoulders and moved on Eck. "You bastard," he whispered. The reaction startled Brian. Apparently Silver wasn't in on everything.

Eck raised his hands defensively. "Skyrm disobeyed my orders! And my wishes. Prometheus is a non-lethal weapon. I did not design it for torture. I designed it to reduce loss of life during warfare."

"I thought you designed it to make yourself rich," Silver said.

"You stay out of this," Eck hissed.

Silver shrugged. "You brought me here, 'to facilitate negotiations,' to help Brian see your side of things."

"Oh, I'd love to see your side of things," Brian said.

Eck looked at him sharply. "Your time on this ride is more valuable than mine, Brian. You shouldn't waste it."

As soon the last word had passed Eck's lips, the gondola lurched to the side and the wind's roar sharpened. "The hell?"

Silver exclaimed as they all lost their balance. Brian and Silver, standing closer to the window, grabbed the rail and remained upright. Eck rebounded off the far-side window before regaining his footing. The gondola swung again, not as violently, and creaked to a halt about one hundred yards shy of the center tower.

A tinny voice squawked from a speaker in the ceiling and spoke in urgent Spanish. Silver translated: "Due to sudden high winds they have stopped the ride until it is safe to proceed again. They apologize for the inconvenience." He looked at Eck. "Did you plan this, too?"

"No," he replied, straightening himself. "But it does give us more time to talk."

"So help me see your side of things," Brian said. "Tell me how your plan is humanitarian and not mercenary."

"I am not doing this for money," Eck said. "My aims *are* humanitarian, I assure you, but the money was—is—necessary for the plan to work."

"I might believe it's humanitarian to steal a weapons system," Brian said, "but to turn around and sell it, no not exactly."

Eck hesitated. "It started with my wife. My late wife, Jessica. The Pentagon considered her a security risk, actually. There I was, designing weapons for them while she was protesting the Iraq war. We always argued about my work. She said if Positive Enforcement, as the Pentagon called it, was meant to save lives, then the U.S. should share it with other governments."

Eck looked out the window toward the Mediterranean as the car rocked again. "I didn't listen to her while she was alive, but after she died—a brain aneurysm, she was gone in an instant—after she died, I saw Jessica's wisdom. I looked for ways to leak information, at least to our European allies, but security was too tight."

"So you faked your death," Brian said.

"Eventually, yes. But as I thought about sharing technology with Europe, a plan crystallized."

"I've figured that much out," Brian said. "Using someone like Professor DeJonge as a front, you could supply the Europeans with your research and technology. You could trick them into building a working prototype, and just as they're about to test it, you switch it with an identical model that doesn't work."

Silver had gone still as a statue, his eyes on Brian. Brian realized this information was new to the man from the CIA. He continued, "So while the Europeans throw their hands up and say, 'Back to the drawing board,' you sell the working Prometheus to someone else."

"To cover costs," Eck said.

"To pay Skyrm and his men," Brian said. "I imagine they aren't cheap."

"No, they are not."

Silver cut in, "You would have needed start-up money. Skyrm would have demanded a hefty payment up front."

"I told you to stay out of this," Eck snapped.

"But I'd like to know where you got that money, too," Brian said. "How did you pay for a fleet of delivery vans, for instance?" Silver's eyes narrowed when Brian mentioned the vans.

Eck waved his hand impatiently. "My wife came from a wealthy family, an old North Carolina textile empire. After her death I used my inheritance to set up a foundation here in Spain for technological innovation."

"And you found a way to will the money to yourself," Silver said.

Eck smiled. "I won't bore you with the details, but you can take it with you."

"And Positive Enforcement became Prometheus," Brian said. "Because you saw yourself as the titan who stole fire from the gods to share with mankind."

"Which is another reason I faked my death. I didn't want this story to end with me chained to a mountain with vultures eating my liver."

"It was an eagle," Brian said. "Not vultures, but a single eagle."

Silver shook his head. "For someone who justifies his intentions with Greek mythology, you sure came up with one Byzantine scheme."

"And deadly," Brian said. He adjusted his feet as the car swayed again. "Heinrich Tetzel, Lenore Harte, the two hikers in the Pyrenees, Eduoard DeJonge, your man Merz—six dead. Any more I don't know about?"

"Those were all unplanned. Tetzel was about to reveal information to him"—Eck jerked a thumb at Silver—"so Skyrm convinced me Tetzel's … removal was necessary."

"One death has a way of leading to another," Silver said. "Something else I learned in my profession."

The cable above them groaned and the gondola moved forward again, slower than before. Brian looked at the oncoming station. It appeared to be an open-air platform atop another skeletal structure, this one resembling the upper third of the Eiffel Tower. He saw the second gondola approaching from the Montjuïc station. The cars would pass simultaneously along the outside of the tower, and passengers would exit onto the platform in the center.

Eck grabbed Brian's shoulders and spoke fervidly. "I never intended to harm anyone. This plan was always about sharing a potentially lifesaving technology with the world. I do not want you or Larissa to be hurt. Help me find a way to keep you safe. No one was ever meant to die."

"No one?" Brian asked.

"No one," Eck replied

"Then who was on the plane?"

"What?"

"When your plane crashed into Long Island Sound, your body was identified. Whose body was it?"

Eck was silent.

"If I could hazard a guess," Silver interjected, "I would say it was a homeless man. They're easy enough to find in D.C. He could have gone shopping along the Mall, looking for a man about the right age, with the right build, the right hair. Of course, they would have had to smash his mouth to destroy the dental records. And burn his hands to remove the fingerprints. But I'm sure Skyrm handled that."

Brian knocked Eck's hands away and said, "So don't tell me you intended no harm, not when this scheme began with one man's death." His voice shook. "And it was supposed to end with Professor DeJonge's death, wasn't it? When they find his car, I'm sure they'll find a note, too. Because his suicide will convince Eurocorps that Prometheus is a failure. You intended to murder Professor DeJonge from the start, and it didn't matter a damn to you that you would destroy Larissa's life."

"I can still save her," Eck said. "And you."

Brian stepped back. "I'll be surprised if you can save yourself," he said.

The car pulled alongside the glass-walled station platform and stopped. Eck was startled when the attendant opened the door.

"Forget to bribe this guy, too?" Silver asked.

"Don't let him out," Eck told Silver, who positioned himself between Brian and the door. The station attendant at first registered confusion to see only three people, then he beckoned them to exit. "I am sorry," he said, "but we have to close down the Transbordador Aeri because of high winds. You will be given a refund at the ticket booth below."

"The three of us are supposed to have a private ride to the Montjuïc station," Eck protested. "Check with your supervisor."

"But, sir, the cable car has been temporarily shut down for safety reasons. I am sorry, but your ride today ends here."

The gondola across the station carried a full load of passengers. Brian watched as they filled the platform. Some stood about, waiting for a chance to talk to the attendant. Others moved toward the elevator. Brian positioned himself so the elevator was in the corner of his eye. He judged the distance, rehearsed a move in his mind, and prayed he got the timing right.

"We will wait until the ride resumes," Eck said.

The attendant cleared his throat and spoke with newfound authority. "Regulations instruct that I clear the gondolas during an emergency shutdown. I insist that you exit the gondola, or I will call security and have you removed."

Eck pulled out his wallet. The attendant eyed it greedily. A passenger from the second gondola tapped him on the shoulder. The attendant frowned as he turned away from Eck. In the corner of his eye, Brian saw the elevator door open.

Now! Brian thought.

He twisted at the waist and threw an elbow into Silver's stomach. Silver staggered back two steps and fell into Eck. They both went down. This result was better than Brian had anticipated, but he wasn't going to question his luck. He pushed out of the car and past the attendant. Brian slipped by startled passengers and into the elevator. Some of them regarded him warily as they filed aboard. He ignored their looks and wished the others would just hurry up and get in. The attendant was inside the gondola, bending to help Silver and Eck up. When the last passenger stepped aboard the elevator, Brian hammered the "close door" button.

Eck's face, purple with rage, popped up just as the elevator doors slid shut.

CHAPTER 44--RAMBLAS

The elevator stopped at a platform one floor above street level. Brian bolted the moment the doors opened and scrambled down the stairs. He oriented himself as he ran. Directly in front of him were a scattering of palm trees and weird, circular metal sculptures—they looked like King Kong's Hula Hoops—springing from the concrete. Snaking alongside the jetty to his left was a tubular walkway that Brian figured was for the passengers of the cruise ship just beyond.

To his right, rising above treetops, was the Columbus Monument. Brian fixed his eye on it and put on a burst of speed. The statue was now as important to Brian as the North Star was to the explorer. It would guide Brian to Las Ramblas, and Las Ramblas would lead him to Larissa. He looked at his watch. It was 5:28. He would miss the 5:30 rendezvous, but he had to reach Larissa by 5:45 to stop her from going to the French consulate. The statue looked close, perhaps three blocks away. Brian wasn't sure how far La Boqueria was from there. No time to consult a map. He had to keep running.

Brian looked back to see that the rising elevator was halfway up the tower. The ride down took less than a minute, which meant that Brian's head start on Eck and Silver was now less than two minutes. Not enough time to look for a taxi, even if he wanted to risk taking a cab during rush hour. Brian's feet were his only reliable mode of transportation. Just keep running.

The jetty ended at a traffic circle that was also an exit for an underground roadway. Brian wondered whether to turn right and stick to the harbor front or to follow the curve of the traffic circle. He saw a break in traffic and dashed across the ring road, deciding to follow it to the next street and approach the Columbus Monument from the side. He crossed to that street, turned right at the corner, then flew toward the monument. He blew past the Museo Maritim, an immense building that resembled a row of aircraft hangars.

Brian skidded to a stop at the next corner and scrambled backward into the museum's shadow. Carter and Voss stood at the Columbus Monument's base. Their eyes, like those of explorer above them, scanned the harbor. If not for that break in traffic, Brian would have followed the waterfront and run straight into them.

Brian watched. The men were concentrating on the Mediterranean approach and ignoring the side streets. Carter pulled a cell phone from his pocket and spoke into it. He put it away, said a few words to Voss, and left, heading in the direction of the cable car tower. To meet Eck and Silver halfway, Brian guessed. Voss watched Carter go. Brian took this as his cue to move. He followed the circular route around the monument, remaining on the far side of the pavement. Brian walked quickly, but not fast enough to draw attention. He was careful to keep a knot of three or four people between himself and Voss.

Slowly, Voss turned toward Brian, and Brian ducked his head. Voss continued his rotation unchecked, then returned his gaze to the harbor.

Brian reached the entrance to Las Ramblas and took in the mass of humanity moving up and down the teeming thoroughfare. Vehicles command almost every major street in the world. Cars and trucks rule the broad center, and people stay on the sidewalks. On Las Ramblas the opposite is true. People young and old, fashionable and unkempt, foreign and native, congregate in the wide central boulevard, while cars are shunted to narrow lanes at the sides.

Brian checked his watch. 5:38. Seven minutes. He took a deep breath and plunged into the crowds, weaving as he ran. No point in worrying about the time again. Brian wasn't certain how much distance he had to cover. Either he would reach Larissa in time or he wouldn't. He just had to run as fast as possible and trust his stamina.

Brian lengthened his stride and angled behind a magazine kiosk. He aimed for the edge of the boulevard, where the line of plane trees marked a clear path. Vibrant tableaux flashed by.

Young men hawked lottery tickets. A woman walked a group of eight toddlers in rows of two on a rope harness like a dogsled team. Street performers were nearly as common as the trees: a violinist, a flutist, another harpist. One tune faded into the next. More abundant than the musicians were the living statues: a man painted silver looking like a junkyard Tin Man; a toga-clad woman painted white posing like a chaste Greek goddess; a man painted bright blue reclining on a bed with sheets that matched his skin.

A teenage girl wearing hippie beads elegantly waved a wand and produced a three-foot-long soap bubble. Brian ran through the bubble, bursting it. The girl yelled in his wake. He felt the sting of soap in his eye. Or was that sweat? He ran his hand across his forehead. It was dripping. What was the temperature? Probably in the eighties.

Brian jinked toward the middle to avoid a pair of guitar-slinging young women in black lipstick singing what might have been Nirvana. Four college-age men wearing identical powder blue jerseys hooted their approval in German. Beneath Brian's feet the flagstones alternated between narrow slate-colored rectangles at the boulevard's edges and a wavy pattern of lighter gray stones in the center.

Suddenly the waves gave way to a tile mosaic—cheerful yellow, red, and blue shapes on a white background outlined in thick black. He remembered this mosaic from their reconnaissance that morning. Brian looked up. The row of trees had ceased, and this little plaza was bright in the early evening sun.

On his left was the towering, black iron entry to La Boqueria. The entrance swept up into a peaked archway to resemble a cathedral, the effect completed by the stained-glass windows that framed the structure. The glass glittered with multiple yellow suns against an azure sky. A large medallion bearing La Boqueria's full name hung beneath the apex, and below that a canopy was suspended to provide extra, perhaps redundant, shelter in the cavernous marketplace.

Brian pivoted sharply toward the entrance. The sudden change in momentum caused him to stumble. An elderly couple parted for him as he regained his balance and ran toward La

Boqueria. "Kid must be hungry," he heard the man say in a Brooklyn accent. Even in his rush Brian noted, as he did earlier that day, that to enter Barcelona's grand marketplace you had to pass the familiar pink and orange sign of a Dunkin' Donuts.

Beneath its canopy La Boqueria was an explosion of scenery and a madness of scents. Stacks of fresh fruit radiated primary colors. The aromatic fruit clashed with pungent fish at a nearby counter. The marketplace buzzed of voices haggling with vendors or ordering meals at food counters down the sides. The sights and smells and sounds overwhelmed Brian. He steadied himself by placing his hand on the edge of a table piled with red onions. Panting, he looked around for Larissa but didn't see her. Panic began to take him. He looked at his watch. 5:43. Maybe she wasn't here yet.

He turned toward the entrance. There she was, wearing her backpack and carrying his in her right hand. Larissa's face brightened with relief when she spotted him. She ran to him. Brian bent over with his hands on his thighs for balance. He breathed heavily, worn out as much by anxiety as exertion. Larissa stooped to peer into his face.

"Brian, are you all right?"

"They're looking for us," he said. "We have to get out of here."

Larissa touched the thin fabric of his jersey and felt the sweat. "Were you chased here?"

Brian gasped heavily. "I don't think so."

"What about my father?"

Brian drew his chin to the right to shake his head, and that simple motion told her the answer. Larissa's knees sagged and her expression went slack. Brian raised a hand to her shoulder. "I'm sorry," he said.

"It … it is not a surprise. The longer I waited for you the more I suspected that … I just hoped not to hear it."

"I am so sorry," Brian repeated, wanting to console Larissa but unable to stop panting like an asthmatic Great Dane. He kept finding ways to fail her.

A tear ran down the side of Larissa's nose. She brushed it away. "I have no time to cry," Larissa said. She hardened her features. "You are here. That is what matters. And now we must leave for the consulate."

"No," Brian said, taking another hard breath before he could continue. "They are watching the French consulate. And by now they must be watching the American consulate. That's why I ran so hard, to stop you from walking into a trap."

"What do you mean?"

Brian recounted his conversation with Eck, and how he saw Voss and Carter watching for him at the Columbus Monument. Larissa bought him a bottle of water while he told the story. By the time he finished drinking, he was breathing normally again.

"Where do we go now?" Larissa asked.

"Madrid, I think."

She shook her head. "Oh, Brian, I am so tired of this running."

"I'm not thrilled about it either, but we take the first train to Madrid, and as soon as we arrive we take a taxi to the American embassy, tell our story, and we're done."

"Are you certain?"

"They can't get to us there. We'll be safe, finally."

"Is there nowhere we can go in Barcelona?"

Brian remembered the ending to *Three Days of the Condor*. He said, "Maybe the newspaper. But it could take hours to convince a reporter of our story, and hours longer to convince his—or her—editor." He pointed to his watch. "And the right editor might not be available until the morning. Frankly, I'd rather go to Madrid. We can sleep on the train."

Larissa frowned. "All right, we'll go. I swear you must love trains."

"I've only been on Amtrak from Milwaukee to Chicago before. And there's not much to love about that." Brian hoisted his backpack over his shoulders. "We should take the Metro to the train station. I think I passed a stop on the way here."

Larissa nodded. "Yes, the Liceu station. Follow me."

She led the way back down Las Ramblas. As they walked across the brightly colored mosaic, Larissa said, "Joan Miró made that."

Brian nodded absently. The name didn't mean much to him, except that it triggered an association with the Milwaukee Art Museum.

The Liceu Metro stop was only a block from La Boqueria. As Brian and Larissa approached it, Mathias Skyrm emerged from its stairwell.

Impossible! Brian thought as Skyrm lunged at them.

CHAPTER 45--BIRDS

As if they had practiced the maneuver, Brian and Larissa simultaneously spun on the balls of their feet, joined hands, and scrambled away from Skyrm.

"How did he find us?" Larissa asked loudly.

"I don't know," Brian said. Had Eck or Silver planted a tracking device on him? Brian doubted it. Had Voss spotted him at the Columbus Monument? Perhaps, but Skyrm should have found them sooner.

Brian looked back as they passed over the Miró mosaic. Skyrm was gaining. He didn't break stride as he shoved aside a dark-skinned man who stepped into his path.

Brian and Larissa ran past La Boqueria and continued down Las Ramblas. He had to release her hand as they dodged through a cluster of people watching a juggler in Marcel Marceau makeup. Brian felt his backpack bump into three people as they wove through the group.

"Lose the backpacks!" he called to Larissa. "They're slowing us down."

Brian shrugged the strap off his left shoulder as he turned to look for Skyrm. It was a mistake. Skyrm was only inches behind. He grabbed the strap that had just come free of Brian's left arm and yanked it so hard that the other strap jerked Brian's right shoulder and sent him spinning.

Brian's momentum carried him forward. He plowed into the juggler, and as Brian whirled away he heard rather than saw the man's three wooden clubs hit the concrete with solid thunks. He made two more drunken revolutions toward a table and a bearded man standing behind it. Brian smashed into the table and dropped to the ground, cracking his head on the table's edge as he went down. Immediately he heard the twittering of birds.

Wow, Brian thought, *just like in cartoons!*

Then he shook his head and blinked his eyes and saw he was in some sort of outdoor pet shop. A wall of fish tanks rose from the sidewalk about ten feet opposite him, and all around were booths selling small animals. Some featured mice and gerbils and lizards, but most of the merchants sold birds—birds of many colors and sizes in a variety of cages. The noise of the birds, their chirps and squeals and squawks, intensified into an alarm to warn Brian of Skyrm's attack.

Brian rolled to the side, dodging the first kick. Skyrm's foot lashed forward again—the second half of a double kick—and missed as Brian twisted into a crouch. Brian delivered a swift knife-hand strike to the soft underside of Skyrm's offered knee. The blow connected but had no effect. Brian jumped backward from his crouch and landed upright. He automatically went into the Guard Stance, left leg back, knees slightly bent, and dukes up in relaxed fists between chin and shoulder level, just as Grand Master Kim had drilled into his head several hundred times.

The stance was sheer bravado. Brian had survived their fight in the Cannes because Skyrm didn't expect his young opponent to have martial arts training. That element of surprise was gone. Long gone. Brian with his red belt in tae kwon do was facing a man who probably had a black belt in everything else. Brian gulped.

A small crowd gathered around them as if they were two more street performers. Skyrm adopted no martial arts stance. He stood with his feet together and his arms loose at his sides. His face, though, was tense. His teeth clenched in a taunting grin, and his eyes locked on to Brian's. Caught once more in Skyrm's cobra stare, Brian's awareness of the onlookers vanished. The red rings around Skyrm's irises flared with fury, signaling that he was no longer following anyone's orders.

Skyrm's lips peeled back from his teeth. He said, "At least you choose to die like a man."

The opening strike came like a missile, a left-handed thrust aimed at Brian's throat. Brian's right hand whipped up to deflect the blow, and his forearm erupted in pain as it took the impact. Before Skyrm could strike again, Larissa appeared behind him and swung her backpack at his head. It clipped Skyrm behind the right ear and knocked him off balance. With this opening, Brian scored a straight punch to the stomach but felt his fist bounce off solid abdominal muscles.

Skyrm pushed Brian back then swiveled into a roundhouse kick aimed at Larissa. His heel connected with her hip and sent her flying across the small marketplace into the wall of fish tanks. She caromed off them and fell, moaning as her left knee jammed into the sidewalk.

Brian reflexively moved to help Larissa, and Skyrm took advantage of this tactical error. He grabbed Brian's shirt collar and belt loop and hurled him at a nearby table of birdcages. Brian skidded down the tabletop, sending cages to the ground with a din of crashing metal and squawking birds. He went over the edge with a large birdcage caught beneath his chest. Brian's ribs seared with pain as he landed on the cage. He rolled onto his back and groaned. The cage, now resting next to him, was eighteen inches wide, a little more than two feet tall, and shaped like a dollhouse. At least it looked like a dollhouse until Brian had landed on it. Now it was twisted out of shape. The impact had snapped and bent the wires on the cage's floor into a jagged hole the size of a small melon. A light blue parakeet hopped through the hole and flew away. Some birds flapped and shrieked in the cages that littered the ground. Others lay still, either in shock or dead. Ten feet away a man, probably the fish seller, was helping Larissa to her feet.

Brian's brain recorded all this information in the second it took for him to stand. He was now on the same side of the table as the bird merchant, the bearded man he had noticed before, who was shouting at Skyrm in Spanish. The screeching birds echoed the man's anger. Skyrm drew a semiautomatic pistol from his jacket and pointed it at the bird merchant. The man went silent. The birds continued their keening protests, joined by the cries of people alarmed at the sight of the gun. The bird man gave Brian an apologetic look and scampered into the crowd.

Skyrm turned and waved the gun at the man aiding Larissa, motioning him away from her. The man shook his head. Skyrm shrugged, raised the pistol, and fired. The bullet cracked into one of the fish tanks on the top tier. The pistol's report sent the birds into frenzy. Bystanders yelled and ran. Water spouted momentarily through the small hole in the aquarium, then the glass erupted outward from the force of the escaping water. Larissa put her hands above her head and leaped to the right to avoid the cascade of liquid and glass. The man at her side took off. Multicolored fish flopped wildly on the sidewalk at Larissa's feet. Skyrm laughed and fired at a tank on the other side of Larissa. She screamed as a second watery explosion barely missed her.

"Stop it!" Brian shouted.

Skyrm wheeled around to face Brian, a table of birdcage supplies between them. Skyrm smiled ferociously. "What can you do to stop me?" he said. "Do you need to be reminded how pathetic you are?"

Skyrm kicked the table over. The impact knocked Brian down. Skyrm cackled as tiny bells and small plastic mirrors rained upon Brian. A heavy wooden object rolled into Brian's forearm. It was one of the juggler's clubs, the type that resemble bowling pins with elongated necks. Brian remembered their name. Indian clubs. He lifted the club to test its weight. About three pounds. He glanced about for the other two clubs but didn't see them. Two weapons would have been better than one, but now he had one weapon, which was better than none.

Brian looked up. Skyrm had his back to him and was threatening Larissa. "Don't move, you little bitch," he said. "Or I won't allow your boyfriend the decency to die on his feet."

Brian stood, holding the Indian club in his right hand behind his back. He stepped to the side so that his hip touched the next booth, its tabletop covered with smaller fish tanks and goldfish bowls. Skyrm was an arm's length away.

"I'm on my feet," Brian said.

Skyrm spun about, his hip followed by his gun arm. Brian stepped inside Skyrm's reach and smashed the Indian club into Skyrm's right wrist. The blow drove Skyrm's gun hand onto the tabletop. His eyes popped as Brian again pounded at his wrist. Skyrm grunted, and the gun discharged. The bullet lodged in the tabletop's thick wood. Brian struck once more. Skyrm spat an obscenity and Brian was satisfied he had broken the man's wrist. Skyrm raised his hand. The pistol dangled from his trigger finger for a second and fell into a fish tank.

Brian swung the club at Skyrm's head, but Skyrm's left hand flashed up and caught Brian's wrist, halting the blow an inch from his head. Skyrm tightened his grip and whispered, "I can fight through the pain, boy. Can you?"

Brian took a step back, which gave Skyrm enough room to raise his foot to Brian's chest. He held his foot in the air for a tantalizing moment, then kicked like a pile driver. The force catapulted Brian backward. He felt the club leave his hand as Skyrm released his wrist and heard it clatter to the sidewalk. Then Brian was falling. Pain jolted across his shoulder blades as he crashed into something metal. His forearm burned as he wrenched to the side and his skin scraped across the sidewalk. Brian twisted the other way and was flat on his back. He glanced sideways to see what he had landed on. It was the same birdcage as before. The second impact had widened the hole at its bottom.

Brian tried to sit up but couldn't. His breath was gone. His heart raced with panic as he tried to pull air into his lungs. Above his wheezes he could hear distant sirens. Too distant. Brian knew he had only a few seconds to live unless he could shake this paralysis. He lifted his chin in time to see Larissa make a grab for the fallen club. Skyrm struck her with a backhanded blow that sent her to the ground. He picked up the club with his left hand and advanced on her. Larissa scrabbled backward, but was blocked by the wall of aquariums. Brian took a deep gasp and felt his lungs fill. Larissa clasped her hands above her head protectively. Skyrm raised the club, and Larissa screamed.

Brian moved. Rage, not thought, drove him as he reached for the nearest object to use as a weapon. He felt his strength return as he came to his feet. He resisted the impulse to yell as he took four unsteady but swift steps toward Skyrm. Brian didn't want to give his enemy any warning as he raised the birdcage high and slammed it down on Skyrm's head. The opening at the bottom of the cage was wide enough to slide over the crown of Skyrm's skull. Brian felt resistance as the cage reached the man's temples. Brian jumped straight up, and as he came down he used his weight to drive the cage's floor to Skyrm's shoulders.

The attack caused Skyrm to swing wild. The club thudded against one of the aquariums and missed Larissa. Skyrm whirled about. The wire cage around his head was like a parody of the old metal diving helmets, and Skyrm should have looked absurd. But the face within terrified Brian. A five-inch scratch stretched from Skyrm's forehead down his right cheek and was just starting to well with blood. His wire-framed glasses, now twisted, hung from his left ear. Skyrm's lips curled into a vicious snarl and the rings in his eyes blazed. He threw the club at Brian's head. Brian ducked and heard the club crash into metal behind him. Birds screeched.

Skyrm brought his hands up to the cage and, even with his crippled right wrist, tried to lift it from his head. For Brian, the next few seconds occurred in slow motion. He saw a stray wire puncture Skyrm's neck and draw a crimson gash across the throat as Skyrm pushed the cage upward. Then came a spray of red, and Skyrm's eyes and mouth went wide with shock. "No," he said, his voice barely a whisper. Skyrm's hands flailed as he instinctively tried to put pressure on the severed artery. But the cage was in his way and his hands slapped uselessly at the wire mesh.

Time returned to normal. Screams of women and birds joined the approaching sirens in an ear-splitting chorus. The sirens were coming from the west, perhaps two or three blocks away. Brian reached down to Larissa and pulled her up. Skyrm howled and came after them. He lasted three steps before dropping to his knees.

Brian watched Skyrm keel over to his side. The cage held his head at a grotesque angle as his body settled and Skyrm's blood spilled out and mixed with the water from the shattered aquariums to form pinkish rivulets in the sidewalk cracks. The rings in Skyrm's eyes faded to slate gray, and the man who was so anxious about his reputation died a ridiculous death.

CHAPTER 46--DESPERATE

The whoop and wail of the sirens pierced Brian's consciousness and forced him to tear his eyes away from Skyrm's broken corpse. The sirens were closer now. The fight had lasted less than two minutes, and the police would be here within seconds. Larissa was tugging at Brian, telling him they had to go. She was right. Brian pulled himself together.

He clasped Larissa's hand again, and they sprinted to the east, away from the sirens. No one tried to stop them. They stepped off Las Ramblas to be engulfed by a torrent of people fleeing the violence. Brian tightened his grip on Larissa's hand as the river of people squeezed into a narrow street. He looked about, trying to determine their new surroundings. They had entered a section of Barcelona that clearly dated back to the Middle Ages. The buildings were constructed of ancient stone, as was the street. Only the neon signs indicated they had not just passed through a time portal.

After they had run about two blocks, Brian felt Larissa slowing. He was starting to drag her. He turned to see her face twisted in a grimace of pain. Brian put his arm around her waist and forced their way to the stone wall on their right. They took refuge in the doorway of a closed pharmacy as people continued to flow past.

"Are you all right?" Brian asked.

"My knee hurts terribly," Larissa said. She pulled up her left pant leg to expose her knee. It was swollen and purple.

On the far side of the street, three police officers wearing black berets with red piping pressed against the crowds to make their way toward Las Ramblas.

"I will slow us," Larissa said.

"Don't worry about it. We'll take care of your knee once we

reach the train station." Even as Brian said that, he doubted himself. They would have to find an ice pack for her bruise, and Larissa would need ibuprofen. Why couldn't this pharmacy be open?

"If we become separated," Larissa said, "promise me you will go to Madrid and stop the men who killed my father."

"Don't be ridiculous. I'm not leaving you. Not after that."

"But if we do become separated, I would find the police and let them take me. I would tell enough lies to buy you time."

Larissa's eyes told Brian she was serious. "Well, let's not worry about it," he said slowly, "because we're not going to get separated, OK? I need you, Larissa."

Larissa pulled down her pant leg and nodded. "You are right, we are a team." She pushed herself away from the stone wall. "We should go now while I can still walk."

Brian looked out at the people still packing the cramped street. The panic couldn't last much longer, and he knew they could best avoid the police by remaining lost in this crowd. He took her hand. "All right," he said. "Hold on tight to me and yell if you have to stop."

"OK," Larissa said.

They thrust their way back into the human traffic, which smelled of sweat and stale tobacco. Brian hoped the pace was not too much for Larissa. A slim alley was coming up on the right and several lines of people were moving toward it like river water racing for a tributary. As they neared the alley, Larissa's hand broke from Brian's. He turned to see her being pulled toward the alley as inexorably as he was being pushed beyond it. Larissa gazed over her shoulder to smile at him, and then she faced forward and disappeared into the alley's darkness.

Brian shouted after her and tried to force his way back. A large man behind Brian jeered at him and shoved him forward. Another man pressed up next to the first man, filling the gap Brian had hoped to squeeze through. Brian turned about face and tried to run ahead, but the people surrounding him were packed too tightly to maneuver past.

The mob began to break up at the next intersection, where the narrow street emptied onto a wider one with room for automobile traffic. Brian turned right and ran, hoping to cut down the next street and intercept Larissa in the alley, if he could find it again.

He reached the corner and was about to dash across the street when a compact car slid to a stop in front of him. Jack Silver leaned from the driver's seat to look at Brian through the open passenger window. "Get in!" he yelled.

"Are you insane?" Brian bellowed back. "Not a chance in hell!" He moved to go around the front of the car. Silver pulled forward to block him.

"Brian!" Silver's voice snapped in a way Brian hadn't heard before. He looked back into the car. Silver was pointing a snub-nosed pistol at him.

"Do you know what this means?" Silver asked.

Brian remembered Silver once describing the only reason he would carry a gun. "You're desperate," Brian replied.

"Right. Now get into the car."

Brian looked toward the alley where Larissa had disappeared, and then he opened the passenger door.

CHAPTER 47--NEED

The first thing Brian noticed as he sat was that the dashboard cigarette lighter was missing. Silver caught the direction of his gaze. "Once bitten," he said. The automatic door locks clicked shut as the window next to Brian rose, and he knew he wouldn't be able to make a run for it at the next red light.

Pistol still in hand, Silver pulled into traffic. A voice on the radio spoke clipped, urgent Spanish then went silent. A flat black box with flashing red LED lights sat on the center console. Brian had seen these devices before. It was a police scanner.

"Where's your girlfriend?" Silver asked.

Brian didn't bother to correct Silver's presumption. "We got separated in the crowd a few blocks back and I saw her going down an alley. I was about to try to find her when you cut me off."

Silver pursed his lips. "All right, we'd better find her. Was she heading in this direction?"

"I'm not about to help you capture her."

"Look, Brian, believe it or not I'm trying to—" A new voice on the radio interrupted Silver. Brian recognized the word *niña*.

"So much for finding your girlfriend," Silver said. "It sounds like the police just picked her up." Brian's spirits sank. Silver continued to listen to the police frequency. "Yeah, that must be her," he said. "Sixteen-year-old girl. Asking that they take her to the French consulate."

Brian snatched at that grain of hope. "Will they?"

"Oh, I'm sure they will. She's a French citizen and a minor. The police wouldn't dare question her before contacting the French consulate. And …" Silver paused and looked at Brian. "Her father's body was found about an hour ago. The French will demand that Larissa be turned over to them. The police will comply. You don't have to worry about her. She's safe now."

Brian nodded. If, as he suspected, Larissa let go of his hand on purpose, she had achieved her goal. She had found refuge, and as a bonus, she no longer had to lie to the police to buy Brian time. That point had become moot anyway, considering that Silver was probably driving him back to Eck. And yet something didn't fit. Silver did not seem upset that Larissa was beyond his reach. In fact, he had sounded relieved.

Silver raised his gun and wiggled it. "It ain't easy trying to shift with this thing. If I put it away, you promise not to try to run off or maim me again?"

"All right," Brian said. Silver slipped the gun into a shoulder holster concealed by his jacket. If Brian wanted to grab for the gun, which did not seem like a smart idea, he would have to reach across Silver's body to get it.

"OK," Silver said. "Now for the big question. I assume you were involved in that fight on the Ramblas that lit up the police band a few minutes ago."

Brian nodded.

"So who's the dead body in the bird market?"

"Skyrm," Brian said.

Silver let out a low whistle. "You'd better tell me what happened."

Brian did. When he finished the story, Silver looked at him with a concern Brian did not expect. "How are you feeling?" Silver asked. "Physically, I mean."

"My chest and back are sore, probably bruised. And my shoulder is hurting again."

"Any numbness?"

"No, I don't think so."

"Good, then we don't have to worry about broken bones."

Brian looked out the passenger window. Silver had been driving in widening spirals with no apparent destination. The buildings they were passing appeared more modern, relatively speaking—nineteenth century instead of fourteenth century. The streets were wider, too, allowing a clearer view of the darkening sky.

"How did you find me so quickly?"

"Same way Skyrm did, I imagine. Your tradecraft so far has

been textbook. So you probably followed the rules to set up a fallback rendezvous with Larissa. Pick a busy place with lots of pedestrian traffic. You've never been to Barcelona before, so you were likely to choose either the Ramblas or La Sagrada Família."

"I was predictable," Brian said. He slouched his shoulders and sank into his seat.

"If it makes you feel better, I was halfway to La Sagrada Família when the scanner went nuts with reports of a man attacking some teenagers near La Boqueria. I did a U-turn on the spot—which, by the way, they don't care for around here—and hauled ass for the Ramblas. When I spotted that mob running from the scene, I hoped to see your face. And there you were." Silver bumped a fist on the steering wheel. "I was terrified it was going to be a repeat of Toulouse, when Skyrm got to that DIA woman before I could."

Brian looked at Silver in surprise. "You were trying to save her?"

Silver sighed. "My moral compass may be wobbly, Brian, but I wasn't going to let them murder a fellow American intelligence officer."

Brian let this sink in. "On the cable car, you knocked Eck down on purpose. You helped me get away."

Silver nodded.

"So you're not working for Eck?"

"Not willingly. Skyrm learned about my financial arrangement with Tetzel. He blackmailed me into helping them find you after they grabbed me in Nice." Silver gave Brian a sharp look. "I was a sitting duck once you caused that fender bender and rabbited."

Brian looked at the gauze wrapped around Silver's right hand. He shrugged. "You kidnapped me."

Silver waved his other hand dismissively. "It probably worked out for the best. Otherwise they would have grabbed us both in Nice. End of story."

Silver took a wide left onto a broad boulevard. The buildings around them were glass and steel. Brian looked up at a skyscraper that resembled a forty-story bullet covered in lights that shimmered from red to blue. They had driven back into the twenty-first century.

"Eck still thinks I'm a member of the search party out to find you," Silver continued. "And from all the times I've felt my cell phone vibrate in the last half hour, I'd say he's getting impatient."

"Then let me go," Brian said. "Take me to the American consulate."

"I can't."

"Why the hell not?"

They were stopped at a red light. Silver twisted in his seat to look squarely at Brian. "I need to know where you hid that Prometheus prototype after you left the warehouse last night."

Brian shook his head. "That's the same question Eck asked me on the cable car, and you just admitted you've been working for him. Do you think I'm stupid?"

"No. You're not stupid," Silver said, accelerating as the light changed. "But you are smart enough to see we both have the same need."

"And what's that?"

"Look, I've spent the last few days collaborating with a traitor to my country and one of Interpol's most wanted criminals. The CIA hasn't heard from me since Switzerland, and if I'm lucky they think I've gone to ground or been captured." Silver jabbed the dashboard with his index finger. "The only way I'm going to get out of this without a prison sentence is to deliver Eck and his stolen weapon system all wrapped up in a nice big bow. I've got to come out of this looking like Foster goddamned Blake."

Silver took a calming breath. "So I need your help, Brian. And you need mine. You want this to be over, don't you? You want to be back with your school friends. You want to call your mother and tell her everything is all right. You want Larissa to be able to return home. Help me bring Eck down, and this could end tonight."

"What about Kralik and those other goons?"

"Once they hear Skyrm is dead, they'll take off. Skyrm was this operation's architect and strong man. Without him, Eck has nothing. He'll want to flee, too, but he's supposed to meet a potential buyer tonight. That's why he needs the prototype. The buyers want the prototype as well as the Prometheus van. So at least tell me the prototype isn't in Barcelona."

Brian studied Silver's face. The CIA man had not pleaded. He had laid out his case logically. The only way to end this quickly was to cooperate.

"We never took the prototype out of the warehouse," Brian said. "We put it in a crate, then I used a forklift to stack it with the other crates. When we stole the van, we wanted Eck to think we took the prototype with us. I guess it worked."

Silver laughed and clapped Brian's shoulder. "Oh, it worked, all right. Eck about had a seizure when they saw the prototype was missing." Silver's laugh faded. "Now we just need to find Eck and the Prometheus van." He looked at Brian. "What were those delivery vans you mentioned on the cable car?"

"You mean you don't know?"

"Eck never took me into his full confidence."

Brian told him about Barcelona Paquete Servicio. Silver pulled an iPhone from his jacket pocket and tapped the virtual keypad while he kept the steering wheel steady with his knees.

"That's the third cell phone I've seen you use," Brian said.

"One for every alias," Silver replied. "Ah, here it is. Barcelona Paquete Servicio has its main distribution center near the port. That's where the Prometheus van should be hiding in plain sight." At the next intersection, Silver turned south, toward the Mediterranean.

"Are you ready for this mission's end phase?" he asked

"Yes," Brian replied. A shiver of excitement shot through him. "Yes I am."

CHAPTER 48--TRESPASS

Brian recognized many of the landmarks as Silver drove along the seafront highway. Lighted by intense beams from below, Columbus blazed atop his monument like a golden specter against the indigo sky. On the left was the cable car's central tower. Brian squinted to see the thick black lines and spotted the cables just as they drove beneath them. He lost them again in the shadows of Montjuïc.

The cable car's path appeared to be a border between the city's tourist and shipping areas. The buildings along the waterfront transitioned to warehouses and fuel depots. The length of an enormous container ship flashed between rows of industrial buildings. Brian took a look at Montjuïc to the right and was puzzled to see tiers of ancient stone battlements—ancient except for clusters of windows—arranged like jumbled shelves from midway up the steep hill to its top.

"That's a cemetery, believe it or not," Silver said. "Those windows are all graves."

"On top of each other?"

"Yeah, they stack 'em up here, just like in New Orleans."

Brian nodded. He could make out roads in the cemetery twisting among the bizarre constructs.

Silver exited the highway and zigzagged among narrow warehouses before finding a place to park.

"I don't suppose it will do any good to ask you to wait in the car?" Silver asked.

"No."

"Of course not, but let the record show I took a stab at playing the responsible adult."

As the automatic locks popped open and Silver got out of the car, Brian considered making a run for it. But where? Silver seemed to read his thoughts. "You could go to the police, of course. But think of the complications. One of your parents will have to come to Barcelona. It would be an expensive trip. You will be tangled in red tape for days, maybe weeks. And while all that is going on, Eck will escape and get away with all the misery he's caused. And the deaths."

Brian thought of Lenore Harte and Professor DeJonge, and the two hikers in the Pyrenees, then got out of the car. "I wasn't going anywhere."

"Didn't think so," Silver said. He stepped to the rear of the car and opened the hatch. Brian followed. Silver stripped off his blazer and took a navy blue windbreaker from the cargo area. As Silver put the windbreaker on, Brian saw its pockets were heavy. "A stylish tool kit," Silver said. He zipped the jacket just high enough to hide the butt of the pistol hanging beneath his armpit.

"Our priority," Silver told Brian, "is recovering the Prometheus van. If we don't see Eck, fine. Once we have the van, his operation is a washout and the CIA should have no problem tracking him down. Understood?"

Brian nodded.

"OK, then let's go."

Silver led him down a series of alleyways. He kept to the shadows without obviously lurking. Brian copied his movements. In a few minutes they were across the street from a low, box-like building about the length of a football field and twice the width. A vast parking lot surrounded the building, and an eight-foot-tall chain link fence, topped by three strands of barbed wire leaning outward, surrounded the parking lot. The side of the building facing them was lined with empty truck bays numbered one to twenty-five. On their left was a gate, now closed. Above the gate, high enough to clear the roof of a semi-trailer, were the words *Barcelona Paquete Servicio*. Just inside the gate was an empty guardhouse.

Silver nodded at the guardhouse. "That we avoid," he said. "Let's find a better way in."

They slinked counterclockwise from building to building. At each alley they slipped into the darkest corner and crouched near the wall while Silver pulled out a small pair of binoculars and studied Eck's base. Silver would nod when he was satisfied, and the pair moved on to the next alley. When a car passed, which happened four times, they retreated down the alleyway to a point where the headlights could not penetrate the darkness.

After roughly thirty minutes they reached the far side of the shipping center. There were no outbuildings, just a set of fuel pumps covered by a metal awning. Beyond the pumps were two large garage doors. Brian presumed the delivery vans were behind those doors.

As they stole around the huge warehouse, Brian counted only two cars in the parking lot. The lot was illuminated by a grid of light poles, each bearing a single cone-shaped lamp. Each lamp gave off a bright yellow glow except one, the one directly across from them. Beneath this broken lamp a section of the fence blended into the shadows.

"Is that our way in?" Brian asked.

"Probably," Silver replied. "I just want to make sure." He raised the binoculars to his eyes. "What have you noticed so far?"

"Nothing," Brian said.

"Yeah, and that's strange."

"Why?"

"A big shipping center like this should be a twenty-four/seven operation, but there's no activity. We've been watching the place for nearly forty minutes and not one truck has pulled in. And not that I expect to see a full parking lot during the night shift, but there should be more than two cars."

Silver lowered the binoculars. "And why is no one in the guardhouse? There should be guards."

"Maybe they're inside protecting the Prometheus van."

"That would make sense. And I know I shouldn't complain because it's much easier to break into an empty building, but things are not as they should be, and that makes us professional spy-types wary."

"So are we going to just sit and watch?"

"No, we go in." Silver looked at Brian soberly. "Unless you want to wait here. I'll grab you on the way out."

"Sit here by myself in the middle of the night by the Barcelona docks? I'll probably be safer with you."

Silver nodded. "OK, here's how we get in." He waved a hand

back and forth to indicate the length of the fence. "No cameras on the perimeter," he said. "We'll have no problems getting through the fence at that nice dark spot. I'm making the risky assumption the fence isn't alarmed, because I'm sure our friend Eck doesn't want to summon the police."

Silver pointed to a door about fifty feet from the garage entrance. "We'll go through that door. There's a camera above it, so we'll have to approach it by sliding along the wall. After you get through the fence, head right there." Silver pointed to a spot another sixty feet to the right of the door.

"Where the electrical box is?"

"Right. Now, once you're through the fence, run fast and straight. None of that serpentine shit."

"Got it."

Silver produced a pair of wire cutters from his jacket. "Sit tight while I deal with the fence."

Silver slipped across the alley to a fence post in the pocket of darkness beneath the broken lamp. Starting at the height of his shoulders and working downward he clipped the strands of the fence where they met the post. After cutting the last link, he pulled the fence up like a page of a tablet and signaled Brian.

Brian shot across the alley and through the triangle that Silver held open for him, then veered toward the electrical box. He heard a metallic shimmy behind him as Silver released the fence. Brian looked over his shoulder to see Silver running fast despite his bum leg.

The wall's shadow hid them once more. Silver took a moment to catch his breath. Then, with theirs backs pressed to the wall, he and Brian edged toward the door.

When they got within fifteen feet of the door, Brian asked, "How are you going to take care of the camera? With an EMP grenade?"

Silver chuckled. "Where'd you get a crazy idea like that?"

"In the Foster Blake video games you always take out surveillance cameras with an EMP grenade."

"No," Silver said. "I have something more old-fashioned in mind." He pulled out his gun and screwed a silencer into its muzzle. He aimed at the camera and fired. A quiet *phut* sounded. Silver swore and fired twice more before the camera jerked and

236

hung from its perch like a drunken bird. Glass from its shattered lens fell to the blacktop.

"Three shots." Silver shook his head. "I'm out of practice."

Then he was kneeling before the doorknob, working at it with a lock pick from his pocket. The lock clicked, and he pushed the door open. "At least I haven't lost all my nefarious skills," Silver said.

They stepped inside to a lighted hallway. Brian didn't like the lights; they meant someone was in the building. He and Silver turned to the left, where they knew the garage bay would be. Silver stopped at a bulletin board next to the door.

"Well, this explains a lot," he said.

"What?"

"This notice says that as of yesterday evening, Barcelona Paquete Servicio will be closed for three days while they install a new computer system. It was posted a week ago."

"Eck didn't want anyone around while he closed up his operation," Brian said.

A door down the corridor opened, and a heavyset guard stepped into the hall. He dropped his cup of vending machine coffee at the sight of the intruders and reached for the holster at his hip.

CHAPTER 49--DELIVERY

Silver charged at the guard, hurling his lock-pick set at the man as if it were a throwing knife. The guard instinctively brought up his left arm to shield himself from the projectile, giving Silver the extra split second he needed to tackle the guard before his pistol cleared its holster. The two men struggled on the ground for a few moments before a crackle sounded. The guard grimaced and arched his back, then went limp. Silver stood, holding the same stun gun he had used against Brian in France.

Silver extracted plastic restraints from inside his windbreaker. "Help me with this," he said. Brian crouched beside him and they bound the guard's wrist and ankles. Silver improvised a gag using the man's socks, which Brian found disgusting. They dragged the guard into the room he had exited, a break room, and deposited him in a gap between the soda machine and the wall. Silver took the guard's pistol, a semiautomatic Beretta, and shoved it into his outside jacket pocket.

"Let's hope he was alone," Silver said as they reentered the hall. They hurried down the corridor to a door at the end, which they assumed led to the garage.

They listened at the door for a full minute, but heard nothing from the other side. Silver drew his own pistol and put his left hand back on the doorknob. "I'll make sure the coast is clear, then let you in." He went through the door and closed it behind him.

Brian counted two minutes before Silver opened the door and told him it was safe to enter. Banks of fluorescent lights hummed overhead. Brian felt vulnerable in the brightness.

The ceiling of the vehicle bay was higher than Brian expected, and the interior dimensions wider. Before them stood several dozen Mercedes-Benz Sprinters parked in five rows. Each was maroon. Each had a ladder on the left rear door. Each had Barcelona Paquete Servicio emblazoned on the side. Each was identical in every detail.

"Looks like there's about sixty of them," Silver said. "Not exactly a needle in a haystack, but it will take a while to figure out which one has the Prometheus gun, assuming it's still here." He slid his pistol back into its shoulder holster and pulled out the lock pick. "We've got a lot of doors to open."

"Slap the sides," Brian said.

"What?"

"You don't have to open the doors, just slap the sides. The regular vans should be empty, so they'll feel hollow. But the Prometheus van will be packed with electronics and the weapon itself. Hit the side, and it will feel solid."

Silver patted Brian on the back. "I knew I brought you for a reason." He nodded at the closest van. "You take the near row, I'll start with the far row and we'll meet in the middle, OK?"

Silver hurried away. Brian took another look around the huge garage as he jogged toward the first van. The expanse smelled of oil, grease, and lingering exhaust fumes. A repair bay with a vehicle lift and red toolboxes as tall as bookcases was in the far corner. Six maroon motor scooters were lined against the wall near the garage doors. Brian guessed they were for delivering small parcels within the city.

He came to the first van and smacked the side. A hollow thunk sounded. Across the bay a fainter version of the sound echoed, signaling that Silver had begun as well. Their quest turned into a call-and-response of thuds and whumps, but the strange percussion ended sooner than Brian expected. He came to the final van in the first row and slapped the cargo wall. The result was a solid thwack that left his palm tingling. He smacked the van again. It was like hitting a steel wall.

"I found it," he called.

Silver was at Brian's side within seconds. He pounded the side of van with the side of his fist. "Cripes," he said. "This must weigh as much as a tank."

Silver dropped to his knees and peered beneath the van. "This is some heavy-duty suspension, and I'd say that's armor plating covering the gas tank." He got back up. "Safe to say this is not an ordinary delivery van. It's Superman disguised as Clark Kent."

Brian rolled his eyes. He had to get stuck with a DC guy.

Silver walked around the van, pulled out his pick again and went to work on the rear door's handle. In less than five seconds the door popped open. Silver grasped the handle, then let go. He turned to Brian. "I believe this honor belongs to you," he said.

Brian pulled the door open. They did not have to stoop when they climbed inside, even though the van's ceiling was two feet lower than normal to accommodate the Prometheus gun hidden beneath the roof. A control center filled with switches, buttons, and lights was built into the cargo area's right wall. A seat, more like an old-time tractor saddle, was attached to the floor on a pedestal. A ten-inch screen was positioned in front of the seat. Beneath the screen was a console with a keyboard and a military-style joystick. There was no barrier between the driver's compartment and the weaponized cargo space.

Silver whistled. "I am satisfied, Brian, that we have attained our target objective." He grinned like a buccaneer who had found a trove of Spanish doubloons.

Silver pointed to the garage doors. "You go open that while I hot-wire this baby." His grin widened. "I'll pick you up on the way out, and mission accomplished."

"What about Eck?"

"Don't worry about Eck. We've got Prometheus and that's what matters."

Brian hopped out of the van. Silver followed. "I thought you were going to hot-wire the van," Brian said.

"I just want to take a quick look at the roof," Silver said, reaching for the ladder. "To get an idea how the weapon works."

Brian trotted to the garage doors and wondered where Eck had gone. He doubted the man would leave Barcelona without Prometheus. If the guard belonged to one of the cars in the parking lot, did Eck belong to the second?

At the garage door, Brian took a closer look at the motor scooters. They were Honda Leads. A helmet and ignition key hung from hooks on the wall above each scooter.

Brian found a pair of buttons six inches from the doors. He

pressed the top one, and the left door rose with a clatter. Brian turned toward the Prometheus van. Silver, his back to Brian, was coming down the ladder. Brian heard the hastening footsteps first, then saw Roland Eck run from between two of the maroon Sprinters holding a large wrench above his head.

Brian shouted a warning, but Eck had already swung the wrench into Silver's midsection. With his hands and feet on the ladder, Silver could not defend himself. He let out an agonized cry as he fell. Eck brought the wrench down on Silver's neck, and Silver went still.

Brian rushed to help Silver. Eck reached beneath the CIA man's armpit and pulled out his gun. He wheeled around and fired.

The bullet ricocheted off the concrete floor fifteen feet to Brian's right. Brian threw himself behind the nearest van. Eck fired again, this time into the rafters. One of the fluorescent lights near the far wall exploded.

"Stay back, Brian," Eck shouted. "Don't force me to shoot you!"

Brian looked beneath the van but couldn't see Eck and Silver. He peered around the rear bumper to see Eck stuffing Silver into the rear of the Prometheus van. Eck spun around again, pistol at his side like a gunfighter, and Brian ducked back. Another *phut* sounded, but Brian couldn't tell where the bullet went.

Brian heard the rear door of the Prometheus van slam shut. He crawled to the cab of the Sprinter that was hiding him, then dropped to the floor and rolled to the next van. Another door banged shut and an engine fired. Brian got up and ran down the row as he heard the sharp chirp of rubber on concrete resound within the vast bay. Then the engine roared as Eck stepped on the accelerator. Brian emerged from between two vans, and Eck waved the gun at him menacingly but didn't fire.

Brian bitterly recalled Silver's assured "mission accomplished" as he stood there and watched Eck speed past him in the target objective and out the garage door he had just opened.

CHAPTER 50--GRAVES

Brian stared into the void beyond the open door as the chill of failure crept across his skin. Then his eyes found the motor scooters parked beside the entrance. He ran toward them. He still had a chance! He squeezed a helmet onto his head and snatched the first key from the wall. Brian hopped on the nearest scooter and started the ignition. While the engine purred to life, Brian aimed the front tire at the door. He twisted the right-grip accelerator and sped out of the garage in time to see the van disappear behind a corner of the warehouse.

Zipping across the parking lot, Brian purged his mind of hopeless thoughts. Sure, the chances of catching the van on this little Honda were slim, but the alternative was to remain in the warehouse and admit defeat. And, anyway, what could he do then? Call the police? Brian knew maybe ten words of Spanish, and they didn't include "stolen American weapon." Call the American consulate? By the time Brian reached someone who would listen, Eck would be out of the country and Silver would be dead (Brian didn't want to admit, not even in his thoughts, that Silver might be dead already). No, Brian would snatch at even this meager chance of catching Eck. He would chase the Prometheus van until its taillights vanished in the distance. At the very least he would memorize the license plate number to pass along to the American consulate.

Brian rounded the building's corner and saw that he had caught a break. The van was slowing as it approached the gate. Brian twisted the accelerator grip to its limit and steered toward the van. The gate opened with a jerk, then rolled smoothly to one side. The Sprinter stopped, waiting until it had enough room to pass. Brian's hope surged. The loud mosquito whine of the Honda's engine bounced off the warehouse wall as Brian cut across the empty lot. Eck certainly had spotted him by now, but Brian didn't care. The distance between him and the van shrank by the second. He was within two hundred feet.

The van bounded ahead the moment it could fit through the gate. Eck would gain speed again, but Brian had made up for the time he lost getting on the scooter. He smiled.

The gate juddered to a halt, then reversed direction. Brian's smile vanished. Was he going fast enough to clear the gate before it closed? He already had the accelerator opened to its max. Brian leaned forward to coax extra speed from the bike.

The gap in the fence was less than five feet and Brian was twenty yards away. The gate seemed to be closing faster than it had opened, but Brian was sure that was his imagination. He had to keep his nerve. He would not lose a game of chicken to a gate. He told himself he needed an opening of only two feet to slip through. Possibly less.

Brian drew his elbows to his rib cage as he rushed at the swiftly shrinking gap. One foot to go. Six inches. Now! With extraordinary willpower he kept his eyes focused straight ahead, even as the gate lunged into his peripheral vision. Was he clear? Brian checked the rearview mirror and saw the gate threaten to clip his rear tire, but it clanged shut without hitting the bike. If he had been one millimeter or millisecond off—

But that didn't matter anymore. He was outside and needed to keep up with the Sprinter. Eck had gone to the left after the gate. Brian turned, but too sharply for his speed. He felt the rear tire slide away. He leaned into the skid, eased up on the accelerator, and tapped the rear brake. Instantly he was upright again and the handlebar stable in his grasp. The van was three blocks ahead. Brian twisted the accelerator.

This was not Brian's first time on a motor scooter. Last September when Tim's older sister, Peggy, got a Vespa for her birthday, she let Tim and Brian take turns riding it around the neighborhood. But those were the familiar streets of Wauwatosa in the daylight, and these were the unfamiliar docks of Barcelona at night.

The Sprinter turned right. Brian followed. He wasn't worried about losing Eck just yet. As long as the chase stayed within the short, narrow streets of the warehouse district, Eck wouldn't find the speed to pull away. Once they reached a main road, though, Eck would escape easily. Brian had to press his advantages while he could. Ahead of him the van braked hard as a tractor-trailer trundled into its path. Brian was within half a block of the van before Eck could move again. The Sprinter turned left.

A house cat chasing a tiger, Brian wasn't sure what he would do if he caught up to Eck. He recalled one his favorite Foster Blake lines. In *To the Point of Insanity*, Regency Sommers asked what their plan would be once they infiltrated Koziakin's heroin processing lab. Brian smiled and repeated Blake's suave reply: "When it happens, I'll know."

Brian remained within a block's length of the van as the two vehicles hurried through a valley of warehouses. The wind sliced through the thin fabric of Brian's FCB jersey. A dark mass loomed ahead. It was not another building, but Montjuïc. They had reached the highway that hugged the bottom of the great hill. Brian's hope sank. He was certain to lose the van in a few minutes. He looked at the license plate: BMT306R with a Spanish EU tag. He fixed the number in his mind.

Eck turned right onto the highway, toward Barcelona. Brian had expected him to turn left, toward the countryside. This could be another break. Brian turned onto the highway just as the van's taillights disappeared behind a bend. Across the highway a stone wall ran along the foot of Montjuïc. It marked the cemetery Silver had pointed out earlier.

Brian rounded the bend, and he saw that the Sprinter had pulled into the cemetery's entrance, an alcove where the stone walls curved away from the road. Eck was out of the van and pushing open the cemetery's towering iron gate. What was this about? Brian remembered Silver saying that Eck was supposed to meet a potential buyer tonight. This could be the meeting site. It made sense. The deal was unlikely to be interrupted in a secluded, darkened cemetery. Eck could have bribed the night watchman to leave the gate unlocked and disappear for a few hours.

Spotting a break in traffic, Brian cut across the highway and swerved into the alcove just as Eck returned to the driver's seat. The van's engine roared as the Sprinter entered the hillside cemetery. Eck had left the gate open—he likely had no choice with Brian so close—and Brian lagged only twenty feet behind as he sped past the tall iron bars.

The scenery racing alongside him was surreal. The graves, as Silver had said, were above ground, regal marble boxes arrayed along the hill. Statues stood solemnly over many of these tombs and reclined sadly alongside others. A few alabaster figures prostrated themselves across graves in eternal anguish. Angels dominated the statue population, as Brian would have guessed, but there also were beautiful, seminude women dancing and laughing. Brian glanced upward. Statues became scarce halfway up the hill, and higher above were the imposing stone and glass bulwarks he had seen from Silver's car.

The road straightened and the van increased its lead. Brian accelerated, but the road had become an incline. He scanned the path ahead and saw that the road was a ribbon that zigzagged through the gravesites and ascended the hillside in a series of hairpin curves and long straightaways. The road had to lead to another entrance at the top of Montjuïc. Brian pictured Eck's buyer waiting within that upper gate.

The van's tires squealed when it entered the first curve. Eck was taking it too fast. The van fishtailed, knocking over a decorative bench alongside the curve. Then the tires found their grip on the pavement, and the Sprinter powered up the first long straightaway.

Brian hoped he could take advantage of Eck's driving error. But by the time Brian rounded the bend, Eck was halfway to the next turn. The Honda's four-stroke engine was no match for the Sprinter on this slope. Brian released the right grip and let the bike slow until he could leap from it safely. The momentum from his jump propelled him toward stone steps at the straightaway's midpoint. These steps rose through the next level of graves and upward. Perhaps if he took this direct route through the tombs he could reach the top before Eck, who had to drive to and fro up the road. Pulling off the helmet, Brian looked toward the van and saw its ruby brake lights brighten as it approached the next curve. It appeared Eck would take each hairpin cautiously now.

And then Brian knew what to do. It had happened, and he knew.

Instead of continuing straight up the stairs, he left them and ran through the tombs, ascending the hill at an angle that would take him to the next switchback curve on the left. Silently asking forgiveness of the souls he might be disturbing, Brian hopped from grave to grave as if they were platforms on a playground jungle gym. His shadow lengthened and danced across a dozen statues as the van's headlights passed above him. He reached the road just as the van rounded the bend about thirty feet away.

Next time, Brian thought.

His destination, the next left-hand bend on the winding path, was up two levels. Brian ran across the roadway and was among the statues again. He hustled through the monuments, climbing them when necessary. He had to squeeze past a weeping angel, her head buried in her hands, before he reached the road's next level. He looked to the right. The Sprinter was nearing the straightaway's end. Brian darted across the road and into another copse of graves. He climbed through them quickly until he reached his destination.

At the edge of the pavement, Brian crouched behind an arch-shaped monument and peered around it. The Sprinter had come around the far curve and was heading upward toward him. Brian moved his head back. The eerie panorama below caught his eye. Sloping away from him were hundreds of statues shimmering silver like ghosts in the moonlight.

The van was almost upon him. Brian tensed his legs. The headlights swept by, and the Sprinter slowed as it approached the curve. Brian emptied his mind of thought that could create doubt. The moment the rear bumper passed him, Brian vaulted from his hiding space and ran behind the van. He took three long strides and leaped for the ladder welded to the rear door.

CHAPTER 51--CLINGING

Brian snatched the third rung with his left hand and the side of ladder with his right. The balls of his feet landed squarely on the three-inch ledge that ran beneath the twin doors. As the Sprinter entered the hairpin curve, Brian locked his right elbow around the ladder and hung on with his left hand. The van rounded the corner and centrifugal force tried to tear Brian away. He hugged the ladder tighter, pressing his cheek into one of the rungs and wedging his feet inside the ladder's frame. Then the force trying to jerk Brian off the ladder ceased and the van accelerated up the next straightaway.

Brian transferred his left hand to the ladder's side and reached for the door handle with his right. He wrapped his fingers around the handle and extended his right leg for balance. He hoped the door remained unlocked after Silver had jimmied it. Brian pressed his thumb into the handle and smiled as the button gave way. He pulled at the door. With the van heading up an incline, gravity took over and the door swung open. Brian didn't let go of the handle fast enough, and the door swatted him backward. He grabbed the inside of the doorframe and regained balance. He repositioned his right foot and slid his face a few inches along the cool steel of the van. When he felt the door's edge against his cheek, he turned his head and looked inside.

Silver was pitched along the floor, his feet pointed toward the door. Brian couldn't tell if he was breathing. Eck was twisted around in the driver's seat glaring back at him. Brian expected to see surprise in Eck's eyes. He saw rage instead.

"Skyrm was right about killing you!" Eck yelled. He reached for something in the passenger seat and came up holding Silver's pistol.

Before Eck could aim, Brian snapped his head back behind

cover. He let go of the doorframe as he heard a silenced shot and lost his balance. His right foot slipped off the ledge, and he reeled into space. He saw the blur of the roadway beneath him and gripped the ladder in his left hand so tightly it bit into his palm. Spread-eagled, Brian flapped behind the van like an idiotic pennant.

Another *phut* sounded. Then another. Brian's left foot was losing its purchase on the ledge. He twisted at the waist and grabbed the ladder with his other hand just as his left foot gave way. He pulled himself hard against the ladder as he slipped downward. His left knee smashed into the ledge. Brian grunted at the sudden jabbing pain, but brought his right knee alongside the left. He thought he heard one or two more shots before Eck began to swear loudly. Was he out of bullets? Brian hoped so, but he had more to worry about at the moment.

He leaned forward and wrapped his arms behind the ladder, locking himself in place by grasping the opposite forearm with each hand. He was now kneeling on the ledge and clinging to the ladder. Muscles that had gone taut with panic relaxed as Brian sensed his balance returning. And then he was yanked to the right as if grabbed by an invisible monster.

The van was hurtling around the next curve. Preoccupied with the gun, Eck must not have had the time to slow down and was taking the left turn at a dangerous speed. The tires wailed like banshees at the abuse, and Brian's knees slid out from under him. His jaw bounced off a rung, but his arms continued to grip the ladder like a vise. The inside of his left elbow felt like it had been kicked. The rear door reeled wide with the centrifugal force. The tires' keening rose in pitch. Brian felt the van tilt tip and feared Eck was going to roll it. He heard a loud whump to his right and turned his head in time to see the door flying right at him. He snatched his legs back just before the swinging door could crush them. A granite cross that the door had smashed into toppled as the van rushed past. Its pieces skidded up the roadway, chasing the Sprinter until they lost momentum.

The van entered the next uphill straightaway. Its suspension resettled with a bounce. The door fell open, no longer a threat. Brian was sitting half twisted. His knees were at his chest, but his feet were still on the ledge and keeping him stable.

He pulled himself up the ladder until he was standing. Eck would have needed both hands on the steering wheel to take that corner, so Brian was willing to bet he had dropped the gun. Had Eck fired its final round? Brian had to put that question out of his mind. Eck's next tactic would be to swerve until he shook Brian off the van. Brian had to get inside before that happened.

He stretched his right leg toward the opening, then grabbed the doorframe's inner edge. He slid his torso along the closed left-door panel and hooked his right foot inside the door. Brian released the ladder and felt an instant of vertigo before his left hand found the doorframe.

Brian heaved himself into the van.

He was wrong about the gun. As Brian landed in a heap behind Silver, Eck turned to face him. He reached into his lap and retrieved the pistol. He pointed the gun at Brian's forehead.

"I'm sorry," Eck said, and he pulled the trigger.

The hammer fell on an empty chamber with a click.

"You're sorry, all right," Brian said. He stood, attempting to demonstrate a sense of control.

Brian expected Eck to throw the gun at him. Instead Eck dropped it into the passenger-side foot well.

"Stop the van," Brian said. "The CIA is after you already. Silver called for backup when we arrived at the warehouse."

Eck returned his attention to the roadway. "Silver wouldn't dare call the CIA," he said to the windshield.

So much for that bluff, Brian thought. "You'll have to stop soon. How are you going to explain me and Silver to your buyer?"

Eck's head snapped around. The shock on his face told Brian he had guessed correctly about the buyer.

"I'll make you regret jumping through that door," Eck said. The engine revved and the acceleration tugged Brian backward. Silver groaned, stirred, and went still again.

Eck continued to accelerate into the next corner and took it hard. The tires shrieked, and Brian bounced against the wall. Silver rolled into Brian's shins, knocking him off balance. Brian threw his hands out to break his fall and crashed into the Prometheus control panel. He grabbed at the joystick and used it to pull himself upright as Eck straightened out the van.

Eck glanced back at him. "Don't touch that!" he cried.

Brian pushed a button next to the joystick. "Stop that!" Eck yelled, then got his eyes back to the road.

"If you don't want me to play with your precious machine," Brian said as he flipped a switch, "come back here and stop me."

Brian's fingers played over more buttons and switches, but nothing happened. The engine growled as Eck increased speed. The only way to force Eck to stop was to turn Prometheus on. Brian studied the panel. Just beneath the video screen he spied a button marked with a bisected circle, the universal symbol for *power*. Brian pressed the button. The circular symbol glowed green, and red LED pinpricks illuminated across the panel as Prometheus hummed to life.

Eck looked back. "Turn it off!"

"Make me," Brian shouted. He pushed a series of buttons on an overhead panel and heard a loud whir and then a whoosh from above. The Prometheus gun was rising through the roof.

Eck jerked the steering wheel back and forth. Brian flew toward the far wall, tripping over Silver. He landed alongside Silver, their faces close together. Silver moaned but didn't move. As Brian sat up his hand brushed against Silver's jacket and felt something hard and metallic. The Beretta Silver had taken from the warehouse guard! Brian tugged the gun from Silver's pocket and stood.

"Stop the van," he said.

Eck looked at Brian, then the Beretta, then back at Brian. "You wouldn't dare," he said. A bead of sweat rolled past his right eye.

"At this point, I think I probably would," Brian said. "Stop the van."

Eck turned back to the roadway. Brian looked past him through the windshield. He saw the fortress-like graves that were near the top of the hill and wondered how close they were to the upper gate and Eck's buyer. The next curve was thirty feet ahead. Eck sped up.

Without hesitating, Brian leveled the pistol and squeezed the trigger.

CHAPTER 52--GATE

Brian had prepared himself for the pistol's kick, but not its bang. Within the Sprinter's compact interior, the shot boomed like a thunderclap. A deep ringing in Brian's eardrums replaced his sense of hearing. He watched Eck's mouth form angry words, but they were lost to the dull tone inside his head.

Brian turned from Eck and saw tiny sparks flicker inside the neat hole he had just shot through the video monitor. Brian marveled that it was a perfect circle, with only a few hairline cracks radiating outward. With one bullet he had rendered the Prometheus weapon unfit for sale. Would a second bullet damage it beyond repair?

Before Brian could try, the entire control panel threw itself at him as Eck angled into the next corner. The impact spun Brian toward the rear door. He dropped the gun as he fell. It skipped across the floor and disappeared through the open door. Brian landed with his head and shoulders sticking out the doorway. The floor shifted as the van hit the straightaway, and Brian slid forward. He threw his hands out but failed to get hold of the doorframe. He slipped again and his torso was hanging in space. Inches below, the road surface rushed by like a deadly, raging river. Brian slipped once more. His center of gravity was nearly over the transom. He closed his eyes and cursed himself for taking off the helmet.

Brian stopped sliding. Something had clutched his ankle. Brian twisted to see behind him. Silver looked back at him, his right hand holding Brian's leg and his left arm wrapped around the control seat's pedestal. Silver pulled Brian inside. Brian mouthed the word, "Thanks," uncertain if he actually spoke it. Silver nodded and looked around the cabin, evidently assessing the situation he awoke to.

To clear his ears, Brian worked his jaw as if he were chewing a large gumball. The ringing subsided. At the threshold of hearing, a monkey's chattering transformed into Eck yammering "I'll kill you!" over and over. But Eck's hatred was directed at the road, not at Brian. Eck yelled, "Kralik, you son of a bitch!" Brian was confused. Why would Eck be cursing Kralik?

Three crooked white stars appeared in the windshield in rapid succession—*Pop! Pop! Pop!*—and Brian knew they were gunshots smacking against bullet-proof glass. The van swerved and a brilliance of headlights washed through the windshield and blinded Brian. The Sprinter shook with a tremendous impact, and a din of crunching metal sounded behind the van.

Silver placed his mouth to Brian's ear and shouted, "Brace yourself!" He sprang toward the driver's compartment reaching for the hand brake. Brian hugged the seat pedestal. Silver yanked the brake, and the van slewed right.

Eck swung at Silver and landed a lucky blow across the bridge of his nose. Silver staggered back toward Brian, who stood and grasped Silver's shoulders to steady him.

The van was threatening to come apart. Tendrils of smoke poured through the bullet hole in the monitor. Sparks flew from the control panel, bringing a smell of burning ozone. The front tires squealed in torment as the van continued to skid, precipitously slowing but refusing to stop.

Eck released the hand brake and the Sprinter slingshot forward. He spun the steering wheel to correct the skid but made it worse. The van lurched at an angle.

"Time to go!" Silver yelled as he tackled Brian, propelling the two of them toward the rear door. The van tipped before they cleared the opening. Eck screamed in terror.

In the brief moment they were airborne, Silver twisted so that Brian would land on top of him. Silver grunted like a wounded bear as they hit the pavement, and the pair tumbled forward with the van's residual momentum.

The Sprinter was on its side, the rear door bouncing and spraying yellow sparks as the van skidded across one of the rampart-like mausoleums. It sailed over the side. The van bounced twice when it hit the roadway below. The impact sent it spinning over the ledge of the next rampart. This time the van crashed nose first and rolled straight over onto its roof. It teetered for a moment on the next ledge, then dropped. The Prometheus gun was sheared from the roof as the Sprinter slid over the verge. The van slammed onto its side and spiraled slowly down the inclined path until it slithered into a gathering of mourning statues. An angel fell, one wing snapping off as it hit the ground. The van remained still except for a spinning front tire. Brian could see nothing through the fractured windshield.

Silver groaned as he sat up. "You all right, Brian?"

Brian held up a palm that was bloody from scraping the pavement. "I'm sore, but I think this is the worst of it. What about you?"

"Left arm's numb; hope it's not broken." Silver looked around. "Why are we in the cemetery?"

"This is where Eck was meeting his buyers." Brian pointed. "I think that was them."

Silver checked where Brian was pointing. The cemetery's upper gate was at the next level, and the bodies of two men Brian had not seen before lay just inside. Brian stood for a better look. One man's left temple and the other man's right were wet with blood. The men might have been seated in a car and fired upon through the side windows.

Brian and Silver turned to find the car that had collided head-on with the van. They saw a mangled, dark gray BMW sedan a few hundred feet below. It rested on its side against one of the mausoleums and had nearly snapped in two. Kralik's body was draped out the broken windshield. Brian could make out the hump of another lifeless form in the passenger seat. Voss or Carter? And was the remaining man's corpse hidden in the wreckage?

"Well," Silver said, "you don't have to be Sherlock Holmes to deduce what happened here. Kralik and friends didn't cut their losses and run, as I figured they would. Looks like they knew about this rendezvous and decided to double-cross Eck." Silver indicated the bodies inside the gate. "They ambushed the buyers—bang, bang—and took their car and their money, maybe a cool five hundred million. And then they waited to kill Eck and steal the Prometheus van, worth another five hundred million."

Brian nodded. He had figured it out as well. He said, "I guess

253

when they saw the van roaring up the hill with the Prometheus gun in firing position, they panicked and attacked Eck. Seems they didn't know the Prometheus van was built like a tank."

Brian shrugged and said nothing more. He regarded the BMW and realized it was the cemetery's newest tomb, containing a fresh consignment of death.

Brian looked down at the van. Was it a tomb as well? The tire had stopped spinning. Smoke seeped from the cargo area. Brian waited for the driver's door to open. It didn't. He spotted a stone stairway leading to the cemetery's lower half. Brian stood and walked toward it.

"Brian, don't bother," Silver said. Brian ignored him.

Brian could see through the windshield when he got to the van. Eck's motionless, twisted form was sprawled across the passenger seat, his face pressed against the cracked glass of the door's window. Brian looked into Eck's eyes and remembered another pair of empty eyes he saw in a Lucerne alley five hundred miles away and several lifetimes ago.

"I told you you couldn't save yourself," Brian said.

He stepped to the side and knelt beside the toppled angel. He caressed its smooth, heavenly face. "I'm sorry," he said. Then he walked back up the hill.

Silver was not where Brian had left him. He was leaning against the gate. As Brian approached, he saw Silver speaking into a cell phone. He had folded his left arm across his chest as if it were cradled in an invisible sling. He nodded to Brian and continued his conversation. From the businesslike tone to Silver's voice, Brian guessed he was using his official CIA phone. Silver said, "We're going to need a level one suppression team."

Brian pulled at the gate and discovered it was locked. The key most likely was inside the BMW, but Brian wasn't about to search for it. He grasped two vertical iron bars and hauled himself up. The gate was about fifteen feet high. Brian climbed. Silver followed Brian with his eyes and continued to speak. "We've got five, maybe six, subjects at the scene, so you'd better get here before the locals." Brian guessed *subjects* meant dead bodies. *Locals* obviously referred to the Barcelona police.

He lifted a leg over the top of the gate and paused to survey the cemetery one final time. The garden of statues below would have been breathtaking under other circumstances, and this undoubtedly was a beautiful place. But it was a home to death, and Brian was sick of death. He needed to put a barrier between death and himself, even if only a few slim iron bars formed that barrier.

Brian eased his body to the other side and lowered himself. Silver continued to watch him. Brian dropped the last three feet, and slumped against the gate. Silver said, "I'm not the only one at the scene." He shot Brian a conspiratorial look. "You'd better wake up the Madrid station chief for this."

CHAPTER 53--DEMANDS

The CIA chose to disavow Brian's involvement. No one but Silver was permitted to speak with him, or even acknowledge his existence.

Brian first sensed this upon the arrival of the "level one suppression team." The team's youngest member, who appeared to be fresh out of college, bandaged Brian's hand without talking or making eye contact. The two other men never looked in Brian's direction.

Brian stood to the side while Silver conferred with the men at the cemetery gate, then Silver borrowed their car and drove Brian to a small hotel just off Las Ramblas. Even though it was nearly midnight, he had no trouble checking Brian in. Silver accompanied Brian to his room and did a quick security sweep.

"It looks like you'll be safe here," Silver said. "I have to go back to the cemetery. You get some sleep. I'll return in a few hours and we'll discuss your immediate future."

"What's to stop me from leaving?"

"The hotel's being watched."

"I bet I could spot the surveillance team."

"If you do they'll lose their jobs, so please don't try." Silver smiled wanly and added, "No one wants to tell the unemployment office he was fired by the CIA."

Once Silver was gone, Brian stripped off his clothes and took the most welcome shower of his life. After that he walked into the bedroom wearing only the white robe he found hanging in the bathroom. Brian picked up the phone. As he expected, it was dead. Brian crawled into the bed and immediately fell asleep.

A sharp knock at the door woke him. Brian looked at the clock on the nightstand in time to see the numbers switch from 6:01 to 6:02. He went to the door.

"What's the password?" he asked.

"Don't be cute," Silver replied.

Brian let him in. Silver's left arm was in a sling. "Sprained, but not broken," he said. Silver tossed Brian's backpack at him. "The Barcelona police recovered this," he said. He picked up a shopping bag and tossed that at Brian, too. "Fresh clothes. Figured you needed some." Brian went into the bathroom and put on the clothes, a new pair of Levis and a red polo shirt. They fit perfectly.

Silver was sitting at the room's writing desk when Brian came out. He drummed his fingers on a leather portfolio. "The good news," Silver said, "is they want to reunite you with your school group as soon as possible."

Brian sat on the bed. "Who are *they*?"

"Best to leave it at *they*." Silver said. "Your group is in Paris now. We should have you there early tomorrow if all goes well. They do want to debrief you, but decided to wait and do it in Milwaukee, at your convenience."

Brian shook his head and chuckled. "My convenience. Can we do it at the Safe House?"

"You talking about that spy bar?"

"Yeah."

Silver laughed. "Sure, set it up. They won't appreciate the irony."

"You won't be the one debriefing me?"

"Oh no, after I drop you off in Paris I am not permitted to contact you in any way."

"Upon penalty of death?"

"I'd rather not find out." Silver tapped the portfolio. "Now the condition for this generous offer of personal freedom is that you swear never to tell anyone what has happened to you or what you have done since we left Lucerne."

"You mean since you kidnapped me?"

"That won't be the official case history."

Brian glared at him before saying, "All right, I won't tell. No one would believe me anyway."

Brian had already considered this. Even worse than the people who didn't believe him would be the reactions of those who did. His parents would be afraid to let him leave the house for years. And if Tim and others believed him, they would think Brian had lived out some kind of exciting action movie. They wouldn't see it as an ordeal filled with desperation and death. As much as Brian hated to give the CIA what it wanted, he knew it would be best to keep his brief espionage career secret.

"Then," Silver opened the portfolio to reveal a document of many pages, "would you please sign this agreement?"

Brian read through it, although the legal jargon often confused him. He snickered when he found a paragraph that declared he would be surrendering all literary, film, and digital rights to his story. He looked up at Silver. "I like this clause where it says by signing this agreement I acknowledge it does not exist."

Silver offered a pen, but when Brian reached for it Silver tipped it back toward himself like the arm of a metronome. He said, "I am not acting in my employer's best interest when I offer you the following advice. It would cause at the least considerable embarrassment to the Agency, and at the most a national scandal, if the public learned of your involvement in this operation. So if you were to make any demands before signing this document"— Silver riffled his fingers to indicate money—"the Agency would probably give in."

Brian mulled this over. After a few minutes, he said, "I have two demands."

"All right," Silver said, "what's your first demand?"

"I presume Lenore Harte will receive a posthumous honor, but those two hikers in the Pyrenees—I think they were British—I want their families to get something. Invent an insurance policy for them. Would one hundred thousand dollars each be too much?"

Silver rubbed a thumb beneath his lower lip. "We can work something out. What's your second demand?"

"I want to see Larissa."

CHAPTER 54--PARTING

As it turned out, Larissa had made the same demand of her government.

Three hours after Brian signed the agreement, Silver drove him to the French consulate. They were led to a small sitting room down the corridor from the public entrance. Their escort turned to Silver. "Monsieur Parker may go in, and you may wait here." He pointed to a chair outside the door. Silver shot the man an ugly look and sat. Brian stepped into the room and heard the escort close the door behind him. A door on the opposite wall opened and Larissa appeared. Brian's breath caught at the sight of her.

She wore a cream-colored blouse and a dark blue knee-length skirt. A pair of leather navy blue loafers replaced her familiar Chuck Taylor All-Stars, and if Brian wasn't mistaken she was wearing pantyhose. Her chestnut brown hair was tied in a cream ribbon that matched her blouse. Her face lit up and she bounded across the room to kiss Brian, slightly limping. She placed her head on his shoulder and hugged him tightly.

"Wow," Brian said, "and I thought you looked good in jeans and a T-shirt."

Larissa looked up at him and grinned. "The consul's wife took me shopping this morning. She wanted to improve my tastes."

Brian returned her grin. "The old you was already beautiful, but I won't argue with the efforts of the consul's wife." Brian looked into her eyes and his smile faltered. Her lower eyelids were puffy and her eyes slightly bloodshot.

Larissa saw his concern and nodded. "I have had time to cry," she said.

Brian wasn't ready to face this subject, so he changed it.

"How is your knee?"

"Much better," she said. "Simply a little sore now."

Brian then told Larissa everything that happened the night before. She clutched his arm when he talked about the runaway van.

"I am afraid my side of the story is not so exciting," she said when he finished. The police had picked Larissa up a few minutes after she ran away from Brian (which she admitted was intentional). She refused to say anything to the police and insisted she speak to the French consulate. By then the consulate knew her father had died, so the consul himself arrived at Barcelona police headquarters to bring Larissa in.

"And I have been here since," she said, "except for my shopping trip. But I have not been alone. Many people from my government want to talk to me."

Brian laughed. "I'm the opposite. I'm poison to the CIA. Silver's the only one allowed to talk to me."

"Have you talked to your parents yet?"

"No. It's still the middle of the night in Wisconsin. I'll call them in a few hours, and hopefully convince them I'm fine. And then I'll have to call my school chaperone, Miss Weninger, and try to calm her down. I guess Silver has been stonewalling them all for the past few days. I'll have to lie to them." Brian frowned. "I'm not looking forward to that."

He explained the cover story the CIA conjured for him, that he had spent the entire time in the safe house in the south of France. Once Silver realized he and Brian were involved in a hostile operation, the CIA decided to put Brian in protective custody. For Brian's own safety, no one was allowed to talk to him or know where he was, not even his parents.

"So," Brian said, "I have to convince everyone I was all secure and happy and spent my time reading comics, watching DVDs, and playing video games. Actually, I don't think I'll have a hard time convincing people of that." He touched Larissa's cheek. "What about you?"

Larissa told him that her aunt who lived in a Paris suburb would arrive in Barcelona that afternoon. Larissa would move in with her aunt's family. She and her aunt would have to spend several more days in Barcelona dealing with bureaucracy and meeting with officials from Eurocorps and the SDECE, France's secret service.

Brian asked, "Are you going to tell anyone else the truth about what happened?"

Larissa shook her head. "*Non*. My government is going to put out the story that my father was killed by terrorists who wanted to steal the weapon he was developing. The government will not say he collaborated." She added quietly, "This is how I want my father remembered."

Brian no longer could avoid the subject. "Larissa, I am so sorry about your father. I don't know how you can forgive me. If I hadn't come to your house—"

Larissa placed a hand over his mouth. "My father was the victim of his own terrible decisions." A tear rolled down her face. She continued to cry, but her voice didn't falter. "If not for you, those men would have succeeded with their plan, and I would forever think that my father committed suicide because the weapon failed. You offered him the chance to save himself, but he realized too late he was dealing with evil people. At the end, he tried to protect me. I will always remember this."

Brian held her, and the two were silent except for Larissa's quiet sobs. When these subsided, Brian said. "I need your e-mail address."

Larissa laughed. Her laughter reverberated through Brian's ribs, and he wished the sensation would never stop. Yet it ended just seconds later as Larissa pulled away to reach for a pen and pad on a nearby secretary's desk. "*Mais oui*," she said.

They exchanged e-mail and snail mail addresses, cell phone numbers, and Facebook and Twitter information. They invented their own cover story in case anyone wondered how Brian had formed such a fast friendship with a girl he met in France. He would explain that he struck up a conversation with a lovely Parisian girl in a bookshop and they really hit it off. "I'll say I was dazzled by your Ramones T-shirt."

She punched Brian's arm playfully and gave him a wide, warm smile. Brian brushed away her last tear. Pressing his forehead against hers, he said, "You are so...*très jolie*." He kissed her. The kiss lasted a long time, and Brian slowly ran his fingers through her hair and down her back. He broke away.

Their lips still close, he murmured, "I don't want to stop kissing you. I'm afraid that once I do, it will mean goodbye."

Larissa leaned back so they could see each other's face. Her deep brown eyes held his as she said, "I can never say goodbye to you, Brian Parker. Never. I can only say *au revoir*."

"Until we see each other again," Brian said.

"I am so pleased you understand my language." She clasped the back of Brian's neck and pulled him close for another kiss. Then, gently, she pushed herself away.

"*Au revoir, cher Brian*." Larissa traced her fingers down his cheek one last time and disappeared behind the door.

CHAPTER 55--GIFT

As Silver told the story, his superiors had debated for hours how to smuggle Brian back into France. Because Brian did not legally enter Spain, he could not legally leave it. They considered putting him in a Zodiac speedboat and depositing him on a beach in France, but decided that would be time-consuming. They considered carrying him out on a black flight, but decided that even blindfolded, Brian might guess the location of the CIA's secret Mediterranean airbase. Finally, they decided the simplest approach was best, so early the next morning Brian crossed into France in the trunk of Silver's car.

It wasn't so bad. Brian didn't have to get into the trunk until they were a few miles from the border. He crawled past the suitcase he had not seen since Nice and into a hidden compartment at the rear of the trunk. Inside were a flashlight and a pillow (Silver was being considerate). The car stopped minutes later and Brian heard muffled voices speaking French, then the car was moving again. After another ten minutes the car pulled over and Brian rejoined Silver in the front seat.

"*Bienvenue vers la France*," Silver said. He tossed that morning's Barcelona newspaper, La Vanguardia, into Brian's lap. The paper was folded to an inside page, and one of the upper headlines contained the word *cementerio*. Brian was able to glean that the headline referred to vandalism in the Montjuïc cemetery.

"The story will start dribbling out today," Silver said, "or at least the version the concerned governments want their citizens to know. The Guardia Civil and the Spanish security services will get the credit for recovering the van with the missing weapon. That's in exchange for erasing Roland Eck's role from the record. The Pentagon insisted that since he died nearly a year ago, he couldn't possibly have been involved in this terrorist plot."

"I like how this became a terrorist plot," Brian said.

"All the bad guys are terrorists these days," Silver responded. "The public doesn't question that. And the terrorist mastermind behind the operation was Mathias Skyrm. The security brain trust decided it would be easiest to blame the whole thing on him. And of course, the Guardia Civil gets credit for killing one of Europe's most notorious criminals."

"I don't recall seeing any of them on Las Ramblas," Brian said drily.

"Oh no, that's not where Skyrm died. He was killed in a shootout at the delivery warehouse, along with his accomplices Kralik, Voss, and Carter."

Brian nodded. So Voss and Carter had both been in the BMW.

"The van was recovered from the warehouse, too," Silver continued. "It was never in the cemetery."

Brian held up the newspaper. "Because vandals ransacked the cemetery."

"You got it," Silver said. "And that other incident you referred to, the one in the bird market, that was just local thugs in another example of the increasing violence along the Ramblas frightening away the tourists."

Brian sighed. He saw how the last few days of his life were being swept neatly under the carpet.

Silver filled him in on other details. Masson, who was still in the San Gregorio brig, started talking as soon as he heard Eck and Skyrm were dead. The CIA had recovered the Prometheus prototype from the warehouse outside Zaragoza. And the Prometheus van was now aboard a container ship bound for Norfolk, Virginia.

Brian watched the rolling scenery of the Pyrenees as they sped along a busy motorway. After a few moments he asked, "How much trouble are you in for dragging me into this?"

"A ton," Silver said, "but that's balanced out by my foiling a conspiracy to steal one of our latest weapons." He glanced at Brian. "Sorry, but I had to take credit for that."

"Take it," Brian said. He was too weary of the whole affair to feel bitter. "Did they discover your financial arrangement with Tetzel?"

"If they did, I'd be on a military flight back to Washington right now. I think I'm safe, though I'd better not touch that account in Liechtenstein for about five years."

Brian paused before asking his next question. "And what about the guy you had watching my family? How much trouble will he be in for domestic spying?"

"He wasn't CIA. He's a private investigator friend of mine from Chicago who owed me a few favors."

"Did your friend know you were using him to frighten a fifteen-year-old boy?"

"No," Silver said.

They lapsed into silence after that. Silver drove to a small airstrip outside of the medieval town of Perpignan. A twin-engine Beechcraft was waiting for them, its propellers already roaring as Brian and Silver stepped aboard. They were airborne within seconds. The cockpit door was closed; Brian never saw the pilot.

After an hour in the air, Silver engaged Brian in small talk. They discussed the chances that the Brewers and the Orioles, which was Silver's team, had for the rest of the season. Silver asked for a fuller explanation of Spider-Girl "because that comic was pretty good." When they were over the Loire Valley, Silver told him to look out the window. Brian watched several châteaux drift past below.

They landed at another small airfield outside of Paris. An empty black Citroën sedan was parked at the end of the runway. Silver and Brian got into the car and drove off. The Beechcraft was in the air again before they reached the road.

Silver called Miss Weninger from the car and learned the group would be at the Eiffel Tower by the time he and Brian reached central Paris. Silver volunteered to drop Brian off there instead of at the hotel. Miss Weninger agreed, saying the group would wait until Brian arrived before going up the tower.

Thirty minutes later Silver found a parking spot along the Avenue Emile Deschanel. Brian saw the Wauwatosa East group exploring the Parc du Champ de Mars, the long, grassy plaza that stretches from the Eiffel Tower and lends it a postcard setting.

Brian stared at the top of the tower and his mouth fell open. "That thing is a lot taller than I expected," he said.

"Let that go to show you that not everything in life will be a disappointment," Silver said.

Brian retrieved his backpack from the rear seat and reached for the door handle, but stopped when Silver touched his arm. The man's eyes held a sincerity Brian had not seen before. "Brian," he said, "you probably won't hear this from anyone else, but I want you to know that you deserve a thank you from the American government. You truly did a service to your country."

Brian scoffed. "Like you did?"

"I only did everything I could to save my own skin."

"That's all I did."

"Not entirely," Silver said. "You could have stayed on the base at San Gregorio. You were safe there. But you left with Larissa and her father to protect them."

"Yeah, fat lot of good I did."

"But you did, don't you see? If you had stayed on that base, Larissa would have been killed with her father."

Brian went cold at the thought of Larissa dying. Quietly, he said, "If you say so."

Silver reached beneath the driver's seat and pulled out a manila envelope. He handed it to Brian. "It's much less than you deserve, but here are some parting gifts."

Brian tore off the edge of the envelope and tipped it. His passport dropped into his lap. Brian opened it to find that his entry stamp into France matched the day he left Lucerne. "Courtesy of your friends at the French consulate," Silver said.

Brian tapped the envelope on his knee and his watch and cell phone fell out. He picked up the phone. "I put a dead battery in there," Silver said. "Fortunately for me, the charging cord you brought doesn't fit European outlets, so you won't be lying when you say you couldn't recharge your phone."

Something else was in the envelope, something flat and rectangular. Brian let it slide out. It was a paperback book. Brian read the title: *Schnefeuer*.

"That's what you were looking for in Lucerne, wasn't it—a German copy of *Snowfire*?"

"Yes," Brian said. "Yes it was." He looked at the painting on the cover. Foster Blake was dead center in a dark blue ski suit, flinty-eyed and poised for action. His right hand held his Sig-Sauer, and his left hand rested protectively around the waist of the ravishing Georgianna Fox, who was wearing the tightest-fitting polar jacket the artist could conceive. Her zipper was pulled low enough to reveal the inevitable cleavage.

"Thanks," Brian said.

"Like I said, the least I could do." Silver pressed a button to unlock Brian's door. "I'll drop your suitcase off at the hotel, OK?"

Brian stepped to the curb. "Goodbye, Brian," Silver said. "I won't be seeing you again."

"Goodbye," Brian replied, and he shut the door.

A familiar voice shouted Brian's name. Tim Gifford was running toward him. The others members of the Wauwatosa East group were looking at him and chattering excitedly, but they were willing to let Tim be the official greeter. Tim reached Brian, clasped his upper arm and leaned in, not quite hugging.

"Dude! What happened to you? I sent you, like, a thousand texts."

"My phone died, and I couldn't recharge it because I brought the wrong kind of cord," Brian said, and realized it wasn't a lie. Not technically.

Brian hitched his backpack over his shoulder and they started walking toward the group. Tim went on, "We heard they were hiding you in the south of France because terrorists were after you because of that dead guy you found in Lucerne. Is that true?"

Brian shrugged. "Nobody really told me anything. I was in a little apartment with the shades drawn. I spent the whole time watching DVDs, playing videogames, reading comics, and wishing I was seeing the sights of Europe with you guys." He punched Tim in the shoulder. "I really missed you."

"No, you know what you really missed?" Tim's eyes brightened. "When we were in Frankfurt they put us in this hotel in the middle of nowhere, just some industrial park somewhere. Anyway, Skip Lewis and Sam Newton somehow managed to sneak a six-pack of Heineken into their room, and they drank it all themselves. So when they come down the next morning they look green as frogs, and then they puke all over everyone's continental breakfast! And Miss Weninger exploded! She screamed at them, 'If you two don't shape up, I will personally drive you to the nearest airport and put you on the next plane back to Milwaukee!' Ah man, you missed all the excitement."

Brian shook his head. "Yeah, I missed all the excitement."

Ahead, Miss Weninger disengaged from the group and walked toward them, relief showing on her face. Brian scanned the pathway leading to her and noticed a trash can to the side.

Tim gave Brian a knowing nudge. "By the way, pal, Darlene Miller found your disappearing act highly intriguing. You're in, man. You are in!"

Brian nodded absently. His thoughts were not on Darlene Miller. He looked around the Paris skyline and wondered which direction would lead him to Larissa's new home.

A car engine started behind them, and Brian turned in time to see Silver pull into traffic.

"Was that that Silver guy?" Tim asked.

"Yeah, that was him."

"So what's his story? Was he a spy after all?"

"I never quite figured out what he was," Brian said as they passed the trash bin.

Without Tim noticing, Brian executed a behind-the-back toss that landed his copy of *Schnefeuer* in the trash. It didn't make a sound.

THE END

Acknowledgements

Because this is my first book, I have many people to thank. Here goes:

To my wife, Jeanette, thanks for the love and support. I couldn't have done this without you.

To my mother and sisters, thanks for being such fabulous cheerleaders. I regret that my father didn't live to see this book published, but I am glad he got to read the first draft.

To Laura Caldwell, thanks for misunderstanding my question about teenage spy novels and responding with the best possible answer: write one!

To Mathilde Bigorgne, thanks for befriending a stranger on the Internet and telling me about your hometown of Toulouse. Any errors pertaining to "la Ville Rose" should be attributed to me and not Mathilde.

To the best copy editor I know, Joan Oliver, thanks for taking your red pen to my first draft.

To my Spider-Girl message board co-mod, Matt "VENOM" Kayser, thanks for reading a later draft and offering advice. Mayday Parker rules!

To my good friend and fellow Bond buff Brian Sheridan, thanks for serving as my Major Boothroyd for tae kwon do.

To the Top Shelf Books Open Mic Night crew, thanks for welcoming me so enthusiastically and giving me a boost of confidence when I needed one. I look forward to buying all *your* books soon.

To the team at Intrigue Publishing, LLC thanks for having faith in my story. Thanks also to editor Lindsey Errington for saving me from several embarrassing mistakes.

Author Bio

Jeffrey Westhoff has served as a film critic, feature writer, reporter, and copy editor in his career as a journalist. Jeffrey wrote his first novel, *The Boy Who Knew Too Much*, while working as a freelance writer.

Jeffrey grew up in Erie, Pennsylvania, where he spent his Saturday mornings at the library and his Saturday nights at the movies. That love of reading and film prepared his future as a movie critic. Seeing *Star Wars* on its opening day in 1977 made him a movie lover, but it was a viewing of *The Spy Who Loved Me* that sealed Jeffrey's fate as a James Bond fan. His first published movie review appeared in the Erie Times News while he was senior in high school.

Also during his senior year of high school, Jeffrey made a campus visit to Marquette University and immediately fell in love with Milwaukee—even though he arrived on a gloomy February day. He enrolled at Marquette the following fall. The first time he visited Milwaukee's famous spy bar, the Safe House, Jeffrey knew the password without knowing it was the password. His favorite Milwaukee hangout was the Oriental Theatre.

After spending a year and a half in Wabash, Ind., Jeffrey took a job at the Northwest Herald in Crystal Lake, Ill. He has lived in the Chicago area ever since. He was a film critic for more than 25 years. During that time he met or interviewed five of the six actors to play James Bond (all except Sean Connery). Pierce Brosnan once wished him a happy birthday. He has contributed to RogerEbert.com and also wrote book reviews for the Chicago Sun-Times. He is a member of the International Thriller Writers and the Society of Children's Book Writers and Illustrators.

Jeffrey lives in Chicago's northwest suburbs with his wife, Jeanette. He is now working on his second novel. Visit his website at www.jeffreywesthoff.com.

CPSIA information can be obtained at www.ICGtesting.com
Printed in the USA
LVOW10s0852210615

443246LV00005B/11/P